WHAT PEOPLE ARE SAYING ABOUT

THE KELLER PAPERS

Ellis Goodman's new novel, *The Keller Papers*, is a story of intrigue, espionage, murder, and mayhem on a grand scale. Its globe-trotting cast of characters include beautiful women, handsome men, spies from east and west, a nefarious ex-Nazi SS officer, and a business executive who occasionally does "little jobs" for M16. With action and suspense galore, Ellis Goodman takes the reader on a wild ride that ends up not only exhilarating but challenging, with informed references to global commerce, as well as European politics, history, and tragedy—the Holocaust plays a sad but prominent role in nearly every character's life. A gripping tale, well worth the reading.
Gary D. Wilson, author of the novels *Getting Right* and *Sing, Ronnie Blue*

The Keller Papers is an exciting read, a worthy sequel to the family saga *Bear Any Burden*, but it stands very much on its own. The well-paced narrative is full of thrills and surprises, and the setting in Eastern Europe during the Cold War in the early 1980s, provides an interesting glimpse into the political and economic turbulence of the times. Highly recommended.
Jian Ping, author of *Mulberry Child: A Memoir of China*

In this groundbreaking mix of fast-paced historical intrigue with heartbreaking genealogical mysteries, Goodman offers a fresh new take on thriller/espionage writing. Incident-filled and packed with edgy details and startling incidents, this book is a thinking thriller-lover's thriller. The suspense never lets up, and each detail moves the plot at a breathless pace. Couldn't put it down.
Suzanne Seed, author of *Saturday's Child*

Testimonial for *Bear Any Burden*

Ellis Goodman has written a gripping, moving, and dramatic story that holds the attention from first page to last. Like all the best fiction, it is deeply rooted in fact; in this case in the realities of Jewish life during stirring, uncertain and traumatic times. This, Ellis Goodman's first novel, is a masterly work of detection and espionage that deserves the widest readership.

Sir Martin Gilbert, London

Winston Churchill's official Biographer and author of 80 books

The Keller Papers

The Keller Papers

Ellis M. Goodman

Winchester, UK
Washington, USA

First published by Roundfire Books, 2016
Roundfire Books is an imprint of John Hunt Publishing Ltd., Laurel House, Station Approach,
Alresford, Hants, SO24 9JH, UK
office1@jhpbooks.net
www.johnhuntpublishing.com
www.roundfire-books.com

For distributor details and how to order please visit the 'Ordering' section on our website.

Text copyright: Ellis M. Goodman 2015

ISBN: 978 1 78535 486 1
978 1 78535 487 8 (ebook)
Library of Congress Control Number: 2016936945

A CIP catalogue record for this book is available from the British Library.

Design: Stuart Davies

Printed and bound by CPI Group (UK) Ltd, Croydon, CR0 4YY, UK

For Diddles

Acknowledgements

There was a Kornmehl family in Tarnów, Poland, to whom my family was related. To the best of my knowledge, none of the Kornmehls emigrated to Scotland. The characters and events in this book are fictitious. Any similarities to real persons living or dead is coincidental and not intended.

This novel was inspired by the award-winning genealogy research by my cousin Leonard Schneider of London, which traced our family history back to 1760 and provided the basis for my first novel, *Bear Any Burden* to which *The Keller Papers* is a sequel.

I could not have completed this novel without the dedication of my executive assistant, Lana Quinn, who worked diligently on typing and retyping my many manuscripts.

I would also like to thank my wife Gillian and my children Sara and Paul, for their continued encouragement, advice and support, and my granddaughter, Jessica Harris, for her research assistance.

I also received outstanding creative advice and support from my friends Jennifer Hou Kwong, and Suzanne Seed.

Finally I would like to thank my meticulous and talented editor Emanuel Bergmann.

Cover Design by Bluewater A&D – Erin Mauterer

"Freedom is never given, it is won."
A. Philip Randolph

Chapter 1

The Imperial Hotel busboy came out of the staff entrance into the chill air, lit a cigarette, cupping his hands around his old Colibri, as he was thinking of his girlfriend Anke, and their plans for the weekend. He pulled up the collar of his leather jacket and hurried towards the bus stop, hardly noticing two men deep in conversation three meters away.

They were both in black ski outfits, standing on the sidewalk outside the palatial Hotel Imperial, on the Karntner Ring in the center of Vienna.

Tall and athletically built, Kurt Rickter was nervously drawing on a cigarette, with beads of perspiration on his forehead. He had high cheekbones and a Slavic countenance topped by short cropped black hair. The other man, Helmut Fischer, was cold-eyed and pale-faced, with a haircut very near the scalp, and had his hand inside his jacket, clutching something bulky. Passers-by took no notice of them. It was Friday, February 25, 1983 and the dying sun cast a golden pink glow in the western sky, giving some hope of spring after a brutally cold winter. The weather forecast was good and snow conditions were excellent for the thousands of skiers who would soon be leaving the city to head for the slopes.

The men watched as a hotel porter put luggage into the trunk of a Jaguar outside the hotel entrance. They also noticed the Audi parked a few meters behind the Jag. Two men and a woman came out of the hotel and stood at the entrance, looking around, as if trying to get their bearings. They were accompanied by another, who headed towards the Jag. Kurt recognized the target and his wife from photos he had studied, but had not expected to see the other man with them, well dressed in a smart blue suit.

"Now!" said Kurt, through clenched teeth. The skiers now looked more like militia as they both pulled ski masks over their heads, revealing only their eyes and mouths. They started running at full pelt toward the hotel entrance. There was a glint of gunmetal as they drew handguns from their jackets. Helmut slammed the first man into the rear door of the Jaguar. Kurt shot the target twice from close range. A woman screamed. The man crumpled to the ground. Kurt and Helmut continued to sprint to the end of the road and turned right onto the road off the Canovagstraße to their parked BMW R80 motorcycle. Two men jumped out of their Audi, but were at least thirty meters behind, as Kurt, with Helmut riding pillion, kick-started the bike into action and accelerated, with a loud growl, up the road to join the traffic on Bosendorferststraße. After a couple of blocks, they crossed Karlsplatz and shortly after turned right into an alley off Friedrichstraße, where a large white van was parked with the shuttered rear area open. Two men in the vehicle slid a metal ramp down onto the roadway as the BMW approached. Kurt accelerated fiercely as he shot up the ramp and then immediately cut the engine. One of the men grabbed the bike and helped bring it to a stop as the other pulled up the ramp and lowered the shutter. The van moved off into the Getreidmarkt and joined the Friday-evening rush hour in the heart of the city.

Within half an hour, they were out of the city and onto the A2 Autobahn to Carinthia in Austria's southwest. They drove through the fading light, and evening mists; and, as the sky turned to black, a brilliant moon bathed the countryside in a silver glow.

They travelled in near silence, not knowing who they had shot or why. They arrived at the mediaeval town of Klagenfurt, and then headed up into the hills, through spruce and beech forests covered in snow. It was past 9:30 p.m. when they finally approached the large wrought-iron gates of a walled estate, and the gatehouse automatically lit up as they arrived; two guards in identical black ski outfits came out and spoke to the driver of the van. The gates swung open to allow them to pass and proceed up a long driveway which continued for over two kilometers through snow-covered woods, eventually arriving at a plateau, on which was located a large mansion in the Baroque style, gloriously lit by carefully positioned floodlights. The van pulled up in front of the house. Kurt and Helmut descended as the van drove off to the east of the house where the stable block and garages were located. Kurt rang the doorbell and after a minute or so, it was opened by a gray-haired man in formal black jacket and bow tie.

"Good evening, Ernst," said Kurt to the butler. "We would like to see Herr von Schuyler. He is expecting us."

Ernst nodded. "I will let him know you have arrived. Come this way." He led the two men across the magnificent marble floor of the entrance hall to a beautifully appointed study. "Please wait here," said Ernst.

The butler crossed the entrance hall once again, and knocked softly on the double doors which led into a sumptuous library with a large table at which nine men were seated. The butler entered, cautiously approached von Schuyler and whispered in his ear. Von Schuyler got up, excused himself and left the room. As he entered his study, both Kurt and Helmut stood to attention and clicked their heels.

"Good evening," he said formally.

"Good evening, Herr Von Schuyler," they both responded, avoiding eye contact.

"Well?"

"The mission has been completed," said Kurt, a smirk on his face, hiding his nervousness.

"Excellent," said Von Schuyler loudly, clearly elated at the news. "Tell me what happened," he continued eagerly. "Is he dead?"

"We shot him twice in the chest. He went down like a sack of potatoes. I don't think he could survive," responded Kurt.

"So, there were no problems," said Von Schuyler.

"No, not really. We recognized the target and his wife. There was a third man with them, but he didn't interfere with us."

"Really?" said Von Schuyler, looking at them critically. "Did he look like some sort of official?"

"I don't think so," said Helmut. "He was quite smartly dressed in a blue suit and that's all I noticed."

"Right," said Von Schuyler. "Well done. Now go and get something to eat."

"Thank you," said Kurt and Helmut almost in unison with relief on their faces, clicking their heels before leaving the room.

Von Schuyler had a slight smile on his face as he reached for the telephone on his desk. He dialed slowly. After a few rings, the phone was picked up.

"Sergei, the mission has been completed," he said, in fluent Russian. "The target was taken out as planned." He paused before continuing. "Perhaps, you could now make the bank transfer as agreed," he continued.

Sergei responded in a dead voice. "It was announced on the news that he has been taken to the AKH General Hospital."

"I don't think he could survive," responded Von Schuyler. "He was shot twice in the chest from close range."

"Well, we'll see," said Sergei. "If all goes well, we'll make the transfer to the Zürich account on Monday, as agreed. We should speak again over the weekend," he continued.

"Fine," said Von Schuyler. He put the phone down and sat back deep in thought as he tapped his desk with a pencil. Karl von Schuyler was a handsome man, six-two, slim, broad shoulders with a permanent deep tan, and white hair closely cut. He wore horn-rimmed glasses in front of cold piercing gray eyes. He looked considerably younger than his sixty-eight years.

When Sergei had phoned him the previous day and asked him to take on the mission, he had readily agreed. He didn't ask who the target was and he didn't want to know. They had a relationship going back forty years, based upon being mutually useful to each other from time to time. That was it. A business relationship; one that had paid off handsomely for Von Schuyler over the years.

The KGB wanted to dispose of someone and would pay one million not to be involved. The one million would help Von Schuyler's political ambitions, and the Russians in return would be quite happy to see political upheaval in Austria and would love to have a highly placed connection in the government. Sergei had sent a motorcycle messenger with a photo of the target and instructions to "eliminate the issue" outside the Hotel Imperial between about 3:00 and 5:00 p.m. Simple, concise, clean. No problems envisaged.

He returned to the library where the meeting was getting heated. The participants were the executive committee of the FPÖ – The Freedom Party of Austria – the right-wing nationalist political party headed by Norbert Stiegler. Although Von Schuyler was not a member of the executive committee, he had been a staunch supporter for many years and exercised behind-the-scenes control, not only of the finances of the organization, to which he gave liberally, but also much of the political strategy and public platform of the party. He was hoping to substantially increase this influence after the May elections. Norbert Stiegler was talking to Jörg Haider, the charismatic, young nationalistic party affairs manager.

"You must not let the demonstrations against Kreisky and the Government turn violent," said Steigler.

"We plan peaceful demonstrations," said Haider. "But sometimes tempers run high. The feelings against Kriesky are fairly widespread."

"When you have too many of these skinhead people or whatever they're called," responded Stiegler, "they look like they're looking for trouble, and some of the recent violence at your demonstrations have seemed more like a Nazi rally. This is harmful to the party, and we can't allow it to continue if we aim to make real progress in the May elections."

"I know, but if we're going to be a force in this election and get rid of that fat-assed Kreisky, we have to be more aggressive on all fronts," responded Haider, forcefully.

Von Schuyler interrupted the proceedings. "I've just been informed that there's been a shooting outside the Hotel Imperial. It appears to be an attempted armed-robbery, and one man has been fatally shot."

"That's just what I've been talking about," said Haider. "While Kreisky has been running around the world as the big shot Chancellor of Austria, his liberal policies have allowed the country to be swamped with immigrants, and this is the result. More violence on our streets, more jobs going to these people, and true Austrians are fed up with that." Haider paused. "But this sort of incident could help our cause. A high-profile shooting outside the Hotel Imperial will give impetus to our platform," he continued. "Nobody is safe. Our demonstration on Sunday will focus on the immigrant problems and I know that people are hungry for change."

"I think the public generally agrees with you," responded Steigler. "But if we're complaining about violence, you must make sure we are not part of it as well."

"Jörg has got a point," said Von Schuyler. "Immigration is a touchy subject and the policies need to be changed. I think this is a weakness for Kreisky and the socialist platform, and it is something we can exploit."

"Well then, Jörg, I think that's it then," said Steigler to Haider, not wanting to argue with Von Schuyler. "I hope you have a good turnout at the demonstration. We agree that your message will focus on law and order and the immigration policies of the Kriesky government."

"Watch the News," responded Jörg confidently.

"Gentleman, I think that concludes this evening's meeting," continued Steigler. "Once again, I'd like to thank Karl for his hospitality and of course his continuing support and advice as always."

The chairs were shuffled back and the eight guests around the table got up, talking casually to each other as they gathered their papers. One by one they moved out of the library, picked up their overcoats from the butler and with a final round of goodbyes they left.

Norbert Stiegler was the last to leave, with a final handshake and pat on the back for Von Schuyler, who then retreated to his study and poured himself a Cognac.

* * *

In London, Sir Alex Campbell could not sleep. Despite being physically and emotionally exhausted, after the ordeals of the day, his mind was racing. He could have been shot, like poor Krystyna Keller, or arrested and in a Polish prison. He was angry. Alex Campbell did not like failure, and he felt this mission had failed in every aspect. Krystyna Keller was dead, Professor Keller could also be dead; his defection to the West had ended up in a bloodbath. Alex`s blood-soaked suit and shirt were in a bag in the corner ready to be thrown out. He was also angry at Tim Bevans and MI6. Why had their intelligence failed? Why was he and Anna not better protected? Who was responsible for the possible assassination of Professor Keller?

And then he was thinking of Anna, and convincing himself he had done the right thing. Substituting for her brother Jan, who had been shot and arrested in the Kraków hotel car park. He had to offer her assistance and refuge when she had come to him in an agitated state. If she had not hidden in his bedroom, she would have been arrested as well and Keller would never have been able to even attempt defecting to the West. He had to offer to share his bed for the night. The room was icy cold and it would have been miserable for either of them to sit up all night. He could still see her silhouette in the doorway of the lit bathroom, wearing one of his shirts as a nightie. Her blonde hair cascading on her shoulders and her athletic long legs and almost-perfect figure clearly visible. He could almost smell her natural perfume as she lay next to him under the duvet in the large bed. Nothing happened. Nothing could happen. She was warm and friendly but probably regarded him as a father figure. And yet... Alex finally fell into a fitful sleep.

* * *

Von Schuyler thought about the evening's events. He believed the FPÖ had a chance to gain a significant number of seats and perhaps be part of a coalition with the Social Democrats. Steigler was more liberal than the previous leadership, and Von Schuyler thought that would give him wider appeal to the Austrian public. Nevertheless, he recognized the FPÖ attracted mainly protest voters and those who desired no association with the other major parties. But the populism and anti-establishment themes that he had promoted were bringing an ever-increasing number of supporters to the cause.

Von Schuyler was to be alone again this weekend. His wife Katarina, a former Miss Austria who was twenty-three years his junior, was once again spending the weekend at their apartment in Vienna. Their marriage was one of convenience. They both led their own lives. Katarina with her interest in the Vienna Opera and of course fashion and design, and Von Schuyler with his various business and political interests. They came together as a couple for parties, special events or when it suited them. Neither one had any restrictions on the other, and so the marriage worked in its own fashion.

Katarina Wempe was born in 1937 in a small village near Innsbruck where her father was a schoolmaster. She was the youngest of six children. Her father, Otto, was an ardent Nazi supporter from the early days of Adolf Hitler and was overjoyed when the Germans marched into Austria in 1938. Pictures of the Führer adorned the walls of their modest house where they lived on the edge of poverty. Katarina was always a beautiful child, and with her white blonde hair, bright blue eyes and perfect complexion, she was the ideal image of the Aryan young woman. Otto was not only a member of the Nazi party but also was an early volunteer to help in the cause particularly when War was declared in September 1939. He applied to join the SS but he was not only quite old, but also suffered from poor eyesight and so was rejected. Eventually, he was given a job in the Wermacht Pay Corps, and posted to Linz, where he rose to the rank of lieutenant by the beginning of 1943. At that time, he was able to move his family from their small overcrowded village house into the former home of a Jewish Doctor in Linz which gave them considerably more room and comfort. For the first time in her life, Katarina did not have to share a bed with her two sisters.

Otto was a brutal disciplinarian at school and at home. His wife, Ute, was terrified of him, often with good cause since he beat her regularly. He demanded complete obedience from his children, and those who disobeyed were given a good caning. There was no warmth in the house, and the children had to fend for themselves. Katarina's two eldest brothers joined the Hitler Youth, and in 1944 were conscripted into the army. They were both killed fighting the Russians as they advanced into Austria. At the end of the war, Otto and his family were forced to leave the comfort of their temporary home and moved back to their small house in the village. Katarina couldn't wait to grow up and get away from this repressive atmosphere. By the time she was a teenager, she realized that her beauty could be the passport to her future. She was the youngest, but there was little feeling of kinship between her and her siblings. Each one was vying for their parents' attention and approval and was quick to run to their father with tales about sibling misbehavior. There was suspicion and mistrust amongst them all.

When Katarina was seventeen, she won first prize in the local village beauty pageant and was encouraged to enter a beauty pageant in Linz. She was just nineteen when she won this competition and went on to other regional pageants, local modeling and sponsorship opportunities. Naturally, her parents disapproved of her career choice. She didn't care, and just before her twenty-first birthday, she left home, moved to Vienna, and never spoke to any of her family again. In Vienna, she obtained some local modeling commissions and eventually entered the national beauty-pageant competition, being crowned *Miss Austria* in 1960. Shortly thereafter, while attending the Austrian National Wine Industry annual charity fundraising event, she met Von Schuyler, one of Austria's leading winemakers and distributors. She was the celebrity for the evening, announcing raffle and silent auction prizes and having her photo taken with industry leaders.

Von Schuyler was struck by her cool beauty, and she was flattered to have this handsome man of the world, with connections in high places, take an interest in her. In the next few months, their relationship developed. He took her to society events where she was often the star attraction for the men and the envy of the women. He bought her expensive couture gowns and designer jewelry. They shared their passions for skiing and horseback riding. He took her to Milan for the fashion shows, the French Riviera in the summer, Paris and London and eventually to the USA. She loved every minute of it. She enjoyed their sexual relationship and became a willing partner to Von Schuyler's unusual sexual appetites. After a while, she became obsessed by many of his unnatural desires.

Eventually they talked marriage. Von Schuyler made it quite clear that he did not want children, but that he would look after her and give her complete freedom to pursue her own interests and the necessary financial backing to do so. This was the life she had dreamed about and found the offer very attractive. She was not particularly interested in children, based on her own childhood experiences, and was quite willing to trade off motherhood for the good life in the hands of this wealthy and worldly man. They were married on her twenty-fourth birthday in Klagenfurt in a small but lavish ceremony.

Von Schuyler was finishing breakfast in his study on Saturday morning when the telephone rang. It was Katarina.

"Hello, Schatzi," she said, using his affectionate nickname.

"How was your opera ladies event, my love? Have fun with all your girlfriends?" he responded somewhat sarcastically.

"It was wonderful," she replied, ignoring his sarcasm.

"Success, I hope."

"Absolutely, we raised a record amount for the opera and the event could not have gone more smoothly. But I've decided to come home this evening." She continued, "I should be home by about six. I'm just doing a little shopping this morning and then will leave after a quick lunch with some of my girls."

"I suppose that will be a post-mortem of last night," said Von Schuyler in a softer tone.

"Of course," Katarina lightly replied,

"Well, I'll tell cook you will be home for dinner," he continued. "Drive carefully."

Von Schuyler picked up the *Neue Kronen Zeitung*, the right-wing conservative newspaper lying on his desk. He read the headline – *Shooting at the Imperial*. He read on:

A guest at the exclusive Hotel Imperial was shot Friday afternoon while leaving the hotel with his wife and an unidentified friend. He was taken to the AKH General Hospital, where he remains in critical condition. At first, the police thought the shooting was an attempted robbery, but they now believe it may have been a Mafia-style contract-killing attempt. The victim, identified by the hotel as Dr. Gustav Bauer and his wife Vera, had checked into the hotel at around 3:00 p.m. The reservation for a luxury suite had been made by a Mr.

Walter Koenig on behalf of the Bauers. However Mr. Koenig informed the reception that there had been a change of plans and the Bauers would be leaving immediately. At approximately 4:30 p.m. their luggage was loaded into a waiting Jaguar outside the hotel; and, as they exited, led by Mr. Koenig and with the third man by their side, two men in black ski clothes ran at the party and shot Dr. Bauer at close range. Mrs. Bauer and the unidentified man were bundled into the Jaguar, which drove off in great haste. Mr. Koenig stayed with Dr. Bauer until an ambulance arrived and took him to the AKH Hospital, where he is believed to be in the intensive care unit in critical condition. At the present time, the police will give out no further information. We understand however that Dr. Bauer comes from Linz, and has been out of the country for many years.

Von Schuyler had already heard both radio and television reports on the shooting. They more or less followed the newspaper report. He was sure the "target" would not survive and was waiting for further news. He was pleased to see that the motive and details of the shooting were still sketchy, and the police appeared to have no idea who could be responsible. He sat at his desk for a while making notes on how the FPÖ could capitalize on this incident in the run-up to the elections. Behind him on an ornate credenza were a number of photographs of Von Schuyler and Katarina on their wedding day, horseback riding, being presented to French President Charles de Gaulle, and Von Schuyler and Kurt Waldheim in animated conversation. In every photo, Katarina looked exquisite, and Von Schuyler displayed a wide engaging smile. There was also a recent photograph of the Von Schuylers in formal dress at the Austrian National Wine Industry Conference last year, with Karl wearing the sash and medal of Chairman of the Board of Governors, to which he had been appointed in December 1980, and Katarina, beautifully bejeweled and gowned, slightly thicker and heavier than her earlier photographs, but still extremely beautiful, her blonde hair somewhat darker, but her blue eyes just as bright. There were no photographs on the credenza of Von Schuyler or Katarina prior to their marriage.

It was a beautiful sunny day. A cloudless blue sky, and the sparkling white snow against the dark green forest made the day a picture postcard.

Von Schuyler decided it was just perfect for one of his regular morning constitutionals. He went into the back hall, where Rajah, his German shepherd, was lying on the floor. He put on his heavy boots, wrapped himself up in a thick jacket and hat and took a ski pole as he ventured out into the clear cold fresh air followed by Rajah, with tail wagging furiously.

He walked across the drive in front of his beautiful Baroque cream and white home. The ten-bedroom Schloss Lendorf had been built in 1810 by Count Klaus von Lendorf, a wealthy landowner from Klagenfurt. In the 1870s, the house had been purchased by Horst von Schuyler, a Bavarian gun manufacturer, who had made his fortune supplying weapons to the Prussian Army during the Franco-Prussian war. He built a factory in Klagenfurt and moved his family to Austria and his 1200-acre estate. The purchase of Lendorf, as the estate was usually called, established Von Schuyler in Austrian society, and his business prospered as he became a leading supplier to the Austrian-Hungarian Empire Army. With the advent of the Great War, Von Schuyler's two sons, Wilhelm and Gerhard, expanded the business by building a giant armaments factory in Linz. In the difficult economic times between the wars throughout the Twenties, the factories nearly went bankrupt. Gerhard moved to Argentina, while Wilhelm struggled on. But with the Second World War looming in the late 1930s, Wilhelm expanded the business further. His factories covered over four hundred acres in Linz and eighty acres in Klagenfurt.

Von Schuyler walked into the woods and followed a beaten-down trail through the snow, with Rajah at his heels. A soft breeze rattled through the pines, and the sharp smell delighted Von Schuyler's senses. The trail wound through the woods, slowly descending after a couple of kilometers or so to the valley floor where the Lendorf dairy farm was located. The farm had 120 cows and state-of-the-art equipment to supply milk, cream and butter products to Klagenfurt and the surrounding area. During the winter, the cows were housed in a giant barn. As Von Schuyler approached, he saw Viktor, the head of his eight-man security team coming out of the milking shed.

They greeted each other, remarking on the beautiful day, as Von Schuyler asked some questions about the daily operations.

Viktor was the oldest and most senior of the Von Schuyler security team. Five of the members were from East Germany and three from Austria. They all had army or commando training, or had served in the police or security forces. They were all nationalist conservatives. They considered themselves simply "political," or as the media would describe them, "neo-Nazis." They shared various duties around the estate, swapping responsibilities on a daily or weekly basis according to an agreed schedule. Two men would be responsible for managing the gatehouse at the entrance to the estate, checking vehicles in and out. Two men were allocated to look after Von Schuyler's four automobiles – the Mercedes 600, the Mercedes 300 SL, the Audi Quattro Estate used by Katarina, and the Land Rover used mainly for driving around the estate. Two other men would be working in the stables where four beautiful horses ridden by Von Schuyler and Katarina were housed, groomed and kept in perfect health. The team also had a supervisory responsibility, not only of the dairy farm but also of the commercial timber business established on nearly one-thousand acres of woodlands covering most of the Lendorf Estate. Although the men were not part of a military unit, Von Schuyler liked them to have the discipline of one. Members were crack shots with a pistol and rifle, and experts in martial arts. They maintained a military bearing and dressed in black in accordance with Von Schuyler's wishes. They had performed a number of missions over the years, ranging from collection of debts to arranging the mysterious disappearances of certain political, media, and business competitors, to unexplained fires in the wine country north of Vienna, which had led to Von Schuyler's advantageous purchases, establishing his V.S. Wines as the leading producer, distributor and exporter of Austrian wines. They always carried out their orders without questions, maintained the agreed code of silence about their activities, and were very well rewarded. Von Schuyler commanded his security team with ruthless efficiency.

Von Schuyler walked around the dairy farm, stopping to talk to the farm manager and nodding or talking to various farmhands. He went into the barn and watched the cows munching on the winter hay, and also visited the milking shed and admired, with satisfaction, how clean and spotless the area was. After spending half an hour or so at the farm, he hiked back up the trail through the snow, which was deep in places, with Rajah at his heels, returning to the house; and, after changing out of his boots and other clothing, he entered his study just as the telephone was ringing.

It was Sergei.

"He is still alive!"

"What?" responded Von Schuyler. "Are you sure?"

"Absolutely, he has come through surgery and is in the IC unit at the AKH Hospital," said Sergei in a cold hard voice.

"I can't imagine how he survived," said Von Schuyler.

"Well, he did. And, you need to take care of it," Sergei continued, emphatically.

"Of course, but I can't do it today."

"Not today! What do you mean?" replied Sergei with his voice rising. "Do you want your money or not?"

"I will need a little time to get my people organized, and the drive back to Vienna on a Saturday afternoon could take five or six hours. But I can take care of it, tomorrow," responded Von Schuyler.

"If we put it off, they may move him out of our reach," said Sergei, now very angry.

"Well, it is also possible he could die," replied Von Schuyler. "I just don't think I can get it done today."

"Okay, tomorrow is Sunday. Maybe it could be the best time because there will be lots of visitors milling around. He's on the third floor and has a policeman outside of his room."

"We will take care of it." said Von Schuyler.

"Make sure that you do," said Sergei.

Before Von Schuyler could respond, the phone went dead. Von Schuyler sat at his desk, and pondered the situation. He couldn't believe the target had survived. Kurt and Helmut had said they had shot him twice at point-blank range in the chest. How could he still be alive? Nevertheless, he would have to deal with the situation and quickly. After a few moments, he picked up a walkie-talkie on his desk and called for Viktor, Kurt and Helmut to come to his study.

Ten minutes later they arrived.

"I have been informed the target has survived," he said, looking at Kurt.

"Good God, that's impossible," responded Kurt, with the color draining from his face, as he started to shake with fear.

"Well, impossible or not, that is the case, you idiot," said Von Schuyler curtly, his voice rising. "You seem to have been incapable of shooting a man dead, from point-blank range." He paused and glared at Kurt menacingly.

"So we need to take care of the situation and quickly," he continued. "I want you all to go into Vienna tomorrow morning and finish the job. The target is in the IC unit on the third floor of AKH Hospital. By early afternoon, there should be lots of visitors at the hospital. I suggest you go down to the dairy farm and take a couple of white coats so as you look like doctors. Do not wear your usual outfits. Choose something casual – jeans, sweaters, something like that. I don't want you to be noticed. Follow the same routine using the BMW and the van. Kurt you can drive the van. Take another couple of men to help. You will have to deal with a police guard outside of the room. Do so quietly, then get into the hospital room, and finish off the target and get out of there as quickly as possible." He paused. "No mistakes. Do I make myself clear?"

"Yes, Herr Von Schuyler," they both responded in unison, fear just behind their eyes.

"Viktor," said Von Schuyler. "Make sure that any life-support equipment is dealt with at the same time."

"Yes, sir," responded Viktor.

"Okay then," continued Von Schuyler. "Go to the tack room, select your weapons, disguises and whatever else you need and make all your preparations this afternoon and evening, so you can leave early tomorrow morning. Get the job finished." He paused again. "No excuses," he said with some finality, his cold eyes seeming to penetrate their skulls.

Viktor, Helmut and Kurt entered the tack room, hidden behind storage shelving on sliding rollers in part of the stable block. This was a large windowless room in which were stored various weapons – AK-47s, Uzi machine guns and pistols, silencers, grenades and detonators. In addition, there was a large rack of clothing including police uniforms, camouflaged army uniforms, and various items of everyday clothing. There was also a makeup counter with wigs, moustaches and numerous styles of glasses. The tack room also contained more basic assault items such as brass knuckles, rubber truncheons, crowbars and road spikes. They all chose their disguises. For Victor, this was a black curly-haired wig and black-rimmed glasses. For Helmut, a lighter brown wig with sideburns and hair of a hippie length, and for Kurt, a fair-haired wig and mustache. They all chose Mauser pistols with silencers.

After making their selections and placing everything in a pile for the following morning, they went down to the dairy and took two white coats.

Chapter 2

Alex Campbell was up early. He had not slept well. He didn't want to wake up Julia so early, so he crept out of the bedroom, made himself a cup of tea and was looking across Regent's Park as the sun was coming up. It looked like it would be a glorious day. The sun was glinting on the dome of the mosque overlooking Rossmore Road. He looked down on Prince Albert Road. It was Saturday morning, so there was little traffic.

He was still angry. He was angry at Tim Bevans, the head of Britain's secret intelligence services – MI6. He was annoyed at himself for putting his life at risk. How quickly he had got into such a dangerous situation. He had been too cavalier in handling these "little jobs" for Tim over the years. Now he wasn't sure he hadn't been used. He and Anna Kaluza had gone through hell and high water to get out of Poland, only for Keller to be shot in Vienna. Who could have possibly known about the plan? Was it MI6? He felt that there must be something Tim Bevans hadn't told him. But maybe it was a KGB hit, or the Polish secret police or even the CIA. His mind was racing. Assassination? Is that how the West would dispose of the one of the world's most renowned nuclear physicists? He didn't have any answers but was determined to question Tim and get to the bottom of this mystery. He felt sick to his stomach. Keller was now probably dead.

He'd been absolutely dumbstruck when Keller unwittingly revealed he was the only survivor of the Holocaust out of the whole Kornmehl family. And yet Alex hadn't been able to tell him they were related before they left the hotel and the fatal shooting took place. He was agonizing over the situation.

And then there was Julia. Of course, she had the right to be furious at him. He'd had to tell her that he'd been doing "little jobs" for Tim Bevans for the past four decades. His suit and shirt were covered in blood. He couldn't just pass it off. After her initial fear and concern, she really let him have it. And why not? She was right. He had put his life at risk for the excitement and the rush of adrenaline of working for MI6.

He waited until about 8 a.m. before calling Tim.

"Tim," Alex said curtly.

"Good morning, Alex, let me call you back on my private line."

A couple of moments later the phone rang. Alex picked it up quickly so as not to disturb Julia.

"Are you OK?" asked Tim.

"Just about. But wiped out as you would expect," responded Alex. Before Tim could answer, Alex continued, "What the hell is going on?

"I don't really know, Alex," said Tim. "We are trying to get to the bottom of it right now. But, I know you've had a really rough time, and I want to tell you how appreciative we are for all that you've done for the service and for the country."

"Never mind that crap," said Alex, his voice rising with renewed anger, as his Scottish brogue came through. "Is Keller alive?"

"Yes," said Tim. "He is in the intensive care unit in a hospital in Vienna."

"What's the prognosis?" asked Alex.

"They tell me it's about fifty-fifty at the moment, but they're hopeful," replied Tim.

Fifty-fifty... How hopeful could they really be? Alex thought, as he continued. "Do you have any idea who was responsible?"

"To be perfectly honest, Alex, at this time we really don't have a clue," said Tim.

"Why not?" shot back Alex in his full aggressive chief-executive voice. "You are the fucking Secret Service. Where is your intelligence on this?"

"I believe it's an inside job, unfortunately."

"You believe!!" responded Alex. "Why don't you know?"

"We're not playing cowboys and Indians here Alex," responded Tim sarcastically, clearly angered by Alex's retort.

"You know we are thin on the ground in Eastern Europe including Poland, since Burgess and Maclean wiped out most of our network. That is why I called on you for help on this mission. We could not miss this incredible opportunity to help Professor Keller and his wife defect to the West. Anna Kaluza has given us a preliminary briefing. We were all shocked to hear that Krystyna Keller had lost her life, and that you had risked yours, in trying to save her. As I said, Her Majesty's government is very appreciative," Tim concluded rather formally.

"Well, Tim, I want to know why there was such an intelligence failure and I would like to meet with you personally to discuss this whole mess in much more detail," Alex responded.

"Of course, I understand," replied Tim, now the calm diplomat. "We need to do that anyway. I`d like you to come into the office for a debriefing session, if that's okay with you, Alex."

"Of course," Alex said in a softer tone and changing the subject. "How is Anna Kaluza doing?"

"She is exhausted, but she is safe and under our protection. We shall be debriefing her as well."

"When do you want to see me?" asked Alex.

"As soon as possible," replied Tim. "Would Monday afternoon at 2:30 work?"

"Yes, that should be okay."

"Then 2:30 at the Lambeth headquarters. Ask for me when you arrive."

"Fine," said Alex, now calmer.

"I'm really sorry you had to go through this ordeal. I had no idea that this mission would turn out to be so dangerous and complicated. It certainly wasn't meant to be," said Tim, lowering the temperature of the conversation.

"Well, I didn't anticipate that either," said Alex somewhat sarcastically. "I came home covered in blood, so I am afraid I had to tell Julia. I know about the 'Official Secrets Act' and all that, but there was no other way."

"I understand," said Tim. "Don't worry about it. I'll see you on Monday. If anything else crops up during the weekend or I have any further news on Keller, I'll give you a ring."

Sir Alex Campbell was someone you noticed. Just over six feet tall, broad shoulders, well built with fair wiry hair, slightly reddish but thinning on top and graying at the side. A pair of large blue-green eyes and a slight suntan complemented his rugged handsome face. Confident, charming, tough but fair, Alex Campbell had achieved success and recognition in Britain's business, political, and social circles.

He was Chairman of the Campbell Group, one of the UK's largest international drinks companies, proprietors of Campbell's Reserve, the world's third-largest-selling scotch whisky, and a variety of international brands through their subsidiaries in the US and France. The business had been founded by Alex's grandfather, Jacob Kornmehl, who had emigrated from Tarnów in Poland in 1892, fleeing pograms, persecution and poverty and arriving in Dundee, Scotland with the intention of moving on to the United States, but eventually staying, putting down roots and building the family business. Since taking over the business in the 1950s, Alex had expanded it dramatically, moving into bourbon, cognac and rum, through a series of strategic acquisitions, in the US, France, and Jamaica. He had been knighted by H.M. Queen Elizabeth for services to British exports in 1976, and taken the company public in 1978. He was a friend of Margaret Thatcher and other government ministers; and despite avoiding publicity like the plague, he was well-known in the City and political circles.

It was not unusual for the MI6 to use British businessmen who qualified for top security clearance to carry out minor tasks in countries where the businessman might have access to the right quarters. Over the years, Alex Campbell, with his network of representatives in virtually every major country in the world, had at Tim's request, carried out some of those "little jobs." They had not been particularly dangerous or complicated, and Alex had been happy to do his bit for Queen and country. In fact, he enjoyed each mission's excitement and the charge of adrenalin that went with each "little job." Alex had a secret security clearance, and had acted on behalf of MI6 in a number of matters over the past four decades, on infrequent occasions when the British government could not be seen to be involved in obtaining information, receiving or delivering intelligence.

Alex had met Tim Bevans at the end of 1944 towards the end of the Second World War, when he'd been transferred from the Royal Scots Guards to the Army Intelligence Corps because of his fluency in Polish and German. Tim Bevans had similarly been transferred from the Middlesex Regiment because of his fluency in German as well. In April 1945, these nineteen-year-old lieutenants had been sent to Bergen-Belsen concentration camp two days after its liberation by British and Canadian forces. The shared horrors of what they saw in those camps were to stay with them for decades. Tim Bevans stayed in Army Intelligence after the war, eventually transferring to MI6 where he worked his way up until being appointed Chief Officer in 1980. Over the past forty years, Tim Bevans had given Alex "little jobs" to do in Argentina, Mexico, South Africa, and many other countries whilst on business trips to visit with Campbell's agents and importers. None of these were very complicated: an envelope in his hotel bedroom; bringing home a local magazine which had been given to him by a taxi driver; buying a large bottle of aspirin at a specific pharmacy. But sometimes the "little jobs" were substantial: smuggling photos of ports and airports, meeting politicians in remote locations and exchanging briefcases. These had certainly made him nervous on more than one occasion, and he had often thought he was crazy to expose himself to risk, however remote.

But, when some three weeks ago while they were having lunch at the Savoy Grill together, Tim had asked Alex whether he would be prepared to do a "little job" in Poland, Alex said he would be pleased to hear more. Alex had already told him that he would be going to Kraków in Poland to sign a new vodka deal, to represent Poland's leading vodka, Walova, in the UK, Europe and USA. Perhaps not surprisingly, Tim apparently already had that information. A few days later, Alex went to Tim's office to hear about the latest mission. After a few minutes of chitchat, tea, and biscuits, Tim got to the point.

"Have you ever heard of Professor Erik Keller?" he asked.

"I think I've heard the name," responded Alex. "But I've got no idea who he is."

"He is a Polish nuclear physicist," said Tim, leaning forward and showing Alex a black-and-white photo of an intense-looking middle-aged man with close-cropped gray hair, and glasses.

"Keller is an expert on nuclear-reaction mechanisms, who spent many years working in both Warsaw and Moscow and is one of the leading physicists in the world and, in two weeks, he will be in Kraków to receive a Medal of Honor from the Polish Academy of Sciences."

"Kraków?" responded Alex, immediately seeing the connection, as he sipped his tea.

Tim nodded and then went on. "About six months ago, his two sons, both of whom were teaching at Warsaw University, were killed. They were active supporters of the Solidarity protest movement which had started in the Gdansk shipyards. Keller had been warned by the Polish secret police that he should keep his sons away from trouble. Apparently, he talked to them, but to no avail." Tim handed Alex a digestive biscuit. Alex accepted it gratefully. "A few weeks later, they were driving to Gdansk and were hit by a large flatbed truck carrying steel girders, which banged into their car as they were crossing a bridge – pushing the car off the bridge and into freefall five-hundred feet to the valley below. Both were killed as the car exploded. The police described it as an accident caused by a malfunction of the truck brakes."

"I think we've heard of those kinds of accidents before?" said Alex.

"Exactly." Tim sipped his tea and then continued slowly. "Of course Keller and his wife didn't believe it, nor did the leaders of the Solidarity movement."

"You think this incident was part of the crackdown?" said Alex.

"Yes, there is no doubt that the Jaruzelski government was behind it." Tim put down his cup as he leaned towards Alex. "Despite their privileged lives, we knew Keller and his wife had been unhappy for years. For the past decade, much of his work was on military capabilities involving long stays in Moscow. We have been courting him carefully for some time. He has no other family in Poland." He stopped a moment and then said quietly, "We now believe our time has come."

"What makes you think that?" asked Alex.

"The Polish economy is in ruins. US sanctions have been crippling, and there is considerable doubt whether Poland will be able to meet its international debt obligations. Life is miserable. The Kellers have apparently had it with the communist system, are traumatized by the deaths of their two sons and want to leave the country." He paused, and then continued in a low voice, "We now know they are willing to defect and come to England." He paused again. "We have made the necessary arrangements." Tim stopped talking, sipped his tea, and munched another digestive, letting Alex absorb this information.

"Sounds like a golden opportunity," said Alex. "How can I help?"

"Alex, it will be of considerable help if you could arrange to be in Kraków the same time as the Polish Academy of Sciences Meeting, which is Thursday, the 24th of February."

"That's no problem," Alex responded, realizing once again he was jumping in headfirst, but he felt a tingle of excitement at being involved in such an important mission.

Tim went on to describe how Alex would be given a small airline shoulder bag in which would be sewn two passports and cash, to pay off anyone that took too keen an interest. He told Alex one of their MI6 agents would meet him at his hotel in Kraków to retrieve the airline bag.

"And when you have handed over the airline bag, you will have done your job," said Tim. "You can then leave on Friday morning and fly back to London."

Tim said slowly but emphatically, "Alex we don't often have an opportunity to bring to the West one of the greatest scientists of our time. This could have a far-reaching effect, not only on the security of this country, but the whole of the free world."

"My god," said Alex. "This is serious stuff."

"Very," replied Tim. "What do you think?"

Alex found himself once again agreeing to do another of Tim's "little jobs," which turned out not to be quite as uncomplicated as Tim had made out.

* * *

Alex went back into the bedroom to find Julia just awakening, her long black hair splayed across the pillow framing her still-beautiful olive-skin complexion and deep blue eyes.

"What time is it?" she enquired huskily.

"About eight. I couldn't sleep," responded Alex.

"After what you've been through, I can't believe you didn't go off like a light."

"Well I couldn't help thinking about what happened in Poland."

"I'm not happy, Alex," said Julia, more awake now and remembering her anger of last night. "I am amazed you would take such risks, without telling me."

"Well, I couldn't tell you. I had to sign the Official Secrets Act," said Alex apologetically. "I'm sorry."

"You may be sorry, but you could be dead in Poland. I want you to promise me, to never do this again," she continued before he could respond. "What time did you wake up?" she asked.

"About six."

"What have you been doing?"

"I made myself a cup of tea and I phoned Tim about twenty minutes ago."

"What did he have to say?"

"Well, of course, he was apologetic, and said all the usual things about appreciation of Queen and country."

"That means nothing. Does he know who was responsible?"

"No. He doesn't seem to know any more than I do."

"Is Keller alive?"

"Yes, apparently he is in critical condition in a hospital in Vienna. The doctors think he has a fifty-fifty chance."

"Did you tell him about the family connection?"

"Not yet. I didn't think it appropriate to talk about family matters. Not just yet, anyway. I have a meeting with him on Monday afternoon, and I will certainly let him know then.

"Maybe you'll learn more about Keller and the whole incident."

"I certainly hope so," said Alex.

Chapter 3

It was a bright and sunny day as Kurt drove the van through light Sunday traffic into Vienna, but as they got near the city, the weather clouded over, and it looked like it could shower again. Kurt parked the van in a quiet side street.

Fifteen minutes later, Helmut, with Viktor riding pillion, parked the BMW motorcycle fifty meters from the side entrance to one of the main buildings in the AKH General Hospital, near a construction fence for the twin towers being built, making the AKH, the Allgemeines Krankenhaus der Stadt Wien, the largest hospital in Europe. They had done their homework and knew the layout and where the IC floor was located. Helmut's hands were visibly shaking as they put on their white coats and marched into the entrance, exchanging nervous glances. It had been quite a while since either one of them had done a "hit" for Von Schuyler. But they were more scared of him and the ruthless punishment they knew he would deliver if they failed. Over the years some members of his "security team" had mysteriously disappeared.

The building lobby was bustling with visitors. Men, women and children of all ages, some carrying flowers or boxes of pastries and cakes. No one seemed to notice Viktor and Helmut who strode across the lobby confidently and headed to the elevator to the intensive-care unit. The doors to the IC unit were closed and a pass-key code was needed to enter. They had expected this to be the case and consequently they stood talking, moving from foot to foot but looking like many of the other doctors and nurses hurrying by, or going in and out of the IC unit. Within a few minutes, they saw their opportunity. The double doors opened and a doctor and nurse walked out slowly and deep in conversation. There was nobody else around, so before the doors automatically closed again, Viktor and Helmut slipped in.

On the right-hand side was a nurses' station with a small seating area facing it. A long corridor disappeared into the distance. Three doors down, Viktor could see a young fresh-faced policeman sitting in a plastic chair lounging back against the wall outside one of the rooms, looking bored and staring into space. He knew this must be the target's hospital room. He nudged Helmut and nodded towards the room. They briskly marched up the corridor; and, as they approached the policeman, Helmut took out his Mauser pistol with silencer attached and shot the policeman between the eyes. He had a stunned expression on his face, and as his eyes slowly closed, he slouched back in his chair. They then entered the darkened hospital room and saw the target covered with a blanket on a hospital bed with an oxygen mask on his face and an IV bag on a stand, dripping into his veins. A heart monitor was beeping and the screen showed his heart rate and pulse.

They both fired three shots into the body, which bounced on the bed. Helmut dragged the oxygen mask and IV off the body, while Viktor put two bullets into the heart-monitoring equipment. This whole process had taken less than thirty seconds. Suddenly, they heard a crash and a scream outside the door. They exited quickly, to see a wide-eyed nurse looking at the policeman who had slid down into his plastic chair. Blood was slowly dripping down his face. She had dropped a tray of instruments. Three white-coated doctors at the end of the corridor turned and looked at the retreating Viktor and Helmut, shouted "Halt!" and started running towards them. Viktor had already identified an emergency exit door just past the nurses' station. They ran towards it, pushed open the door, setting off a loud alarm, and started running down the three flights of stairs. Two of the doctors continued to chase after them yelling "Halt!" again. They were nearly at the bottom when one of the doctors fired a shot at them which bounced off the metal banister. Viktor looked at Helmut with surprise and shock in his eyes. They burst out through the emergency door onto a path some fifty meters from the BMW motorbike, and started running with the doctors on their heels.

"I'll cover," yelled Helmut, turning and dropping on one knee as he fired at the two doctors who dove to the ground as Helmut was up and running after Viktor. They were just twenty meters from their bike when another shot rang out and Helmut stumbled and fell into the snow-covered grass. Viktor looked around with alarm. Helmut was not moving, and blood was oozing into the snow. He hesitated a moment and then ran on towards the bike, jumped on and kicked it into a quick start as the sound of police-car sirens cut the cold air, and Viktor saw two cars approaching the car park at great speed.

He shot across the car park as one of the police cars braked and swerved across the entrance, blocking his exit, but he accelerated onto the sidewalk, around the back of the first police car and was on Wahringer Gürtel Road before the second car turned and gave chase, with sirens blaring. He was a good eight-hundred meters ahead of the police and swerving in and out of the traffic at a fast pace. He took a couple of quick turns to try and shake them. Within five minutes, he was on Alser Straße where the van had been parked in a quiet alley next to a warehouse. It being Sunday afternoon there was little traffic. Viktor zoomed up the ramp and cut the engine as he entered the rear of the van. He could hear the police sirens fading in the distance. The roller shutter was brought down, and the vehicle moved out into the empty streets eventually crossing the bridge and linking up with the E 49, which would take them out of Vienna and back to the Autobahn to Carinthia.

"What the hell happened? Where's Helmut?" asked Kurt.

"I think he is dead," responded Viktor, and then gave Kurt a full description of the events.

"This could open up a whole can of worms," said Kurt after listening to the story. "The boss will not be happy."

Von Schuyler had watched the six o'clock television news. The lead story was that Dr Gustav Bauer, the Imperial Hotel shooting victim, had been shot dead in his hospital room at the AKH Hospital intensive-care unit. One of the assailants had been fatally shot by a plainclothes policeman as they were attempting to escape. A police spokesman stated that, while they did not know the motive for the murder, it had the trappings of a contract killing by the Mafia or similar criminal elements. On hearing this news, Von Schuyler's face reddened as his anger rose within him. How could this possibly have happened? He had instructed Viktor and Helmut to be in and out of the hospital room within a few seconds. One of them was now dead. This could present a real problem, although he knew that neither of them would carry any identification in accordance with strict policy for all missions. Nevertheless, perhaps they could be traced to the Lendorf Estate at some stage, and embarrassing questions might be asked.

The second lead story on the news was about the FPÖ demonstration bringing out an estimated 50,000 supporters marching in the streets with banners demanding law and order, changed immigration laws, and the removal of Bruno Kreisky, the Austrian Chancellor. Von Schuyler was happy to see that the march had gone off peacefully and that Haider's speech and rallying of his supporters did not bring about any violence. The timing was excellent and would undoubtedly bring additional votes to the FPÖ in the forthcoming elections.

Three hours later, Viktor and Kurt were back at Lensdorf. Within a few minutes of their arrival, Viktor was in Von Schuyler's study.

"Well then, let's have a full report," said Von Schuyler curtly, with a withering stare.

"We carried out the mission in accordance with the plan, Herr Von Schuyler," said Viktor, shaking with fear. "We fired six bullets into the target, removed the IV support, and destroyed the heart-monitoring equipment. We shot the policeman sitting at the door of the target's hospital room, but there were three doctors in white coats at the end of the corridor, and two of them started chasing us. They shouted at us a couple of times as we burst through the emergency exit and raced down the stairs. One fired a shot at us, which missed, and then we were out into the open some fifty meters from the BMW. We had covered about half that distance when another shot was fired, and Helmut staggered off the path and into the snow. I stopped for a second to check. He was lying still and blood was oozing from a wound. He appeared to be dead. I then raced to the BMW, jumped on, and kick-started the engine, just as two police cars arrived. One blocked the exit to the car park, but I got past it and was out of the car park before any more shots could be fired."

"Your three doctors were probably policemen," interjected Von Schuyler.

"Probably, but we had no way to know that when we were carrying out the mission."

"I want to make sure that you carried out normal procedures and that neither you nor Helmut were carrying any identification. Was that the case?" Von Schuyler continued, sharply.

"Yes, neither of us had any ID on our clothing."

"This is a mess. I can't believe you fucked up a simple 'hit.' Where was your training?" continued Von Schuyler, controlled anger in his voice. "We shall have to see how this develops. In the meantime, I want you to take the BMW and put it in the tack room and leave it there until further notice. Also, remove your disguise, clear out Helmut's room; and, if any enquiries are made about him now or at any time in the future, he was a former employee and left our employment a few days before this incident took place. Is that clear, Viktor?"

"Yes, sir," responded Viktor, eager to agree. He and most members of the "security" team had been on the receiving end of Von Schuyler's violent outbursts on many occasions.

"Make sure that the rest of the security team understands those instructions. Now go get cleaned up. My instructions are to be followed to the letter. To the letter – do you hear?"

"Yes, sir," responded Viktor as he clicked his heels turned and left the room.

Von Schuyler sat at his desk for a few moments pondering the situation.

Like all of Von Schuyler's security team, Helmut Fischer had forged papers and an alias. His real name was Gunter Foch and he came from Leipzig. He had been a former Stasi undercover agent and had lost his job due to his neo-Nazi leanings. Von Schuyler had hired him nearly three years previously, giving him his new ID and papers. He had been – for the most part – an efficient and ruthless operative for the security team. He had never been in trouble with the East German police, nor was he known in the West, and Von Schuyler felt reasonably confident that the Viennese police authorities would not be able to trace him to Lendorf.

After another couple of minutes, he picked up the phone and dialed.

"Sergei," he said to the voice at the other end. "The mission has been completed."

"Yes, I saw the news," came the response. "Your man – shot dead so they say," he continued.

"Yes, that's a bit of a blow, but it is highly unlikely he could be traced back here. He carried no ID, doesn't have a record, and has been operating under an alias for the last three years."

"Well, that's your problem," continued Sergei, dismissively. "As long as you feel confident, that's fine with me."

"I'd like the bank transfer to be made as soon as possible," continued Von Schuyler.

"I am sure you would," said Sergei sarcastically. "The money will be transferred when we are confident there are no other problems. Maybe in a couple of days."

"Fine," responded Von Schuyler, seething at Sergei's insulting tone. There were no further niceties as they both put the phone down.

Von Schuyler got up from his desk, left the study and walked across the hallway to the living room. He entered the elegantly furnished room with its large mantelpiece, above which was a portrait of Katarina painted in 1972 by Franz Koch, one of Austrian's leading portrait artists. A log fire was roaring in the fireplace. The room was elegantly furnished with overstuffed settees and armchairs and soft lamps, the walls adorned with French Impressionists and other works of art, including a Pissarro, a small Degas and a Henri Lebasque. Von Schuyler was in his Sunday-casual clothes, a knit camel cashmere cardigan with leather buttons, over a pale-check cream shirt with green corduroy trousers and heavy brown leather shoes. Katarina was sitting in one of the armchairs reading a *Vogue* magazine, elegantly dressed in Loro Piana beige pants and a silk and cashmere pale blue twinset. Her blonde hair was swept up above her forehead and pulled up in a loose bun, her blue eyes heavily made up with mascara. She was lavishly powdered, her lipstick a bright orange as bright as her style. She looked up with a smile.

"Do you know Helmut?" asked Von Schuyler.

"Helmut who?" replied Katarina.

"Helmut who works for us," said Von Schuyler patiently.

"No, I don't think so. Which one is he?" Katarina had always been disinterested and dismissive of all of the staff, and always maintained very formal relations even with the head house-keeper, Adela. She was too much involved in her own life to have any interest in the "servants."

"Well, Helmut is one of my personal team," replied Von Schuyler.

"Oh, the men in black," said Katarina, with a slight wicked smile.

"Yes," replied Von Schuyler. "Anyway, Helmut was the one

with the pale face and close-cropped hair. I know that he's driven you before, and probably helped you on various chores from time to time," continued Von Schuyler.

"Well, maybe," said Katarina. "But I don't know one from the other. They're always dressed in black and look exactly the same to me," she said dismissively.

"Anyway, Helmut is no longer with us," continued Von Schuyler.

"Oh?" said Katarina quizzically.

"And I want to make sure, Katarina, that, if you are ever questioned about his employment, you deny knowing who he is or what he did on the estate, and you confirm that he left our employment early last week, on the 20th or 21st of February."

Katarina looked puzzled.

"It's a business issue, my dear," said Von Schuyler. "But it is essential that we distance ourselves from Helmut if his name ever comes up in the future. Is that understood?" he said in a hardening voice, his cold gray eyes looking directly into hers.

Katarina knew that voice and recognized that it was time to acquiesce to all requests and ask no further questions.

"Of course, my love," she said sweetly. "I shall definitely follow your instructions if the need arises."

"Thank you, my dear," Von Schuyler said with a soft smile, flashing his famous grin. At that moment, there was a knock on the door and Ernst, the butler, came in.

"Your dinner is ready to be served in the morning room, sir," he said.

"Thank you, Ernst. We shall be there in a minute."

Chapter 4

Alex and Julia had dined with their friends, the Lewis's, at Mimmo's restaurant in Belgravia on Sunday evening. Alex was still feeling exhausted from his ordeal and his mind kept wandering. He was preoccupied with Keller and not in the mood for friendly chatter. When they returned home, there was a message from Tim Bevans. Alex called back early Monday morning. Tim's secretary, Fiona, informed Alex that Mr. Bevans was meeting with the minister and would not be available until at least 2:00 p.m. She confirmed Alex's appointment at 2:30, so Alex had no choice but to wait for Tim's update.

Frank, Alex's chauffeur, pulled the Mercedes up to the Lambeth Headquarters of MI6 a few minutes before 2:30. Alex checked in at the Commissioner's Desk and shortly thereafter was escorted to Tim Bevan's large corner office on the ninth floor, with spectacular views across the River Thames from the Houses of Parliament to Chelsea.

Tim, a tall slim handsome man with an engaging smile and sleeked back graying hair, greeted Alex warmly. His blue suit, white shirt and dark red tie set off his intelligent bespectacled face. They were still good friends. Or were they? After the Keller debacle, Alex no longer felt certain whom he could trust.

"So nice to see you, Alex," said Tim, smiling, perhaps too extravagantly, as he held out his hand and ushered Alex to a comfortable armchair in the large seating area by the plate-glass window.

"Good to see you again, Tim," responded Alex, with his own charming smile. "Well, what was the message?"

"Good news and bad," responded Tim. "The good news is that Keller is now in London. The bad news is there was another attempt to murder him in Vienna."

"Good God," responded Alex nearly jumping out of his seat.

"What happened?"

"We've been working with the Viennese police, and had agreed with them that we should both take every precaution to protect Keller. We had Toby Harris from our embassy assigned to them. I think you met him in Vienna, Alex."

"Yes I did."

"Harris and a couple of plainclothes policemen dressed as doctors hung around in the corridor of the intensive-care unit where Keller was receiving treatment. We also made arrangements for a uniformed officer to sit outside a hospital room where a recently discovered dead vagrant was placed, with various intensive-care heart-monitoring and IV equipment set up to appear operational, in case there was an attack on Keller." Tim paused as Alex anxiously leaned forward in his chair, and then went on to tell Alex what had transpired at the hospital.

"Unbelievable," said Alex. "Sounds like a Hollywood movie."

"Sometimes fact is stranger than fiction," responded Tim. "But this was serious stuff, Alex. The other assailant got away on a motorbike, similar to the shooting outside the Hotel Imperial." Tim paused. "The man they shot has not yet been identified. In fact he had no ID on him. Nevertheless, Interpol has been informed and, if he has any sort of police record, we shall be able to identify him. That should give us a big clue as to who is behind the attempted assassination of Keller."

"Well, how come Keller is now in London?" asked Alex.

"Despite his delicate state of health, we decided that we couldn't risk yet another attack on his life," Tim responded. "He's obviously very important to somebody who recognizes the damage he could do to the Eastern bloc. So, we decided to move him to London. We arranged a private ambulance plane. We took a big risk; he's in critical condition, after all. We flew him to Northolt yesterday evening and transferred him to the London Clinic." Tim paused. "That's when I called you, Alex."

"Thanks. How is he doing now?" Alex responded anxiously.

"Not too badly, considering the ordeal we put him through. We've got the best people at the clinic looking after him and they think there are some signs of improvement today. We'll know more in the next 48 hours, but the prognosis is looking slightly better at the moment."

"That's a relief," said Alex.

"Alex, I can't stress enough how important Keller's defection is to the West. I had a meeting this morning with the Prime Minister, Foreign Secretary, and my minister, and they are very anxious to hear the outcome of this mission. Your help has been invaluable."

"My role was minimal, Tim, but I have to tell you, this mission proved to be even more interesting from my point of view." He cleared his throat, paused and then he said, "Erik Keller and I are closely related."

"What?" said Tim, looking puzzled. "What you mean?"

"I think you know that my grandfather, Jacob Kornmehl, left Tarnów in Poland in 1892 and emigrated to Dundee."

"Yes. Go on..."

"He came with my grandmother, who was pregnant at the time with my father, but he had been married before. He had a child with his first wife who died of cholera a few months after the birth. That son, Isaac Kornmehl, was brought up by his maternal aunt. She married a man called Kellerman. Isaac took his name. His son, Erik, shortened it to Keller after the War. We believed that all the Kornmehl family had perished in the Holocaust, but apparently, Erik Keller survived." Alex paused. "You will have to get him to tell you his story," he continued, but then paused again, holding back his emotions. "It's quite amazing, Tim," he said quietly.

"Good lord," Tim went on. "None of this is in his file. We thought he was a Catholic, brought up in Warsaw, educated at Warsaw University after the war, and married Krystina, who I understand was tragically shot dead as you escaped Poland."

"Yes, Tim," replied Alex somberly. "An awful accident. I will give you all the details, later."

"Have you told Keller of your family connection?" asked Tim.

"No, I didn't really have a chance. After all he has been through, he may get some comfort from finding out he has a large family here." He paused, then rubbed his temples. "Anna doesn't know either," he continued. "By the way, how is Anna?"

"She's doing well," responded Tim. "We sent her shopping with one of our agents this morning because, of course, she had hardly a stitch to wear. Just her ORBIS outfit and a rather bedraggled fur coat that I understand belonged to the unfortunate Krystina Keller."

"Yes, that's right," said Alex. "Anna took that from Krystina in order to cover up her uniform."

"Well we debriefed her this morning," said Tim. "God, what a life!"

"Really," said Alex with genuine interest. "I didn't know."

"Didn't she tell you about her early life and being born in a Russian labor camp?" asked Tim.

"No," replied Alex. "We were together less than 24 hours and really didn't have time to chitchat. We were completely focused on how to get the hell out of Poland and Czechoslovakia and into Austria."

"Of course, of course, I understand," responded Tim. "We're going to debrief her again on Wednesday afternoon at 2:30," he said slowly. "I would really appreciate your sitting in and watch the proceedings."

"Sure," replied Alex. "But why two debriefing sessions?"

"To be honest, Alex, we've got no idea where the leak came from. At the moment, we also have no idea who shot Keller. So you will appreciate we can't be too careful. We'd like to see if Anna's story on the second briefing is exactly the same, more or less word for word as her first. If this is the case, we would have reason to be suspicious."

"Surely you can't be thinking that Anna could have anything to do with Keller being shot," said Alex, his voice rising, as he was thinking, *What the hell are they talking about?* "After all, she risked her life on more than one occasion. She got us out of Czechoslovakia and into Austria," he continued firmly.

"I know," replied Tim. "But we have our protocol."

"Of course, your protocol," he responded, still annoyed. "A little more intelligence and a little less protocol, might be more productive."

"Well," Tim responded somewhat uptight. "This is how we operate and it has served the country well, for the last one-hundred years."

"Okay, I'll be there," said Alex, now lowering the tone, to his old friend. "But I do have a couple of questions for you."

"Fire away," said Tim.

"Who is Jan Kaluza?" asked Alex.

"Jan is Anna's brother and also works for the SIS. In fact, he's been one of our agents since the early '60s," replied Tim, looking at Alex quizzically.

"I just wanted to make sure that there was a Jan. Do you know what happened to him?" Alex continued, probing once again to see if Tim had told him everything. He still had a nagging feeling about trusting Tim and the SIS. He had never felt that before, but perhaps he should have.

"Well, according to Anna, he was shot in Krakow and taken away by Polish secret-service agents. We know not where. It's early days yet and, it will take us some time to find out if he's still alive and where he is located. All we can say so far is that our people don't appear to have been compromised; this morning at least, they are still in place. So either he isn't talking or they arrested him for something entirely different. Anyway, that is our thinking at the moment, Alex." He paused and looked out the window. The sky was now brilliant blue. For a moment, Tim seemed lost in thought, then he said, "Were you aware of the luggage that the Kellers brought out of Poland?"

"I think they had a rather battered old leather suitcase and a very large canvas-covered holdall."

"Did Keller have a briefcase, attaché case, backpack or something like that?"

"No, I don't remember anything like that," said Alex.

"Well that presents a bit of a problem," said Tim somberly.

"Why?" inquired Alex, looking anxious, and thinking, *Not another bombshell after all I've been through.*

"Keller was supposed to bring his notes, sketches, and mathe-matical calculations covering more than twenty years' work on nuclear-fusion techniques. Even though he's probably got a lot in his head, it is imperative that we have sight of those notes and plans. We've been through his luggage and there's nothing there. So, we believe, for some reason, he must have decided to leave those papers behind, and that puts a whole new slant on this mission. Obviously, we can't question him at this time but, hopefully if he starts to improve, this will be one of our first questions."

"Do you mean this whole mission could fail because we didn't bring back the papers with us?" asked Alex, truly aghast.

"I wouldn't say that but the papers are extremely important."

"Does Anna recollect seeing anything – some package, large envelope, backpack?" asked Alex.

"No she gave the same answer as you," said Tim.

"Well, I sincerely hope you get to the bottom of this," said Alex, feeling not for the first time, that he wanted to kick himself for getting involved. "After all we've been through, I'd hate to think we didn't come up with the goods."

Tim got up from his chair and started pacing up and down in front of Alex, in deep thought, and almost talking to himself.

"Our friend Keller seems to be fit and strong. He was shot at close range and yet somehow he has survived. So far at any rate." He stopped and looked at Alex. "Can you tell me what happened,

Alex?"

"Well, of course it was all so quick. A bit of a blur really. But, I think Keller saw them first," said Alex.

"Go on," said Tim, now standing directly in front of Alex.

"There were two men in black. I think they wore ski masks. I suddenly saw one of them run at Toby Harris, and shove him into the rear door of the Jaguar. I then felt Keller push me, or really sort of bounce off me as the other man ran in front of us. Keller had turned sideways toward me as the man fired two shots at point-blank range at him. The two men carried on running, Keller fell into my arms and was bleeding profusely. Anna and I tried to tend to him, but Harris hustled us in to the back of the Jag. And that was it really. It was all over in a minute or so."

"Thanks," said Tim. "That's very helpful. I think Keller may have saved his life, by 'bouncing off' you and turning sideways. I understand one shot entered his abdomen at the side and exited without causing too much damage. The other bullet, however, hit a rib and tore part of his lung, which collapsed. That's the one that caused most of the problems, but he had successful surgery in Vienna to remove the bullet, and his heart seems to be holding up." Tim started pacing again, looking pensive.

"Alex, we would really like to hear the whole story," he continued. "I wonder whether you would be good enough to come with me down to the basement, to a debriefing room, and you can fill us in. We won't keep you long," he said reassuringly.

"Of course, if it won't take long," said Alex warily, getting up from the armchair, and looking out of the window at a glistening River Thames. "What a beautiful afternoon," he said to Tim, changing both the tone and subject. "Perhaps spring is coming at last?"

"I hope so," Tim responded. "The bloody gray weather of the past two weeks is really miserable. But, you know what they say – March comes in like a lamb and goes out like a lion."

They both chuckled, friends again, as Tim led the way out of his office to the elevator that would take them to be basement of the Lambeth headquarters.

Tim escorted Alex into Interview Room B, a stark, bare, white-walled windowless room. "I am sure you'll have no difficulty with this interview, Alex," he said. "Just try not to leave anything out."

"I will try," said Alex, now feeling distinctly uncomfortable in the menacing surroundings.

"Alex," continued Tim. "I'd like you to meet Bob Stewart who will be conducting the interview."

"Pleased to meet you," said Alex, sizing up his interrogator.

"Likewise, Sir Alex," said Stewart, a large red-haired Scotsman. Stewart motioned for Alex to sit at the small bare table in the well-lit room. Alex immediately noted the large mirror on the left-hand wall. He knew he was being observed through a two-way mirror and facetiously gave a little wave and smile. In front of Stewart was a large tape recorder, with two small micro-phones placed on the table next to a tumbler of water and two glasses.

"Right, Sir Alex," said Stewart. "I shall ask you some brief background information for the record and then ask you to describe in detail your experiences during the recently completed mission to Poland. Do you have any questions?"

"No, fire away," said Alex, not liking this one bit.

Stewart turned on the machine.

"This is debriefing Part I to file number 10643. Sir Alex Campbell starting at 3:17 p.m. Monday, 28th February 1983."

Looking up at Alex, he continued. "Would you please tell me your name, date of birth, and current address?"

"Alexander Campbell born January 27, 1926 in Dundee Scotland. My current address is Flat 17 Courtney Lodge, Prince Albert Road, St. John's Wood, London, NW8."

"What is your profession?" asked Stewart.

"I am the chairman and CEO of the Campbell Group of

companies. We are an international drinks company, distillers of scotch whisky, bourbon, and other spirits and importers and marketers of a range of spirits brands around the world."

"Thank you," said Stewart. "Would you now describe in detail your experiences during the mission to Poland?"

"Do you want me to start with the briefing I was given by Tim Bevans, or should I start when I arrived in Poland," questioned Alex.

"No, Sir Alex, we want a description of the whole mission from start to finish," replied Stewart.

"Okay," said Alex, realizing that it is going to take a lot longer than Tim made out.

"Mr. Bevans and I lunched at the Savoy hotel about four weeks ago. During our lunch, he asked if I would come to meet him at his Northumberland Avenue headquarters office to discuss a 'little job.' I had been involved in a number of Tim Bevans' 'little jobs' over the past thirty years or so."

"Good," said Stewart. "Go on."

"He already knew that I was planning to go to Kraków in Poland to sign an exclusive import deal for Walova Vodka. He asked if I would be able to go on 23rd February, to which I said there would be no problem. He then described the mission. I was to deliver an empty airline bag to an MI6 agent, who would call at my hotel last Thursday evening, the 24th February, and swap an identical empty airline bag for the one that I had delivered, which I understood contained a secret compartment, containing Polish zlotys and two Austrian passports. Tim Bevans had already briefed me that these would be for Professor Erik Keller and his wife Krystina, who were planning to defect to the West. They would be escorted from Kraków through Czechoslovakia and into Austria on Friday, 25th February. I was told that Professor Keller was being honored by the Polish Academy of Sciences, with a gold medal at their conference held at my Kraków hotel on the 23rd and 24th of February. Having delivered the airline bag as instructed, my mission would be complete and I could return to London as planned on Friday 25th of February flying from Kraków to Warsaw and Warsaw to London." Alex paused.

"That's fine, Sir Alex. Please continue," said Stewart.

"I completed my business with Vodka Walova by the evening of 24th February and was getting ready for a banquet to celebrate the signing of the contract that we had just concluded, when there was a knock on my bedroom door." Alex took a sip of water. His mouth was dry, and he was feeling nervous about describing his meeting with Anna.

"I opened it to find MI6 Agent Anna Kaluza dressed in an ORBIS tourist-guide uniform and holding an airline bag similar to mine. We swapped the bags and that appeared to be the end of my mission." He paused again. It was important he get this bit right. "But an hour later as I was just about to descend to the bar of the hotel prior to being collected for the banquet, there was another knock on my door and I found a very distressed Anna in a high state of agitation. I could see she had been crying. I sat her down, calmed her, and she explained that her brother Jan, with whom she had arranged to have dinner that evening and who apparently would be responsible for taking the Kellers out of Poland into Czechoslovakia, had just been shot in the hotel car park by the Polish secret service or as they say in Poland the 'ferrets.'" Alex breathed in, gathering his thoughts. "Do you mind if I have another glass of water?" he asked Stewart.

"No, of course help yourself, Sir Alex."

Alex poured himself a full glass from the jug on the table. The bright white lights and stark white walls of the room were beginning to press down on his head which had started to throb. However, he still had a long way to go.

He spent the next half an hour describing the events that led to their escape from Poland and arrival in Vienna.

As Alex paused for another drink, Stewart suddenly shot him

a question.

"Anna Kaluza, in her debriefing said that she spent the night in your room. Is that correct?"

"Yes," said Alex. This was just the situation that he did not want to talk about, and made him nervous and uncomfortable. "Of course, she had nowhere to go. Where else could she have been safe?" He stumbled on, a little embarrassed, and not wanting to give the wrong impression.

"Just wanted to clarify the facts, Sir Alex," said Stewart in a rather brusque manner.

Alex was irritated by this personal question. Did they think he had slept with Anna?

"Thank you, that was very helpful," Stewart continued in a softer tone. "Perhaps we can call you if we need any additional information."

Stewart stood up and Alex realized that the interview had at last come to an end. He was exhausted and his shoulder was throbbing, always a sign of stress. The door of the interview room opened, and Tim came in. "Thank you so much, Alex, your contribution will be invaluable," he said with a warm smile on his face.

"Any time," said Alex, wanting to tell Tim, nothing happened between him and Anna.

"So, I hope to see you Wednesday afternoon at 2:30."

"Absolutely. I'll be here," said Alex, thinking, he never really knew what Tim or these other SIS people had on their minds.

Tim escorted him up to the main lobby where they said their goodbyes. Frank was waiting and Alex thankfully got into the rear of their Mercedes as they headed out into the evening traffic. When he got home, it was after six and Julia was waiting.

"Well, how did it go with Tim?" she asked, after greeting him with a kiss.

"It was good. Tim was thorough as always. Very intense," he replied, not wanting to tell Julia how unpleasant and stressful an afternoon, he had endured.

"Did you tell him about Erik Keller being related to us?"

"Yes, amazingly that was something he didn't know. He didn't have all the information on Keller's background."

"Really? So much for the great MI6," continued Julia with a little laugh. "I hope that's the end of it for you though, Alex."

"Well, he wants me to go back on Wednesday afternoon to listen to Anna's debriefing. So, I've agreed to do that."

"Did you tell him no more 'Little Jobs?'" asked Julia.

"Yes. He understood. Don't worry, the way I feel now, I wouldn't even contemplate anything new," said Alex, trying to avoid an argument.

"Well, I hope that's the end of your spy days," said Julia, as she took her husband's arm and led him into the dining room.

Chapter 5

Alex arrived back at the Lambeth headquarters fifteen minutes early on Thursday afternoon. He was immediately escorted to a basement anteroom with a two-way mirror window that looked onto one of the interview rooms. The anteroom contained a television console and a long table at the window with two microphones.

Within a minute or two, Tim Bevans arrived.

"So good of you to come, Alex," he said, holding out his hand and with his warm diplomat smile on his face.

Alex noted how tired and drawn his friend looked, his eyes deep in their sockets and his complexion wan. Tim had always been the "true blue" reserved Englishman, cool, calm and charming, but with a ruthless streak beneath the diplomat's veneer.

"I'm pleased to be able to help," said Alex. "What's the latest on Keller?"

"Well, Alex," replied Tim, "I didn't want to call you, but it's been a tough few days for Keller. His damaged lung had to be drained and he got an infection. However, I just got an update, and he seems to be responding to antibiotics. He's a little more stable. He's not out of the woods by any means, and will have to stay in the IC Unit at least over the weekend. Perhaps, we will have some better news next week."

"I hope so," said Alex with a worried expression on his face. He was genuinely concerned and felt quite emotional about his newly found cousin.

"I thought you'd find this interesting, Alex," Tim said, changing the subject. "This is today's newspaper from Vienna." He handed Alex *Der Standard*, Vienna's leading quality newspaper.

"Have a look on page three," said Tim.

Alex immediately saw the headline – *Shooting Victim Buried at Linz*. Underneath there was a photograph of three men in dark suits and a woman dressed in black, with a veil over her face and hair, holding a bunch of lilies. Alex read on:

Dr. Gustaf Bauer was buried at a private funeral at St. Anton's Church in Linz yesterday afternoon. Dr. Bauer was shot outside The Imperial Hotel last Friday afternoon, and was then murdered in his hospital bed in the Intensive Care Unit of the AKH Hospital on Sunday. The police are continuing their investigations into the cause and possible perpetrators of this murder.

The small family funeral was attended by his widow, Frau Vera Bauer, and family friends. Although Dr. Bauer grew up in Linz, there is no registration of his birth in that city, and nor was he apparently well known by any residents. It was known, however, that he lived and worked for many years outside of Austria. The pastor, Dr. Frederich Gunter, said that the funeral arrangements were made by telephone from Vienna. Payments for the funeral were made in advance, and a generous donation was made to the Church.

Inquiries of the Viennese police as to progress on the murder investigation received a minimal response. "We are continuing our investigation and pursuing a number of leads," said an authorized police spokesperson. "We have not as yet identified the assailant who was shot dead by one of our officers," he continued. The police spokesperson would not confirm whether this murder was considered a revenge killing, contract killing, or a mafia-style execution.

Alex handed the newspaper back to Tim.

"How did you arrange all this, with the widow and everything?" questioned Alex.

"We had to move quickly," replied Tim. "We got some of our people to 'stand up' at the funeral. We want to try and dampen down newspaper speculation and hopefully let this story die while the police, Interpol and indeed ourselves try and get to the bottom of this."

"Well, it seems you've done a good job," said Alex. "From the newspaper report, it doesn't look like they're going to be digging much further."

"I hope you're right," said Tim. "Now let's turn to the debriefing session," he continued. "I think you know the format by now?"

"Yes, I think so," responded Alex.

"Take a seat," said Tim, motioning Alex toward a number of chairs, looking out through the two-way mirror.

"We shall be debriefing Anna for the second time on the Keller mission, and we will also ask her to give us details of her life from birth. I would like you to carefully listen to her description of the mission," Tim continued. "We may interrupt the interviewer from time to time to ask questions. Hope that's okay with you, Alex."

"Of course," replied Alex.

Bob Stewart strode into the room a few seconds later and proceeded to prepare the debriefing table, placing a jug of water and a glass on one side, and checking the microphone. Almost immediately, Anna came into the room, escorted by a female agent.

"Nice to see you again, Miss Kaluza," said Stewart holding out his hand with a smile. "Please take a seat," he said, indicating the chair at the table.

"Good day," responded Anna. She settled onto the chair folding one leg under her bottom, in a casual comfortable position. "Good to see you again, Bob," she said in her broad Australian drawl, with a sweet smile, looking right at him with her clear blue eyes.

Alex looked down into the interview room and was immediately reminded of Anna's outstanding beauty. Her blonde hair was cascading around her shoulders. She was dressed in an Irish knit cream roll-neck sweater and blue jeans secured with a fabric belt. White sneakers and socks completed the casual outfit. As she leaned forward towards the desk, a patch of white skin was revealed between the bottom of her sweater and the top of her jeans. She wore no makeup and looked more like twenty-three than her forty-three years. Alex felt his heart beat increasing.

"I think you know the procedure," said Stewart.

Anna nodded.

"Remember," Stewart continued, "this is not an interrogation. Think of it as an informal chat." He paused. Anna looked skeptical. "I shall start this time by asking you to give us details of your life history and then get into your description of events in Poland last week. Are you ready?"

"Yes," she replied looking at him intently.

"As you know, this interview will be recorded." She nodded again.

Stewart proceeded to talk into the mike. "File number 10343S, second debriefing, Anna Kaluza, starting at 2:42 p.m. Wednesday, 2nd March 1983. Please give your full name and date of birth and location," Stewart continued.

"Anna Majana Kaluza-Zyradowski. I was born 23rd of February 1940 in collective labor camp 165, south of Stalingrad, in the Soviet Union."

"Are you married, divorced or single?"

"Divorced."

"Will you please give details of your family background?"

"I already did this at our previous interview," said Anna, looking perplexed.

"I know," said Stewart. "But at this second debriefing, we will require you to give a much more comprehensive description of your life."

"Why?"

"It is our normal protocol and nothing for you to worry about. Just give us the full story."

"Okay.," said Anna resignedly, still looking puzzled. "My name is Anna Majana Kaluza-Zyradowski. My father, Marius Kaluza-Zyradowski, was the nephew of Count Frederic Kaluza-Zyradowski from of one of the oldest families in Poland and the founders of the town of Zryadow, west of Warsaw. My father's family owned over nine-thousand acres of agricultural farming land, houses and villages in that area. My grandfather died in a horse-riding accident in 1934 and my father inherited eleven-hundred acres and the seven-bedroom 19th-Century Kaskia Lodge. He had recently married my mother, Maria Elena Rostowski, whose father was one of the leading doctors in Poland and whose family had been Court physicians for centuries."

She paused. "Is this okay so far?"

"Perfect," responded Stewart. "Please continue."

"On 1st September 1939 when the Germans invaded Poland, my mother was at Kaskia Lodge with my three-year-old brother, Jan. She was four months pregnant with me. My father had joined his regiment, the Second Cavalry division a few days earlier. The massive German onslaught completely overwhelmed the Polish defense forces; and, by 16th September, the retreating Polish forces were being pushed back towards Warsaw. On that morning, two German vehicles arrived at Kaskia Lodge, with a dozen soldiers and officers. My mother was told that they were requisitioning our home for their local headquarters and gave her one hour to prepare some personal belongings and leave the property. She had no choice but to comply; she was not allowed to take one of our motor vehicles, so she loaded up a horse and trap, and left the estate with the intention of traveling fifty kilometers or so to some cousins near Janki south of Warsaw. However, she quickly found herself in a vast column of fleeing refugees, Polish Army remnants, ambulances and foot traffic. They were continually strafed by Stuka dive bombers as they inched their way towards Warsaw. But as they got nearer, police diverted them away from the city because of thousands of fleeing inhabitants, and they were pushed further east." Anna paused, gathering her thoughts, pushing her hair back behind her ears, before continuing. "After two more days, they were approaching Siedlce whenthe refugees were stopped at a major roadblock, and my mother suddenly found herself facing Russian soldiers and tanks. Over the past couple of days, the Russian Army had moved into eastern Poland following the signing of a secret agreement with the Germans partitioning Poland, with every-thing east of the Bug River being apportioned to the Russians. But the Polish defenses collapsed so quickly, the Russians had found themselves well beyond the Bug River, trying to organize the seething mass of Polish refugees pushing into the town. The men were separated from the women and children, and my mother joined a long line leading to a desk at which a Russian officer together with a Polish policeman asked for names and identities. She gave her name as Maria Kaluza, deciding that the Zyradowski name was too well-known. She was instructed to follow a group of women and children to a platform at the station where they would be boarding trains and taken to safety in the countryside. She was too tired and exhausted to question this instruction, so she grabbed her belongings and with my brother Jan holding onto her skirt, joined the lines of women and children being loaded onto freight cars by Polish police with armed Russian guards looking on. She and Jan were ushered up a gang plank with 40 or so other women and children, and eventually the long train slowly moved out of the station."

Anna stopped and helped herself to a glass of water.

"You're doing fine," said Bob Stewart.

"Do you really want to hear all this stuff?" said Anna.

"Yes, Anna," replied Bob. "Please continue."

Tim Bevans leaned into the microphone on the table in front of him as he looked through the two-way glass.

"Ask her how she knows her mother's story so clearly," he said into Stewart's ear-piece.

Anna was still drinking the water as Bob Stewart questioned her. "How do you know this story in such detail, Anna?" he asked.

"Ha," responded Anna with a laugh. "My mother told me the story a million times. My mother is a Polish aristocrat, who has always had difficulty coming to terms with a post-war world. She never felt comfortable in Australia and moved back to Poland as a result, and she yearns for the 'good old days.' When I was young, she described her war experiences over and over and over again. In the end, I knew her story, which of course is also my story word-for-word."

"I see," said Stewart without further comment. "Please continue, Anna."

Anna, wriggled around on her chair and then continued. "They soon realized that the train was not heading to the Polish countryside but was on a long journey across the low plains of Ukraine towards Kiev where they arrived the following morning. They were given food and water but didn't stay, and their journey continued until they arrived the following day in Stalingrad. Once again they were fed and loaded back onto the train which in less than two hours pulled into the station at Kapustin, where the passengers were told to unload by numbers, and groups of about fifty boarded open trucks with their children and possessions. Within an hour and a half, they arrived at the People's Socialist Soviet Republic collective farm number 165. They moved into filthy barracks, which they had to clean up before being put to work on the farm, replacing former political prisoners who had been drafted into the Soviet Army. I was born in that camp and lived there for the first five years of my life. I remember very little other than running around with bare feet and always being hungry."

Alex leaned over to Tim. "My God, you were right, what an incredible story."

"It certainly is," responded Tim. "I'd only heard a brief

summary up to now."

Anna continued. "Many women and children died in the brutal winters at that camp where there was little or no medical assistance and people were malnourished and sometimes even starving. My mother, brother and I survived. In April 1945, the survivors were told that Poland had been liberated, the victorious Russian Army was advancing on Berlin and they should pack their belongings as they would begin their journey home. A few days later, we were taken to Stalingrad where we boarded a long freight train with two-thousand other women and children from similar collective farm camps and set out on a journey that would take us across the steppes of southern Russia around the Caspian Sea and eventually to British-occupied Baghdad. After a five-day journey, we all arrived more dead than alive to be greeted by Polish soldiers in British Army uniforms. After a few days of good food, rest and medical checkups, my mother and the other refugees were informed they would be transported to a temporary camp in Uganda in East Africa, where they would await resettlement back to Poland, as soon as stability returned and it was possible to make the move."

Anna paused and took another sip of water, as she again gathered her thoughts.

"Please continue," said Stewart to Anna. "You're doing fine."

Anna continued. "Of course I don't remember much, but this is what my mother told me many times. We were to be temporarily housed in a former British Army camp near Kampala. We sailed from Basra and apparently, again according to my mother and Jan, we had a great time running around the decks in the sunshine, teasing the crew and playing with other children bound for the Polish refugee group."

Anna adjusted her position on the chair. "We spent nearly two years in Uganda in the camp. It was there I think that my mother finally gave up on the hope that my father had somehow survived the war. Even though the British had intended to send us back to Poland at the earliest opportunity, the political uncertainty and unrest in what was rapidly becoming a Russian-dominated Communist country continually put off the move. Eventually, my mother was given a choice: spend another few months to a year in the camp while she filed an application to move to England or Canada, or take advantage of an Australian government offer of immediate transportation to Australia with the promise of accommodation and a job at the other end. She took Australia and we arrived there in November 1947. The Australians were true to their word and put us in a little flat – maisonette, as they called it. I vaguely remember how excited Jan and I were to be able to share a room for the first time and have our own garden to play in."

Anna paused again. "Do you really want this much detail of my life story?" she asked.

Bevans leaned into the microphone again. "Tell her yes, absolutely, every detail," he said.

Stewart responded, "Yes, and we want every detail. It will be very helpful to us."

Anna looked perplexed. "I can't understand what interest you could possibly have in my life story and how it affects the mission to get Keller out of Poland," she said a little defiantly.

"Please go on, Anna," said Stewart gently.

Anna shrugged. "OK," she said. "Jan and I loved Australia. We loved the sunshine, the beaches, and the sports. We had already learned English at the British camp in Uganda and we settled into school, losing our Polish accents quickly. For my mother, it was much tougher. Although she gradually learned English, she could not avoid a thick Polish accent. She frequently felt embarrassed. The Australian government had promised her a job, but the best thing they could offer her was house-cleaning work, a 'daily,' as they called it out there. So she found herself working for women, often younger than her, cleaning their homes. It was another large painful step down for my mother with her aristocratic background and her previous life of supervising a slew of servants and an eleven-hundred-acre estate."

Anna stopped, clearly emotional, but fighting back the tears.

She continued in a husky voice. "However, by chance, things quickly looked up for her. One of her employers told her to apply for a vacant music teacher's position at a local school. My mother was an accomplished pianist and jumped at the opportunity. She got the job and for the first time in a decade. I believe she was happy."

Anna paused again, thinking of her childhood, a teardrop ran down her face, but she continued in a stronger voice. "Jan and I moved through the school system. Jan was three years older than me and left high school in 1955. I left in 1958. Our mother of course wanted us both to attend university and follow a serious profession, law, medicine, something like that. However, the chances of going to university were very slim in Australia at that time and neither of us were particular academic. Jan was great at sports. He loved to be outdoors. He got a job working for Fosters brewery, initially in their warehouse and subsequently delivering beer. For my part, I spent a little time attempting to be a model, I represented a French perfume in Sydney's department stores, and then I was accepted to be trained as an airline stewardess for Qantas. I loved that job. It opened up the whole of Australia for me. It was through Qantas that I met Jack."

"Who?" interrupted Stewart.

"Jack: Jack Gray my former husband," responded Anna.

"Oh yes," said Stewart. "Your former husband – how long were you married?"

"We were married for three years from 1964 to 1967. Unfortunately, Jack was not really the marrying type; and, although he tried hard to be a good husband, it was beyond him."

Anna paused again and took another sip of water, to cover her emotional reaction to some painful memories. "It was in 1963 that my mother and brother, Jan, decided to return to Poland," Anna said with renewed focus.

"Why would they want to do that?" asked Stewart. "Surely things were still very tough in Poland. It was a brutish communist regime under Russian influence, and the standard of living was way below that which you were enjoying in Australia."

Anna nodded. "Yes, you are right and that's exactly what I told them, but my mother was homesick. She was in communication with her sister, who assured her that things were getting better, and she also had unrealistic hopes of being able to return to her family estates. Jan, I think, realized that his job was going nowhere and also harbored thoughts of the possibility of owning and managing the family estates once again. I tried to persuade them otherwise, but they wouldn't listen; and, so in October 1963, they moved back to Poland. Of course at that time I didn't realize you guys had recruited Jan."

"What do you mean?" asked Stewart.

"Well, you know," Anna replied. "MI6 recruited Jan before they moved."

"How did you know that?" asked Stewart.

"Well, I didn't know at the time," replied Anna. "I first heard about it in 1967, when they recruited me. I was stunned, of course. But anything Jan did was okay by me," Anna responded with a sweet smile. She paused again, awaiting Stewart's response.

"Carry on," said Stewart, without further comment.

"Well, after my divorce, I have to say I was pretty miserable. It was embarrassing to keep going to my job. After all, 'handsome' Jack Gray was a very popular and well-known senior pilot and I was just a "trolley-dolly" as they called me. I became depressed and missed my family. My mother and brother were very supportive, and my mother wrote to me regularly, pressuring me to return to Poland. In 1967, she was told by the authorities that they were considering her application to return and live on her former estate Kaskia Lodge, which had been turned into an orphanage after the war run by an order of nuns. She was eventually allowed to live in the former gardener's cottage and employed as a music teacher. She was in seventh heaven. Even though the estate no longer belonged to her – it had been requisitioned by the state – she felt she was at home. She was very happy tending the garden, teaching music, and enjoying her surroundings once again. I was so happy for her. We had our conflicts and arguments, particularly as I became an adult used to the free and open life of Australia, but I love my mother dearly and I would do anything for her happiness. It had pained me tremendously to see her suffering. I knew she had adored my father, who, of course, I had never met, and his loss was something she would never recover from."

Anna stopped for a moment and looked directly at the two-way mirror, before continuing. She was tired and the oppressive lighting and bare walls made her head throb.

"You guys had found Jan a job as a driver for ORBIS, the Polish National tourist office, and I guess with the money you were giving him, plus his salary, he was able to live a pretty good life by Polish standards. Within a year or two, he met the lovely Ava whom he married. They had two kids." Anna paused, and let out a big sigh.

"Okay," said Stewart. "Now tell us about your time in Warsaw."

"Well in 1967, I returned to Warsaw to be with my mother and brother. In some ways, I thought I was crazy, but Australia had nothing for me anymore and it was painful to continue my life there. You guys enlisted me just before I left the country and found me a job with ORBIS, the same as Jan. I spoke Polish, Russian, and English, and became one of the ORBIS drivers for visiting dignitaries mainly from Eastern Bloc countries. Jan had the same job, but he had a Z permit which allowed him to drive dignitaries over the border to surrounding countries.

"I got a nice little flat near the center of the city, made some friends and was very happy to visit my mother and Kaskia Lodge when I could get away. I became close with Ava and Jan's kids and my life settled down into an acceptable routine. From time to time, I was given instructions to do various jobs for MI6. These were never too demanding, usually involving my dropping off packages at pickup points in the local park. It wasn't a bad life," she said almost to herself.

"Tell us about the Russian Defense Minister, Anna," interrupted Stewart.

"Ah, Ivan. That was different," responded Anna with a chuckle. "That was my claim to fame, wasn't it?" She threw back her head with another large laugh, her blonde hair falling over her shoulders as she repositioned herself, taking her leg from under her bottom and putting it on the ground for the first time since the interview began.

"He was actually the Deputy Russian Defense Minister, Ivan Chetterkov. I was allocated as his driver for the four days of the conference he was attending. My instructions were to try and photograph the contents of the briefcase he carried to every meeting. Initially, this seemed an impossible task because he usually had one or two aides with him in the vehicle. However, I started flirting with him and showing off a bit of my kit."

"What? What did you say?" said Stewart looking puzzled.

"My 'kit,'" said Anna. "You know, cleavage." She laughed again.

"Oh, I see," said Stewart, looking a little embarrassed.

"I know how to flirt," Anna said.

Alex watching the proceedings thought, *She does. Was she playing me?*

Anna continued. "I could see he was interested. On the third day, he asked me what time I finished work. I told him, my time was his time and I had been instructed to be available for as long as he wanted me. I said this to him with a come-hither smile and he seemed... interested. I thought he was repulsive, but this was my MI6 job, so I did as instructed. The conference ended on the fourth day, and he pointedly told me that his assistants would not be in the car with him after the end of the conference and perhaps he and I could spend some time together and have a drink. I told him that would be wonderful and I heard him tell his aides to follow in another vehicle after the conference. I drove him to an unused factory parking lot followed by the car with his aides. We stopped and I parked. I got out, waved provocatively to the guys in the car behind and climbed into the back of the vehicle. I was very nervous, of course, because I had no idea how this guy would behave. I had a flask of vodka to which I'd added one of your sleeping draughts. You know, the stuff you hand out to all your agents I presume."

Stewart did not respond.

Anna continued. "Well, he was hot and started to rip off his clothes and wanted to rip off mine. But I calmed him down and told him that we should both have a drink first and then passed the flask of vodka. He took big swig and gave it back to me. I pretended to drink but of course did not swallow anything. Returning the flask to him, he took another swig and started to get glassy-eyed. He looked very puzzled and then keeled over. I opened his briefcase with a key I found in his jacket pocket. I took out all the documents and started photographing them with the miniature camera you gave us – you know the one that looks like a matchbox and you pull it in and out."

"Yes," said Stewart a little impatiently. "Please continue."

Anna smiled and leaned back in her chair. "That's about it really. I photographed everything I could and put the documents back in the case and the key back in his pocket. He was still undressed as I got out of the car. I waved to the guys behind and then drove off to the hotel with them following. When we arrived, I got out of the vehicle, went to the car behind and told them that their boss was in a pretty poor state. They came and helped him out of vehicle. I gave him a big lipstick kiss on his cheek and told him how wonderful he was. He looked totally out of it and off they went. A couple of days later I received instructions where to drop my matchbox camera, which I did. I heard afterwards you guys were pretty pleased with the contents."

Bevans leaned forward to his microphone. "Tell her we were very grateful," he said into Stewart's ear piece.

"Yes and we were very grateful," Stewart repeated.

"Quite a story, eh, Alex," Tim said.

"Quite a woman," responded Alex. "Are all your female agents this talented?"

Tim chuckled. "I wish."

Chapter 6

Bevans leaned into his microphone again. "Okay, Stewart, ask her to turn to the mission last week."

"All right, Anna," Stewart said. "Let's turn to your mission last week." He paused. "Would you like a break?" he asked.

"No, I'm fine," Anna replied. "Let's get this over with... I've already given you a report on the mission last week. Do I have to do that again?"

"Yes. As I said at the start, it's part of our protocol."

"Okay," said Anna giving a resigned sigh. "Let's go."

Anna leaned forward, forearms on the desk and hands clasped in front of her. Alex noticed as he looked down into the room that Anna had started nervously tapping her left foot on the floor.

"About two weeks ago, I was called into the supervisor's office at ORBIS." She paused. "My god," she said. "Has it only been two weeks? It seems like a lifetime.

"Anyway I was told that I would be assigned to escort a group attending the Polish Academy of Sciences conference in Kraków. My main responsibilities would be to escort the group on a coach from Kraków airport to the Reymonta hotel and to make sure they all got checked in, and help during the conference. I was given a package of instructions with a list of attendees. In my group, there were about fifty people. There were two other ORBIS employees responsible for two other coaches. I understood that the total conference would be about a hundred and fifty. Three days before my departure to Kraków, my supervisor asked me to come and see him."

"Were you concerned?" Stewart asked.

"No," she said. "It didn't strike me as unusual. I went to his office and he handed me a sheet of paper and indicated I should read it silently. These were my instructions. I was to make contact

63

with Professor Erik Keller and his wife Krystyna, part of my group. I was to advise them that they would be escorted from the hotel by my brother, Jan, at 7:00 a.m. on Friday, the 25th, February." Anna paused again. "Last Friday," she said, almost to herself, realizing that it was only a few days ago.

She placed her hands flat on the table and looked at them, as if seeing them for the first time, as she concentrated on remembering what happened in Kraków.

"On Thursday evening, I was to go to Sir Alex Campbell's room at the hotel, and deliver an airline bag to him, exchanging it for one he would give me, which apparently contained a secret compartment with passports and money. I was to give this airline bag to my brother. Jan would join me for dinner on Thursday evening and would then depart with the Kellers on Friday morning." She paused.

"Go on," said Stewart slowly.

"Jan's mission was to deliver the Kellers over the Polish border into Czechoslovakia where an MI6 agent would pick them up and transport them through Czechoslovakia and into Austria – the Hotel Imperial in Vienna. My mission was to return with forty-eight passengers on the coach to Kraków Airport, but sign off as if I had the full complement of fifty passengers. I would then return to Warsaw and if and when questioned about the Keller's disappearance, I should feign total ignorance and assume that they had gone on a different coach. That was to be my mission. Certainly not as complicated as some missions in the past, but nevertheless...quite a responsibility. I had no idea at that time who Professor Keller was or why my brother was driving him across the Czech border."

Anna paused again and took a sip of water.

"How did you know about the money and passports," Stewart asked. "And that the Kellers were being taken to Vienna?"

"I didn't..." she said. "Not until Alex told me, when he agreed to help with the mission."

"Okay, go on," said Stewart.

"Well, I followed the instructions," said Anna, "And went to Sir Alex's room around 5:30 p.m. He answered the door, we exchanged some pleasantries and swapped our airline bags. I went back to my room. I had a service room, more like a box really, which overlooked the rear car park of the hotel. I was waiting for my brother to arrive. It was..." She sighed, and ran her hand through her hair. "It was nerve-wracking. Sometime after 6:00 p.m., I saw him drive into the car park. I was so relieved. He parked and started to trudge across the snow. I then saw two men get out of another vehicle. I immediately recognized they were probably 'ferrets,' – that's the slang word for the secret police in Poland. They approached Jan and started an animated conversation. Jan tried to walk around them but they grabbed him. My relief turned to horror, as I watched. There was a scuffle and then I saw one of the 'ferrets,' who had a pistol in his hand, shoot him. I saw Jan fall in the snow, and bloodstains start to appear. I was absolutely terrified. I was in utter panic, and wanted to scream. I was standing at the window, and shaking like a leaf. I felt my legs were stuck to the floor. The two men picked Jan up and bundled him into the back of their car. One of them went to his car got in and started the engine. The other car left the car park quickly with Jan's car following."

Tears welled up in Anna's eyes and started rolling down her cheeks, but she kept talking, huskily. "We still don't know if he's alive or dead," she stopped again.

"I know, but we'll find out soon," responded Stewart gently. "I'm sure he's fine," he continued somewhat unconvincingly.

"I have to admit I was totally freaked out," Anna continued, trying to keep a tremble out of her voice. "I didn't know what to do or who to turn to. I knew the mission was important, but seeing my brother shot, and not even knowing whether he was dead or alive was a terrifying experience. I turned to the only person that I knew in the hotel – Sir Alex Campbell. I ran to his room, knocked on the door, and tried to explain what had just happened. Of course Alex had no idea who my brother was or his involvement in the mission. I was probably totally incoherent. Alex didn't know what I was talking about. I panicked and tried to run out of the hotel. I don't know what I was thinking. I didn't know where I was going, but I thought I had to find Jan. Alex chased after me and caught me at the top of the stairs, calmed me down and took me back to his room."

She paused, emotionally drained and wiped her tears away with a tissue, and then took a sip of water.

"Do you want a break," asked Stewart.

"No, I'm fine," responded Anna, breathing heavily.

"We then discussed what we needed to do to save the mission. Alex was wonderful," said Anna, glancing at the two-way mirror. "After a while, we came up with a bold plan. I would try and obtain the car keys from the chauffeur to the chairman of the Polish Academy of Sciences, who had a room next to mine. He had a large Zil sedan sitting in the car park. If I was able to achieve that, then I would drive the Kellers on Friday morning to the Polish border and try and get them across so as they could meet up with an MI6 agent. I knew this was a long shot and I was putting my life at risk, so I implored Alex to help. I felt he might be able to bribe the border guards or use his British passport as some sort of authority. Of course once I was there, I had no idea how I was to get back to Warsaw or even if the 'ferrets' were now looking for me, having got Jan. If they'd been watching him perhaps they were watching me." She stopped, reflecting on this statement, trying to gather the sequence of events.

"Sir Alex had to go to a banquet with his vodka people so we agreed that, if I could obtain the keys to the chairman's car, I should return to Alex's room and stay there until he returned. He felt that I would be safe in his room but probably not in mine. I understood perfectly. Anyway I was lucky that the chauffeur was in his room when I knocked on his door. Alex had given me a bottle of vodka. I suggested that we had a drink together because neither of us was allowed to leave the hotel and were in no way involved in the evening's proceedings. He was excited at the thought of having me in his bedroom. I gave him the come-on, and my biggest smile, and we started in, on the vodka. Of course I was not really swallowing mine but he was drinking lots of his." Anna paused again trying to remember all the details.

"It took me a long time to get him totally drunk but just as I thought he was going to pass out, we heard a loud banging on the door of my room next door. It was the 'ferrets' screaming for me. He was still aware enough to realize that something was going on and he grabbed my arm in a vice and asked me what the hell was happening. I was terrified. I knew I only had a few seconds to save myself, so I picked up the vodka bottle and smashed it across his head. He went down like a ton of bricks." She smiled as she recollected her swift action. "I pulled out the cords of the curtains and trussed him up like a chicken as best as I could, and poured even more vodka down his throat. I thought he would be out for a few hours probably until morning, by which time we would have gone. I stuffed his handkerchief in his mouth, blind-folded him with his tie, and tied a scarf across his mouth and round the back of his head. I then sneaked out of his room. I saw the door to my room had been smashed in by the 'ferrets' and that they had turned over the room. It was a total mess. Luckily, I had taken my ORBIS overcoat and my pistol, when I went to the chauffeur's room. I crept back to Alex's room, unlocked the door with his key, which he had given me, and waited in the dark until he returned. I was terrified the 'ferrets' would find me and that they would be ransacking every room in the hotel in their search. I was quiet as a mouse and didn't dare move. I knew it would be impossible to escape. About 10:30, I heard a quiet knock and I knew it was Alex. I opened the door still holding my pistol. He of course was wide-eyed at seeing the gun, but I quickly told him not to worry and that I'd got the car keys. He was really delighted. He kept encouraging me and telling me that we had a real shot at success. Without his encouragement, I could never have carried out the mission and we would never have had a hope in hell of getting out of the country."

Anna paused again, gave a slight smile to the two-way mirror, wriggled around a bit in her chair and pushed a wisp of blonde hair, back behind her ear. She then continued. "We both knew that the 'ferrets' would be looking for me and so I had no real alternative but to stay in Alex's room for the night. He of course was a perfect gentleman," she added with a slight smile on her face. "We were both up about six the next morning. Alex went down to breakfast and to check out. He also wanted to see whether there were 'ferrets' crawling all over the hotel. Luckily there was no sign of them. He grabbed some extra food for me and the Kellers from his breakfast and we met at the entrance to the car park in the basement right on time at seven. The Kellers, of course, had no idea of the dramas that had taken place overnight. We did tell them, however, that there had been a change in plans and that Alex Campbell would be in charge of taking them over the border. Krystyna Keller was highly agitated. She looked ill, gaunt and terrified. Professor Keller tried to comfort her. We moved quickly across the car park, opened the trunk of the Zil sedan and put the Keller's and Sir Alex's bags in."

Bevan leaned forward to his microphone and said to Stewart, "Ask her if she remembers what luggage the Kellers had with them."

Stewart interrupted Anna and asked, "Do you remember the Keller's luggage?"

"Um! The Keller's luggage." She paused, thinking hard. "Yes, let me see, they had a battered old leather suitcase, together with a large canvas bag both of which were stuffed to the brim."

"Was there anything else: briefcase, backpack, something like that?" Stewart asked.

"No," responded Anna slowly. "I am pretty sure those two

cases only."

"Okay, please continue."

"Well, we left the hotel car park and headed to the Polish border. It's only about 70 km from Kraków and we made good time."

Anna, paused and took a sip of water.

"We'd been driving for about forty minutes and were nearing Wadowice when an armed soldier of the MO – the Militoiya – Paramilitary stepped out on the road waving a red and white round paddle. It is part of everyday life in Poland for vehicles to be waved down by the MO, who usually do a cursory search, examine ID cards and wave you on your way. It was just routine so I wasn't really panicked. We were motioned into a small lay-by, and another soldier carrying a machine pistol over his shoulder came up to my driver's window and asked for my papers. I gave them my ID card and told them I was with ORBIS, and I was driving guests of the Polish Academy of Sciences from their Kraków meeting to the Czech border. The soldiers seemed disinterested but asked me to open the trunk, which I did. We were all asked to exit the car and produce our passports which were handed over to the soldier. He seemed happy and pretty disinterested and then told us we could proceed.

"We just started to move back to the car when the officer shouted, 'Halt' and then 'Wait.' I think he was bothered by the Kellers' appearance. They just didn't look Austrian. In fact, they looked Polish in every way. We all turned, to see the officer bringing his machine pistol off his shoulder. I noticed that Krystyna Keller was totally panicked, and my heart was thumping like mad. All I saw was the barrel of his gun. I realized we'd been caught. Alex asked the officer in Polish what the problem was. The officer was surprised that Alex had spoken in Polish and turned his gun towards him. I realized it was now or never, so I brought my pistol out of my overcoat and shot the officer in the chest. He crumpled into the snow and didn't move, but I saw out of the side of my eye that the other soldier was taking his Kalashnikov off his shoulder and was pointing it at me. I also saw Alex spring forward to try and grab the barrel of the rifle; but, at the same time Keller lunged at the officer's back and had his arms around his neck. The weight of Keller's assault pushed the soldier to the ground, as a shot went off. There was a muffled crack. Keller twisted the soldier's head, and he fell to the ground in a heap. But then I noticed Krystyna falling, and I turned to see her lying face down in the snow, shot by the stray bullet from the Kalashnikov. A small trickle of blood was settling into the snow. It was an absolute nightmare."

Anna's voice started to tremble and tears began to flood her eyes. "It was an accident," she said quietly, her voice turning husky with emotion. "I didn't know what was happening. I think I was rooted to the ground and shaking uncontrollably like a leaf. I know that both Keller and Alex rushed over to Krystyna, but she was obviously dead. Keller started sobbing."

Anna paused, wiped her eyes with a tissue and took a sip of water with a shaking hand. Stewart said nothing, giving her time to recover. After a few moments, she carried on. "Alex was the first to get things under control and told us that we'd better get moving, otherwise our lives would be in jeopardy. He took Keller to the car and put him in the rear seat. The poor man was totally traumatized... There were three bodies lying on the ground and he pushed me to help him pick up the bodies and lay them in a ditch behind the officers' sentry box. At the last minute, I suddenly realized that Krystyna might be the answer to my problems. I took her purse with her passport and put on her fur coat in exchange for my ORBIS overcoat. I thought it would improve our chances if I became Mrs. Keller, and it would certainly help me if I could follow Keller to Vienna. Alex took over driving the sedan, and I got into the rear seat and tried to comfort Professor Keller. He was looking into space and moaning to himself. We drove on towards the border. We were now fugitives. We had to get out of Poland. Less than an hour later, we were approaching the border crossing at Cieszyn."

Anna paused again with a large sigh.

"Are you OK?" asked Stewart.

"Yes," replied Anna. "I'm just trying to remember every-thing," she continued.

"As we had foreign passports, we were instructed to pull our car over to a wooden building, which was signed 'Passport Office' on the right-hand side of the road overlooking the border crossing plaza from an elevation of twenty feet or so. I agreed that I would do all the talking as I was now Mrs. Keller and would tell them that I spoke Polish. I was praying that Alex and a cash bribe would get us across the border. We walked up the wooden steps to the Passport Office, where we gave our passports to an official behind a counter. An armed guard ushered us into a rear office where an officer in a border security uniform was seated behind a desk, facing a long bench seat. He had our three passports opened in front of him. Eventually, he looked up and asked in German to no one in particular where we were going. I can't speak German, but Alex said that we were going to Vienna and explained the whole thing about Kraków and the Polish Academy of Sciences. The officer didn't seem to believe us. He told us to sit down. He was looking intensely at the passports. I'm not sure, maybe he was trying to come to some sort of decision... and then the telephone rang. He seemed to be responding to a Colonel somebody or other and, even from we were seated, we could hear a loud voice shouting through the phone. Our official didn't seem to be impressed, but he kept looking backwards and forwards at Keller, myself and Alex. And then after a moment, he looked at the passports, and said the names "Gustav Bauer and Vera Bauer" into the phone.

Anna paused and sighed deeply.

"My heart hit my stomach at that moment, and I thought we were done for. And then to make things worse, he was asked a question about ORBIS, to which he replied 'no,' but when he put the phone down, he looked at us with a slight knowing smile and said slowly in Polish to the professor, "So, you're Professor Keller."

Anna paused again, creasing lines on her forehead, reflecting her painful memory.

"I had visions flashing through my mind," she said, "of being tortured and then shot. I could see no way out. We'd been caught red-handed. Both Alex and Professor Keller seemed to be rooted to the ground waiting for the ax to drop. And then miraculously, the officer took three slim green cards from his desk, scribbled something on them and then put one in each of our passports."

"'You better move quickly,'" he said to Keller. "We all started saying thank you at the same time. Alex took out a wad of money from his overcoat and dropped it on the desk. Without looking up, the officer swept the money into the top desk drawer."

"'Now get out,'" he said. "We had no idea why he was letting us go and I still don't understand it. Perhaps he was aware of Professor Keller, or maybe knew of his recent tragedy, losing both his sons. Perhaps he was a supporter of the Solidarity movement. Or maybe he just sympathized with Keller's obvious desire to get out of Poland. Anyway, for whatever reason, we were thankful, elated, but still very nervous."

"Amazing," said Stewart. "Go on."

"We got back into the car and passed through the Polish border. As we entered Czechoslovakia, the border guard took out the three green cards from our passports and waved us on. I started driving furiously, aware that perhaps we only had a thirty-minute lead. After about seventy-five kilometers, we ran into traffic and then slowed to a crawl. Alex thought there might be some sort of roadblock ahead. He thought we should get rid of the Zil sedan as quickly as possible and also get off the main road. So I turned off and headed into the countryside. We knew we had to dump the car and get a new one as quickly as possible.

After a few kilometers, we came to a large café with a number of cars and vans in the car park, and I pulled in. Alex told me to use my charm to try and hijack another vehicle, but I felt more comfortable using my pistol." Anna paused and smiled, before continuing.

"We looked at potential victims and their vehicles; and, after about ten minutes, a middle-aged man came out of the restaurant wearing a hat, gray raincoat and a scarf around his neck and carrying a battered briefcase. He was wearing thick glasses and walked towards an old black Skoda. Alex decided that he was our man. I reversed the Zil out of our parking space and moved alongside the man. I rolled down the window and said, 'Bitte?' and flashed him a wide smile. He came towards me eagerly, resting his hand on the top of the driver's door. I produced my pistol, and jammed it under his chin, and Alex told him to get in the car. The man was totally terrified. We told him if he did what he was told, he would not get hurt. Alex got him to hand over his car keys and went to the Skoda and started it up. I followed Alex in the Zil and Keller, with the gun at the man's head, sat in the back as we went out onto the main road again. After a few kilometers, Alex pulled off into some woods. We parked about five-hundred meters from the road. We unloaded the luggage from the back of the Zil and put it into the Skoda and then we told the poor man to get into the trunk of the Zil. At first he wouldn't move, but after we told him to move or be shot, he climbed in, trembling like a leaf. Alex told him he would be fine because we would leave the Zil lights on and they would be seen from the road as soon as it got dark, and he would be rescued."

Anna paused and took another sip of water. She then continued. "From then on, we took the back roads heading towards the Austrian border. When we got to about ten or fifteen kilometers from the border, we decided we needed to stop and hatch a plan as to how we were going to get into Austria. We all agreed, there would be roadblocks at every border post and we certainly couldn't take a chance that the Polish and Czech authorities were not cooperating with each other in the search.

"A few kilometers from the border, we pulled into a large transport café. The car park was full of trucks, with license plates from Poland, Austria, Czechoslovakia and Germany. We agreed on a plan. I would tart myself up a bit and try and find a Polish driver in the café who was going to Austria. I knew this was a dangerous proposition but I thought I could handle it. After all, I've been working for you guys for fifteen years," she said with a chuckle, looking at the glass mirror on the wall. "If I could find the right source, we would bribe him with eighty-thousand Szlotys to take us across the border. So with a lot of makeup and plenty of cleavage showing, I ambled into the restaurant and, after chatting up a few of the drivers, eventually found Karol."

She paused again, gathering her thoughts.

"Karol?" said Stewart.

"Yes. He made a regular run from Katowice in Poland to Vienna, delivering baths, basins, and toilets made in Poland, to their distributor in Vienna. Karol said he knew all the Czech border guards and had been doing this run for nine years. He was confident that there would be no problems and that we could sail through. The eighty-thousand Szlotys was a big enticement. I took him to meet Alex and Keller waiting in the Skoda. We abandoned the car and climbed into the back of Karol's truck.

"We unloaded two baths from two wooden crates and Professor Keller and Alex climbed in. I sat in the driver's cab as I was to play Karol's girlfriend. I had Krystyna's passport in the name of Vera Bauer with me. As we drove off, I spilled some coffee purposely on the passport and then with the help of a razor blade from Karol, changed the name from Bauer to Eaver. It was just as well we had taken precautions, because as we got to the border all hell broke out. Traffic was narrowed down to one lane by armed personnel carriers, backed by a couple of tanks. Army personnel were directing the traffic. The border was sealed completely. They were letting through ten trucks at a time. Each one had to be physically searched. We were directed into one of the parking bays and, luckily, Karol knew the officer who came over and asked for his papers. Karol introduced me as his girlfriend. He said I was a singer with a band and I had drug problems. I was clean now and he told the officer, Hans, that he could meet my sister. She was very good-looking, apparently. Hans seemed eager to make a date and looked me up and down as he compared my face to the passport with Krystyna's photo in it. He must have thought the passport photo had been taken when I was deep into my drug addiction. I mean, I looked very different. Although there was a resemblance between myself and Krystyna. Karol was told to raise the metal shutter at the rear of the truck, and Hans and a couple of soldiers climbed in and started kicking the crates. He asked Karol to open the one with Alex in, and Karol started banging with a hammer and a screwdriver. After a few moments, he told Hans that this particular crate was really stuck and asked if he could open another one to which Hans agreed. Of course when they opened the crates, they found nothing but a bath encased in straw. He then gave Karol the okay. He rolled down the shutter, climbed back into the driver's seat, and we were waved through the border and fifteen minutes later, we were safely in Austria."

Anna paused with a long sigh. Bevans, Alex, and Stewart had been glued to Anna's amazing story.

"What a relief," Anna continued. "I nearly passed out. I was so excited to be free. I gave Karol a big kiss and told him how wonderful he was. I'd seen how scared he was as we were waved down at the border. He realized that the search and all the problems at the border had been because of us, but he didn't ask any questions. He dropped us at Vienna airport and we took a cab to the Imperial Hotel. After cleaning ourselves up, relaxing, and having a meal in the café, we were leaving the hotel when two men dressed in black ran at us, one man pushed the guy from the embassy into the back of the Jaguar car, which was waiting for us, and one shot Keller, who fell to the ground as he grabbed Alex. It happened so fast," Anna said, starting to tremble, with tears welling up, again.

Tim Bevans leaned in to his microphone. "Ask her to be more specific if she can about the shooting," he said into Stewart's earpiece.

"Anna," said Stewart. "Can you be a little bit more specific? Can you remember exactly what happened?"

"It was all so quick. The man from the embassy, I think his name was Harris, came to tell us that a car was waiting to take us to the airport. I think it was about 4:30. Keller had been telling us his remarkable story of his life during the Nazi occupation. He lost all his family. You have to hear his story. It is truly incredible. I was deeply moved and shaking with emotion when Harris appeared. So, I'm afraid I wasn't really concentrating as we left the hotel. I was just following Alex and Keller out into the street. I know there were two men. They were dressed in black and had masks, and one of them pushed Harris firmly into the side of the Jaguar right in front of me. Alex was to my left and Keller to his left. The other man was running right in front of our noses, and then I heard a crack, not very loud, more like a plop really, and I suddenly saw Keller grab Alex as he fell to the ground, and I could see a lot of blood. Harris was yelling at us to get in the car. I wanted to stay and help but he was pushing and yelling at the driver of the car so we got into the back seat. It seemed to be covered in blood as we headed to the airport."

She stammered on. "I had no idea how long the trip took. We were immediately escorted onto the plane, and the next thing I know we were on our way to London. Alex was covered in blood and in shock, and neither of us spoke for ages. Eventually, I asked him what had happened and whether he thought Keller was still alive. He really didn't know and couldn't understand how this could have happened. He was deep in thought most of the flight.

When we arrived in London, we were met by one of your representatives. Alex went off with his driver – home I suppose – and I was taken to the apartment building where I'm now staying, which I suppose belongs to you guys."

She paused again, and leaned back in her chair as she completed her story.

"That's all I can really tell you about the mission. What happened to Keller..." Her voice trailed off. She started crying and was unable to continue for a few moments. "It was an accident," she said quietly again. "I feel terrible. The whole mission has been a waste."

Bevans leaned into the microphone, and told Stewart to thank her and call it a day. Stewart leaned forward over the desk and touching Anna on the arm, said, "Thank you, Anna. That was very helpful and that will be all for today."

Inside the room Bevans turned to Alex and said, "Well what do you think? Was that an accurate description?"

"Yes, I think it was," said Alex. "Pretty much word for word as I would describe the events. Surely, you don't have any more concerns about Anna."

"Ha," said Tim. "I really wouldn't know, Alex. It's not up to me. Every bit of that interview was being filmed, and we have a whole department who will be looking at body language, repetition and whether the story unfolded exactly as her previous report. Anyway we don't have to think of that now. It's probably fine."

"It seems she has been a fantastic agent," said Alex. "I can't believe anyone could have done more than Anna did. She risked her life more than once in order to get this mission completed."

"Yes, that she did," said Bevans. "Would you have time to come up to my office?" Bevans continued, deftly changing the subject.

"Of course," said Alex. They made their way from the interview booth up to Bevans' fifth-floor office. As they walked through the anteroom to his office, Tim asked Fiona for some tea with milk and lemon and a couple of digestives.

"Make yourself comfortable," said Tim as they walked into his office, motioning towards the comfortable sofa in front of a roaring fire.

"Thank you, Tim."

"I've asked Anna to join us," said Tim. "I thought you'd like to see a friendly face," he continued, quizzingly.

"Fine," responded Alex. "What are you going to do with Anna?"

"We're going to put her into the translator's pool next week, and then, at the end of the month, we will send her on a refresher course. "

"A refresher course?" Alex asked.

"Yes," responded Tim. "We like to give ongoing training to our agents, and it's been years since Anna has been updated on our procedures because she's been in the field. Personally, I'd like to see how she does during the course as well."

"A school for spies," said Alex with a chuckle.

"You could call it that," said Tim. "But it really is quite rigorous. The location is a remote castle in North Wales and we have monthly programs throughout the year."

"Really! What do they learn?" asked Alex, genuinely interested.

"First of all, we always plant two counter-intelligence agents within the group. They know that they are in the group but nobody knows who they are. That means they have to learn to survive on their own, can't make friends, and become total loners for four weeks. Quite difficult, I would say."

"Yes, I don't like the sound of that," responded Alex.

"Well, then they're given a tough course in killing with and without weapons, survival, sleep deprivation and torture procedures, body language, poisons, sleeping draughts, and all sorts of other nasties," said Tim.

"Certainly not a vacation by the sound of it," said Alex.

"Not at all," agreed Tim. There was a knock on the door and Heather entered with a tray with three cups and saucers, a pot of tea, lemon and milk, and a plate of digestive biscuits. After placing these on the coffee table between the two couches in front of the fire, she handed a sheet of paper to Tim. "I believe you were waiting for this. It is the latest report."

"Thank you," responded Tim. "Mind if I take a minute to look at this, Alex?"

"No, of course not," responded Alex.

Tim sat at his desk and concentrated on the report. After a minute or two he got up just as there was another knock and Heather came in and announced Anna Kaluza.

Anna strode into the room. "Oh my god, Alex, it's you," she said, bounding over and throwing her arms around Alex's neck, while tears welled up in her eyes. Tim looked on without any emotion.

"Lovely to see you," said Alex rather stiffly, hugging her and then pushing her away gently.

"I knew you were here, Alex," said Anna. "I just felt you were behind that mirror during my interview." Then realizing she had not addressed Tim, "I'm sorry, sir," she said as she realized she was in the presence of the big boss. "It's just so good to see Alex again."

"I understand," said Tim. "Help yourself to some tea and biscuits." He motioned for Anna to sit on one of the sofas.

"Thank you," said Anna, now much more calm and gracious. "Excuse me, sir," she said to Tim. "Have you heard anything about my brother?"

"Well as it happens, I have. I just received an updated report from Poland. He's fine and you don't have to worry."

"Oh God, thank you," she said, putting her hand to her mouth in horror as more tears ran down her cheeks. "I've been so worried." She could hardly speak.

"I have been told he was shot in the thigh. Nothing too serious. In fact, it looks like the shot may have been an accident. He's in a prison hospital in Kraków at the moment, although we think he might be transferred to Warsaw soon."

"May, I ask, sir, what is happening over there now?" said Anna.

"On Monday morning, the secret police arrived at ORBIS offices and announced that they had made three arrests in connection with a crackdown on cross-border smuggling. Jan was one of those arrested. It was also announced they were looking for you, an accomplice in the smuggling ring."

"But that's ridiculous," said Anna.

"Maybe so. It's possible that there were not telling the truth at that stage... However, yesterday they changed their tune somewhat. We understand that they broke into your apartment and turned it over, and they also arrested your sister-in-law and your mother."

"Oh my god," said Anna, her face immediately registering fear and shock. "How could they do that? They've got nothing to do with this."

"I know," said Tim. "But I think it means that they know about Krystyna's death and that of the two soldiers. They also clearly know about Keller's disappearance. We also understand that today they eased restrictions at the Polish border into Czechoslovakia and the Czech border into Austria. I think they realize Keller has left the country."

"I'm so sorry, sir," said Anna. "I have not asked about Professor Keller."

"Well, he's still in critical condition," said Tim, not saying too much. "We will know more after this weekend."

"When do you think we can see him?" asked Alex. Tim gave him a quizzical glance and Alex realized he'd made a faux pas. It was not common knowledge that Keller was in the country. However Tim didn't comment.

"We shall have to see what progress, if any, he makes over the next few days," said Tim with some finality.

"I'm off to Paris and Milan," said Alex. "I'll contact you upon my return if that's alright Tim."

"Yes, please do," said Tim.

"And maybe we can get together for lunch on my return," said Alex to Anna.

"That would be lovely, Alex," Anna replied with a glittering warm smile. "I'm not sure where I will be or what I'll be doing," she said turning to Tim.

"You'll be relocated to a translator's pool next week, and we will be moving you into an apartment."

"That sounds great," said Anna. "But somehow I've got to go back to Poland and make sure that Jan and his family are okay."

"Well, I don't think you can contemplate that at the present time," said Tim. "Remember, you're probably wanted for murder."

Anna looked quickly at Tim as the color drained from her face. "Yes, you're right," she said quietly. "I probably am."

"Well in any event," said Tim, "we will keep you quite busy here. More tea?" he enquired.

"No thank you," both Alex and Anna replied. With that, Tim got up signaling that the meeting was at an end.

In the anteroom outside, an agent was waiting for Anna and all three of them walked to the elevator. Both Anna and the agent got off at the third floor, saying their goodbyes, while Alex descended to the ground floor, exiting the building where Frank was waiting in the Mercedes. Alex climbed into the back and sat back, feeling suddenly exhausted. There was a steady drizzle falling. Spring seemed to have disappeared. It had been a long week. He was looking forward to a quiet weekend with Julia.

Chapter 7

The following Monday morning, Alex flew to Paris. It was a bright and crisp day and Paris had the look of an early spring. He was met at Charles de Gaulle Airport by Gaston, Jean-Paul Cruze's driver, and they immediately headed for the Cruze Cognac offices on Faubourg Saint-Honore. Cruze was one of the Campbell Group's subsidiaries, and Jean-Paul Cruze was the chief executive. Alex attended a meeting with Paul Cruze and his executives followed by a small private dinner. The next day, he flew to Milan to meet the Campbell Group importer Armando Innocenti, and twenty-four hours later he was back to London and went straight to his Sackville Street offices. After a few hours' work, he was more than ready to go home. Julia said he had received a message from Tim asking him to call the following morning. Alex was apprehensive, and very worried about Keller's progress.

First thing in the morning, he spoke to Tim who shared some encouraging news about Keller, who seemed to be making good progress.

"Well, we hope that his progress continues and, if this is the case, I'd like you to join me at the clinic to see Keller on Monday afternoon if that would work for you," said Tim.

"Sure," said Alex. "I'm anxious to see him as well. Shall we say 3:00 p.m.?"

"I should tell you Alex that one of the reasons I'm anxious to talk to him, is to find out what happened to his papers. Having Keller here is one thing, but without his papers, his defection to the West does nothing for us."

"I understand," said Alex, again frustrated and annoyed that he may have risked his life for nothing. But, he responded calmly, "I'm sure there's an explanation. Keller is no fool, and I think he knows exactly why you are helping him defect."

"Well, if he's up to it, I'd like you to ask him that question first, in Polish," said Tim.

"Okay," said Alex. "And I still want to tell him about our mutual family history."

"I know," said Tim. "That's a fascinating story. It will be amazing to see his response."

"I shall break it to him gently," said Alex.

They arrived at virtually the same time on the following Monday afternoon.

They were escorted to the third floor by one of Tim's agents providing protection for Keller.

There were two large bodyguards at the entrance to the corridor and two more outside Keller's room. Alex thought, *Tim is taking no chances.* The guards all nodded to Bevans as they walked down the corridor. They got to Keller's room just as a nurse was coming out.

"Please don't say too long," she said quietly. "He is still very weak."

"We understand," said Tim, turning to Alex.

They entered the small dark hospital room. Keller was sitting up in bed with various pieces of equipment attached to his arms and his neck. Alex was immediately shocked by Keller's appearance. He had wasted away in the ten days since he last saw him. He was pale as a ghost.

"Good afternoon, Professor Keller. Do you remember me?" said Alex slowly in Polish.

"Of course, Alex," replied Keller with a slight smile and a more than croaky voice. "Good to see you," he continued.

"Well, I'm relieved to see you," said Alex with a smile. "You've certainly been through the mill these past couple of weeks," he said cheerily.

"I know, but I'm a tough old boot," responded Keller. "So I'm still here – just about – I think."

"I'd like to introduce you to Tim Bevans, who is the head of the British Secret Service and was responsible for getting you out of Vienna to safety in London," said Alex.

Keller immediately stiffened, and Alex saw his eyes go hard and cold.

"You people promised that you would protect me and my wife. My wife is dead and I was shot and nearly died as well." He said to Bevans in heavily accented English. "What happened? Where was the great British Secret Service? I think I have a right to know," Keller continued, as his voice weakened to a husky whisper.

"Of course, you do. I'm sorry, Professor, but at this time, I don't have an answer. I don't know what went wrong, but we are doing everything in our power to get to the bottom of this issue. As soon as I have more news, I will of course let you know. But now the main thing is to get you better and stronger. As to the tragedy with your wife, I can only express my sincere condolences and that of the British government." Tim was in full diplomatic mode.

"Mr. Bevans" said Keller in almost a whisper. "I've heard excuses throughout my whole life. The Poles, Nazis, and the Communists are experts at making excuses and blaming others. 'Just following orders.' How many times have I heard that over the years? A few months ago I lost my two sons. They said it was an accident. Plenty of excuses. Plenty of condolences and you can imagine what that did to my wife and myself." He paused, trying to control his emotions. "I decided there was nothing left for us in Poland, and that we should try a new life of freedom in the West. So we made the most momentous decision to abandon our homeland, and our memories, and defect." He paused, again trying to control his emotions, looking directly at Bevans. "I thought the worst part of my life was over when the war ended after the horrors I'd seen, and the murder of my family by the Nazis. But now I've lost the love of my life, Krystyna and I'm all alone once again. Condolences and excuses don't help." Keller had the look of abject despair in his face and eyes. He looked like he was ready to die.

"Professor," interjected Alex, speaking in Polish and gently seizing the opportunity. "You're not as alone as you think. I'm about to tell you an amazing story." Keller's eyes flickered with interest. "When you told me the moving history of your life" continued Alex, "and the horrors you endured under the Nazis as a teenager in Tarnow, I was astounded. Partly because you told us that your father was able to arrange for you to flee to freedom and join the partisans in the woods, only because the Nazis couldn't reconcile his papers. This was because your father's name was really Kornmehl and not Kellerman." Alex paused. "Professor," said Alex slowly but dramatically, "you and I are cousins."

Keller was now sitting up and taking notice. A mixture of confusion hope and fear was on his face.

"What?" he said huskily. "Did you say cousins? That's impossible. All my family was murdered in the Holocaust." Even Tim Bevans, struggling to understand the Polish, was moved.

"I know, Professor. But the fact is my grandfather was a Kornmehl, and in fact, we had the same grandfather. He was married to your grandmother, who died three months after giving birth to your father who I know was named Isak."

"That's right – Isak," responded Keller, now much more awake and eager to hear more.

"When our grandfather, Jakob, remarried and had other children, including my father Aaron, he emigrated to Dundee in Scotland, and it was there that he brought up his family, and my father and I were born. My grandfather, Jakob, often talked about your father Isak. He felt very guilty about leaving him behind with his maternal grandparents, but he was in no fit state financially or physically to take a two-year-old on a hazardous journey of immigration to a new country."

Alex paused. "As it happens," he continued as Keller looked

on in wide-eyed amazement, "he returned to Tarnów in 1926 with my father and had hoped to meet your father Isak, and indeed you, who I believe was two years old at that time. However, you and your family were away at a wedding in Kraków and they were unable to get together. After the war, my father and grandfather made every effort to trace their family. They knew that Isak and his wife and family had perished in the Holocaust as had all the other Kornmehls. He assumed that you had perished as well, but for the rest of his life he never forgot your father. Even on his deathbed he talked about Isak and the Fogler family who had agreed to look after him. Your aunt adopted your father and then married a man called Kellerman."

"I know, I know, the Foglers," said Keller, excitedly, his voice now stronger.

"It is an amazing story," said Alex. "I wanted to tell you at the Imperial Hotel in Vienna...

"Anyway," he continued, "I wanted you to know, Professor, that you have a large family here in Britain. Lots of Kornmehls who are now called Campbell. As soon as you are fit and well, I will introduce you to many of them in London and Scotland. One thing I want to make clear, from now on, you will not be alone."

Keller, was speechless with emotion. "Thank you, Alex. Thank you so much," he replied with difficulty, tears welling up. "This is incredible. I can't tell you how grateful I am to know that there are other members of my family here. I want to meet all of them. I can't wait." Keller now had tears running down his cheeks and couldn't continue.

After a few moments to allow Keller to recover, Tim said in faltering Polish, "I hope you don't mind, but there are some questions that I'd like to ask you. I've asked Alex to be my translator since his Polish is so much better than mine."

"Of course," responded Keller with a wan smile, but now friendlier to Tim.

"I am sure I know what those questions are." Again Tim look

at Alex.

Alex, still speaking slowly and gently, said, "Mr. Bevans and MI6, which is the British Secret Service, expected you to arrive in Britain with a large package of your private scientific papers. We understood you were going to bring these with you. Of course they are very important with regard to your defection and being accepted to live in Britain."

"I know, I know," said Keller wearily. "You want to see all my papers, research, drawings and mathematical calculations in connection with my theories on nuclear fusion. The whole story. However, when my wife, Krystyna, and I..." he said as his voice drifted off and tears welled up again in his eyes. He paused for a moment, then looked again at Bevans with a frosty expression. "Krystyna and I discussed this at length. We were concerned with what would happen if we were caught. I knew that, if I had incriminating papers with me, I would probably be shot within twenty-four hours. I also wanted to use my papers as an insurance policy not only for my defection to the West, but also in the event that I was arrested in Poland."

"I can understand your concern," said Alex, trying to be diplomatic and helpful.

"I did have real concerns," said Professor Keller. "I had no idea what defection would mean. Was I going to be protected by the British Secret Service? Apparently not." He again stared at Bevans. "Would I be handed over to the KGB in some spy swap? Would the Americans be involved? Would I be killed on either side of the border? Well that nearly happened. I just didn't know, but I thought I should give myself some protection. It seems I was right. Your MI6 or whatever you are called apparently is more interested in my papers, than my safety."

Bevans understood enough of this, to respond in poor Polish. "That is not true, Professor. I can assure you, Her Majesty's government considered your safety as the highest priority."

"Well, Mr. Bevans, that is good because I may disappoint

you." He paused again, perhaps savoring the moment, despite his weakened state. "In answer to your question, I left all my papers with my closest friend and scientific peer at Warsaw University, Jaroslav Kopacz. We entered university together just after the Second World War, became firm friends and have been close ever since. Like me, he was on the faculty of the university. He's an eminent professor of physics in his own right. He's done some incredible work and has a worldwide reputation. He is the one person I knew I could trust with my papers and indeed my life."

Bevans turned to Alex, looking aghast. "Did he say all his papers are still in Warsaw?"

"I am afraid so," replied Alex. He could see Tim thinking, *We did all of this and the papers are still in Poland? Are we all mad?*

Keller turned to Alex. "I could give you a note which you could give to Professor Kopacz, which he would know was genuine, and he would hand those over to you or your representative," he said, having taken note of Tim's expression, perhaps realizing his defection might be in jeopardy.

"I see," said Alex. "We will have to give that some thought." He turned to Tim. "Are you getting all this?"

"I think so," Tim replied, tight-lipped and clearly angry.

"One other thing," said Keller. "All my papers are in code."

"In code?" responded Alex, now thinking like Tim, *This is turning into a nightmare.* He turned to Tim. "He said all his papers are in code."

"In code!! Bloody hell, we risk lives and spend a fortune to plan and prepare for Keller's defection, and he leaves his fucking papers in code and in Warsaw!! What a disaster." Tim was red-faced and about to explode. Alex knew his friend was really furious. His diplomatic façade had fallen. He never used profanities.

Keller, not understanding all of Tim's tirade, ploughed on. "Yes, I've used a code that I created to describe all of my work, all of my scientific experiments, all of my theories for the past thirty years."

"That's incredible. Why did you do that?" questioned Alex, trying to rescue something from this encounter.

"Because I needed some security. You may not understand, but I lived and worked in a Communist State. I could have disappeared, any moment, and never been heard of again." He paused. "It happens."

"Well, Professor, we have a lot to think about." Alex looked at Keller and saw he was fading fast. His pale face now seemed even more ashen.

"I think we should leave you now," said Alex. "But, we will come back again soon. I want to hear all about your family history and I'm sure you will want to hear about ours. We've got lots to talk about. What we need now is for you to get stronger and healthier."

"Thank you so much, Alex. I am so pleased to see you again," he said in an ever-weakening voice but with a smile. "By the way, I meant to ask, how is the beautiful Anna, who saved our lives?"

"Anna's fine," said Alex. "I saw her last week."

"Please give my best wishes and thank her once again for her bravery and courage in getting us to safety in Vienna. Although in my case, it wasn't quite as safe," the professor said, looking at Bevans.

"I will," responded Alex with a smile. He turned to Tim and said, "I think we should leave now." Tim nodded.

As they walked down the corridor Tim said to Alex, "What the hell do we do now? The professor is here but his papers aren't."

"Somehow you will work out how to get hold of Kopacz, and the professor's papers," said Alex.

"Everything is coded?" said Tim.

"Yes, you didn't get that. Apparently he's been coding all his papers, experiments, and everything else for the past thirty years and only he knows the code."

"Christ. What a mess. My minister will not be happy, nor will the FO and PM. I think your cousin played us. I don't like that, Alex," said Tim, still seething.

"I am sorry, Tim, but don't worry," said Alex, giving his friend a pat on the back. "I know you'll find a solution."

"Well, we better. Otherwise they may take my head," said Tim. They reached the ground floor, exiting the building onto Devonshire Place. Both cars and drivers were waiting for them. They stood and shook hands. "Thanks for coming, Alex." He paused. "It is quite a family story," said Tim, now the diplomat again. "Really amazing."

"I know," said Alex. "I'm really moved by it all. Keller looked very weak, but I hope he won't have any more setbacks and makes a good recovery. Then perhaps in a few weeks he'll be able to meet the Campbell family for the first time."

"I'll keep in touch with you over the next week or two and let you know if we have any further information on what's happening in Poland," said Tim.

"Please do so," said Alex. "By the way," he said to Tim as an afterthought. "Would it be okay if I took Anna to lunch in the next week or so?"

"Certainly, but do me one favor, Alex," he said looking serious. "Don't tell her about our meeting today or about Keller being in London."

"I won't," said Alex. "I'm sorry about that. It was really stupid of me."

"Not to worry," said Tim, but making his point. "See you soon." He turned and got into his car.

Ten days later, Alex was in the bar of L'Ecu de France, a French restaurant on Jermyn Street, waiting for Anna. A couple of minutes later, she walked in, shoulders back, and strode quickly across the floor, gave him a big smile and threw her arms around him. "It's so great to see you, Alex," she said, her bright blue eyes and flashing smile dazzling him into speechlessness for a moment. Everyone in the bar had turned to look at this beautiful woman striding across the room.

"Thank you so much for inviting me to lunch, Alex," she said, holding onto his hand as he sat down.

"It's lovely to see you, Anna," he said with a smile. "Now what would you like to drink?"

"It's lunchtime so I think I'll just have a small glass of white wine. Sorry it's not Campbell's Reserve," she said with a smile and a laugh.

"That's fine," said Alex. He ordered his whisky and a glass of Chardonnay for Anna.

"Well now," he said. "What have you been up to?"

"They've been keeping me busy," said Anna. "I am working in the translators' section, reading cables from Poland and also looking at Russian information from time to time. It's quite interesting but needs a lot of concentration. And of course I am deskbound, which really is not me, Alex," she said with a chuckle. "But, I love being in London. It is so alive and exciting, beautiful and overcrowded. After dull and drab Warsaw, this is like living on another planet."

"I'm sure of that," said Alex.

"But, I would like to be out and about. In fact, it so happens they are sending me on a course at the end of the month."

"Well that should be fun," said Alex. "A change of pace."

"I know, and I'm looking forward to it, although I understand it's quite grueling. Not like a beach holiday or anything like that," she said with a laugh.

At that moment, Mario the maitre d' appeared with two large menus. "Sir Alex and madame," he said. "Can I recommend our sole goujon today?"

"Thank you, Mario," responded Alex as he took the menu. "Now, I know you're hungry," he said to Anna.

"Me?" Anna replied. "I am always hungry. I can always eat,"

she said with a grin.

"Well that's great," said Alex, relaxing in the company of this confident, beautiful young woman. He had to admit, he was excited to see her; visions of her framed in the bathroom door at the Hotel Reymonta, flashed across his mind. But he showed no emotion as he calmly ordered.

He chose a plate of smoked salmon followed by sole goujon, and Anna chose crab cocktail followed by a sole bonne femme. He ordered a half bottle of Pouilly-Fuisse, and they settled down to a comfortable lunch. This was the first time they had a chance to really talk to each other. Her experiences in Poland and escape to the West hadn't allowed much time for conversation. Alex told her how amazed he was to hear her life story, and she wanted to know all about Alex's family in Poland. When he told her that he was actually closely related to Professor Keller her blue eyes widened in amazement.

"But that's incredible. What a story," she said. "How is Professor Keller doing?" she inquired anxiously.

Alex hesitated a moment and then responded. "I don't really know. Last I heard, he was still in intensive care. I haven't spoken to Tim Bevans for the last week, so, I'm not really sure."

"Well, I hope he comes through," said Anna. "It will be terrible if he doesn't."

"I know," said Alex eager to change the subject. "Have you heard anything more about Jan?"

"I got a message from Mr. Bevans, saying Jan had been moved to Warsaw. He's in a prison hospital outside of the city somewhere. That's all I know. I'm really worried about him, but I suppose the mere fact that they moved him shows that he's not too badly hurt."

She then turned to Alex and looked at him intently. "I've got to get Jan out of Poland, Alex," she said.

"I don't think you can handle that," responded Alex. "It's not your job. You'll have to leave it to the MI6. They will find a way

– a prisoner swap or something like that, over the next year or two."

"A year or two!" exclaimed Anna clearly horrified. "Jan incarcerated for a year or two? I am not sure he could survive." She continued. "I've got to find a way."

"Well I don't know how," said Alex. "It's up to Tim Bevans. MI6 understand these things better than we do." Anna didn't pursue the subject further.

They continued their pleasant lunch, talking about their amazing experiences in Poland, Anna's mother's estate, Jan's family and Alex's life in London and Scotland.

After nearly two hours, they said their goodbyes. Alex put Anna in a taxi as Frank pulled up in the Mercedes. They kissed each other on the cheeks.

"We'll keep in touch," said Alex.

"Please," responded Anna, with a sincere smile.

Anna sat back in the taxi as it weaved its way down Jermyn Street, past Simpsons, all the custom shirt shops, and Fortnum and Mason, turning left at the Cavendish Hotel and heading for St James's Square and ultimately the Mall and Victoria. She loved the sights and smells of London. She had known for many years that it had been a mistake to leave Australia for Warsaw. But she had decided to follow her mother and her beloved Jan, who had always been her hero. The protector and father that she had never had, her patient friend and play pal, from the days of the Collective Labor Camp 165 in Russia, right through their teenage years in Sydney. He had protected her when his boyhood friends made jokes about her trailing along, and then as she matured into a beautiful young girl, provided a different type of protection against his more mature friends. She had always felt he was the strong solid and reliable rod that held her family together.

For Anna being near her mother and brother compensated for the drab and restrictive life of living in Poland. She had been quite content, however, as her ORBIS salary was also supplemented by an MI6 stipend. She had also enjoyed a satisfying affair for over ten years with Wladyslaw Starzec, which had only come to an end a year or so ago, as a result of his retirement and a wife in poor health in Wroclaw. Wladyslaw Starzec was twenty-three years older than her, but that did not deter her love for him, nor his for her. She had always been attracted to older men. Jan had often said she really wanted a father figure. She knew she was beautiful, and attractive to all men. But she was natural and unassuming. Nevertheless, she knew how to use her sexuality when need be, to get her own way or to achieve a dedicated goal. She was confident in her ability to use her beauty and charm to extract almost anything she wanted from most men, as she had done in the past and would do again in the future.

As the taxi made its way through the clogged traffic of London towards her new apartment, she was thinking of one thing only. How could she get Jan and his family out of Warsaw and to safety in London? She couldn't leave him to rot in prison. She was sure that if they connected him to Professor Keller's disappearance, the "ferrets" would torture him. She had to find a way. There was no alternative. She must do it, and she would.

* * *

Von Schuyler came into the house with Rajah at his heels. It was late afternoon on a crisp sunny Saturday at the end of March. He had enjoyed his walk up the hill from the dairy farm. Ernst came to the front entrance and took his coat. "You received a telephone call, Herr von Schuyler," he said.

"Yes."

"A gentleman called Sergei."

"Thank you, Ernst." Von Schuyler went into his study with Rajah padding behind. There was a roaring fire in the fireplace, making the room warm and cozy. He picked up the telephone and dialed Sergei.

"Sergei, it's Karl," he said.

"Karl," said the voice at the other end. "You owe me one million dollars."

"What?" said von Schuyler loudly.

"Your target is still alive."

"Impossible," responded von Schuyler, feeling his temper rising. "The funeral was in the newspaper."

"Fake," responded Sergei curtly.

"How do you know?" responded von Schuyler aggressively.

"He is alive and in London."

"In London?" von Schuyler barked into the phone. "How could that be?"

"Never mind how," replied Sergei. "We've been informed by our people in London. There's no mistake. He is alive and being protected by the MI6."

Von Schuyler felt a sinking feeling in his stomach. "I don't understand," he said. "My people pumped the body full of lead in the hospital."

"I'm sure they did, but it was not the target. It was somebody else."

"But there was a police guard outside of the hospital room."

"A decoy," responded Sergei. "They were taking precautions. And it worked."

"I can't believe it," said von Schuyler.

"Well believe it or not, Karl," said Sergei, his voice rising. "It's true. And you owe me one million dollars. You have ten days."

"Ten days," responded von Schuyler. "What's the rush?"

"Ten days," said Sergei, and put the phone down.

Von Schuyler was furious. He thumped his desk and swept some papers onto the carpet. He stood up, as did Rajah disturbed by the noise. His face was red and his temper was broiling. "A fucking million," he told himself, as he launched a kick at Rajah's rear. The dog yelped in pain and scampered away to the corner of the room. "A fucking million," he repeated. He had already donated the money to the FPÖ. Their campaign was in full swing. The money had made a big difference. Now he would have to dig into his own assets to find the million. He knew there would be no arguments with Sergei. It was pay up or else. He was furious. At that moment, his study door opened and an elegant Katrina walked in, loaded down with bags from shopping in Vienna.

"Hallo, Schatzi," she said not realizing she was walking into hell. "How was your day?" She didn't appear to notice Karl's flushed face.

"Not good," he responded in a loud voice. "What the hell is all of this?" he said pointing at her shopping bags.

"I just did a little shopping. I bought some beautiful clothes. You will love them."

"You think I'm made of money?" he roared, rising from his desk. "That's all you're interested in. Spending, spending, spending," he yelled. She backed away.

"Schatzi, calm down," she said. "What's going on?"

It was too late. He was a red-faced roaring animal. He charged at her. "What's all this garbage?" he screamed, ripping the bags out of her hands and throwing them across the room. She was caught unaware and staggered back. "All you're interested in is spending money," he yelled. Suddenly he launched his right arm at her face and hit her forcefully. She fell to the floor with a cry, and scrambled away from him cowering in fear.

He came after her again as she got to her feet, this time with a backhand swipe to her left eye. She went down again with a cry of pain. He then kicked her viciously in the back. "You whore!" he yelled. "I want you to take all this garbage back and get my money back." She tried to stagger to her feet, holding her face and her aching back. He stood over her deciding whether to launch another kick, but then he stormed out of the room, still yelling.

Wincing with pain, Katarina slowly made it back to her bedroom, where she took off the jacket of her suit, which had a long tear at the seam. She went into her large marble-covered bathroom, and looked at the swelling on her eye and cheek. She took some witch hazel from the medicine cabinet, and carefully dabbed it on the angry bruise. Her makeup was smudged, her lipstick spread down her cheek, and her mascara had run. She stared in the mirror and shivered at the thought of what she knew would come that night.

She had not shared a bedroom with Karl for fifteen years. When she had first met him, she had been swept away by his good looks, strong macho personality, and worldly sophistication. She enjoyed the rough sex, and she was a willing partner to some of his more bizarre sexual demands. Katarina was no stranger to sex. She had learned at the age of seventeen that, if you wanted to win beauty pageants, it helped if you were willing to sleep with the leading judge. Most of the men she had known had been bowled over by her beauty, and had treated her as a delicate flower, timid and often apologetic, as they made love to her. She saw sex as a means to an end, and had learned a few tricks of her own as she made her way through the Austrian beauty pageants. Karl was different. He was in charge. He knew how to arouse and pleasure her, and she returned the favor. However after they were married, he became ever more demanding, forcing her to cater to his expanding bizarre tastes. The rough sex became more brutal and the encounters became less frequent and, for Katarina, painful and frightening. She decided she had enjoyed enough sex to last a lifetime. She persuaded Karl that they should have separate bedrooms, and to her surprise he did not object. Of course, she had to be available and willing when he did appear. For the past few years his visits, for the most part, had coincided with his loss of temper, tantrums, and punishment for Katarina.

She knew what to expect later that evening. He would appear in her bedroom in his silk robe, totally naked underneath, with the handcuffs in his pocket, and maybe a riding crop, or rubber truncheon. He would tell her to take off her night dress, or sometimes if he was really angry, he would tear it off. Then he would roughly throw her onto the bed face down, grab her wrists, pass the handcuffs through the bars of her bed headboard and clamp them onto her. He would then tell her that she had to behave as he hit her forcefully across the face and to make sure she did, he would strike her across her naked buttocks and back, with the riding crop or rubber truncheon until deep red welts appeared. If she yelled or screamed, he would hit her harder. He would then disrobe, and force himself into her rear, bringing tears to her eyes and often blood to her lips, as she cried out in pain. Sometimes he would pull her hair back until she thought her neck would break or more often, he would bite into her shoulders until he drew blood, and climaxed. When he was satisfied, he would unlock the handcuffs, put on his robe and leave the bedroom without another word. Katarina would crawl or stagger into the bathroom, where she would shower under a hot stream of water, deal with her wounds as best she could, take some sleep and pain medicine and fall back into bed.

But tonight, Karl would be even more brutal than usual.

Chapter 8

Alex visited the clinic a couple of times the following week and then took to "popping in" on the way back from his Sackville Street offices for half an hour to see Keller's progress. In fact, Keller was making remarkable progress. Within a week, he was walking up and down the corridor. He started to put on weight and his color improved dramatically. Alex enjoyed these visits and he felt a bond of friendship, or maybe it was family. Erik Keller was a tall, strong-looking man, with close-cropped gray hair, intelligent gray eyes and apart from a large scar on his right jaw, he had a handsome visage. Alex found Keller an intriguing and interesting fellow and particularly enjoyed hearing about life in Tarnów, the Kornmehl family home for centuries until Alex's immediate family had left in 1892.

Tarnów is located approximately forty-five miles east of Krakow in southern Poland. It had always been a crossroads for trade between East and West, and for hundreds of years had a large Jewish population. Even though there had been pogroms, poverty, high taxation, discrimination and persecution, the population of 50,000 in 1939 was nearly 50% Jewish. Keller described a small attractive town originally walled and containing rows of brightly painted old houses, some with Venetian-style balconies surrounding the Rynek – the market square, a smaller version of the famous square in Krakow. Through the centuries, there had been periods of stability, peace and prosperity, even for the Jews, and there was a strong feeling of family, and religious tolerance within the Jewish community itself. Keller of course had never known the Kornmehl part of his family, but his maternal grandparents and the aunt who had raised his father Isak, spoke in glowing terms of the Kornmehls.

As Alex and Keller traded questions and answers about their respective lives, Alex realized how fortunate he had been to be born in Scotland where he and his family had been able to live, prosper, and build their lives without discrimination. Keller's life from 1939 onwards had been one of fear and persecution first, under the Nazis, then under the Communists. It was only Professor Erik Keller's brilliance as a nuclear physicist that had allowed him and his family to enjoy a comparatively comfortable life within the Communist system.

On 19th March, Erik Keller was discharged from the London clinic and sent for recuperation and rehab to a nursing home on Hampstead Heath.

He was accompanied by two bodyguards at all times and was registered at the nursing home as Mr. Pollard. Within a couple of days, Alex visited him to make sure he was comfortable. The following day, he phoned Tim, to update him on Keller's progress and inquire about the future.

"What are you going to do with him?" asked Alex.

"Well," said Tim. "If he continues to make such good progress, then within a couple of weeks or so, we'll have him discharged, and then we plan to send him to Aldermaston. We've got a nice 'safe house' – well actually a pretty cottage on the edge of Reading where we think he'll be very comfortable, and then we can get him working with the other 'boffins.' Alex knew that Aldermaston was Britain's atomic-weapons establishment and the headquarters of the UK's nuclear-weapons program.

"Do you think he'll cooperate?" asked Alex. "He wasn't too happy about working on Moscow's nuclear-weapons program."

"I know," said Tim. "But I shall talk to him first. He's no fool, and he knows why we helped him defect to the West."

"I was wondering, Tim," said Alex tentatively. "Do you think it would be okay if I had Keller join us for our family Passover dinner on 28th March?"

"I don't see why not," said Tim. "We will need to have one of our people in your flat and also at the entrance to your block for security purposes. I'm afraid Keller's life in the future will be one of bullet-proof cars and twenty-four-hour security watch."

"I understand," said Alex. "I just think it would be great for Keller to meet the rest of the family."

"Wonderful," said Tim. "I think it will do him good to know that he has a close family in this country."

"I also wonder whether it will be alright if I asked Anna to join us," continued Alex. "She doesn't know that Keller is in the UK, or that he's recovering so well. I know she would love to see him, and I think he wants to thank her for all her help. Do you think at this stage it would be okay to include her in the group that knows that he's safe in London?"

"I think the Poles and the Russians probably know by now that we've got him," said Tim.

"Really?" questioned Alex. "What makes you think that?"

"Well, we don't underestimate our opposition. They're very good, Alex, and it's been four weeks now. We know that the Poles have opened up the borders, as have the Czechs, and have stopped searching for him. Polish security and the KGB have got their people here, whether we like it or not, and I think this sort of information has probably got back to them. So, I don't really see much harm in letting Anna in on our secret now. After all, Keller has made a good recovery physically and I hope, with your help, mentally, and I think we've got him well protected." He paused again. "The real issue is going to be how to get hold of those papers."

"Well, thanks, Tim. I'll ask Anna to join us," Alex said, pointedly changing the subject. "Perhaps we can get together for lunch in a couple of weeks, by which time you may have some ideas about getting Keller's papers out of Poland."

"Fine," said Tim. "I'll call you in a week or two to make a date."

It had become a tradition over the past fifteen years or so for Alex and Julia to host family and friends for the Passover Seder dinner in their London or Edinburgh homes in alternate years.

This year 1983, Julia was planning for twenty-four guests – now twenty-six – with Erik Keller and Anna Kaluza. Alex's three aunts, Rachel, Esther, and Lillian – all in their eighties, but remarkably energetic and feisty – would be coming down from Scotland with their husbands, Bobby Marks, and David Woolf. Rachel's husband, Bill Silver, had passed away. Most of their children and a lot of grandchildren, many who lived and worked in the London area, would be there. Alex and Julia's daughter Laura was coming down from Glasgow University. Their eldest son Paul was in Kentucky, working at a Campbell Group subsidiary company, and younger son Mark was traveling in South America. Seder night was always a joyful family occasion with lots of talking and laughing and of course, eating. Julia was already making the Matzo balls for the chicken soup, gefilte fish, and the traditional brisket and roast chicken, together with a compote of fruit, macaroons and cinnamon biscuits.

During the service, which was led by Alex and lasted about an hour, the youngest child, Emily Marks, would ask the four questions – "Why is this night different from every other night...?" And the guests would partake of four glasses of wine with bitter herbs to commemorate the years of slavery in Egypt, eggs and saltwater for a new beginning, and the Matzo (unleavened bread) representing the haste in which the Jewish people left Egypt.

This year Alex asked all the family to come early, so they would have an opportunity of meeting Erik Keller, the sole survivor of the Kornmehl family from the horrors of the Nazi Holocaust. Many of the family were amazed to find out that there was a Kornmehl survivor, since it was well known that, despite every effort after the war to trace survivors, no one had appeared.

Alex told the family that Keller was a professor of physics and had obtained permission to take a sabbatical year, teaching in the West, having lost his wife and children in a dreadful accident. He told everyone to be understanding and sympathetic since Keller's loss was recent. A bodyguard had arrived an hour before Keller, to check out the Campbell apartment and then ensconced himself discreetly in the kitchen. Another bodyguard delivered Keller safely to the Campbell apartment block and then stayed in the vehicle with the driver, watching the entrance.

When Keller arrived, there was a buzz of excitement, nervous laughter and tears. Many family members spontaneously hugged and kissed him. Keller was overwhelmed and had tears in his eyes. Aunt Esther, in her usual fashion, was sobbing uncontrollably. It didn't take much to get the aunts emotional. Alex introduced Keller to all the family. Alex was surprised that all three aunts were able to speak to Keller in Polish. He didn't realize that they had retained their knowledge of the language so many years after Papa – Jakob Kornmehl – had passed away.

Fifteen minutes after Keller, Anna arrived. She was wearing a figure-hugging black suit, high heels, pearl earrings and little makeup. Alex introduced Anna to Julia and other members of the family, as an employee at the Foreign Office who had helped Keller with his move to the UK. No one questioned Anna's Australian accent.

Alex quieted all the family down. "We're all happy to welcome my cousin, Erik." Chuckles and laughter from the family. "A long lost member of the Kornmehl family. For those younger members of the family who are here tonight, I should just take a minute or two to explain our connection." Alex paused, gathering his thoughts.

"Jakob Kornmehl – Papa – my grandfather, emigrated from Tarnów in Poland to Dundee in 1892.

"The Kornmehls had lived in Tarnów, since the early seventeen hundreds. By the 1890s, continued pogroms, persecution and poverty had forced thousands, particularly young people, to emigrate mainly to the United States but also to European countries. Papa was a peddler like his father, hauling boxes of soap and flour, candles and cooking oils, to the small

Jewish-dominated villages around Tarnów on a rented horse and cart. It was a hard living, backbreaking, but they earned enough to put food on the table. In January 1888, Jakob married Yentl Fogler, a neighbor, whom he had known since she was a young girl. In December 1888, their first son Isak was born, but a few months later, Yentl contracted cholera and within a week she died." Alex paused. He could have heard a pin drop. The family was transfixed.

"Of course, Jakob and the families were distraught and overcome with his loss. He now had an infant son to support but through the kindness of the Fogler family, his in-laws took on the responsibility of raising Isak."

Alex looked around the table, before continuing. "After a year of mourning, the local matchmakers were eager to marry Papa off again. He was an eligible young man and was introduced to Freidel Rappaport, one of four daughters of Solomon Rappaport, a hat maker from Zabno, a Hassidic village near Tarnów. Freidel did not particularly want to marry Papa. She knew that he was still in mourning for his wife Yentl, and had an infant son. However her father was eager to marry off at least one of his four daughters as quickly as possible. Eventually they met and Freidel was surprised to find she liked him. She was particularly inter-ested when he told her of his plans to move to America and start a new life away from the pogroms and persecution of Tarnów. She did not want to lead the life of a Hassidic wife, in a deeply religious home with lots of children. So Papa's plans were an exciting alternative.

"They married in July 1890 and moved into a two-room apartment in the center of the Jewish quarter of Tarnów. The pogroms got worse and, in the spring of 1892, they felt they had enough money to pay for the passage out of Poland. They were following Jakob's brother, Herman, who had already gone to America. Freidel – Mama – was already four months pregnant when they said farewell to their respective families. The Foglers agreed with Jakob that he could not take his two-year-old son with him, with an uncertain future and no money. So they agreed to continue to raise him. Their daughter Faye was getting married and had taken to the young two-year-old Izak."

Everyone was captivated by Alex's history of the family. Nobody moved. Alex paused again and looked around the table, before continuing. "Papa and Mama left Tarnów for Warsaw where they were met by members of the Jewish Agency, who informed them that they didn't have enough money to get to America. Passage prices had gone up. Their only choice was to take a passage on a ship leaving the next morning for Dundee. That's how Mama and Papa came to Scotland. When they arrived, immigration officials were unable to understand the name Kornmehl, and having been instructed to either shorten or change all these Polish names, they converted Kornmehl into Campbell. So now you know the story," concluded Alex. All the young people around the table were in rapture. Some started clapping excitedly. This was the first time many of them had learned of their background.

"Tell us more," said young Roger Woolf, Lillian's twelve-year-old great-grandson.

"Well," continued Alex. "Papa became a peddler and worked very hard visiting all the villages around Dundee the same as he had done with his father in Tarnów. Sometime later he was contacted by a supplier in Dundee who offered him rum, which he thought he could sell quite easily to the taverns and inns in the small mining villages. He started with rum and eventually added scotch whisky, which is how the Campbell Group of companies was born. My father, Aaron, was born five months after Papa and Mama arrived in Dundee and eighteen months later Auntie Rachel, who is sitting here with us this evening, was born, followed by Auntie Esther and Lillian. We're all pleased to see them in such good health and joining us for yet another Seder." Alex paused.

Some family members said, "Hear, hear," while laughing.

Alex continued. "Faye Fogler continued to look after baby Isak, and after she married a man called Kellermann, they agreed to adopt little Isak as their own child. My father Aaron visited Tarnów with Papa in 1926. He wanted to see his mother and his son Isak. Unfortunately, when they got to Tarnów, Isak and the Kellermanns were in Kraków for a cousin's wedding and so they never got together. Papa maintained an active correspondence with his sisters, throughout the 1920s and 1930s as the situation in Europe deteriorated and Hitler and the Nazis came to power. One of Papa's sisters was living in Vienna and another one in Warsaw. They both returned to Tarnów as the Nazis marched across Europe and annexed one country after another. Unfortunately, none of them survived the Holocaust." Alex paused, feeling the emotion of that statement, as the grand-children looked on uncomprehending.

"After the war," Alex continued shakily, "I know that every effort was made to find surviving members of the Kornmehl or Fogler family. Eventually, we received long lists of those who died, but we could not find one survivor. Papa never forgot Izak and even on his deathbed talked to me about what had happened to the family, including his son Izak."

He looked around the table. All the women were tearful, including Anna who was seated next to Keller and holding his arm. A deathly hush had come over the group.

"But one member of our family did survive," Alex continued more jauntily. "And it is an absolute miracle that we have found each other. I'm sure you will want to know how our cousin, Erik Keller – my first cousin – survived the Holocaust and what happened to his family." He paused. "I know this is a serious and daunting conversation before the joyful Seder, but I think it will highlight how important the celebration of Seder is, not only for the freedom of the Jewish people from the slavery of Egypt, but our own personal family connection to freedom now that we have our long-lost cousin amongst us."

He turned to Keller. "Professor, perhaps you would like to take over from here." Alex sat down as Keller looked around at the tearful members of his family.

"I am sorry," he said in a thick Polish accent. "My English is always not good. I will have to ask Alex for help with my talking," he said slowly.

Julia thought how much he sounded like Papa.

"I wish to thank you for welcoming me into your house. This important night of nights, we celebrate the flight of the Jewish people from slavery in Egypt from thousands of years." Keller was struggling with his English. "This is the first Seder night for me since I was fifteen years in 1939 in my hometown of Tarnów." He turned to Alex. "My English is understood?"

"It is fine," responded Alex softly, nodding approvingly.

"Shortly after the war started in September 1939, the Germans marched into Tarnów. The Polish defense forces had collapsed. I remember looking through the curtains of our apartment as I saw the first German soldiers and tanks pass by on the street below." Keller paused trying to get his English together. "I was old enough to know that my father was very frightened. The same with the rest of the Jews in Tarnów, and the thousands of Jewish refugees from other Polish cities. He knew of the Nazi brutality and the regulations and restrictions that they had imposed on the Jews of Germany, Austria, and more recently Czechoslovakia." Keller stopped, as if remembering those terrible days. "Quickly there were beatings, shootings, and disappearances. The Jewish leaders of the city were powerless. Jewish schools were closed, including my own school, the Baron Hirsch High School, where my father taught maths and sciences." He stopped, gathering his thoughts.

"My father Izak was a brilliant mathematician and physicist. Had it not been for restrictions on Jews and advanced education, he would have been a professor at a leading university or maybe even more." He paused again. "I won't go into gruesome details on a night like this and with so many young people, but I will tell you that over the next two years, conditions got worse, and the Jewish population was thinned out by killings, forced labor, and the concentration camps at Plasnow and Auschwitz." The mention of the camps moved the older members of the family. They squirmed uneasily on their chairs.

Keller stopped and let out a big sigh, before continuing.

"During the late summer of 1941, the Jews were forced to erect a fence around the Jewish neighborhood. A ghetto into which all the Jewish peoples of the town would be herded. This ghetto quickly became a prison. We lived far from the center of the Jewish community, and my father decided we should not voluntarily move to the ghetto. If we were forced to do so, we would have no choice, but many other families made the same decision, trying to put off the evil day."

Keller paused again, clearly moved by his recollections and trying to muster his thoughts. He continued slowly. "The Germans were methodically searching the town for Jewish families who had not moved into the ghetto, and one Sunday afternoon we heard a loud banging on the front door of our apartment." The aunts gasped.

"My sisters were playing at a neighbor's home and I was in the apartment and went to the door and found three uniformed Germans, two in SS uniforms and one in the light beige uniform of the German police. They demanded to see Izak Kellermann and his ID card. My father came forward holding his ID, and they quickly grabbed him and marched him out of the apartment. They said they would be back later for my mother." Keller looked around the table. Not a sound from anyone. "You can imagine how frightened we were. I remember that feeling as though it was yesterday. I will never forget the fear in my stomach. I couldn't move. I couldn't talk, and my mother and I were staring into space. We didn't know what to do. Eventually she said we should pack some bags and wait. We did this more or less mechanically. My three sisters were still playing with a neighbor's children and had no idea this was going on."

Keller stopped, fighting back tears and unable to speak.

"Take your time, Erik," said Alex in Polish.

After a moment or two, Keller continued. "Very few people ever came back from being interviewed by the SS. But a miracle happened. The Germans in their true efficiency had a record of every Jewish family born and living in Tarnów. But there was no Izak Kellermann registered. My father like all of you, Kornmehls, as I now see, looked Aryan – blonde hair, blue or green eyes, pale and slim. He was beaten and hauled before an officer who demanded to know why they couldn't find him registered as a Jew in the city of Tarnów. He quickly realized how their mistake had happened. He wasn't a Kellermann because he'd been born a Kornmehl; and, even though he'd been brought up by Faye Fogler, now Kellermann, they had not informed the authorities of his change of name. He jumped at the opportunity and told the interrogating officer that he was actually from Leipzig and that he wasn't Jewish, even though his wife was. He continued his story by saying that he had continually been asking the authorities to issue him with a new ID card that did not restrict him as a Jewish citizen of the town. Amazingly, the officer believed his story, while warning him that the fact he was married to a Jewish woman would mean that he would be arrested unless they divorced. He was issued with an ID card that gave him complete freedom of movement. He came back to us with this incredible story, bruised, beaten, but alive and excited at the opportunity that had arisen." He paused, as the younger members of the family, looked on with eyes wide.

"Over the next few weeks, my father and mother sold everything they owned down to my mother's gold wedding ring and our silver candlesticks," he said, fighting back the emotion of the statements. There was complete silence around the table.

"They used the money to pay for my three sisters to be smuggled out of Tarnów to Hungary where they would be placed with a farming family, not far over the border. Even though at that time, Hungary was allied with Nazi Germany, they had not been carrying out the Nazi decrees against their Jewish population. My father felt that my sisters would be safer, which indeed they were until 1944 when Adolf Eichmann arrived in Hungary." The name Eichmann brought angry muttering from the older members of the family. "He carried out the Nazi policy of rounding up all the Jews in the countryside and large numbers from Budapest and the other main cities and transporting them to Auschwitz and other camps."

Keller paused again before continuing quietly and emotionally. "Unfortunately, my three teenage sisters were shipped to Auschwitz in late 1944 and were dead within a few weeks. As for me, my father paid to have me smuggled out under the false floor of a vegetable cart that came in from the countryside and unloaded vegetables in the Ryneck, the market square of Tarnów. He had arranged for me to join Jewish resistance fighters, operating from the woods near Tarnów, sabotaging German lines, along with other Polish partisan groups. I lived rough in the woods with small Jewish groups for nearly two years. We were never more than eight or ten so as we wouldn't attract attention. Often we were starving; sometimes we killed for weapons, sometimes for money, sometimes for food that the Germans had. Eventually I think our group was betrayed, because we were ambushed by a German patrol." Keller stopped. The family was hanging on every word. "Most of my group was killed, but I escaped. I ran and ran through the woods, believing that any minute a bullet would cut me down, but somehow God was good to me, and I ran right into a Polish partisan camp. I didn't tell them I was Jewish because they might have killed me on the spot. I did tell them about my escape from another group after a German ambush and they took me in and I stayed with them until the Russians advanced into Poland in the early weeks of 1945, and the Germans retreated from Tarnów once and for all. I went back home except it wasn't home." Keller paused again, holding back his tears. "It wasn't home," he repeated shakily.

"My family were gone. I didn't know whether they were alive or dead. There were no Jews in the town. Our apartment had been taken over by Poles who were, to say the least, unfriendly. I didn't know anybody and couldn't find one friendly face, so I set off north to Warsaw. Most of the city had been destroyed. There I helped young people clear the rubble and slowly bring the city back to life. Eventually Warsaw University opened its doors and I applied for a science scholarship. I changed my name to Erik Keller and in my application said I was a Catholic whose family had been killed in the war. It was a common story. Nobody questioned my background. I got my master degrees in physics and became a teacher at Warsaw University. It was there that I met my wife Krystyna. We married in 1956 and had two sons. I enjoyed my teaching at the university which slowly recovered from the ravages of war. New buildings were developed, and new faculty was added. Unfortunately, my wife Krystyna and my two sons were killed in recent accidents within a few weeks of each other." Keller couldn't continue. Everybody around the table gasped again. Tears welled up. Auntie Esther was of course sobbing quietly, but uncontrollably. Lillian and Rachel were holding hands and dabbing their eyes, with small handkerchiefs. Most of the other adults were wet-eyed and trying to control their emotions. Erik Keller had suffered more than his share of tragedies.

"Take your time," said Alex. "We understand." Keller nodded still unable to speak.

"Anyway," he eventually continued. "The authorities were sympathetic to my situation and as I'm approaching retirement age, they agreed that I could have a sabbatical year in the UK where I had been offered teaching positions."

Alex was amazed at how quickly Keller had spun this plausible explanation.

"Alex, and Anna from the British Foreign Office, were extremely helpful in accompanying me out of Poland a couple a weeks ago. I am indebted for their kindness and help. I am sure you can understand that leaving the graves of my family was extremely emotional for me." He paused again, for a moment or two, again unable to speak.

There was a complete silence around the table, and then Julia got up and went over to Keller and hugged him. Anna, with tears in her eyes, gripped his arm encouragingly and pecked him on the cheek. All the aunts came over, talking in rapid Polish to him, kissing and hugging him, and other members of the family did the same, even though they were different generations.

Alex started the Seder service, and the evening then continued in song, laughter, stories and a special understanding of the celebration of freedom, which this year had much more meaning. The evening ended in hugs and kisses and farewells at about 11:00 p.m., with many of the small children asleep, being carried out by their parents. Eventually, only Keller and Anna remained. The policeman came out of the kitchen as Keller said goodbye with thanks again to Julia and Alex, and Anna joined in, before leaving to meet her own driver downstairs.

"Your driver will take you back," said Alex to Keller. "I'm sure you're tired." Indeed Keller looked exhausted. It had been a highly emotional but enjoyable evening for him. He was now part of the Kornmehl family again.

Chapter 9

Otto Langer was not happy. The chief investigator of the Bundeskriminalamt – the BK – was sitting in his Vienna office in a pall of blue smoke. Although it was not yet 2:00 p.m. there were eighteen cigarette stubs in his ashtray. His nicotine-stained fingers were turning over the report and photos, which he had received from Interpol Inspector Vogl who had called him earlier that morning.

Langer had been a policeman for over thirty years. He was a thin angular man, with brown hair streaked with gray, bushy brown eyebrows and a nicotine-stained, droopy mustache. He had a pale complexion, typical of a heavy smoker, and always looked rumpled and untidy, his suits hanging off his bony shoulders, sometimes covered in ash, and his shoes scuffed and in need of a good clean.

His wife of twenty-five years, Angela, had long given up trying to smarten him up, but Otto Langer was an extremely capable homicide detective who had risen through the ranks to become chief investigator. He was well respected by his superiors for his considerable intellect and the quick observations of his darting brown eyes. Otto Langer didn't miss much and had a reputation for persistence.

"We've got some good news for you, Langer," Vogl had said with some sarcasm in his voice. "You seem to have been beating your head against a brick wall on the AKH case, but maybe we have a breakthrough."

Langer mumbled, "Well."

"We have some photographs... looks like your dead assailant."

"Good, anything will help at this stage," responded Langer.

"They're from our Berlin office," Vogl continued. "I'll send them over."

Indeed, Langer had been banging his head against a brick wall for the past ten weeks. He had tried everything to identify the dead assailant. He had interviewed every possible employee at the Imperial Hotel, including a busboy who had left work a couple of minutes before the shooting. He had also been in touch with every informant source from all the police forces in Austria, sent out photographs of the dead man with a full description, checked out all his clothing sources, posted photographs and requested information from every police station in Austria, all to no avail.

On top of that, he knew this was an important case, the deputy director of the BIA – Federal Bureau of Internal Affairs – had kept asking for a progress report. This wasn't just a normal murder case, of the kind on which he had built his reputation over the past thirty years. The BIA, the Austrian Secret Service, and Interpol were all involved. When he asked for more information about the victim, Dr. Gustaf Bauer, he was told that information was not relevant and that he should concentrate only on the homicide.

So be it, he had thought to himself. *If I find the murderer, the whole house of cards may come tumbling down.*

He was now looking at the photographs through his old bone-handled magnifying glass. One photo of a man with long hair at some sort of rally, and another face-on photograph of the man with close-cropped hair. The report identified the man as Gunter Foch, age thirty-seven, born and raised in Leipzig. A former Stasi undercover agent, he had been fired four years previously, had managed to cross from East Germany into the West and had resurfaced in Frankfurt, where had he taken a job as a security guard. Two years ago, he abruptly left that position. His where-abouts are currently unknown. He has no record with the German police. There was no record of him entering Austria nor was there any ID issued by the Austrian authorities in the name of Foch.

Langer looked closely at the photographs. He puffed away on

another cigarette.

Now, he thought. *We have a clue.*

He phoned Vogl.

"So soon. You must really like the sound of my voice," said Vogl, teasingly.

"Thank you," said Langer, ignoring Vogl's jibe. "This could be very helpful."

"I thought so," responded Vogl, now more serious. "It seems our friend mixes with skinheads or has neo-Nazi leanings. Maybe that's why he got thrown out of the Stasi. He has been identified at a number of illegal rallies in West Germany. He doesn't appear to have any connections with those groups in Austria."

"Well at least we've something to go on now. Leave it to me for a few days and I'll get back to you," responded Langer.

"Please do," responded Vogl. "The big cheeses are pushing from the top."

"I know I know," responded Langer resignedly. "Don't worry, I'll keep in touch."

He pressed a button on his intercom and called in his assistant, Investigator Johann Dorner.

"You and I are going to Carinthia."

"Why?" responded Dorner.

"Here, look at these," he said to Dorner, handing over the photographs and report.

"Neo-Nazi leanings," continued Langer.

Dorner was a fresh-faced young man of twenty-seven. Tall, fair, thin and very serious. Nevertheless he was extremely bright and capable and Langer found him to be a very good assistant.

"Nazis in Austria?" Dorner said. "I thought they'd all gone, long ago."

"Ha!" responded Langer. "You're kidding, right? That's the Austrian way. We put our heads in the sand and pretend it didn't happen. There are thousands of Nazis or former Nazis in Austria," he continued, a little irritated at his young assistant.

"They were the founders of the FPÖ. This young man Georg Haidar and his lot, are all former neo-Nazis. That's why we are going to Carinthia," Langer said firmly.

"I know the FPÖ headquarters are in Klagenfurt," said Dorner. "But I regard the FPÖ as a nationalist party. In fact I think I might even vote for them this time."

"What!" said Langer incredulously? "These guys are right-wing lunatics," he continued, as Dorner flushed a little.

"Well, I don't think so. In fact, I agree with their immigration policies. We're getting flooded with immigrants. We have to support them and their families. They don't understand our culture. They are a burden on society."

"You sound like an FPÖ pamphlet," responded Langer, smiling condescendingly. "In any event, we are off to Klagenfurt, first thing in the morning. Make sure you bring clothes for a couple of nights. I think maybe if we get lucky we may find someone who recognizes our assailant."

The next day was a perfect spring day, clear blue sky, trees, bushes and flowers beginning to bloom, and the first warm day in May. Dorner drove the Audi 4 Quattro that they had taken from the car pool and comfortably covered the journey to Klagenfurt in just over four hours.

With national elections less than three weeks away, the town was smothered in political posters and flags. It was clear that the FPÖ was the strongest party in Carinthia. The latest polls indicated that Bruno Kreisky's government would fall and the FPÖ could hold the balance of power if they could get a sufficient number of seats. They checked into a modest three-star hotel not far from the railway station, changed into more casual clothes, had lunch and commenced their search. They visited a number of bars and cafés around the Alter Platz, and other areas in the center of town. They discreetly showed their police ID, seeking someone who would recognize Gunter Foch's photograph. But they had no luck.

Later in the evening, after a light dinner in a café on the Hauptplatz, they started to work the bars again. Now they were seeing younger crowds, noisier bars and cafés, some with music. It was past ten o'clock when they entered a noisy bar, called Lapponia – full of young people. They started to question the barman and waitresses, showing their ID and Foch's photograph. Much to their delight, one of the waitresses nodded.

"I know that face," she shouted over the noise and music, a dark-haired skinny girl in a halter top and miniskirt carrying a tray of drinks that looked like it weighed more than she did.

"That's Helmut, Astrid's boyfriend," she continued. "Astrid Kronburger. She is a good friend of mine"

"Really?" questioned Langer. "Are you sure?"

"Oh yes, absolutely," she continued. "My boyfriend and I went out with them on a number of dates. Then Astrid said he just dropped off the edge of the earth, a couple of months ago. She never heard from him again. She was really upset."

"Really?" said Langer, now very interested. "And where can we find Astrid?"

"She works at the Alpen Bar and Restaurant on Kleinstraße on the hill; just as you're leaving Klagenfurt to go north... But she won't be there tonight, it's her night off."

"Would she be working tomorrow?" questioned Langer.

"Yes I think so," responded the waitress. "Tomorrow she'll be on the 11:00 to 7:00 p.m. shift."

"That's very helpful," responded Langer. "Thank you very much." he said, smiling graciously at the girl.

They left the bar with music pounding in their ears. But Langer felt elated. At last some sort of breakthrough.

"With any luck, we may have a good source about our assailant and what he was up to," he said to Dorner.

"Yes," said Dorner. "But, she called him Helmut. He may not be the same man."

"That's possible," responded Langer. "But she did seem pretty positive."

After a leisurely breakfast the following morning – another beautiful sunny day – they made their way to Kleinstraße and easily found the Alpen Bar and Restaurant on a slight hill looking down on the old part of the town. It had an attractive beer garden in front of the entrance to a building in the alpine style. It was just after noon and there were very few people around. They entered the restaurant, showed their ID and asked the barman whether Astrid Kronburger was on the premises.

"Yes," he responded, and pointed to a corner of the dining room where two young women were laying up a table. "That one on the left – the blonde," he said. "What's she been up to, then?" he asked with a slight leer on his face.

Langer ignored the question and lit his tenth cigarette of the day with the Alpen book matches on the bar. They approached the two young women who were dressed in traditional Austrian red dresses with puffed sleeves and white petticoats showing underneath, and scooped-out necklines, revealing plump breasts. White aprons were tied around their waists.

"Excuse me, Astrid Kronburger?" Langer asked, pleasantly, his cigarette hanging from the corner of his mouth.

One of the girls turned. "Yes that's me," she said. "Can I help you?" she continued politely.

"Yes, I think you can," responded Langer, showing his police ID as he identified himself and Dorner. "We are looking for information relating to the whereabouts of this man," he said, producing a photograph of Gunter Foch. "Do you know him?"

She stiffened at the sight of the police ID, and Langer could see she was thinking whether she would cooperate or not.

Astrid was a tall, country girl with bleached blonde hair and dark roots starting to show. She had large green eyes, a pleasant smile and a buxom, voluptuous figure, amply proportioned. Even though she was an attractive woman, maybe twenty-seven to thirty years old, Langer could see that within ten years she'd look like a real heavy Hausfrau.

Astrid started to flush.

"Yes, I know him. That's Helmut Fischer," she responded quickly, the polite smile gone. "What's he done?"

"We would just like his help in connection with some enquiries," responded Langer smoothly. "Do you know where he is?"

"No, I don't," she responded sharply. "I haven't seen him for weeks, even though we were supposed to go to Velden together for a weekend, back in March. He has just disappeared off the face of the earth," she said, her face getting more flushed as her anger rose. "I thought we had a good thing going," she rattled on. "We've been seeing each other seriously for about four months or so." She paused reflectively. "I've been dumped before," she continued. "So this is not the first time, but never anything like this," she said. "One minute he is all lovey-dovey and planning weekend trips, and the next minute I don't hear a word and that's the end of him. I've got no idea where he is," she continued, clearly upset as her large eyes watered up.

"Do you happen to know where he worked?" Langer asked.

"Yes he worked at the Lendorf Estate," she responded.

"Lendorf?" questioned Langer.

"Yes, Schloss Lendorf, the home of Karl von Schuyler."

"Ah, yes," replied Langer, now quite eager. He had heard of von Schuyler, a leading Austrian businessman.

"Do you know what he did at Lendorf?" Langer continued.

"Yes, he was in some sort of security team. I know he did some driving for him and his wife and he also had other duties on the estate. He has a farm up there and some other businesses, I think," she continued.

"Do you know how long he worked there?" continued Langer.

"I think a couple of years."

"Did he like his job?"

"Well, he didn't really talk about his work too much, but I

think he liked it. He did say he was well paid and he had plenty of time off, so it wasn't difficult to make plans with me – or so he said," she continued sharply.

"Well, Astrid, you've been very helpful," said Langer. "Thank you very much."

"When you find him," said Astrid, "you can tell him that I don't want to see him again. I will never forgive him," she continued angrily.

"I understand," responded Langer. "Here is my card. In case you think of anything else, please don't hesitate to contact me."

"Ok," she said, tucking the card into her ample cleavage.

"Would you like a beer before you go?" she asked.

"Thank you, Astrid. It is very kind of you but we're working, unfortunately."

They turned to go. Langer stopped and turned back towards Astrid. "By the way," he said. "Did Helmut have a motorbike?"

"Yes, he did as a matter of fact. A big BMW," she said. "I'm not sure it was really his or whether he shared it with some of his mates, but I loved it. He was really a good driver and we zoomed through the countryside. It's great. The wind blowing through your hair."

"I'm sure it is, Astrid. We'll be in touch."

When they came out of the restaurant, Langer said to Dorner, "Well now, that really is a breakthrough. Karl von Schuyler," he mused. "Very interesting."

"Who is he?" responded Dorner.

"You must have heard of him. He's an industrialist, very wealthy and very well connected. He is reportedly the financier behind the FPÖ. He is in property in a big way, and he's the largest wine producer in Austria."

"Oh. Yeah. Now I know the guy," said Dorner. "He was recently honored as chairman of the Board of the Wine Institute or something like that. I think I saw his picture in the paper not so long ago."

"Yep," replied Langer, "That's him. I think we should pay him and his wife a visit. She is a former Miss Austria."

"Really? That should be fun," said Dorner. "Should we do that now while we are in the area?" he continued.

"No, we will head back to Vienna now. I want to complete a report on our discussions with Astrid and then we'll plan when to call on Herr von Schuyler and his pretty wife."

The following morning surrounded by a haze of smoke, Langer completed his report and contacted Vogl. He requested urgent information on Helmut Fischer. Within an hour he received a copy of Helmut Fischer's ID, and some background indicating that Fischer had been born in Vienna in 1948. A list of schools and his university were attached. He had earned a degree in marine engineering at Graz University of Technology. He was unmarried and he had been working for the von Schuyler Group for the past twenty-one months. There was no criminal record or indeed a run-in with the law at any level. His ID certainly looked like Gunter Foch. Langer, however, felt there was some undisclosed information they needed to dig out. He asked for the school and university records as well as any photographs other than the ID. He received back a copy of his passport application made seven years previously to which a passport photo had been attached. There was a resemblance to Gunter Foch and yet they were not quite alike. He knew that the photograph had been taken some years previously, but even so Langer was not convinced it was Fischer. He then asked for the records of Helmut Fischer leaving and entering the country. From those responses he found that Fischer had last left the country in March 1981, flying from Vienna to Berlin. He returned to Austria three weeks later. Further enquiries revealed that both of Fischer's parents had died in a car accident twelve years previously and his one sister had been living in Indonesia for the past fourteen years. They appeared to have very little contact. Langer was convinced that Helmut Fisher and Gunter Foch was the same man.

"Put a tail on both von Schuyler and his wife," Langer told Dorner. "And make sure I receive a daily report."

Over the next few days Langer received daily reports on the whereabouts of von Schuyler and his wife and then he got the information he was waiting for. While von Schuyler was staying at Lendorf, his wife was spending a couple of nights at their luxurious apartment above the von Schuyler Group offices in Singerstraße in Vienna. He wanted them to be separated as and when he conducted interviews and not be able to communicate with each other. That way he thought he might get the truth.

Dorner and another assistant investigator, Hans Weiber, would call on Frau von Schuyler at 8:45 a.m. on Tuesday, at the same time Langer together with a further young assistant, Bernhard Gartner, would be arriving at the Lendorf Estate to interview Karl von Schuyler. Langer told Dorner to arrive at the von Schuyler residence fifteen minutes earlier, guessing that Frau von Schuyler would keep them waiting at least fifteen minutes. Similarly he allowed fifteen minutes to pass through the security gates and drive up to the front entrance of Schloss Lendorf.

Promptly at 8:30 a.m., Dorner and his assistant arrived at the von Schuyler residence sitting on top of the beautiful building on Singerstraße that served as the headquarters of the von Schuyler business empire. They took the private elevator to the top floor and were greeted at the door by a pretty little maid dressed in a black uniform with a small white hat, looking like something out of a 1930s Hollywood movie. Dorner showed his ID and presented a card to the maid. "We would like to see Frau von Schuyler please," he said, firmly but politely.

"Of course, please come in," said the maid. "I'll see if Frau von Schuyler is available," she said discreetly, guiding them into beautifully appointed apartment. The sunlight was flooding a large living room with a terrace overlooking the old part of Vienna. Beautiful art adorned the walls and the room was full of plumped-up furniture and Biedermeier antiques.

"Wait here please," said the maid as she scuttled off. Dorner and his assistant stood awkwardly in the middle of the room looking at the art and a range of photographs adorning a grand piano in the corner. The maid returned promptly.

"Frau von Schuyler will be with you shortly," she said. "Would you please follow me." She then led them out of the living room into a small study, which also overlooked the terrace. The study was more modern, but exquisitely furnished with a bookshelf crammed with bestselling novels.

Dorner looked at his watch anxiously. It was 8:40.

A couple of minutes later Frau von Schuyler came into the study, wearing a long white house coat, tied at the waist. Her blonde hair was pulled back, but Dorner immediately noticed that she had discreetly completed her makeup. The former Miss Austria was still a very attractive woman and her brilliant white smile, as she greeted Dorner, was captivating.

"Officer, what can I do for you?" she said sweetly. "Please sit down and make yourself comfortable," she said to both of them as she moved behind the desk sinking into a deep leather office chair.

"I apologize for disturbing you so early in the day Frau von Schuyler," said Dorner. "We do however need your assistance."

"Of course, I shall be pleased to be of help if I can."

Dorner took out a photograph of Gunter Foch, from his file.

"Do you know this man Frau von Schuyler? We believe he worked for your husband."

Frau von Schuyler looked intently at the photograph.

"No, I can't say that I do," she responded.

"But we believe he has worked for your husband for nearly two years," pressed Dorner. "And we understand he has been your chauffeur on many occasions."

"That's quite possible," responded Frau von Schuyler. "My husband has many employees. I am often driven by them but I can't say that I could recognize one from the other. Indeed," she continued, "they all look the same to me." She chuckled conspiratorially.

"This gentleman is Helmut Fischer. Does that ring a bell?" Dorner pressed on.

"No it doesn't," came the response "As I said, they all look the same and I really don't talk to my chauffeurs."

Dorner believed that Frau von Schuyler was telling the truth. He recognized the sort of woman that she was. Arrogant and self-absorbed. Full of her own importance and unlikely to talk to a chauffeur or indeed any member of the staff other than to issue instructions. She certainly wasn't betraying any recognition of the photograph. He decided that they had drawn a blank.

"Well, Frau von Schuyler, we will not be disturbing you further. Thank you so much."

"Sorry I couldn't be more helpful."

"If you have any second thoughts would you be kind enough to call me. I left your maid my card," Dorner continued.

"Of course I will." They all rose and Frau von Schuyler led them out of her study back into the living room where the little maid was waiting. "Berta, will you show these gentlemen out," she said imperiously.

"Thank you once again, Frau von Schuyler," said Dorner, being unnecessarily polite, as they were escorted to the elevator.

It was 8:40 a.m. when Langer and Gartner rang the doorbell of the Schloss Lendorf. Ernst answered the door aware of their pending arrival. "Good morning, sir," he said politely to Langer. "Please follow me." He led them both into Karl Von Schuyler's study where they waited awkwardly in the luxurious surroundings. A couple of minutes later von Schuyler entered, greeting them with a big smile.

"Good morning, gentlemen. What can I do for you on this beautiful day? Please sit down," he said, motioning towards the two large leather chairs facing his desk.

"We would like to talk to you about one of your employees,"

said Langer.

"Of course," responded von Schuyler. "How can I be of help?"

Langer took out from his file, a picture of Gunter Foch and handed it to von Schuyler. "This gentleman, Helmut Fischer works for you."

Von Schuyler took a moment or so while he studied the photograph intently.

"Yes," said von Schuyler. "This gentleman did work for me but is no longer my employee,"

"I see," responded Langer. "When did he leave your employment?"

"I'm not sure," responded von Schuyler, his forehead creasing in thought as he tried to remember. "You'll have to ask my estate manager, but I think it was some time in the middle of February."

"Do you know why he left?" asked Langer.

"No, I couldn't say, but again, my estate manager will be able to answer those questions."

"Could I ask you what Mr. Fischer's duties were?"

"Yes, of course, Fischer was one of my security team," responded von Schuyler.

"Security team?" said Langer.

"Yes I have a large estate, and many business interests, as you may know. We have a security team with rotating duties that vary from manning the entrance gates through which you came this morning, to chauffeuring myself and my wife, on occasion, to helping in the management of our various businesses on this estate. We have a large timber business here as well as a dairy farm. I also have a number of vehicles which the security team looks after and maintains. There are house-maintenance matters, a market garden, gardeners to be managed, and a variety of other headaches in looking after a large old estate like this one." Von Schuyler gave a wide grin and a chuckle.

"Of course," responded Langer, dutifully with a smile.

"Perhaps I could meet your estate manager?" continued

Langer,

"I'll arrange that right away," responded von Schuyler with another wide smile. He picked up the phone and asked Viktor to come to his study immediately.

"May I ask why you have this interest in Helmut Fischer?" asked von Schuyler.

"We would just like to interview him in connection with some other enquiries we're pursuing at the moment," said Langer, noncommittally.

"I see," responded von Schuyler pensively.

There was a discreet knock on the study door and Viktor entered.

"Good morning, Herr von Schuyler," he said, slightly kicking his heels, Langer noticed. Tall muscular and dressed totally in black. Very much a military figure, thought Langer.

"Good morning, Viktor," Von Schuyler responded. "I'd like to introduce you to Chief Investigator Langer. He has some enquiries about our former employee Helmut Fischer and I thought you would be in the best position to answer them."

"Good morning, I'm Viktor Eigner, the Lendorf Estate Manager," said Viktor without flinching. "How may I help?" he said.

"I understand that Helmut Fischer has left your employment," Langer asked.

"Yes, that's true," responded Viktor.

"May I ask when that happened?" continued Langer.

"Yes, I think it was the middle of February but I will have to check my records."

"You have records of all employees?" asked Langer.

"Of course, we're very meticulous with both our hiring practices and maintaining proper employee records in accordance with regulations," responded Viktor without a flicker of concern.

"How long was Helmut Fischer in your employment?"

continued Langer.

"About two years, I think. I'll check the exact dates for you later."

"May I ask why he left your employment?"

"I think it was love," responded Viktor with a smile. "He had some girlfriend who he had fallen for and decided he wanted to leave."

"And how much notice did he give you?" questioned Langer, careful to not being drawn into the love life discussion.

"It was all rather abrupt. Actually we were quite surprised."

"So he didn't really give you any notice?"

"No, he just said that he decided he wanted to leave and when an employee tells us that, we don't like to stand in their way. We found in the past that it's better just to let them go straightaway and not work out a notice period."

"I understand," said Langer, rather dubious about this answer. "Do you happen to know who the love of his life was?"

"No, I don't," responded Viktor. "I try and keep out of love matters of our employees."

"Of course," responded Langer. "Maybe some of his other colleagues would know."

"Possibly," said Viktor as a flicker of concern crossed his face. "Although it's not common practice to talk about personal matters amongst our employees."

Langer felt that Viktor was stumbling about.

"I can make some enquiries for you," Viktor continued.

"That would be very helpful."

"May I ask why you are seeking Helmut Fischer?" continued Viktor.

"We want to interview him in connection with some other enquiries that we're pursuing," said Langer, again noncommittally.

"I could have our employees' records here in a minute," said Viktor.

"Thank you," responded Langer.

Viktor turned to von Schuyler. "May I call the office, sir?"

"Of course."

Viktor went over to the desk, picked up the phone and asked whoever was at the other end to bring over the personnel file for Helmut Fischer.

"We shall have it in a minute," said Viktor.

"Thank you," said Langer. "How many security-team employees do you have?"

"Eight," responded Viktor. "Well, seven at the moment."

"I see," said Langer, thinking that the security team was more like a private army.

"By the way, Viktor, did Helmut Fischer have a motorbike?" Langer continued quickly.

He saw Viktor falter for a moment at this question, clearly thinking how best to answer.

Langer sized up Viktor, realizing that perhaps he could have been the second assailant – the one that got away. If not him, possibly one of the other members of the security team, who he also suspected would be of the same ilk.

"Yes, I believe he did," he continued. "A big BMW machine."

"Was it owned by Fischer, or does he share the ownership with other members of the team?"

"No," responded Viktor quickly. "It was his. None of the other team members have a motorbike." He nodded his head to himself.

"What process do you follow when you're hiring a new employee?" asked Langer, moving the discussion in a new direction as he turned towards von Schuyler.

"We're very meticulous about our hiring procedures," responded Von Schuyler. "We have to be in this day and age. I and my family could always be a target of kidnapping or burglary. This is a large estate with very valuable possessions and so we only employ the best, particularly when it comes to our security team."

"So how do you go about this?" asked Langer.

"Well, when we are seeking a new employee, we advertise in the Vienna and local Klagenfurt newspapers or from time to time use headhunters. Generally, however, most of our employees have come from our ads. We ask for a full history and references and we conduct at least three interviews before we proceed."

"And what credentials are you looking for?" asked Langer.

"Well, of course it is helpful if the prospective employees had military, police, security, or personal-protection experience. Most of our security team has one or the other."

"You seem to be fortunate in being able to find these particularly talented employees," said Langer with a very straight face.

"Yes, we are fortunate," responded Von Schuyler. "We have an excellent qualified team led by our friend Viktor here and they do a great job. It's unusual for us to lose an employee such as Fischer. But when love is in the air we can't compete," responded von Schuyler with some finality, another wide grin on his face.

Another knock on the door. A young woman came in and handed a file to Viktor who opened it, looked at the contents and handed it immediately to Langer.

Langer had the distinct impression that these papers had been prepared for just this visit. Maybe not today, but certainly they were expecting these questions to be asked.

Inside the file were copies of advertisements placed at the end of 1980. There was then an application form completed by Helmut Fischer in his own handwriting. Langer thought this might be useful at some stage. In addition there was a photograph very similar to his passport photograph that Langer had already seen and then notes on the three interviews conducted by Viktor and finally von Schuyler himself. Each interview result was typed up and initialed. There was then a copy of a letter of offer of employment together with the terms of salary and bonus, which Langer noticed was extremely generous. Surely a security officer would not receive such generous rewards. Langer immediately suspected that these employees were expected to do a lot more.

"Thank you," said Langer to Viktor. "Do you think I could take this file with me and return it when we have taken copies?"

Viktor looked a little taken aback. He stammered, "We don't usually allow files to go out of our office." He turned towards von Schuyler, who nodded his approval. "But of course in this case we're eager to help," Viktor continued in a stronger voice. "Perhaps you'll be able to return the file within a few days."

"Absolutely," responded Langer enthusiastically.

"Well," said Langer turning again to von Schuyler, "we certainly don't want to take up any more of your valuable time, sir. Thank you so much for your help and cooperation. It is much appreciated." Von Schuyler came round his desk with a big smile and patted Langer on the back as he led him to the door of the study.

"Glad to have been of help," he said.

Langer turned to him. "Here is my card in case there's something else you may remember, Herr von Schuyler; and here's one for Viktor as well."

"Thank you," responded von Schuyler. "If anything else crops up, we shall certainly let you know."

Langer extended his hand to Viktor and said, "Thank you, Viktor."

"Of course, any time," responded Viktor with a smile.

"Perhaps you might like to talk to the rest of your security team in case they have more information about Helmut Fischer's love life and his BMW. We'd certainly like to know," said Langer. "Particularly the name of the lucky lady who is the object of his love."

"I shall make enquiries," said Viktor helpfully. "And if anything comes up I shall let you know immediately."

"Thank you," said Langer once again as von Schuyler escorted him through the hallway to the front door. With that, both Langer and Gartner stepped out into the sunshine.

Langer was deep in thought as they got into the Audi, and the driver scrunched over the driveway and headed down the hill to the security gates at the entrance to the estate.

"That was very interesting," he said emphatically to Gartner.

"Yes it was," said Gartner, not quite sure why he was agreeing. "Why didn't we search for the BMW or meet the other security-team members?" he asked.

"They were clearly very prepared. They've been expecting this visit and were well rehearsed. I've got no doubt about that," said Langer. "So even if the BMW is on the estate, you can bet it's well hidden. As for the rest of the security team, they will have been fully prepped. But maybe we'll go back and interview them at a later date."

"Yes, I see, and I think you're absolutely right," said Gartner, a little too eager to please.

"Now the mystery is what possible connection there could be between Herr von Schuyler, one of Austria's leading businessmen, and the murder of a physics professor?"

Chapter 10

The weather had been glorious the first two weeks of May, and Alex had taken to walking through Regents Park to his office in Sackville Street, enjoying the trees in full blossom and the flowers a palette of spring colors.

Frank picked Alex up from Sackville Street and deposited him just before 4:00 p.m. on a sunny Tuesday afternoon at the MI6 Lambeth Headquarters. Within a minute or two he was in Tim's office.

"How is Keller doing? I haven't spoken to him in a couple of weeks," asked Alex.

"Remarkably well," replied Tim. "He seems to be getting stronger by the day, has settled into his new home, and is working very well. In fact, from what I hear, they all think he is absolutely brilliant and are amazed at the detail of his nuclear theories. In addition, Alex, he seems to have a remarkably deter-mined streak. He signed up for the intensive Berlitz course to improve his English and even after four weeks or so, there has been a dramatic improvement."

"Well that's good news," said Alex.

"Yes," replied Tim, raising an eyebrow with a smile. "And he also asked to see Anna a couple of times."

"Really," responded Alex, involuntarily feeling a pang of jealousy.

"She seemed quite keen to see him," continued Tim. "Perhaps they have a bond based upon their shared experiences. But in any event, we are happy that he is seeking friends. It's a good sign that he is getting settled."

"By the way," asked Alex, "how did Anna get on with her course?"

"Incredibly well," responded Tim. "One of the best we've ever had."

"Amazing," said Alex, with a smile.

"She ended up in the top five percentile of anyone that has ever taken this course. Turns out she is a crack shot, quite capable of surviving on her own, self-motivated, very tough, and has an almost photographic memory."

"My God," replied Alex. "That's quite a list."

"Yes, I think we've been underutilizing Anna and we shall address that in the future. We are quite excited to have someone with her aptitude," said Tim. "Of course, having done so well on the course, she is now pestering me to return to Poland. She wants to complete the mission and also, of course, help get her brother Jan out of the country."

"Are you going to use her?" asked Alex a little anxiously.

"We are giving it serious consideration," replied Tim. "We have concerns about her safety. We know she's wanted for murder. However, we have created a new identity for her, which would help."

"A new identity?" said Alex raising his eyebrows.

"Yes, Anna is now Janet Clark born in Sydney, Australia, aged forty-three, previously married and divorced and now working for the British Foreign Office in international cultural relations. If we decide to use her for the mission to recover Keller's papers, we shall send her to work at the British Council in Warsaw."

"Good lord," said Alex with true surprise. "That is big news. You're really considering sending Anna back into Poland?"

"We will give her every protection. Her new identity has given her a new hair color and glasses," said Tim.

"My God," said Alex with a chuckle. "Real spy stuff!"

"Of course," replied Tim with a smile. "We know how to look after our people. But seriously," he said, "you know we're thin on the ground in Poland and she probably is the best person to get this mission completed. She knows Warsaw very well, she knows Keller; she knows what she's looking for and providing her new identity can hold up, there should be no problems. Anyway as I said, we are giving this consideration."

"Well, I shall have another lunch with Anna, and catch up on all the news," said Alex, hiding his genuine concern for Anna's safety and the feeling that MI6 wanted the Keller papers at any cost.

"We've also had a breakthrough in the Vienna shooting," said Tim changing the subject.

"Really?" said Alex.

"The Vienna police appear to have identified the dead assailant who tried to shoot Keller at the AKH Hospital," said Tim. "Their chief homicide investigator is pretty certain that they have a positive identification, but we still don't know who the other assailant was – the one that got away, nor do they have any idea of the motive or who's behind the attempted killing. But it's a start."

"Do you have any ideas, yourself?" asked Alex.

"We can't really be seen to be too involved in the situation, Alex, that's the problem. We really need to know who was behind the attempted assassination, and in addition we also need to understand where the leak came from. These are very worrying issues, as I'm sure you understand, Alex."

"Of course," said Alex, as he drank his tea.

"The report says that there might be a connection to Karl von Schuyler," said Tim. "Do you know him?"

"No," responded Alex. "Should I?"

"He's in your business. Well, not exactly your business," said Tim. "He is, among other things, the largest wine producer and exporter in Austria."

"We're not in the wine business," said Alex.

"Yes I know, Alex, but I thought you might know him through the sale of his brandies and schnapps, of which he is also a leading manufacturer and exporter."

"That's a possibility," said Alex. "But I can't say that I know of him. What's the connection?"

"It appears the dead assailant had a false name, false ID, false passport and had worked for von Schuyler until a week before the attempted assassination. It also appears that von Schuyler employs a small army as his private security team and there is a possibility that the assailant that got away was part of that team."

"Presumably the Austrian authorities will get to the bottom of this," said Alex.

"We're not sure," responded Tim. "It's a delicate situation and they have national elections coming up. When you have a leading industrialist and businessman like von Schuyler in a small country like Austria, it's possible these enquiries won't be taken any further, even if they have a homicide department eager to do so."

"I see," said Alex thoughtfully. "So what do you intend to do?"

Tim leaned forward while he poured himself a second cup of tea.

"I know you're very keen to see a resolution of this mission involving Keller," said Tim looking intently at Alex. "So I was wondering if you would be able to do a 'little job' for me?"

"Ha, another 'little job,' Tim. You're kidding. I'm still recovering from the last one," Alex responded.

"I know," said Tim. "I fully understand it was not a pleasant experience, whichever way you look at it. But this would just be a question of a few days in Vienna. Nothing sinister – just a couple of meetings." Tim waited to see whether Alex would respond positively. His words hung in the air.

Alex was thinking rapidly. The adrenalin was starting to flow again. He did enjoy the excitement of Tim's "little jobs." But he thought about the near death experience he had just been through. How would he explain another "little job" to Julia?

"What you have in mind, Tim?" said Alex, slowly.

"Von Schuyler is reputed to be the main source of finance for the FPÖ," said Tim. "We'd like you to meet with him."

"The FPÖ?" questioned Alex. "Who are they?"

"They are a right-wing political party centered in Carinthia in southwest Austria, founded by former Nazis and running on a platform of anti-immigration and anti-EU rhetoric. However, the polls show they could be quite successful in the upcoming elections. If they get five percent of the vote, they could hold the balance of power in Parliament, as part of a coalition with the SPÖ, the Social-Democratic party, in which they will have a pretty active role. This is a big breakthrough for the FPÖ," continued Tim. "It's also the end of an era. Bruno Kreisky, the leader of the SPÖ, will retire and there will be a changing of the guard." Tim paused.

"What has any of that got to do with Keller?" asked Alex.

"We don't really know, but we would certainly like to find out. That's where you come in, Alex."

"Oh, yes, Really!" said Alex with a smile.

"Do you know Simon Wiesenthal?" Tim asked.

"Yes… the Nazi hunter," said Alex. "I happen to know him quite well. I chaired a committee that held a fundraiser for Simon and the Wiesenthal Center last April at the Inn on the Park. He's an amazing man."

"I know," responded Tim. "He's devoted his life to tracking down all the Nazi bad guys that got away and has had tremendous success."

"Absolutely," said Alex. "But how could he help in the Keller case?"

"We really have got no idea at this stage, but we thought if you could spend a day talking to Simon Wiesenthal or looking at his files, you may find some connection between von Schuyler and the Nazis and maybe a motive for an attempt on Keller's life. Although I should tell you we understand von Schuyler didn't come to Austria until 1956. He spent the previous thirty plus years in Argentina, where his father was a successful wine producer. Still, we think it's worth a visit to Wiesenthal. I know you understand, Alex, we can't really ask the Austrians to do this. In fact we shouldn't be involved in this investigation at all. That's why I'm asking you."

"I see," said Alex, thinking fast. "Well it's possible. I haven't visited our importer and distributor for a few years now, so a couple of days in Vienna wouldn't hurt," he continued.

"In addition, Alex, I'd really like to know what you think of Karl von Schuyler. You are experienced in intelligence work and I know you'll have a good feel, if you have a chance to meet him. Do you think that could be arranged?" said Tim, with an innocent expression on his face.

Alex paused a moment while he thought through the situation. "I suppose a meeting could be arranged. After all, we could be a possible importer of his Austrian brandy and more likely his range of schnapps. So I could drop him a line and arrange to meet him during a visit to Vienna. If I can spend an hour or so with him, I should be able to give you a reasonable assessment."

"That would be terrific," responded Tim enthusiastically. "I really can't tell you how much help that would be, Alex. We've got to get to the bottom of this. You know what I mean, don't you?"

"Yes, of course I do," said Alex.

"Well, when do you think you could take a few days to go to Vienna?" asked Tim.

"I'll have to look at my diary and see what my plans are over the next couple of weeks, but possibly in two or three weeks. I'll need that time to settle my appointments."

"Of course," said Tim. "But this job will not be even remotely dangerous," he continued earnestly.

"I hope you're right. I don't want to go through another experience like Poland. I'm getting too old for that stuff, Tim."

"Aren't we all," said Tim with a chuckle, now much more relaxed. "Could you let me know when you set up the visit,

Alex?"

"Absolutely. Just give me a few days." With that, Tim stood, they shook hands, and Alex departed.

The following Monday, Alex was at Scotts restaurant on Mount Street for his lunch date with Anna. She bounded into the bar and it took Alex a moment to recognize her. She now had reddish-brown auburn hair and black horn-rimmed glasses, and as she moved nearer, he noticed her new blue-green eyes. She was dressed in a green and beige suit and high heels and looked spectacular. Whether she was blonde or brunette she still turned all the heads in the bar.

"Oh, Alex, it is so good to see you again," she said, throwing her arms around his neck and giving him a strong hug. Alex stood stiffly, conscious of the envy in the men's eyes who were looking at them, but excited to see her.

"Lovely to see you, Anna. Or should I say Janet."

Anna laughed. "Yes it's Janet now," she said. "Do you like the new look?"

"Well... Anna or... Janet," said Alex with a chuckle. "Whatever they do, you will always look beautiful."

"Thank you, kind sir," Anna said with a little coy smile, as she sat down next to Alex.

"Madam will have a Chardonnay," said Alex to the waiter who handed them the menus.

"I hear you had outstanding results on your course," said Alex, prodding the conversation forward.

"I worked my butt off, Alex. I really wanted to make an impression on Mr. Bevans."

"It appears you have done so. I understand you landed up in the top five percentile on the course."

For a moment, Anna looked perplexed, wondering why Tim Bevans had told Alex about her success on the course. Had she done too well? But she quickly recovered. "It was really grueling but I was determined. I want to go back to Warsaw. I want to complete the mission and I want to get Jan out of Poland."

"That's a pretty tall order," said Alex. "And I have to say, dangerous as well. As I said before," he continued solemnly, "as far as Jan is concerned you should leave it to MI6. They're good at that sort of thing. You know that he's safe and I'm sure that they will get him out sooner or later."

"Sooner or later is not good enough for me," said Anna. "I worry about him. I can't sleep. I can't imagine what he is going through. Maybe torture, maybe worse. We don't really know if he is even alive." Tears were welling up in her eyes.

"Don't get carried away," said Alex. "I think the MI6 information is pretty good. We know that he wasn't seriously hurt in Kraków and is now in a prison in Warsaw. I'm sure he's doing just fine... I hear you saw Erik Keller recently," he continued, deliberately changing the subject.

Anna looked up, quite surprised. "How did you know that?"

"Tim Bevans told me. I also hear he's doing very well."

"Remarkably so," responded Anna. "I went to see him at his little cottage outside of Reading a couple of times. He's really charming and I'm so pleased he's making such a strong recovery," she continued. "And he thinks I should go back to Poland," she said defiantly. "He believes I am the best person for the job, and uniquely he can instruct me exactly how to get hold of his notes and papers."

"Maybe so," said Alex. "But you are also wanted for murder and – disguise or no disguise – if you get caught, you would really be in hot water."

"I know," Anna said slowly, thinking about that possibility, "but I'm willing to take the risk," she continued in a quiet voice.

The rest of their conversation was pleasant but superficial. After lunch, Alex stood on the pavement in the sunshine and got another big hug; and, as he returned to his car and Frank opened the door, he saw Anna hailing a cab and running down to the corner of North Audley Street.

On Monday, 5th June, Alex took the BA flight to Vienna, landing just after 1:00 p.m. on a gray overcast day. He was met by his Austrian agent, a red-faced little round man, Rudolph Henning, who had worked in the U.S. liquor industry for ten years, and spoke perfect English.

"Hi, Rudy," said Alex warmly. "So good to see you again."

"Good to see you again, Sir Alex," replied Rudy. "I've got my car waiting," he continued. "Where are you staying on this visit?"

"I'm staying at the Palais Schwarzenberg," said Alex, having decided that a return visit to the Hotel Imperial might not be too prudent at this time.

"Very good," said Rudy. "A lovely hotel with spectacular grounds and only a couple of blocks from the center of things."

"Precisely," replied Alex as Rudy threw Alex's small bag into the trunk. They got into the car.

"I have an appointment to meet Karl von Schuyler Wednesday morning at his office at ten o'clock," said Alex.

"Ah yes," responded Rudy. "I got a copy of your correspondence. He has confirmed then?"

"We are all set. What do you know about von Schuyler?" asked Alex.

"I did a little research for you," said Rudy. "He controls almost fifty percent of the Austrian wine business and something like sixty-five percent of its exports. He is also the leading brandy producer in Austria – Imperial Reserve is his leading brand. You may have heard of it, Alex."

"Only from my own research," said Alex.

"He is also the major schnapps producer in Austria and owns a majority of the small boutique producers in Friesach, which is in the Carinthian Alps near where von Schuyler lives. He also has major property interests. In Linz, I understand that he has over 400,000 square feet of warehousing, most of it rented to the Austrian Post Office. He also owns a number of buildings in Vienna, including a five-story office building on Singerstraße, where he also keeps a penthouse apartment."

"He seems to be quite a success," said Alex.

"Absolutely. Von Schuyler is undoubtedly one of the leading businessmen in Austria, well connected politically... and very rich," Rudy said with a chuckle.

"I'm looking forward to meeting him," said Alex.

Alex and Rudy spent the evening discussing the Austrian market for the Campbell Group brands, over a heavy Austrian meal. Alex was up early next morning and took a walk in Schwartzenberg Park in the sunshine.

Alex left himself plenty of time for the walk across town, marveling at Vienna's glorious architecture, its wide boulevards, and numerous palaces and churches. The city mainly built during the glory days of the Hapsburg Empire seemed far too grand for the country that Austria had become – a small but prosperous nation of fourteen million, no longer encompassing the grandeur of the Austro-Hungarian Empire.

The Jewish Documentation Centre operated by Simon Wiesenthal at Salztorgasse 6, was ironically on the site of the former Gestapo headquarters. He arrived a few minutes early for his 10:30 appointment. He had purposely asked for a meeting at 10:30 believing that, if there was nothing to discuss about Karl von Schuyler, they could have a pleasant chat and perhaps an early lunch. However, if Wiesenthal was able to throw some light on von Schuyler and his background, Alex had plenty of time to review whatever files and information was available.

On his arrival, he was immediately struck by the modest and cramped quarters of the Wiesenthal Center. The three rooms and two staff were overwhelmed with files, papers, and boxes piled high on the few desks and tables.

Wiesenthal greeted him warmly. "Alex, how wonderful to see you. It is so kind of you to call on me," he enthused.

"It's lovely to see you again, Simon," said Alex with a warm smile as they shook hands. "Thank you for giving me some of your valuable time."

"Nonsense, nonsense," said Wiesenthal. "You're always welcome. You are such a great supporter of my work and were so helpful with the fundraiser in London. I want to thank you once again for that."

"It was my pleasure," replied Alex.

"Come into my office," said Wiesenthal, leading the way through a mound of files into a small room with bookcases on either side of a modest desk covered with papers. "Try and make yourself comfortable, Alex," said Wiesenthal with a chuckle. "I'm afraid our offices are not built for comfort."

"This is fine," said Alex, settling himself into a battered leather chair opposite Wiesenthal.

"How about some coffee or tea?" asked Wiesenthal.

"Tea with lemon would be very nice," said Alex.

"Of course," said Wiesenthal, calling in his assistant Heidi.

Simon Wiesenthal was a small man with a little moustache and a twinkle in his eye. A survivor of the Holocaust after escaping twice from concentration camps, he had established the Jewish Documentation Center in 1946, with a view to seeking out many of the thousands of Nazis who escaped through the Allied forces net at the end of the War. He had been responsible for hundreds of prosecutions against ex-Nazi camp commanders and officials who had responsibility for the genocide. His most successful prosecution had been Adolf Eichmann, who had been tasked by Adolf Hitler to pursue the extermination of the Jewish people of Europe.

Wiesenthal said that his job was not to prosecute the Nazis that he identified, but to prepare the necessary facts and documentation so that others could complete the job.

"Well," said Wiesenthal, folding his arms on the desk. "What can I do for you, Alex?"

"I have a meeting with a gentleman named Karl von Schuyler tomorrow morning," said Alex. "And I've been told that he is the main financer of the FPÖ – the neo-Nazi political party. We may become an importer of his brandies and schnapps, but if he is a Nazi, I would definitely take a pass."

"Well, I don't think the FPÖ today would want to be identified as a neo-Nazi party," said Wiesenthal. "Even in Austria that might be too hard to take," he said with a smile. "However, the party was set up by ex-Nazis and it is true that von Schuyler is one of the main financers of the party. They did well in the recent elections. They are now a part of the ruling coalition within the SPÖ." He paused thoughtfully before continuing. "We are currently investigating two thousand cases in these small offices. It takes years of painstaking work," continued Wiesenthal, slowly. "But we have extensive files on von Schuyler." He paused. "But they are under the name of Franz Stueben," he said dramatically.

"Franz Stueben?" asked Alex. "Who is he?"

"We believe von Schuyler and Stueben are the same person," Wiesenthal replied. "Alex, I will let you review all the files, which are quite extensive, but I think it would be helpful if I gave you some background of our investigation."

"Yes, that would be helpful," said Alex, amazed that Wiesenthal had any information on von Schuyler.

Wiesenthal paused again, gathering his thoughts, before continuing.

"Franz Stueben was born in Paris in August 1914. His parents were Klaus Stueben, a diplomat working as an assistant secretary of trade in the German Embassy, and the beautiful Anastasia Irena Romanov, the daughter of a Russian diplomat who was a distant cousin of the Czar. She was nineteen and he was twenty-five when they married in July 1912.

"Klaus Steuben was the third son of Horst Steuben, an old-established wine importer and distributor in Bremen, with over one-hundred years of trading relationships with the Bordeaux region of France. With the advent of the First World War, the

Stuebens were shipped back to Berlin and then to Bonn, where Klaus spent the War in various administrative positions. With the reopening of the German Embassy in Paris in 1919, Stueben was sent back to his old job, as Assistant Secretary of Trade, and they brought up young Franz, an accomplished pianist, and a top student, who became fluent in French, Russian, and English, in addition to his native German. Klaus had two elder brothers who were killed on the Western Front during the war, and so Horst was left to run the business on his own during the most difficult economic times in Germany. Eventually, he was forced to sell the Steuben Wine business in 1932 to the Hapag Shipping Group owned by the Warburg banking family. He was retained as managing director, but died three years later. Meanwhile, Franz completed his education by taking a chemical-engineering degree at Stuttgart University, where he was exposed to the budding National Socialist movement and became an ardent admirer of Adolf Hitler. In 1935, on graduating from university, he became a full-time member of the SS with the rank of Obersturmführer."

Wiesenthal paused as Alex leaned forward on the edge of his seat, intrigued by the story that was unfolding.

"In March 1939," Wiesenthal continued, "Franz married Eva Eckhart, the daughter of a right-wing newspaper proprietor from Dresden who was a committed supporter of the National Socialist movement from its earliest days. When war broke out in September 1939 with the invasion of Poland, Franz was drafted into an SS commando unit whose job was to take control of the security and administration of the captured towns and villages as the German Army advanced, identifying and separating Jews and Communist officials, homosexuals and other others who the Nazis considered a threat to the advancing German war machine. There were, of course, mass killings, rape, torture and other atrocities carried out by the invading German armies. Although Franz was not responsible for those decisions, he was extremely efficient, filing the necessary reports to his headquarters on all aspects of those activities.

As the German armies advanced into Ukraine, Franz and his SS commando units followed closely. When the German Third Army finally occupied Kiev in September 1941, after a major battle for the city, which lasted for many weeks – 500,000 Russians were killed – and Franz and his SS had the mammoth task of trying to organize and control a further 500,000 Russian prisoners. He was also very much involved in the interrogation of Russian officers, as he was fluent in the language."

Wiesenthal paused again. "I hope I'm not going on too much, Alex?" he asked with a smile.

"No, on the contrary," replied Alex. "It is a fascinating story. Please continue."

"Franz ran into a major problem when six NKVD Russian officers – that's the former KGB people – somehow escaped shortly after his interrogation. He persuaded his commanding officer that their escape was nothing to do with him, and was due to the negligence of two of the guards, and his senior officer had them shot on the spot. This itself was against German regulations and added to the scandal. We know from examination of documents that this issue went all the way to Himmler's office. It could well have been expected that he would take strong action against the young Franz, but somehow nothing happened and he was able to continue his career.

"A few weeks later, Stueben was called back to Berlin and because of his chemical-engineering background was seconded to liaise for the SS with the Degesch Company. They were the manufacturers of the Zyklon B chemical, which originally was created as a liquid pesticide to exterminate vermin. Plans were already prepared to increase the strength of Zyklon and incorporate the chemical into mass-extermination procedures for Jews and others at the concentration camps."

Wiesenthal paused and gave a sigh as he contemplated his

own concentration camp experience. After a moment, he continued. "In May 1942, Steuben was sent to Auschwitz to work with the IG Farben Company, which was building a plant, using Jewish slave labor from the camp. He worked diligently, identifying chemical engineers and scientists, who would be the most useful to Farben and oversaw the transfer of prisoners and reviewed their performance.

"As the Germans advanced into Russia on the southern front towards Stalingrad in the summer of 1942, Stueben was sent back to his unit to resume his duties of interrogation and reporting. We know that he was in Rostov in the summer, when thousands of Jews and other political prisoners were rounded up and massacred. He continued to follow the German advance towards Stalingrad and, by the end of September, was on the front line inside the city itself. The ferocious fighting inside the city swung back and forth with attack and counter-attack. Sometime towards the end of October, Stueben and some aides were sent into the badly damaged tractor factory to interrogate some NKVD officers who had just been captured. During the interrogation, the Russians counter-attacked and their location was overrun. Steuben was shot in the thigh, but apparently managed to escape. All other members of his unit died. He was flown out of Stalingrad with other wounded, eventually landing up in a hospital just outside Berlin. He was treated as a hero as one of the very few prisoners ever to escape the Russians. For his bravery under fire, he received the Iron Cross Second Class and was promoted to Sturmbannführer. As a result of his fortunate wound, he missed the gruesome winter of the siege of Stalingrad and the eventual rout of the German armies by the Russians. Stueben spent most of 1943 at the SS headquarters in Berlin, on a variety of administrative positions including the allocation of slave labor to the ever-hungry German war machine." Wiesenthal paused and took a sip of water.

"In the summer of 1944 he was added to Adolf Eichmann's

team and sent to Budapest where the Germans had taken control of the Hungarian Army operations and had decided to institute a 'final solution' to the Jewish population of Hungary. As the year progressed, and the Jewish population diminished with the shipment of hundreds of thousands to the concentration camps, the war news was getting worse for the Germans and Stueben probably realized that the war was lost. It had been far easier to round up the Jews in the Hungarian countryside than to deal with the 150,000 or so that lived in Budapest, many of whom were well-established in business and society. He could obviously see an opportunity, and since he had the power of life or death over so many members of the Jewish population of the city, he gave hope to those that could pay. He made it clear that, if sufficient money and assets were given to him, he would give those selected Jewish families the necessary passes and even false passports to allow them to escape the ever-tightening SS net."

"Incredible," interjected Alex. "I never even heard of this."

Wiesenthal nodded knowingly and then continued, "Apparently from this scheme he collected vast sums of money, gold, silver, bearer bonds and jewelry from, we believe, over three-hundred families. For the most part, he issued the passes that he promised, as his game continued through the summer, but it also appears that many of those passes turned out to be only a temporary refuge and eventually many families fell into the hands of the SS and were shipped off to the camps. Meanwhile, we know that Stueben was taking some regular vacations, which took him from Budapest to Zürich in Switzerland, where we believe he deposited his loot, in a Swiss bank. If the war went very wrong, he would try and make his way back to Zürich and get out of Europe. In fact we believe that's exactly what transpired. Particularly because of events that took place in February 1945." Wiesenthal paused for a moment, looking up at the ceiling, as he tried to remember the sequence of events. Alex waited for him to continue as he finished his tea.

"He was back in Berlin on leave. Berlin, by that time was a shattered city, and like many members of the SS and Hitler's hierarchy, families were panicking, trying to move to safer cities. His wife and two children went to her family in Dresden, which had been spared the Allied bombing.

"On the 13th of February, Steuben took the train from Berlin to Dresden to meet up with his family and spend a few days with them. They were only a couple of miles from the main station in Dresden, when the British Royal Air Force and United States Army Air Force commenced the first of four raids that, over the next forty-eight hours, would drop over 3900 tons of high explosive bombs and incendiary devices, destroying fifteen square miles of the city center. The train was stuck while the raid was going on, and Stueben could see the city engulfed in enormous flames. He apparently sent a message to his superior officer, with a dispatch rider who left the train for Berlin, informing him that he was in the midst of a major air raid in Dresden and that he might be delayed in returning to Berlin, because he was anxious to find his family. We believe that, along with many other passengers, he got off the train and walked into the city, and somehow made his way through the firestorm. We know his wife and two children had been killed, along with his in-laws and his wife's brother.

"We're not sure when he returned to Berlin, but we do know that he went to Vienna in March, just as the Russians' advance was entering Austria. In early April, he retreated with other SS units heading back to Germany. He left the SS headquarters in Vienna with an aide and a driver and, we believe, a lot of files. The main roads were clogged with retreating German forces and equipment and were continually being strafed by the Allied air forces. Equipment was strewn across the roadsides as the air forces took their toll and thousands of soldiers and civilians were killed as the retreat continued. Stueben's aide and driver were identified as 'killed in action.' Neither his vehicle nor Steuben's body were ever found, and he was classified as missing in action."

Wiesenthal paused. "Interesting story?" he said.

"Incredibly so," responded Alex. "But how do you remember all of this?"

"We have hundreds and hundreds of cases in our files," said Wiesenthal with a smile. "But I have always found this one intriguing because it is close to home. Karl von Schuyler is an extremely successful, powerful and rich businessman in Austria. I have spent many years pursuing this case"

"But how are von Schuyler and Stueben connected?" asked Alex

"Well, you can make your own judgment by looking at our files," said Simon with a chuckle. "It will keep you busy, I promise," he continued. "But now how about some lunch? I have been talking far too long."

"Thank you, Simon. That would be wonderful."

"We will go to the Julius Meinl Café across the road. You'll enjoy it. It is well known for the apple strudel and chocolate torte, but they have some less-fattening things as well," Simon said with a grin.

"Sounds delightful," said Alex.

They crossed the street to the Meinl Café, one of many in the city. As they entered, Simon was greeted with a big smile and a cheery hello from the manager. Alex could not help but reflect on how different that greeting was from the story he'd heard about his aunt and uncle. Henrik and Cypora had been forced to leave Vienna in 1938 and sell their very successful jewelry business for a fraction of its worth. Unfortunately, they had chosen to make their way to Prague which itself fell into Nazi hands, and then made the fatal mistake of deciding to return home to Tarnow in Poland, where eventually they died in the Holocaust. Alex remembered hearing Henrik's story of how, within a few days of the Nazis marching into Vienna, he was unable to use his regular café across the street where he'd been going for twenty years for coffee and lunch because a sign had been placed in the window saying "No Jews or dogs allowed." *How times have changed in Vienna,* he thought, or had they?

Alex ordered a delicious open-faced sandwich followed by Simon's recommendation of apple strudel and a coffee with cream, and Simon had a similar lunch.

"If you have these files and all this information on von Schuyler," Alex said, "why don't you go to the Austrian authorities and expose him?" He sipped his coffee.

"Ha," responded Simon with a big grin. "This is Austria. There are no Nazis here," he said sarcastically. "The Austrians, unlike the Germans, have still got their heads in the sand. There are many former Nazis in government and in powerful positions throughout the country. Nobody would be very interested in von Schuyler, especially now that the FPÖ is in the coalition," he continued, "and although we have evidence that Steuben was a member of the SS, eventually promoted to Sturmbannführer and that he was undoubtedly involved in many massacres and killings, there is no evidence that he actually ever issued the final instructions or was the responsible person for the deaths of Jews or any others. We know he was there and we know that he reported on what was going on. We know that he worked on the plan to supply slave labor to IG Farben and other projects, but none of that would necessarily get a conviction. There are still more important fish out there that did pull the trigger and did make the decisions for mass killings, murders, rapes and whatever. Nevertheless I find this story particularly interesting," continued Simon. "Because I believe it involves theft on a massive scale, intrigue, and murder. But," he said in a much more light-hearted manner, "Alex, you must make up your own mind. Let's return to the office and I'll give you the files."

Chapter 11

Alex was eager to return to the office where Simon had set him up in a small area of the conference table. One of his assistants brought him four box files labeled Franz Steuben, and underneath, Wilhelm Schmidt and Karl von Schuyler.

The box files were marked 1914–1939, 1939–1945, 1945–1956, and 1956–.

Inside each box file were neat folders. He opened the first; inside was a wedding photograph of Klaus Steuben and a very beautiful young Anastasia Irena Romanov, dated 17 July 1912, as well as an attached photocopy of an article in both French and German newspapers announcing the marriage. There was also an announcement of the birth of Franz on 2nd August 1914 in Paris, and articles in German about the Steuben wine business in Bremen and a Christmas price list from December 1922. The folder also included an announcement of the sale of the Steuben wine business to Hapag shipping company, and a notice in the Bremen press about the subsequent death of Horst Steuben. There were university photographs, including Franz Steuben during his time at Stuttgart University, and a more informal photograph of a group of students about that time. Alex immediately noticed Franz's appealing impish grin, compared to the serious faces of his fellow students. Also in the folder was another photograph of Steuben in an SS uniform dated March 1936, and in group SS photographs in 1937 and 1938. He was also in the background of a photograph in Nuremberg at some event with Adolf Hitler and Goering in the foreground. The folder also contained the wedding announcement in March 1939, of Franz and Eva Eckhart, accompanied by a photograph of Franz in his SS uniform and an attractive blonde, Eva, with her stern-looking parents, standing in the background. Finally, the folder contained a report signed by Franz's superior officer in September 1939, praising him for his confidence and pointing out how his knowledge of French, Russian and English would be of valuable service to the Reich.

Alex leaned back in his chair, trying to visualize Franz Steuben and wondering whether he and Karl von Schuyler were really one and the same. Not much to go on so far.

He took out box number two, covering the period 1939 to 1945. Inside was a thick folder containing photocopies and typewritten communications on flimsy paper: he quickly found references to Obersturmführer Steuben and his SS commando unit, with orders to proceed to Lvov and onto Kiev. He also found filed reports signed by Steuben of actions taken in various towns and villages to round up Jews, Communists and others. There was a signed report concerning a roundup in Lvov and a chillingly statistical report, a few weeks later, signed by Steuben, listing the execution of 330 men of military age. There was a series of reports about the fighting and the commando units' experiences during the siege and battle for Kiev. He was really shaken when he came across special orders issued to regimental officers, revealing collective measures against villages in areas of partisan activity and the "commissar order." Soviet political prisoners and officers, Jews and partisans were to be handed over to the SS. There was a copy of Field Marshal von Routledge's order dated 28th April 1941, laying down ground rules for relations between army commanders, the SS commando units, and security police, operating in combat areas. Documents described the special tasks which would form part of the regulations covering the two opposing political systems, which included a jurisdictional order depriving Russian citizens of any rights of appeal and effectively exonerating German officers and soldiers of crimes committed, including murder, rape, or looting. He found a report signed by Steuben to a superior officer, confirming cooperation from Sixth Army headquarters, who had provided troops to assist in the roundup of Jews in Kiev, which sent a further cold chill down Alex's spine. He paused, gathering his thoughts. This was not easy reading.

But Alex was then riveted by a neatly typed report from Steuben on the incident relating to the escape of a number of NKVD officers. The report on the interviewing and interrogation of six NKVD officers captured by the Sixth Army on 17th May 1941 was comprehensive and concise. The names were listed as Kuchin, Yelten, Prolakov, Fradkov, Lebedev and Malenkov. After interviewing the prisoners for five hours, he took a break, leaving the prisoners under guard. He claimed that when he returned thirty minutes later, the cellar in which the interview had taken place was empty. Two of the SS guards were dead and two missing. He found them outside the building unaware of what had taken place in the cellar and denying any knowledge of the escape. He immediately reported them to his superior officer, who carried out an investigation into the negligence of the two remaining soldiers, who were then shot on the spot for deserting their post. It was clear from the number of stamps and initials on the document that this description of events by Steuben had been read by many parties, and he saw that the document had been stamped as being received at Himmler's headquarters. Alex was intrigued. He wondered what had really happened in that cellar in Kiev. He had spent months at the end of the war, interrogating captured German officers, and knew the process. He could put himself in Steuben's shoes.

Alex rummaged through additional documentation and found orders to Steuben to proceed to Rostov with his SS commando unit and then he came across another chilling reminder of those terrible times. There was a picture of Steuben, with the charming grin, and four other officers standing casually in the foreground of an area identified as Rostov. In the background was a long line of men standing in a dejected fashion over what appeared to be an open trench.

He also read documentation confirming Steuben's assignment

to assist IG Farben in the establishment of their chemical works outside Auschwitz concentration camp in July 1942. A letter of introduction to the management of IG Farben identified Obersturmführer Steuben as an officer with fluency in German, Russian, French, and English and a chemical engineering background. The letter of introduction went on to confirm that Steuben would be assisting in selecting work parties from Auschwitz prisoners, with particular focus on scientists and administrators who may have a chemical or engineering background. Alex was horrified, recognizing Steuben had the power of life or death over those poor prisoners. His heart was palpitating and he was sweating profusely, as he read the orders issued to Steuben to rejoin his SS commando unit on 18th September 1942 as the German assault on Stalingrad commenced. Skipping through a number of Stalingrad related documents, he found a report signed by Steuben's commanding officer, Hauptsturmführer von Helder, describing Steuben's capture and escape. Alex read the document with intense interest.

On the morning of 12th October as German forces engaged with the Russians in a battle for the Tractor factory in the center of Stalingrad, a number of Russian officers and NKVD were captured and brought to the basement of the damaged building where Steuben was asked to interrogate them. Three other SS commandos joined him. The battle was raging back and forth. After the interrogations had been going on for about an hour, the Russians counter-attacked. The German position was overrun and Russian soldiers burst into the basement. The three SS were killed instantly and Steuben was shot in the thigh. However, he managed to shoot two of the Russians and threw himself through a broken window, falling fifteen feet into a trench. German forces were responding to the Russian counter-attack and after two hours or so, Steuben, bleeding from his wounds, was able to come out from his hiding space and return to his own lines. He was sent to field hospital 8 and airlifted to Berlin on 16th October.

Killing two Russian officers and his daring escape resulted in his being recommended for a medal.

Alex also found two stapled documents with a front cover highlighted in yellow stating, *This is a personal statement dated 23 July 1973,* and underneath: *Heidi Kohlberg, secretary to Franz Steuben, December 1941 to March 1944,* and an address in Munich with her telephone number. The attached document read as follows:

My name is Heidi Kohlberg. I served as a secretary in the SS headquarters in Berlin to Hauptsturmführer Franz Steuben until August 1942. I was only twenty-one at the time and was totally committed to Adolf Hitler, the Nazi party and the Third Reich. In my starry-eyed, naïve innocence, I believed Hitler was near God and that Germany was destined to be the leader of the world. I was thrilled when I was offered the job at the SS headquarters.

Franz Steuben was a tall, handsome, charming officer in the true Aryan mold. He had a cheeky grin, which endeared him to all of the female staff. He was looked upon as a rising star in the SS but was not nearly as serious as many of the other young officers. His charm and good looks brought him to the attention of the senior officers, and so I was not surprised when he was invited to the Wannsee Conference in January 1942. Although we didn't know it at the time, it was there that the Nazi Party adopted the "final solution" and put into practice the extermination plan for the Jews in Germany and other European countries. A somber Franz Steuben returned from the conference with a pile of papers and asked me to set up new files for the SS plans and instructions.

I well remember when he turned to me and said, "Heidi, I am not sure we're doing the right thing. I believe this might set off a world reaction that could harm the Third Reich."

Hauptsturmführer Steuben was sent to the southern front in the spring of 1942 and I only saw him occasionally after that. He returned to the Berlin headquarters in the summer but was then shipped off again to the Eastern Front as his SS commando unit advanced on Stalingrad. I was sent back into the secretarial pool at that time, and did not see Steuben until January 1943, when he returned to the Berlin headquarters walking with a cane as a result of a wound received in the Battle of Stalingrad, for which he had received the Iron Cross second-class, for bravery, as well as a promotion to Sturmbannführer. The story of his escape was all over the Nazi newspapers, and he was treated as a hero, particularly as the grim news of the loss of the Battle of Stalingrad filtered through to the people. I worked for Steuben throughout 1943. During this time, he had assignments to IG Farben & Company, and was frequently sent on trips to interrogate captured Russian officers, and worked closely with Albert Speer, becoming a liaison officer between the various labor camps and Speer's office.

I also believe that Steuben had meetings with Adolf Eichmann and was eventually seconded to his staff in Budapest, Hungary, in the spring of 1944. After that transfer, I never saw Sturmbannführer Steuben again.

The SS administrative offices were bombed many times during 1944. We moved from pillar to post, but I was just part of the secretarial pool at that time.

As the Russians advanced on Berlin in the spring of 1945, I fled to the countryside and spent the rest of the War with an uncle who had a farm near Cologne.

The document was signed and dated by Heidi Kohlberg.

The second document was similarly labeled and highlighted in yellow as the personal statement of Anke Wenger, secretary to Sturmbannführer Steuben in Budapest Hungary from May 1944 to February 1945. The document was dated 26th March 1977:

My name is Anke Wenger and I was twenty-three years old in the spring of 1944, when I volunteered to join an expanding SS presence in Budapest, Hungary, controlled by Adolf Eichmann. I was working at the SS headquarters in Prague at the time. I was an idealistic and ardent supporter of Adolf Hitler and the Third Reich. When I arrived at my new location, I was told that I would be working as secretary to Sturmbannführer Steuben, who was an Administrative Assistant to Adolf Eichmann tracking the roundup of Jews throughout Hungary for shipment to labor camps.

Sturmbannführer Steuben was a tall, good-looking officer with blonde hair and gray eyes. He was very charming and had an endearing grin. He was very popular at the Budapest headquarters, as he always seemed to be more light-hearted and less serious than the majority of SS officers. I also knew him to be a hero who had been awarded the Iron Cross for bravery under fire during the Stalingrad campaign.

The war news at that time was not good. The Russians were continuing a steady advance and the German forces were falling back on many fronts. Steuben was particularly upset when news of the Allied D-Day landings came out in June 1944. He told me, albeit in a light-hearted manner, this was probably the beginning of the end. He said, "Anke you'd better start thinking of getting back to your family and safety." But he never mentioned the subject again.

I knew that the SS were rounding up Jews in Budapest. Towards the end of the summer they started arriving at our office. They were mostly older people, somewhat disheveled, wearing a yellow star of David on their clothing. They all looked terrified. I usually ushered them into Steuben's office two at a time. I don't know why he was interviewing these people but sometimes he came out his office with a smile on his face and a slap on the back for his guests, and they left the offices clutching some pieces of paper still looking anxious but with hope in their eyes and eagerly shaking Steuben's hand.

Although I was not aware of exactly what had taken place in his office, I was pretty sure that he had given them some sort of exemption from the roundup that was taking place. I was also sure that he was receiving something in exchange. Many of the visitors were clutching envelopes and documents and in some cases velvet bags of coins or jewelry. On one occasion, one woman accidentally dropped from her coat pocket a small bag that burst open revealing rows of pearls, diamond bracelets, earrings and some Hungarian gold coins. I felt that most of the visitors were carrying similar treasures. These visitors kept coming almost daily for about six weeks.

Sturmbannführer Steuben never spoke to me about these people and, of course, I would never dare raise the subject. However, he did have a private safe in his office, and on one occasion I saw a large envelope that appeared to be stuffed with US dollars, sitting on his desk. Steuben started taking short vacations at that time. He joked that the news was so bad, he needed the break. I had no idea where he went on his trips, but one of the other girls in the secretarial pool said that she had once received train tickets for Steuben for Vienna, and on to Zürich in Switzerland.

Steuben generally was good to work for but on occasion, if things went wrong, he displayed a violent temper. Once, I remember, he had some junior officers meeting in his room and I could hear him screaming through the door at them. I don't know what the discussion was about but he landed up throwing a lamp across the room, screaming at the top of his voice and physically throwing one of the young officers out of his office. The man was totally shaken up.

On another occasion, I remember Steuben yelling at two of the Jews who came to his office. They were an elderly couple, with the usual fear in their eyes. I don't know what they said to him. Or perhaps they just did not come up with enough money and jewels. He started screaming and insulting them, then came to the door, pushing them in front of him, red-faced and yelling at the top of his voice. He screamed for the guard and told him to take them to the transport immediately. From that, I gathered that their offerings did not satisfy him, and he was arranging for them to be shipped to a labor camp immediately.

As the year progressed, the war news got worse. The Russians were advancing rapidly into Hungary and by the end of 1944, we were told we would evacuate to the SS headquarters in Vienna. Sturmbannführer Steuben went back to Berlin and I never really saw him again, although I know he did reappear in Vienna early in 1945, before we evacuated once again in the big retreat to Germany. I had family in Austria and I went to stay with them in the countryside until the war ended.

The document was signed – Anke Wenger – 26th March 1977.

There was a third stapled document with the yellow highlight on the front page. The document referred to a personal statement from Ilse Krause and was dated 20th April 1976. Alex read the document:

My name is Ilse Krause, and in August 1944 I was a resident of Budapest, with my father Aaron. He was a scientist and owned one of the major chemical companies in Hungary. Our lives as Jews had become increasingly intolerable. Our assets had been taken. We were required to wear the yellow star, but we still had some freedoms and could move around within our own Jewish community. When the Nazis arrived in the spring of 1944, things got significantly worse. We soon learned that Adolf Eichmann and his SS units were rounding up Jews in the towns and countryside and shipping them off to the concentration camps. There was considerable panic in Budapest, as Jewish families tried to protect their children, parents, and the elderly. In August we learned that one of the SS senior officers was handing out passes, and ID cards, which would give immunity from the shipment to the camps. The officer's name was Sturmbannführer (Major) Franz Steuben. A friend from the Jewish Council arranged for us to have an appointment with Steuben. We were told that we would need at least $100,000 of bonds or jewelry, or US dollars in order to obtain the necessary passes. We had sold nearly all our valuables just to survive, but my father arranged to sell his valuable stamp collection, the rest of our art collection and the last pieces of jewelry that I owned from my late mother, and we converted our reichmarks into US dollars on the black market at a very unfavorable rate. We believed our valuables totaled just over $100,000.

We went to the SS headquarters which was located in a beautiful mansion, which had belonged to a Jewish family. I was absolutely terrified, thinking that my father and I were walking into hell, and might never come out. We were escorted into an ante-room and were greeted by his secretary, the only other occupant. She was an attractive young girl with blonde hair pulled back into a bun, wearing a light khaki uniform with a black tie and a little swastika pin on one of shirt lapels. We were kept waiting, but eventually were ushered into Sturmbannführer Steuben's office. Amazingly he stood up from behind the desk with a pleasant smile and came around and shook hands with my father. The whole scene was unreal. He sat us down into comfortable chairs, and started asking my father questions about his chemicals business. He said he had studied chemical engineering at university. Steuben was a tall, handsome, blond-haired Aryan, but with cold gray eyes. After the chitchat, he asked us to place all our valuables on his desk. He counted the US dollars, looked at the jewelry and the bearer bonds and told us our offerings were adequate. We were too terrified to say anything. He then took out a pad, and wrote something down, tearing off the two sheets, stamping them with a seal and handing them to us. He said, "These passes guarantee that you will not be arrested or trans-ported." He indicated that we should now feel quite safe.

He stood up, indicating that our meeting was at an end, and gently ushered us out. We left the building clutching our passes, but somehow I didn't feel we were really any safer.

Three weeks later we obtained access to Raoul Wallenberg, the Swedish Ambassador, who was granting Swedish nationality to many Jews and issuing as many Swedish passports as possible, so they could leave the country. Fortunately, we were able to join that group, finally arriving in Stockholm two weeks later. I subsequently heard that many of Steuben's passes did not stand the test of time, *and the majority of Jews were eventually transported to the camps.*

I don't know how many Jewish families paid off Sturmbannführer Steuben, but he must have collected millions over a matter of weeks.

I never heard what happened to Steuben, nor was I particularly interested.

The document was signed Ilse Krause.

Alex paused and put his hands over his eyes as he absorbed all the information he had read. His analytical mind was pigeon-holing a variety of salient facts about Franz Steuben. He was beginning to get a clear picture. A handsome SS Nazi officer, with great charm and certainly some intellect, as evidenced by his interest in music and his talent as a pianist. Nevertheless, Alex could feel the arrogance, cruelty and violent temper that was just beneath the surface.

Alex turned to box number three, covering the period 1945 to 1956, which had the name Wilhelm Schmidt under that of Karl von Schuyler.

He opened the box to find a pile of papers, press cuttings, photocopies, and photographs. These were in chronological order. The first item that caught his attention was a photocopy of a newspaper article dated 28th September 1926, in the Mendoza *Los Andes*, newspaper showing a photograph of Gerhard von Schuyler and his wife Marta, standing in front of a large Spanish colonial house and walled garden with a backdrop of snowcapped mountains. The article said that von Schuyler had purchased seventy hectares of land in Oak Hill Valley, outside of Mendoza from the Pinelli family. Part of the land was planted with vines, in an area that was considered quite high for the creation of good wine. The articles said some of the land purchased was as high as six-hundred meters in the foothills of the Andes. Gerhard was quoted as saying that he would expand the winery, and focus on creating quality wines.

Alex looked closely at the photograph of von Schuyler, a large man with a bushy moustache and a floppy hat on his head. His diminutive wife Marta stood next to him, a rather pale and sickly-looking lady.

There were a series of subsequent photocopies of newspaper and magazine articles from time to time throughout the 1930s, as von Schuyler expanded his winery and developed his expertise in successfully planting vines in higher elevations. His VS Wines brands achieved some success in the domestic Argentine market.

Alex read a copy of a 1941 magazine article about the VS Winery, Gerhard's expertise in developing Malbec and other wines in the foothills of the Andes, and specifically the opening of his new sales office in Buenos Aires, where his son Karl was to head up the sales organization.

Alex also found a photograph and newspaper article dated 30th September 1948, highlighting the VS Winery winning the Bronze Medal, from the Argentine Wine Society for their Malbec. Alex looked closely at the photograph which had Gerhard von Schuyler sitting next to his son Karl but also included Wilhelm Schmidt standing in the second row. Wilhelm Schmidt was a tall, well-built man, with what looked like brown hair and a thick moustache. He wore horn-rimmed glasses.

The next article was the announcement of the death of Marta von Schuyler from unspecified causes in June 1949. There was commentary about her background in Austria, and her contributions to Mendoza charities, and the local Lutheran church.

Alex scanned many other documents in 1950, 1951, and 1952 about the exploits of Karl "Charlie" von Schuyler, at the La Plata Polo and Country Club, where he was part of the polo-playing team. There were numerous photographs of a tall fair-haired smiling Karl with members of the team, usually with a beautiful girl on his arm. Other press and magazine comments and photos included Karl with a variety of different women at social events in Buenos Aires and the Argentine Grand Prix and at the

Concours d' Elegance standing next to a dark Lagonda car.

Alex's attention was particularly drawn to a photograph dated 28th September 1954 in the *Los Andes* newspaper, announcing that VS Winery had been awarded the Gold Medal from the Argentine Wine Society for their Malbec wines. What caught his attention, however, was the photograph of an aging and more fragile Gerhard seated, with his son Karl on his right side and "general manager" Wilhelm Schmidt, to his left. Apart from their physical statures, there seem very little similarities in appearance between Karl and Wilhelm. The article again referred to Gehard's expertise and his developing domestic and international reputation.

On 17th January 1956, there was a further article in the *Los Andes* newspaper about the death of Gerhard von Schuyler, from a heart attack while horse riding with his general manager Wilhelm Schmidt.

A couple of weeks later there was another article referring to rumors that Karl von Schuyler intended to sell the VS Winery and estates, followed by a number of articles, announcing on 28th April 1956 that the VS Winery had been sold to Arturo Diez Family Estates, one of the largest wine producers in the Mendoza region. The Buenos Aires article speculated that the sales office of the VS Winery Company would probably be closed, as Karl von Schuyler was not going to stay with the company.

Next, Alex found more personal statements, the first being from Lizette DeRosa dated 28th August 1974. Alex read on:

My name is Lizette DeRosa. In the early 1950s, I was a professional photographic and fashion model in Buenos Aires. I met Karl "Charlie" von Schuyler in December 1955. Although he was 14 years older than me, we started dating and developed a close serious relationship – or so I thought. I knew that Charlie had a reputation as a "man about town" who was very much involved in Buenos Aires society, the La Plata Polo and Country Club and motor racing.

I never met his father who died a couple of months after we started dating. Charlie told me that he intended to sell the VS Winery that they owned in Mendoza. A few weeks later in April, he told me he was going to Mendoza to negotiate a deal for the sale. I read about the finalized deal but I didn't hear from Charlie. I tried contacting him by phone, without success. He wasn't back in his apartment in Buenos Aires and after a couple of weeks, I contacted a couple of Charlie's friends, but they hadn't heard from him either. About the middle of May, I received a typed letter from Charlie, saying that he was selling up and going to Europe for a few months. He said he would keep in touch. The letter was signed with a big C and a couple of kisses. I never heard or saw him again which I thought was really odd.

Alex read and re-read that document and then turned to the second one dated 19 January 1976, a personal statement from Carlos Fernandez. Alex read on:

My name is Carlos Fernandez and I worked for the VS Winery in their Buenos Aires sales office from 1941 until 1956 when the company was sold upon the death of Gerhard von Schuyler. Although Gerhard's son Karl was nominally put in charge of the sales office, in the position of executive vice president, my responsibility was to show him the ropes and really run the business. Karl was never really interested in VS Winery and preferred mixing with the polo-playing set and motor racing, spending a lot of time with many beautiful women over a number of years in Buenos Aires, and I also believe in Punta del Este, Uruguay where he and a group of pals, had an interest in a horse ranch. Karl was a tall good-looking guy able to charm the ladies, but was never a serious businessman.

Naturally, I was very upset when Gerhard died and Karl announced his intention to sell the VS Winery business. He assured me and our other employees that he would do everything to protect the Buenos office but I didn't have much faith in his assurances.

Subsequently, the business was sold to Arturo Diez and by the summer of 1956, the sales office was closed and we were paid off and lost our jobs.

Karl went to Mendoza to conclude the sale, but for some reason, he did not come back to Buenos Aires. In May, I received a letter from him explaining that he had decided to spend a few months in Europe, returning to his roots in Austria. I never heard another word from him, nor did I ever see Karl again.

Alex thought about the two statements. Certainly Karl von Schuyler's behavior seemed out of character and mysterious. Why would this playboy with a beautiful girlfriend, lots of money from the sale of the family business, a position in Buenos Aires society and an obvious "man about town," decide to leave for Europe without telling his friends or business associates of his plans? Nevertheless he still found it difficult to connect Franz Steuben, Wilhelm Schmidt, and Karl von Schuyler. He would have to ask Simon Wiesenthal how he believed they all came together.

Alex then turned to the final box file commencing 1956. He opened the file to find a mass of papers, newspaper cuttings, photographs, magazine articles, and additional personal statements.

The first document was a copy of the *Klagenfurter Zeitung*, dated 28th July 1956 announcing that *Von Schuyler Returns to Lendorf*. The article referred to the recent arrival of Karl von Schuyler at the Lendorf Estate, and went on to state that Karl von Schuyler was a nephew of Wilhelm von Schuyler. His father Gerhard had left Austria in the early 1920s, and had established a major wine business in Argentina. The article then outlined Karl's plans to revive the Lendorf Estate, modernize the dairy, improve the woodlands, and redevelop the Klagenfurt former munitions works, which had been totally destroyed towards the end of the Second World War. Von Schuyler was quoted as saying he was prepared to invest millions of schillings to achieve these objectives. There was a photograph of Karl, which Alex looked at closely. Karl was tall, handsome fair-haired with clear eyes and a big smile on his face.

A few weeks later, the same newspaper announced the death of Astrid von Schuyler, Wilhelm's widow. The newspaper pointed out that Astrid had been sick for many years and apparently was suffering from dementia. Since her children had died during the war, Karl von Schuyler was now the heir to the Lendorf Estate.

Alex read various other newspaper and magazine articles covering the next few years about Von Schuyler and his progress at Lendorf, including the installation of a state-of-the-art dairy at the estate, improvements to the woodlands, the establishment of a timber business, and architectural plans for the development of the former munitions works into warehousing and distribution centers. There were pictures of Karl with the chairman of the Chamber of Commerce in Klagenfurt, and Alex noted his appealing grin that appeared in every photograph.

Then, in 1958, there were magazine articles about von Schuyler and his new girlfriend, the former Miss Austria, Katarina Wempe. Shortly thereafter, he read the announcement of their engagement and subsequent marriage. The happy couple, handsome Karl and beautiful Katarina, appeared in numerous magazines, while the gossip columnists talked about their Riviera honeymoon and Katarina's plans to modernize Lendorf.

Alex read an interesting article from March 1951 in the *Wiener Zeitung*, referring to the acquisition of two of Austria's major wineries by the Karl von Schuyler companies. The article went on to refer to Karl's previous family background as a major winery owner in Argentina. Karl was quoted as stating he wanted to develop the quality of Austrian wines and would be seeking to establish more export opportunities.

Skipping through the endless gossip columns and magazine articles in the early 1960s about the von Schuylers, and particularly the beautiful former Miss Austria, Katarina, and her newfound interest in the Vienna Opera, modern art, and Klagenfurt social events, Alex found more interest in the announcement of the completion of eight-thousand square meters of warehousing in Klagenfurt, which had already been rented to Alpine Construction, Henkel and Vasko. The article also referred to von Schuyler's plans for the forty-thousand square meters of destroyed buildings which had been the former munitions works in Linz. It said von Schuyler was negotiating with the Austrian Post Office for the development of a major regional warehousing and distribution center on that site.

Skipping through the file, Alex's attention was caught by an article about Karl joining the board of the Viennese Symphony. The article described Von Schuyler as an accomplished pianist with a deep interest in classical music. Alex had never seen any similar reference in all the other articles and news clippings that he'd read to date.

Alex read an article, dated August 1975, about the acquisition of the Heligmann Winery and Estates, one of Austria's largest in the Burgenland, north of Vienna, following a mysterious fire that had taken place the previous May. The article described how the acquisition would further secure VS Wineries and Estates as a leading producer and exporter of Austria wines. A similar article in May 1978 covered a further acquisition following the death of Kurt Schafter, the fifth-generation owner of a famous winery in the Danube River region. The article went on to say that Kurt von Schuyler now controlled over fifty percent of the production of Austrian wines and over sixty percent of Austrian wine exports.

One more major article caught Alex's attention. This was in the *Vienna Neue Zeitung*, dated 26th February 1983, and was headlined, *The Rise and Rise of the FPÖ*, with the subheading of, *The man behind the success*. Alex read the article closely. It referred to the establishment of the FPÖ in the mid-1950s, the struggles to survive for the first few years, the poor showing in elections; changes were made in the leadership and the party was finally able to focus on its main themes of law and order, and immigration. The article referred to Karl von Schuyler as the man behind the scenes. He was pulling the strings and had the power to direct the party strategy. The article said that recent successes and a disillusioned Austrian public could mean that the FPÖ would get a larger percentage of the votes in the upcoming May 1983 elections and could hold the balance of power as part of a coalition with the Social Democratic Party (SPÖ). The FPÖ had distanced itself from its former Nazi image, and the charismatic youth leader, George Haider, had a more universal appeal. The article estimated that Karl von Schuyler had spent millions to finance the party, and to bring it to its current position. The question now was, the article went on, how much power he would wield with the new Austrian parliament. The article described the many political connections that von Schuyler had with existing ministers, with current and past presidents. Would he use these connections to further his political ambitions?

Alex paused while he thought about the power – political and financial – that von Schuyler had. Enough to get away with murder?

Alex read on, as the article commented on how far von Schuyler had come since he had arrived in Austria in 1956 from Argentina. There, the article went on, he was regarded as a playboy, but the challenges of Lendorf, the death of his aunt, Astrid, and the responsibilities of turning around the estate had clearly bought out his serious side and led to enormous success. There were pictures of Karl von Schuyler in 1956, and shortly after his wedding with Katarina, smiling happily in the company of President Bruno Kreisky, and most recently with the sash of the chairman of the Austrian Wine Institute across his chest at a black-tie event.

There were a few more articles and comments about the elections in May, as Alex came to the end of the box. Just as he was closing the file, Helga appeared and asked if she could do anything further for him as she was leaving.

"No, Helga," Alex said. "Thank you very much. I hope I haven't kept you."

"Not at all," replied Helga. "Herr Wiesenthal will probably be here for another couple of hours. He always works late. If you need anything further, I'm sure he can help you."

Alex got up stretched, and went into Simon Wiesenthal's office.

"Come in, Alex," said Simon. "How did you get on?" "Fascinating," said Alex. "I can't believe you've been able to accumulate so much information on one person."

"Well," said Simon, "that's what we do. German efficiency gave us a mountain of war records. But I must admit that this person, because he's a local boy," Simon continued, "generated a lot of material."

"It's all very interesting," said Alex. "There is clearly some intriguing mystery about Franz Steuben, Wilhelm Schmidt, and Karl von Schuyler, but even though the facial expressions and smiles are similar, I'm still not sure how Steuben became von Schuyler. What's your theory, Simon?" asked Alex.

Simon smiled. "You may think this is a bit far-fetched Alex" said Simon, "and I'd say this only as a possibility, but it is an explanation that I think has credibility." He cleared his throat.

"I believe Franz Steuben recognized that the war was lost in late 1944, and that Germany would be defeated. He and his fellow SS officers would probably be imprisoned, particularly because of his involvement with the concentration camps. By offering wealthy Jewish families in Budapest the chance of freedom, he accumulated a fortune, all of which he deposited in a Swiss bank account in Zürich. He probably planned an escape for himself and his family, but when his wife and children died in the Dresden bombings, he only had to think about his own escape. When he joined the great retreat from Vienna with his two aides, he probably had already planned how to get over the border into Switzerland and had no intention of returning to Germany. I think it is a possibility that he shot both of his aides, eliminating any witnesses to his activities in Budapest. He then made his way over the border into Switzerland and from there, to Argentina. He worked there, probably quite contentedly, for many years at the von Schuyler wineries in Mendoza, until he saw an opportunity with Austria becoming independent in 1956 and the withdrawal of the Allied occupation forces. He would have known that Karl was a playboy with no interest in the business and he may have plotted at that time how he could get control of both the business and Karl's identity. Maybe Gerhardt did die of a heart attack while they were horseback riding, but it is also a possibility that, with his chemical-engineering background and knowledge of interrogation techniques, he may have given Gerhardt a lethal dose of something, maybe through an injection... or a bottle of wine. This could have brought on the heart attack." Simon paused, as Alex looked on, riveted to this theory.

"He then probably calculated that Karl would want to sell the business pretty quickly, and he might even have been the adviser who helped that transaction along. Karl went to Mendoza for the closing and was never seen again. Steuben as Wilhelm Schmidt would have been at the closing and could easily have celebrated with Karl after the event, murdered him, hid the body, took over his identity, changed his appearance a bit, and with the money from the sale, headed to New York and then on to Zürich. Within a couple of weeks, he popped up in Klagenfurt and announced to the world at large that he had come home. He knew that his cousins had been killed in the war and that Astrid von Schuyler was demented and sickly. It would not have been too difficult to kill her with another lethal dose in her medications, or even suffocation, or something similar. Because of the state of her health, the doctors wouldn't have looked too closely at the cause of death. So there, within a few weeks of returning to Austria, he now owned the Lendorf Estate, had a vast fortune in a Swiss bank, and also had the proceeds from the sale of von Schuyler wineries and estates, in Argentina. He would now start a new life and establish himself in Austrian society, politics and commerce. The marriage to Katarina would have been the icing on the cake. The trophy wife and a suitable mistress for Lendorf."

Simon paused. "That's my theory, Alex. I may be way off, but I'm pretty convinced that Karl von Schuyler, as we know him today, is really Franz Steuben."

"Phew, that's quite a story, said Alex. "But it could well be the truth. There are many unanswered questions. One thing that struck me in an article I just read, was that Karl von Schuyler is a member of the Board of the Viennese Philharmonic Orchestra and is an accomplished musician himself, a dedicated pianist with a deep interest in classical music. That appears to confirm the information about Franz Steuben's early life. Nowhere did I see any reference to the Karl von Schuyler of Argentina having any interest in music. His interests seem to have been polo and beautiful women."

"You're right," Simon said with a chuckle, "and there are many more similar mysteries and unanswered questions."

"So, Simon, why don't you report all this to the police?"
"Ha," said Simon, "and what good would that do? First of all, I have no evidence. Secondly, von Schuyler is a very well-known and successful businessman in Austria, who is believed to be the financier of the FPÖ, which, since last week's election, are now part of the coalition with the SPÖ. Nobody will want to upset von Schuyler at this time. My theories are all circumstantial. I don't have one piece of paper or anything else to back them up. Finally, as I said earlier, this is Austria. We don't like to talk about the Nazis. We would rather put all that behind us."

"I think I agree with your theory," said Alex. "Maybe not all of it is correct, but certainly there seems to be an incredible likeness between Franz Steuben and Von Schuyler – Austrian version. I can't wait to meet him tomorrow. I'll let you know if anything comes up. But either way, I want you to know that I've already decided that the Campbell Group will not be doing business with von Schuyler."

"Good luck," said Simon, "and, yes, please let me know if there is anything you can add to my theory. Otherwise, I hope you have a wonderful trip home. Give my love to your charming wife Julia, and I hope to see you again shortly, maybe in London or elsewhere."

"I hope so," said Alex. "And thank you, Simon, once again for your hospitality and the use of your files. I hope you will continue to do your great work for many years to come."

They shook hands and Alex left, coming out into the sunshine of a beautiful summer's evening. He took a leisurely walk through the old town, watching the serious Austrians rushing home from work and mingling with the tourists. Eventually he found himself at the Hotel Sacher Café and sat down ordering himself a light chicken salad, complemented with a glass of VS Riesling which he found a little sweet. He could not resist a Sachertorte with his coffee. But, sitting in this landmark café in the center of Vienna, he felt the chill of the Nazi era, and could envision the fear of the well-established and prosperous Jewish community as their world fell apart in the spring of 1938. They were robbed of their possessions and, within a few short months, their very lives. He did not feel comfortable in Vienna and never would.

Chapter 12

Alex was up early the next morning. Another sparkling brilliant day. He took an early-morning stroll around the grounds of the Palais Schwarzenberg and went back to the terrace for a full Austrian breakfast. Fortified, he decided to walk through the old town to the VS Group offices at Singerstraße 10, a beautiful whitewashed 18th-century building. There was a brass plate on the wall with the simple letters VS Group. The door was polished wood, light oak perhaps, and next to this were garage doors, which just as he was about to press the doorbell, opened to reveal a black Mercedes coming out from an underground car park within the courtyard of the building. He caught a glimpse of a black-suited chauffeur and a blonde lady in the rear seat. Alex recognized Katarina. The car sped down the street. He rang the doorbell and was buzzed in. The old oak door opened on to a small foyer and modern reception area, and within a few steps Alex was at the desk, looking at an attractive receptionist in a severe cut business suit.

"Good morning," Alex said in German. "My name is Alex Campbell and I have an appointment with Herr von Schuyler."

She looked down at a pad and responded, "Ah, yes Sir Alex, please take a seat."

He crossed the marble floor and sat down on a modern brown leather bench seat. Before he could take in his new surroundings, a small elevator opened and a tall attractive young lady approached. She had sweptback brown hair in a bun and wore a tight-fitting gray skirt, matching gray shoes and a white blouse. She wore very little makeup and no jewelry. An almost military look, thought Alex.

"Good morning, Sir Alex," the young lady said in English. "I am Anke Grefelmann, Herr von Schuyler's personal assistant. Please follow me." And without a further word, she turned and

Alex followed her into the elevator.

"Another beautiful day," Anke said. And nothing more. Probably her attempt at small talk. The elevator quickly rose to the 4th floor.

Alex noticed the elevator only stopped at two floors – 4 & 5. *A personal elevator for dear old Karl,* Alex thought.

The doors opened onto another reception area. The walls were painted white and the floor was polished wood, looking to be the original. Color was provided by a Lichtenstein painting behind the receptionist's desk. Anke turned right and led Sir Alex through double white painted doors into the large office of Karl von Schuyler. Similar to the reception, his office had polished wooden floors, white walls and modern furniture. Von Schuyler was seated behind a large Herman Miller desk, on a brown leather swivel chair. The windows to his left, which were part of the original building, overlooked Singerstraße. To his right was a clustering of comfortable linen-covered furniture; a sofa and two armchairs with a glass topped coffee table in between, and behind the sofa a large picture window with a view of the courtyard. Behind von Schuyler was a very bright Pollock painting, and on the opposite wall, a David Hockney. Quite a famous one, thought Alex as he took in Schuyler's surroundings. His feet echoed on the floor as he crossed to shake hands with von Schuyler, who got up from his seat.

Alex felt his stomach turning as Karl von Schuyler extended his hand and gave one of those impish grins that Alex had seen over and over in Wiesenthal's files. Alex studied von Schuyler closely. He was a tall well-built man, with white close-cropped hair, a suntanned face, and cold gray eyes. "That smile" revealed a set of good, white teeth. He looked younger than his years. He was wearing a light gray, well-cut suit, with a white shirt and light, blue-striped tie.

"Sir Alex, so good to meet you," said von Schuyler in good English with only a slight Austrian accent.

"I am pleased to meet you, Herr von Schuyler," replied Alex.

"Please," said von Schuyler gesturing towards the sofa and chairs. "Make yourself comfortable."

Alex settled into one of the armchairs. "Well, it's good to finally meet you," said Alex. "I've heard so much about your success in the wine business," he continued.

"Please, call me Karl," said Von Schuyler, oozing charm.

"Thank you," said Alex. "And you should call me Alex."

Von Schuyler sat himself down on the sofa and turned to Alex. "I feel privileged to have the chairman of one of the major international drinks groups, the Campbell Group, here in my offices," he said.

"It's my privilege to be here," responded Alex, playing the game.

"So, what can I do for you?"

"Well, Karl," said Alex. "I will come straight to the point. We would like to discuss with you the representation of your schnapps brands in the United States. We believe there are opportunities for growth in that area, particularly in states which have a strong European ethnic background."

"I wouldn't have thought there was much of an imported schnapps business to warrant such arrangements," said Karl, somewhat warily.

"Yes, there is," said Alex. "Cordials, as they are called in the US, or liqueurs as we call them, are an expanding and profitable niche in the US. Domestic schnapps do well, particularly on the East Coast and the upper Midwest, and they are growing."

"That's very interesting," responded Karl. "We've never looked at the export potential of our schnapps business, although we do a bit of business in Germany and Switzerland. You may know, Alex, that we own the majority of the boutique schnapps producers from the village area of Friesach in Carinthia. This area has traditionally produced flavored schnapps which I can only describe as being out of this world. But it is a fairly small production, which we sell domestically. I'm certain that discerning American customers would love the quality and flavor."

"We don't expect to see high volume, initially," said Alex. "But we do see this as being a profitable business. It would certainly be for the discerning palate. We would probably restrict our introduction to no more than three flavors, and would stress the heritage and quality, as the products would be priced at the high-end. That's our thinking, anyhow."

"I would certainly like to explore this with you, Alex, and I would also like you to visit Friesach, to see for yourself the incredible craftsmanship that goes into this traditional distilling process. Being a distiller of fine scotch whiskies, I'm sure you would enjoy the experience. How would you like to proceed?" von Schuyler continued, now quite interested.

"Perhaps we could ask you to send some samples of your leading schnapps to our offices in London, together with packaging information and a proposed export price list. We would then analyze the opportunities, send the product and pricing on to our US subsidiary and see where that takes us."

"Yes, I think that sounds very sensible," said Karl. "We can organize that without any problem."

There was a quiet tap on the door, and Anke entered with a tray containing a pot of coffee and biscuits.

"Do you take cream and sugar, Sir Alex?" asked Anke.

"Yes, thank you," responded Alex. Coffee was poured and the conversation turned to light chatter. "This is a beautiful building," said Alex.

"Yes, it was built in 1790," said Karl. "Of course, we really gutted it, and the building now serves as a modern center of our operations. We also have an apartment on the top floor."

"How lovely. I know you are the leading vineyard owner and marketer in Austria and I also believe you have some real-estate interests," said Alex, probing.

"That's true," said Karl warily, his gray eyes going very cold. "But I also have considerable investments around the world, in bonds, stocks, other financial instruments, and commodities. So we have a trading floor in this building which also serves as a sales office for our wine business and administrative offices for our other businesses. A dairy farm, lumber business, and my charitable foundation," said von Schulyer. *Just stating facts, but not showing off*, thought Alex.

"Congratulations on your success," said Alex. "From what I hear, you transformed the family estates when you came here from Argentina and have gone from strength to strength in the wine business... and other activities."

"We've been very fortunate," said Karl, now defensive and unsmiling. "It's taken a lot of hard work by a talented team," he continued. "As I'm sure you recognize in your own business."

"Yes," responded Alex lightly. "I always say that it is people that create success, not businesses."

"Ah, yes," responded Karl. "Very wise."

Alex could feel that the meeting was not going to achieve anything further. It was time to leave. He finished his coffee.

"I won't take any more of your time Karl. I will have my operations director follow-up on this meeting. Perhaps you could put us in touch with your head of operations and they can arrange for samples of those schnapps products to be sent to London."

"Of course," responded Karl, getting up from his chair. "In fact, I'd like to introduce you to our head of operations. He is waiting for me in the reception right now." He got up and went over to his desk and buzzed the receptionist.

"Come on in, Jean-Robert," said Karl effusively as the door opened. "I'd like you to meet Sir Alex Campbell, Chairman of the Campbell Group."

Alex stood and shook hands with Jean-Robert. "Pleased to meet you," he said.

"Jean-Robert du Sable is originally from Bordeaux and is the head of our wine operations," said von Schuyler rather proudly.

Alex looked at du Sable, a squat stocky man with dark hair and a ruddy complexion that one often sees in French country people. Du Sable gave a slight smile, revealing nicotine-stained poor teeth. Alex had already noticed that his red hands were rough and calloused. A man who had worked in the vineyards and the winery.

"Jean-Robert is a miracle worker," said Karl with a cold smile. "In the past five years he has increased our yields some seventy percent, and as a result, our exports are booming. But we have managed to maintain our high quality."

"That is some achievement," said Alex. "How did you manage to boost your yield so dramatically?"

"You have to know your vines," responded Jean-Robert a little nonsensically, "and know how to maximize the yields from the earth that you have," he continued, with a satisfied grin on his face, basking in the limelight.

Alex took an instant dislike to du Sable. He decided he had shifty eyes and there was something about him that looked dishonest. His ill-fitting suit and short stocky figure made him look ridiculous and out of place.

"Keep up the good work," said Alex, terminating the conversation, as he turned to Karl von Schuyler.

"Very nice to meet you, Karl," he said in true English fashion. "I hope that we can develop our conversation further and if so, no doubt we shall meet again shortly."

"That would be very pleasant," replied Karl, with that smile on his face again.

Von Schuyler escorted him to the door of the office, where Anke was waiting. She took him down in the elevator, and he was able to look out into the courtyard and across to the modern offices behind the glass wall on the other side. Karl von Schuyler was really running an empire from these headquarters, Alex thought, perhaps on the back of murdered relatives and terrified Jews.

"What a thought," Alex said to himself as he shivered somewhat, leaving the VS Group building behind him.

He took a taxi to the Palais Schwarzenberg, picked up his bags and headed to the airport for his flight back to London.

Chapter 13

"Thanks. Is that all he had to say?"

"Well," Langer responded sarcastically. "He said I did a good job, but it was out of his hands, national security and all that."

"National security?" Fritz said in disbelief. "Sounds like a good reason to get you off the case, perhaps you were getting too near to some sensitive people."

"Maybe so. Maybe they don't want me getting close to Karl von Schulyer. Especially after the elections."

"That's it," said Fritz. "With the FPÖ as part of the coalition, von Schuyler could be pulling all the strings. If that's the case, the last thing the new government will want is you poking around and asking questions."

"Probably, Fritz," said Langer. "Those fucking politicians are only interested in themselves and preserving their jobs and the good life. Anyway, I'm off the case and I'm really pissed. I spent weeks and weeks, trying to get to the bottom of this case, and just when I dig up some evidence, they whip me off. That Vogl is a real prick. There's nothing I can do about it, at the moment, but I am not going to roll over and play their game."

Bernhard Langer and his friend Fritz Muller were having their usual Friday night drink, at the Braukeller bar near the Metropolitan police headquarters. Langer and Muller had been friends since the first day that they had both entered the Police Academy thirty years ago. Langer had progressed up the ranks in the homicide department, while Muller had been in various departments, finally landing in the Serious Fraud squad, of which he was now the chief investigator. Muller looked like a policeman; he was dark, slim and always well-dressed, with intelligent blue eyes behind his wire-rimmed glasses. Langer looked the opposite, but they were firm friends with a deep respect for each other's abilities. Langer trusted Muller implicitly, and that trust was returned. So they both felt comfortable talking about their respective cases, commiserating with each other about Austrian bureaucracy and politics, and occasionally socializing with their wives, which had for the past twelve years, included a week's skiing in the Alps.

Langer had told his friend about the Bauer murder investigation, and the breakthrough that had led him to Karl von Schuyler. Fritz thought the case was fascinating.

"Did you ever manage to trace the widow?" he asked.

"No. So far, we have nothing. She seems to have disappeared off the face of the earth. We have a photograph of the funeral, by a BDM photographer from a local Linz newspaper."

"BDM?" asked Fritz.

"Yes. Birth, deaths and marriages."

"Oh. Yes, I see," said Fritz.

"Anyway," continued Langer, "we have also been unable to identify her escorts at the funeral. She doesn't appear to have left the country, certainly not by air, but of course she may have left the country by train, or she may be staying with family or she's just keeping a low profile out of fear. One thing we have established," Langer continued, "is that Gustav Bauer was not born in Linz, as we first thought. We've checked all the relevant births information and cannot find him, nor can we find anyone who knew him."

"Well," said Muller, "another mystery."

"It is," responded Langer. "It's just one of many. There are too damned many unanswered questions." Without waiting for any response from Muller, he continued. "Who is Gustav Bauer, and what is his connection to Linz if any? Who were the two men accompanying Frau Bauer at the funeral? Where is Frau Bauer? Who is the person that made a reservation at the Imperial Hotel? It's possible he was English. We got that from the hall porter. It is also possible that the Bauers were accompanied by an Englishman, as they were leaving the hotel. What is the connection?" And finally, as he slammed down his glass of beer, spilling some on the table Langer continued, intensely, "Who killed Gustav Bauer and why?"

"I may suffer the same fate with my latest case," said Fritz, changing the subject.

"Really," responded Langer, realizing he had dominated the conversation with his friend. "What are you working on?"

"I've just been handed an enquiry into the Austrian Wine Industry, or more specifically a couple of companies in the industry. There may be a case of labeling fraud, although it's probably small fry compared to what you've been doing."

"It sounds petty to have the Serious Fraud squad involved," responded Langer.

"I know," said Fritz, "but the only reason I'm involved is because the complaint came from the German government. They take these things pretty seriously, but at this stage, I can't believe it's a big deal. I'm just reviewing the papers. Not much to go on. However, I thought it was interesting, I may end up interviewing your friend Karl von Schuyler," said Fritz with a big chuckle.

"I hope you do better than I did," responded Langer, now more relaxed. He removed his umpteenth cigarette of the day from his nicotine-stained moustache and stubbed it out in an ashtray on the bar.

"Time to go home to the good woman," said Langer looking at his watch.

"Me too," said Fritz, "but I'll see you next Friday. Don't let Vogl get you down," he said as he picked up the tab and left a generous tip. "See you next week, Ute," he said smiling at the buxom blonde behind the bar.

"Yes, have a good weekend."

The two friends waved goodbye and stumbled into the bright sunshine from the darkened bar.

Chapter 14

"He could be your man, Tim," said Alex, sitting in Tim Bevan's Northumberland Avenue offices, looking out over the Thames on a bright but cloudy day. He had returned from Vienna a few days ago. And he had delivered a comprehensive report to Tim.

"But what would be the motive?" asked Tim, clearly puzzled and unconvinced. "You've got one of the most successful businessmen in Austria, the supposed power behind the throne of the FPÖ. It seems extremely difficult to link von Schuyler to the murder, or attempted murder, of an Eastern European scientist."

"I know," responded Alex. "It is hard to make the connection, but I've told you about Simon Wiesenthal's theory—"

"That's a bit of a stretch," said Tim interrupting.

"I've seen the files," responded Alex firmly. "I believe that Karl von Schuyler is really the former Nazi SS officer Franz Steuben. If Simon's theory is correct, murder would present no problem for Steuben. As to the motive, I agree that is difficult to understand."

Tim interrupted again. "That's the point, there is no motive, Alex. This is too farfetched for me," he continued condescendingly. Alex was taken aback by Tim's negative response, but Tim continued talking. "The man has plenty of money, and his politics appear to be at the other end of the spectrum from the Eastern Communist countries. It's also difficult to make a connection between Steuben and any Communist officials."

Now it was Alex's turn. "We know Steuben spoke Russian, as the son of the beautiful Anastasia Romanov, and he interrogated lots of Russian officers during the war. I agree it is hard to find a motive, Tim, but if you were to see the photos and the Press over the years, you might be persuaded by Simon's theory... Have you had any more feedback from the Austrian police?"

"No," said Tim. "They seem to be closing down the case. My concern continues to be the possible leak. We might have more problems down the line."

"I understand, Tim," replied Alex, leaving Simon's theory up in the air. "Where do you go from here?"

"Our parallel concern is, of course, to get hold of Keller's notes and papers and somehow squirrel them back to the UK. Keller has told us that he gave the papers to his closest friend, a science-faculty teacher at the University of Warsaw, named Kopacz. We have decided to send Anna back to Poland with the objective of recovering those papers."

"What! You're kidding?" questioned Alex, now feeling very worried. "You couldn't find an alternative to Anna? After all she's wanted for murder in Poland. It seems a big risk sending her back into the lion's den. Her life could be on the line. Are you really serious about this?"

"I know. Of course we considered all of those issues," responded Tim with his diplomatic speak in full flow. "But in the end we came to the conclusion that she is the best person for the job. She knows Keller, she is fluent in Polish, she lived in Warsaw until a few weeks ago, she has a deep desire to finish the mission that she started, and she feels that, if she succeeds, we will move mountains to get her brother, Jan, back to the West."

"Did you spell that out, as an incentive?" asked Alex in a serious questioning tone. "I wouldn't like to think that MI6 would put that young woman's life at risk, with an incentive package so to speak, to spring her brother from captivity." But that was exactly what he did think.

"No, of course not," said Tim equally seriously. "We would never do that. We have given her a new identity, a new appearance, and will get her a diplomatic job at the British Council. She should arouse no suspicion."

"When is she going?" asked Alex, totally unconvinced, and with his mind racing on how he could talk Anna out of this life-threatening venture.

"In a couple of weeks," said Tim. "We're sending her to work for Rupert Brookes-Walton, Lord Chadwick's younger brother. You might know him, Alex."

"I know Lord Chadwick, Charlie Brookes-Walton," responded Alex. "The government's Industry Secretary, reporting to Patrick Jenkin. He is a good solid chap."

"His brother is a little flowery, if you know what I mean," said Tim with a slight chuckle. "But nevertheless I understand he's doing a good job in Warsaw. He has a big responsibility over the next few weeks, with the first visit to Poland by the London Philharmonic Orchestra... I believe you are on the Board, Alex," asked Tim innocently.

"Yes, I am," replied Alex. "Although I'm not very active, I confess."

"I understand there's a group from the Board going to Poland for a concert."

"I believe that's true," said Alex warily. "That is quite normal on foreign concert tours."

"Were you thinking of joining them?" asked Tim.

"Noo!" said Alex, realizing that Tim was about to pounce.

"Well," said Tim, "I wonder if you could do a 'little job' for me?"

"Ah," responded Alex. "Another 'little job,' Tim? Haven't you got anybody else?"

"I'm afraid not, Alex," said Tim getting serious again. "I need someone in Warsaw, when the London Philharmonic Orchestra finishes its tour. If Anna is successful, she would pass Keller's papers on to you, and you could smuggle them out of the country as you return to the UK as part of the Orchestra's entourage. It shouldn't be a difficult job and really not at all dangerous."

"I seem to have heard that from you before, Tim," said Alex with a smile. "How am I supposed to walk out of the country with those papers? I'm sure there will be heavy security at the airport."

"We will brief the British Ambassador on our mission, and we have some resources on the ground. That should help, and we will firm up a plan with you over the next week or so. But, Alex, you are really resourceful as well. I know you could find a way."

"Well, what happens if Anna doesn't get the papers?" said Alex.

"You will have a nice few days in Warsaw, enjoying some great music," responded Tim somewhat flippantly.

"And if she gets caught, Tim?" asked Alex, annoyed at Tim's response.

"Then we will abort your trip," said Tim, seriously.

"I'll have to think about it Tim," said Alex. "What are the dates that you're talking about?"

"The orchestra is going on a fourteen-day tour, leaving London on the 6th of July. They will be in Warsaw on the 20th and 21st of July, and will be flying back to the UK on the 22nd. I only need you to go to Warsaw for a couple of days, say, on the19th of July."

"You know, Tim, I left Poland, a few hours after those two soldiers were killed, one shot by Anna," said Alex. "We got through the border, but my passport was stamped, and who knows, maybe I'm now connected to that murder?"

"I am positive that's highly unlikely," said Tim. "We've heard nothing from the Polish authorities. Although they were looking for Keller, I don't think they have any interest in you. We will create a new passport for you, from your existing one. There will be no Polish stamp."

"I'll have to speak to Julia about this," said Alex, letting Tim roll on, but unconvinced that he should put himself in a life-threatening situation, however remote.

"I understand," said Tim. "Under the circumstances, that will be fine. I know she can be relied on not to discuss these matters with anyone else."

"Of course, but in the meantime, perhaps you could fill me in on your plan for Anna."

"Absolutely," said Tim. "We're giving Anna an intense two-week briefing, plotting out on a daily basis, how she could meet up with Professor Kopacz, and arrange for the delivery of the package of papers. The orchestra arrives on the 6th of July, and Anna will be in Warsaw on the 30th of June. The orchestra will have a couple of days rest and then rehearsals, before proceeding on a tour, and returning to Warsaw. Rupert Brookes-Walton has responsibility for this tour, and Anna will be an extra pair of hands, to travel with the orchestra and smooth out any problems that occur along the way. She will be the liaison between the orchestra and the various towns that are to be visited. Within the first day or two of her arrival, she will try and make contact with Professor Kopacz, and work out a way for him to deliver the papers, hopefully before the orchestra arrives. The orchestra will return to Warsaw on the 19th of July for the final two concerts. Anna will deliver the papers to you when you arrive from London on the19th of July. Either you or we will work out a method of bringing them out of the country when the Orchestra returns to London on the 22nd."

"That plan seems to leave out a lot of details, Tim," said Alex thoughtfully. "If Anna gets the papers in the first couple of days, what will she do with them until I turn up? And how is she going to find Professor Kopacz and convince him to hand over the papers? This sounds much more difficult than you are making out," Alex said in his questioning chief executive's voice.

"I know, Alex, but at this stage I can only give a rough outline of the plan. We will certainly tighten things up in the next couple of weeks, and I'll give you a much more detailed briefing before you head off to Warsaw. I should tell you, however, that Keller has given us a code that will be communicated by Anna to Professor Kopacz, to prove our legitimacy, and also has advised us where Anna would find the professor during his normal workday at Warsaw University. We know what he looks like, so making contact should not be a major problem. What we have to do, however, is make sure that Anna can slip any Polish security people who may be covering her every movement. That's where the training comes in."

"You've got a lot of planning to do," said Alex, "but I will let you have my decision as soon as possible. I will also make a date with Anna, to make sure she understands what you are getting her into. I'm truly concerned for that girl's life."

"Of course, Alex," responded Tim. "We are as concerned as you are, but Anna is extremely capable and very tough, and I'm telling you, she is really keen to go. Having you there in Warsaw, Alex, will help Anna feel more secure. You know how much she admires you. She knows she can trust you to protect her and look out for her back," continued Tim, aware of Alex's weak spot.

"I'm sure I'll have some further questions for you, Tim," said Alex, realizing Tim had pounced, using Anna's safety as an incentive.

"Thank you," replied Tim. "I know I've said this before, Alex, but this time your country really does need you."

"Yes. Well, we will see," said Alex with some finality.

With that, both men stood up and shook hands as Alex departed.

Frank was waiting for him downstairs in the Mercedes, but Alex decided to go straight home and not to the office. He felt a real obligation to discuss this fully with Julia, before he could make a commitment. On the face of it, he agreed with Tim that the mission didn't seem to present much danger, but he had been through this before, and he didn't want to put himself or Julia through that ordeal again. In addition he had a nagging feeling that Anna was being used by MI6, and was going to be in much more danger than Tim made out. After all, there was an unsolved murder case in Poland, their world-famous nuclear physicist had defected to the West, and the Russians were breathing down their necks. Into this cauldron was being sent this boisterous beautiful, woman on an extremely dangerous mission.

Julia was home when Alex arrived at Prince Albert Road.

"You're home early, dear," Julia said with a welcoming smile on her face.

"I know," replied Alex. "I just had a meeting with Tim and I decided to come straight home rather than go back to the office."

Julia's forehead creased with a worried expression. Her blue eyes became brighter and she slipped her dark shining hair over her shoulder looking Alex straight in the face.

"Tim? What does he want this time?"

"I'll come straight to the point," said Alex. "Keller left some very important papers behind in Poland. Tim wants Anna to go back to Warsaw, recover those papers, and hand them to me and I'm supposed to squirrel them out of the country."

Before he could continue, Julia said, her voice rising as her Scottish brogue became more pronounced, "Alex, I hope you're not even thinking of getting involved in this nonsense. You just came back from Poland and could easily have been dead by now. You were covered in blood when you returned to London, and now Tim wants you to go back there. That is totally crazy. I hope you've told him so," she continued defiantly.

"Well," Alex said, looking a little sheepish. "It's not nearly as bad as it seems. I will be joining the London Philharmonic Orchestra on their tour of Poland for the last couple of days in Warsaw. I'm supposed to meet up with Anna who will hand over the papers and I will work out a way of bringing them out when the orchestra and we, the Board, returns to London on the 22nd of July. I'll only be there for three nights," he continued a little hopefully.

"Three nights is quite long enough for the Polish police to arrest a murderer," said Julia, raising her voice again. "How could Tim even think of asking you to go back?"

"Tim is convinced that if I was wanted for murder or had been implicated in any way we would have heard through the MI6 contacts, the police or the Polish government. Everybody knows they are looking for Keller and Anna, but nobody has mentioned me or even the fact that I was there. He's pretty confident that there are no worries from that source."

"Pretty confident," said Julia going slightly red in the face, her voice raised again. "Tim is pretty confident. He was pretty confident when you went off to Kraków on a business trip also for three days – and look what happened. No, Alex you should not go under any circumstances," she said defiantly.

Alex could see that he wasn't getting anywhere with Julia at the present time.

"I told him I would talk it over with you and would give it some consideration. But of course I have not committed to go."

"I would like you to tell Tim tomorrow you've decided against it, Alex."

"I can't do that, Julia," said Alex. "I have got to give the matter further thought. I need to ask more questions but I know how important this issue is to not only Tim, but also to the British government and possibly Western democracy."

"Don't be so ridiculous," said Julia irritably. "You're supposed to be the savior of the Western world. Utter nonsense."

"Well, I know where you stand Julia," he said reasserting his authority.

"This is not one of your office review meetings," she said now very annoyed. "This is your life, my life, and that of your children, all of which could be affected by this foolishness. You better take that into account, Alex. You're too old to take on these spy games."

They shared a frosty evening together.

Chapter 15

A few days later, Alex was sitting in one of the wooden booths in the bar area of Bentleys Oyster bar on Swallow Street, just around the corner from his Sackville Street offices, waiting for Anna. He had a glass of Chablis on the table as he looked out of the window onto the street, where heavy showers had been followed by a cool damp morning. This was Royal Ascot week, and he and Julia had been invited as guests of Samuel Montagu, the Campbell Group's investment bankers, to their box in the Royal Enclosure.

Julia hated Royal Ascot. "All that dressing up," she said, "to sit in traffic for two and a half hours both ways, and freeze to death in that wind tunnel, at the Royal Ascot boxes," she went on, "and on top of that, the food is awful and the drinks are exorbitantly priced." Alex smiled to himself. Personally, he enjoyed the pageantry; seeing the Queen and the royal family up close and, if the weather was good, the scene of the ladies in their finery and pretty hats, and the men in their formal top hat and tails... it was something that could not be repeated anywhere in the world. It was quintessentially English, and he always thought that if Royal Ascot was abandoned it would be the end of England. His thoughts were miles away, hoping that Ladies Day on Thursday would be sunny and warm, although the forecast did not look good. But he and Julia would be there come rain or shine.

Suddenly he noticed that Anna had arrived. As usual, she swept into the bar area, turning all the men's heads. She was taking off her light raincoat, as she crossed the bar area to greet Alex with her usual hug, and bubbling enthusiasm.

"Lovely to see you Alex," she said. "You're looking well."

"Thank you, Anna. I'm drinking a Chablis," said Alex. "Would like to join me?"

"Thank you, a Chardonnay," said Anna. Alex called over the

waiter and ordered the drink and menus.

Alex ordered fresh asparagus followed by a plate of smoked salmon. Anna chose lobster bisque, and dressed crab.

"I wanted to see you, Anna," said Alex, lowering his voice to a whisper and turning serious after a few minutes of chit-chat, "because Tim Bevans told me that you are returning to Warsaw shortly."

"Yes, I am," replied Anna brightly. "I want to complete the mission. I think I'm the best person to do it."

"You may well be," said Alex, not much louder. "But I'm concerned that maybe Tim Bevans has not spelled out the dangers that you face. You are wanted for murder. They have your brother Jan in prison, and maybe are watching your mother, to see if you show up there. I know that you've been given a new identity and appearance, but I urge you to take no chances, and especially not to try to use this visit to get Jan released," said Alex, aggressively. "You surely know MI6 is focused on getting Keller's papers, and is not concerned about much else, including you."

Anna was surprised by Alex's outspoken criticism of "The Firm," but she knew he was trying to protect her. "You're very sweet, Alex," said Anna, reaching across the table and putting her hand on his, as she looked directly into his eyes. "Given my life experiences, there have been very few people I trust, other than my mother and Jan, but I knew from the moment we met, I could put my trust in you. So I appreciate your genuine concern," she continued. "But I shall be careful. I won't be in Warsaw for very long, and will be travelling around the country for most of the orchestra tour, and the whole mission is less than four weeks." She stopped and took a sip of her wine and a couple of nuts.

Alex, was momentarily shocked, that Anna had opened up about her feelings and trust in him. He did feel protective and felt she was telling him the truth.

Before he could respond she continued. "I understand that

you're going to be there for the last few days to hold my hand," she said with a smile. "That will be very reassuring."

"I'm going to see Bevans again this week," Alex said, barely above a whisper. "I haven't really made up my mind." He paused. "I would also like to see the mission completed, and I know it's very important we recover those papers, but coming so soon after our recent experience you can understand that I was not expecting a quick return to Poland. But mainly, I need Tim to lay out the strategy, and what fallback options we have if things don't go according to plan." He paused. "I need to be convinced and so should you."

"I understand, Alex," said Anna, speaking as quietly as Alex. "I don't underestimate the task ahead, but it would certainly make me feel more confident if I knew you were going to be there. You gave me the strength to see us through our last challenge, but I think this one is going be a lot simpler."

"I certainly hope so," said Alex with a wan smile.

"I'm going to be leaving early next week," said Anna. "I would really like to know what your decision is."

"I promise to let you know before you leave," said Alex softly, looking into Anna's eyes, as he put his hand on hers. He felt warmly protective and he decided there and then, he would go to Warsaw to help her.

On Friday afternoon, another blustery very cool June day, Alex met Tim at the Lambeth MI6 headquarters. Tim welcomed Alex with his usual warm handshake.

"Make yourself comfortable, Alex, I've ordered some tea for you."

"That's very kind Tim. I certainly need it today. It's more like November than June."

"How was Ascot yesterday?" asked Tim.

"Overcast, damp and cold," said Alex. "Julia hated it as usual, and moaned all the way there and all the way back. I must admit,

I couldn't argue this year, it was a pretty miserable day out."

"Oh dear, I'm sorry," said Tim, moving on. "But Alex, I'm anxious to know your decision about Warsaw."

"I have been giving serious consideration to your request Tim," responded Alex. "But I'd like to know a few more details."

"Of course," Tim replied. "We have now fleshed out the plan. First of all, we're sending one of our people to keep an eye on Anna. He will be sent in as a driver at the consulate before she gets to Warsaw, and we will decide later whether he stays or comes back with the orchestra. His job will be to see that Anna doesn't get into any trouble. Her mission will be to find and approach Professor Kopacz within a couple of days of her arrival in Warsaw. Assuming she can accomplish this, she will arrange for him to deliver the papers to her, hopefully before she departs for the orchestra tour and she will then take the papers to the embassy where they will be stored in the Ambassador's private safe. Do you know the ambassador... Sir Miles Stanford?"

"No," replied Alex.

"Good chap," said Tim continuing. "Anna will then accompany the orchestra to the various concerts around the country, and will not be in Warsaw again until they return three days before departure, when I hope you will arrive. If you follow this plan, the Ambassador will contact you on your arrival, and will hand over the papers to you on the day of your departure to London – or earlier if you desire. We will have a number of suggestions before you leave, about getting the papers out of the country, and will brief the Ambassador as well, but once you are on the ground there you may work out the safest way to squirrel the papers out of the country. Really Alex, this should be a piece of cake. Not at all dangerous. Nothing like your recent experience."

"Okay, Tim," said Alex, "a couple more questions. Why doesn't the Ambassador just send the papers out in his normal diplomatic bag?"

"I'm afraid the diplomatic bag from Eastern European countries is just not safe anymore, particularly from Poland. Of course, we could raise havoc if something did happen, but that would not get the papers back. No, Alex, we have to separate this whole mission from the normal diplomatic channels, and indeed our normal personnel. We have a leak somewhere in Warsaw that could jeopardize not only this plan, but all our future activities. One of the reasons we're sending in one of our men is to try and get to the bottom of that particular issue. It is vital that we come up with the right answer."

"My second question, Tim, is what happens if Anna is arrested, possibly with Professor Kopacz?"

"Well, then, we've lost, and lost badly. If that happened before your departure, of course you wouldn't go. Quite frankly that would be a disaster not only for our government, but also as I said previously for the safety of the West."

"I discussed this with Julia, Tim," said Alex. "And, to say the least, she is extremely unhappy at the thought of my returning to Poland. In fact we have had some blazing rows. She feels 'The Firm' didn't do enough to protect me, Erik Keller and Anna on the last mission, so she isn't confident about your assurances now." Alex was using his arguments with Julia to have a dig again at Tim and MI6.

"I understand Julia's concerns, Alex," said Tim. "Kraków and Vienna was an unexpected blow. We were not prepared. But this mission is a lot simpler, and I can assure you we have a well-thought-out plan. Your safety and Anna's is paramount. I can assure you, there will be more than adequate security and resources at your disposal."

"I would hope so," said Alex. "I need to feel a hundred percent confident that the plan will work and that Anna and I have the protection of 'The Firm' and the UK government." He paused as Tim nodded. "But I have given this considerable thought and I would also like to see the mission completed, and

Keller's papers returned to the UK. I believe I have a responsibility to see this through, so I'm willing to go to Warsaw."

Tim's face lit up. "Alex, thank you. I can't tell you how pleased and appreciative I am about your decision. I promise when you safely return, I will personally express my gratitude to Julia as well. I truly believe we can successfully conclude the mission. Anna is now well trained to meet any unexpected challenges and we shall keep tabs on her every movement."

"I sincerely hope so, Tim. I understand Anna leaves for Warsaw next week, and I shall follow a couple of weeks later."

"Yes, Alex, but I would like to meet with you for a final briefing before you depart. By that time, we should know whether Anna has been successful in recovering Professor Keller's papers. I will keep you posted, as soon as I have some news."

"A lot is riding on that young woman's shoulders, let's hope it all goes smoothly," said Alex slowly, but emphatically.

"I can assure you, Alex, from the PM down, everyone will be holding their breath, and praying quietly."

With that comment Tim got up, walked Alex to the door of his office with his arm on his shoulder. "I won't forget this, Alex, I promise, and I'm confident you're the man to get the job done."

"We shall see," said Alex. They shook hands and Alex headed down the corridor, and took the elevator to the ground floor and Frank and the Mercedes.

Chapter 16

On Thursday, 30th June, BA flight 169 swooped from brilliant sunshine into overcast gray clouds as it approached Warsaw's International Okecie Airport. Anna suddenly felt very nervous. What was she getting herself into? Maybe she *was* crazy to be returning to Poland. She could feel her stomach tightening, as she thought of the possibility of her immediate arrest, as she went through the airport formalities. Maybe they were waiting for her. She tried to put these thoughts out of her mind as the plane landed with a slight bump and approached the airport gates.

"Welcome to Warsaw," said the pretty little dark-haired BA stewardess. "We hope you enjoy your stay in the Warsaw area or wherever your future plans may take you," she said in an automatic voice. Anna grabbed her airline bag and, clutching her passport a little too tightly, with its official letter of introduction, she followed the other passengers into the dimly lit terminal. She lined up for passport control and pushed her passport through the glass screen to the official, who looked Anna in the eyes and compared her face to the passport photo.

"How long you in Poland?" he asked disinterestedly, in broken English.

"About four weeks," Anna responded croakily, her heart thumping and her throat dry.

"Why are you here?" he asked. "Tourist?"

"No. I'm here with the British Council," replied Anna as she handed him the official letter from the British Foreign Office, trying to control her shaking hand. *This is worse than I anticipated,* she thought to herself.

He read the document and left his booth, with Anna standing there, and went over to a cubicle a few meters away and spoke to another officer, who stood up and looked at Anna over the cubicle wall. She thought she was going to faint with fear. The official returned to the booth and without a further question, stamped her passport and handed it back to Anna. She felt the air rushing out of her lungs and she moved away.

She took the documents and proceeded to a currency booth where all the passengers were required to change pounds to zlotys. She then followed the signs to the baggage claim, collected her suitcase and proceeded to Customs where an officer again requested her passport, and asked the same questions. She handed him the Foreign Office letter and he asked her what work she would be doing for the Royal Philharmonic Orchestra tour, and then before she finished her answer, shot back another question. "How do you speak such good Polish? Have you lived in Poland? Have you visited many times?" She responded, sticking to the agreed script, but conscious that she had neglected to make some pronunciation errors and misuse of words, as she had been practicing in London. He looked at her suspiciously and insisted on opening her case and going through all her personal belongings. Very carefully, he looked at labels, opened her makeup bag, and examined the contents of her creams and lipsticks. And then, without another word, he closed her bag and waved her on. She happily grabbed her belongings and as calmly as possible walked out into the grayness of Warsaw's airport. She immediately noticed the armed guards every fifty yards or so, the passengers scurrying by with their heads down, and suddenly realized that even though she had only been out of the country for four months, she had adapted, almost without thinking, to the freedom of movement, expression, and individualism of a Western democratic country. Now she had returned, and immediately felt the oppression of the political system. Almost immediately she saw a sign with her name on it – Janet Clark – held up by a tall dark-haired young man who gave her a big grin as she approached.

"Janet Clark?" he asked.

"That's me," she responded lightly, now calmer at seeing a

friendly face.

"Hi, my name is Neil Jordan, and I'm going to be your escort and driver while you're in Poland."

"Really?" said Anna with some surprise. Tim Bevans and his team had not informed her that she was to have an escort. "That's very nice. I wasn't expecting such service," she continued with a smile.

"I shall be discreet, I assure you, but now my job is to drive you into town and deliver you to the British Council offices."

"That's great. Thank you."

Jordan took her bag and they crossed the road to the car park and a black Skoda. They exited the airport quickly, and Anna began to relax even though within a mile or so she saw the paramilitary waving down vehicles to be searched, which brought back horrific memories of her experiences when Krystyna Keller had been shot dead.

"First time in Poland?" asked Jordan.

"Yes," replied Anna, comfortably lying now. "It looks a bit gray and grim after leaving sunny London today."

"Everything looks better in the sunshine," responded Jordan. Anna liked his laid-back English manner.

He dutifully pointed out buildings and places of interest as they drove into the center of Warsaw. She of course knew everyone.

Jordan drove through the archway into 59 Aleje Jerozolimskie, the British Council office building since 1948, parked the car, retrieved Anna's suitcase, and led her into the building. He walked up to the receptionist and said, "I've been asked to take Miss Clark directly to Mr. Brookes-Walton's office, Maria. Can I leave her case with you?"

"Fine, Neil," the receptionist answered. "I'll call his secretary and tell her you're on the way up."

Jordan led Anna into the elevator. They ascended to the fifth floor and were greeted by a middle-aged lady with gray streaked hair wearing a black suit and white blouse. Every bit the formal secretary.

"Nice to meet you, Miss Clark. I'm Emily Paige-Madison, Mr. Brookes-Walton's assistant," she said, extending her hand.

"Nice to meet you," said Anna.

"I'll leave you in Emily's good hands," said Neil, "but will see you later."

"Thanks," said Anna.

She followed Emily into Mr. Brookes-Walton's office – a light airy room decorated with English furniture, a comfortable couch and an antique partner's desk.

Brookes-Walton stood up. "Ah, Miss Clark, please take a seat," he said, gesturing to one of the leather chairs in front of his desk. "I hope you had a pleasant journey. This is your first time in Warsaw?" he continued before she could answer.

"Yes, to both of those questions," said Anna.

"Well, Miss Clark, I have to be honest, I was looking for an experienced male assistant, with at least some knowledge of classical music and orchestras." Anna raised an eyebrow, and Brookes-Walton realizing how sexist his comment was, tried to recover. "Well, not necessarily male of course but someone to help me through what is probably the most important cultural exchange between the UK and a Communist country for over fifty years," he continued rather pompously, as his face reddened.

Rupert Brookes-Walton was a slim, handsome man with sleek black hair in his mid-forties, wearing a gray chalk stripe suit, a purple-striped shirt with white collar and cuffs, matching mauve tie, and a purple silk handkerchief flouncing out of the breast pocket of his jacket.

He looked at Anna, with gray-blue eyes, clearly expressing his distaste and frustration at not receiving the assistance that he had requested. *What a prick,* Anna thought.

"I'm sorry, Mr. Brookes-Walton," said Anna evenly, "but I'm

sure that I can do a satisfactory job for you. If our superiors in London did not believe I was up to the task, I'm sure they wouldn't have sent me."

"Well," responded Brookes-Walton, looking down at the paper on his desk, now backpedaling. "I see you speak Polish, and that will be a big advantage. We will be moving more than a hundred people – musicians, stage staff, and administrators – around the country on a tight schedule. It won't be easy, but you'll have to do as best as you can."

"Quite frankly, it doesn't sound like rocket science," replied Anna coldly, now feeling a bit testy. "I'm sure I can handle it."

"Miss Clark, you've never been to Poland before, and this is a country still under martial law, with services that are quite primitive. You have to respond very quickly, in order to survive. We have a few days before the orchestra arrives, which will give you a chance to get your bearings, understand the schedule and follow through on the arrangements that have already been made. I'm going to introduce you to another young lady, Stefania Piatkiewicz, who has been here about four weeks and has been working as an assistant to Miss Paige-Madison. She will now be your assistant. You will be staying in her apartment when you're in Warsaw. She will brief you on the schedule and arrangements that have been made with the orchestra and get you up to speed." With that, he pushed a button on his intercom. "Miss Madison, can you come in with Miss Piatkiewicz?"

He paused before continuing, and Anna braced for another verbal onslaught.

"As part of your responsibility, Miss Clark, you will be attending various formal functions for the London Philharmonic Orchestra in Warsaw and other locations. I hope you have got some suitable attire," he continued arrogantly, looking at Anna's loose M&S blouse, hanging over her gray skirt, and sensible shoes. She was wearing very little makeup and her outfit and horn-rimmed glasses made her look somewhat dowdy, an impression she was trying to create. She could see him thinking, *Not only did they send me a woman, but she dresses like a bag lady.*

"Yes, sir" she replied. "I was briefed in London, and I think I have an adequate wardrobe."

At that moment, Emily Paige-Madison entered the office accompanied by a pale, tall, slim girl in her early twenties. She had straw-colored hair, partly hiding her blue eyes, a long, somewhat crooked nose, thin lips with just a touch of makeup, and an angular, slightly stooped posture. She was flat chested, and her green short-sleeved shirt, and dark green skirt below her knees did nothing to add to her appeal.

"Ah, Miss Piatkiewicz," said Brookes-Walton. "I would like you to meet Janet Clark, who will be helping us with the Philharmonic tour. I believe Miss Paige-Madison has already briefed you on how you will assist Miss Clark with her responsibilities. As you know, she will be staying with you as well, so now I shall leave her in your very good hands. You can show her around the offices, introduce her to everyone and then leave the office early in order to make her comfortable in your flat."

"Yes, sir," responded a timid Stefania.

"Good luck, Miss Clark," he said with a final flourish, clearly meant to dismiss everyone.

Emily Paige-Madison turned and left the office with Stefania and Anna following.

"I'll start by showing you around the offices," said Stefania, with a strong South London cockney accent, in contrast to her very Polish appearance. They spent the next half an hour roaming through the British Council offices, and getting her photo taken in the basement for her British Council ID card. Anna was introduced as a special assistant for the upcoming London Philharmonic Orchestra tour. She was pleasant and cordial to all. Stefania was clearly happy with her newfound authority.

After completing the tour, they returned to the ground-floor reception where Anna picked up her suitcase. Neil Jordan was waiting to take both Stefania and Anna to the apartment.

"Wow," exclaimed Stefania. "You seem to be getting the royal treatment," she said as they walked towards the Skoda. "Nobody drove me around when I arrived."

"I know," said Anna in a loud whisper. "I was surprised as well." She didn't let the discussion go any further.

Jordan drove for about ten minutes, until they reached the apartment building on Bielanska Street, the other side of Ogrod Saski Park, and only a few hundred yards from the apartment Anna had left in February. As they drove past, she anxiously looked to see if anyone was still watching. She saw a car perhaps seventy-five yards from the entrance to her former apartment. Were they "Ferrets?" Would they still be watching to see if she returned? She again felt a clammy nervousness down her back, as she thought about the possibilities.

They parked outside her new accommodation, and Jordan carried her suitcase as they trudged up three flights of stairs before saying their goodbyes. The flat was in a classic Warsaw pre-war building, desperately in need of repairs, maintenance and a good lick of paint.

Stefania was chatting away. "You'll meet Maggie later on," she said, referring to the third member of their shared flat. "She's really sweet. She's a secretary to the British Consul. She's worked all around the world," she continued, her voice clearly indicating the awe in which Maggie was being held. Stefania retrieved the keys, and opened one of the double entrance doors to the apartment. They walked into a large light airy room with high ceilings, fireplace and a kitchenette. Stefania was chattering on. "I'm afraid you've got the smallest bedroom," she said. "But you're only here for a few weeks, and most of that will be out of Warsaw."

Anna could already see that this flat was much superior to the average Warsaw apartment. "That'll be fine," she said as Stefania escorted her into a small narrow bedroom. Behind the bed was a large window, covered with a lace curtain. The hardwood polished floor had a thin rug over it, and there was a wardrobe and a small chest of drawers.

"We have to share the bathroom, I'm afraid," said Stefania, "and there is only a hand shower, which is a bit of a pain. We take turns to use the bathroom and the loo. I'm sure we can work it out" she continued enthusiastically.

"It's a lovely flat, and I think it'll be fun," said Anna encouragingly.

Anna unpacked her things, such as they were. A few not very glamorous M&S outfits, jeans and T-shirts, and her one glamorous cocktail dress that she had bought on sale at Harvey Nichols. She heard the door of the apartment open and close, and Stefania talking to the third inhabitant of their flat. Anna returned to the reception room and was introduced to a petite, pretty, dark-haired woman about Anna's age with large green eyes and a big smile.

"Janet Clark," said Stefania. "This is Maggie Mason."

"Pleased to meet you," said Anna, smiling and moving forward to shake hands.

"Me too," responded Maggie. "Welcome to our humble digs."

"Not so humble," said Anna. "It's a lovely flat, very bright and airy."

"Yes," said Maggie. "But I'm sorry that you've got a rather pokey bedroom."

"That's fine," said Anna. "I'm here on a short assignment."

"Oh, yes, Steph told me," said Maggie. "I've heard BW has got his knickers in a twist. Although that's not too unusual for him. He's a bit of a poofter you know, and they are inclined to panic and get emotional," she continued with a big laugh, her Yorkshire accent coming through.

"Well, I will have to be on my best behavior. I don't want to be the cause of any meltdown," Anna responded with a laugh. She had immediately taken to Maggie. "What do you do, Maggie?"

she asked.

"I'm the assistant to the British Consulate General in Warsaw," she replied.

"Sounds like a big job," said Anna inquisitively.

"Well, not really," responded Maggie. "I've been at it a long time in various parts of the world, so I know the form pretty well by now."

"Which cities have you worked in?"

"Let's see," said Maggie. "Buenos Aires, Mexico City, Cairo, Chicago, Vancouver, Milan, and now Warsaw."

"My God. That's quite a list. How long do you spend in each posting?"

"Usually three years, and for the most part, it's been interesting and fun. You're an Aussie?" asked Maggie.

"Yes, born and bred."

"How long have you been working for the Foreign Office?"

"About twelve years," said Anna, keeping to the script that she had been given in London.

"How did you get this job?"

"Mainly because I speak fluent Polish. My mother is Polish, from Poznan, and we always spoke Polish at home when I was growing up, even though she left Poland in the 1930s."

"Oh, I see," said Maggie. "Your job is to smooth the way for the round the country tour."

"Yup, that's me," quipped Anna. "I'm sure there will be a few cock-ups, and BW is warning me about everything from martial law to terrible hotel service. So I've been forewarned, and I'm prepared to face the music if you excuse the pun."

They all laughed.

"Any husbands in the picture?" asked Maggie.

"Yeah, I tried it for a while but it didn't work out," replied Anna. "How about you?"

"Same thing," said Maggie. "He was a bit of a stick in the mud. He also worked in the Foreign Office. Maybe you know him, although he left about four years ago. Ronnie Mason," she continued.

Anna shook her head. "Nope."

Maggie continued. "At the time, I wanted to see the world, be adventurous, and I had some lucky breaks that led me to these consular jobs. It's been great, but not very helpful if you want a serious relationship."

"I know what you mean," said Anna. "But I guess the ad is wrong, maybe we can't have it all," she concluded.

"Well," said Maggie with a laugh, "I intend to make the most of it. I believe we're only on this earth once, so enjoy every minute."

"I'm with you, Maggie," Anna said, giving a salute. "Let's party while we can."

She went to the Council's offices the next morning with Stefania, and to her surprise was allocated an office of her own, albeit without a window. Stefania bought her a pile of files and placed them on her metal desk.

"I've opened a file for each location of the tour. I think it will be helpful, and I've put in all the hotel-reservation information and as much logistics as I could find so far. The guy in charge of that part is Charlie Adams. I spoke to him on the phone a couple of times. He seems like a good bloke. Anyway, take a few days to get settled and fill in some of the blanks that I've left out. I was a bit cheeky and asked Miss. Madison whether I could travel with you on the tour, since I'm supposed to be your assistant. But they said no. So I've got to stay here and hold the fort for you and also help them with the Warsaw arrangements, which they regard as the most important part of the tour."

"That's very helpful. Thank you," said Anna. "I guess from your name that your parents are Polish. Were you born in England?"

"Of course," replied Stefania with a roar of laughter. "Wot! Can't you tell I'm from Souf London through and through?"

"You speak Polish?"

"Yes, of course. They didn't give me this job for my good looks," responded Stefania with another cheeky laugh. "My parents came to England in 1939, with their families when they were small children. They planned on returning after the war, but then the country came under Communist control, and they decided to stay put, which was just as well."

"So, Warsaw is a great experience for you, as it is for me?" said Anna. "This assignment should be fun, although I'm sure it'll be hard work as well."

"Well, call me when you need me, Janet," replied Stefania as she bounced out the door. "I'm just in the cubicle round the corner."

Anna started studying the files. The London Philharmonic Orchestra was traveling with eighty-five musicians, and seventeen technicians, lighting, sound, music planners, and controllers of the instruments. She found out that Charlie Adams would be arriving forty-eight hours before the orchestra. BW had told her this, and she thought it would be helpful to have a couple of days with him and make sure they were on the same page.

She worked diligently for the next couple of days, reading through the plans for the performances, and schedules, tying them into rehearsal times, travel times, transportation, hotel reservations and food. Permits had already been granted for the free movement of the orchestra around the country, but she found that the Polish authorities had allocated two "assistants" to help with communications. Of course she knew that these "assistants" were supposed to spy on every movement of the orchestra and its management. It was part of the political scene in Poland. There was nothing to be done.

Chapter 17

It was just after eight in the morning when the doorbell rang. Anna was in the bathroom, putting on her makeup, when Stefania burst in.

"It's that handsome hunk Neil whatshisname again," she said excitedly. "He's here to pick you up."

"Really?" said Anna.

"Shall I ask him in?"

"Of course. You can't leave him out in the hall."

"Okay," said Stephanie. "Cor blimey. I didn't realize."

Anna finished her makeup and slipped back into her bedroom; she quickly dressed in another M&S outfit, light gray cotton skirt with a large white blouse covering all her curves, secured by a wide belt – Cossack style.

"Good morning, Neil," she said as she entered the lounge. "Would you like something to eat?"

"No, thanks, Janet. I had my breakfast a couple of hours ago."

"Well, this is a pleasant surprise," Anna said. "I had no idea you were coming to pick me up. Where are we going?"

"I have been asked to take you to the embassy to meet with the ambassador."

"Really? What fun."

Stefania stood wide-eyed watching the proceedings but couldn't resist. "Cor blimey. The ambassador himself?"

Anna and Neil both laughed.

"We're not going to Buckingham Palace," said Neil with a chuckle.

Maggie, who had left for work earlier, had left a pot of tea on the kitchen counter and Anna quickly popped some bread in the toaster and chatted pleasantly to Neil while she waited. She couldn't leave the flat on an empty stomach. It was one of her rules. Within a minute or so she was eating her toast and marmalade with a hot cup of tea, feeling content. As soon as she gulped down a second cup, she was ready to go.

"I will see you later at the office," said Anna to Stefania. "I don't suppose I'll be too long."

It only took ten minutes to drive to the British Embassy, located in a 19th-century palace at Number 1 Al.Roz, romantically named Alley of the Roses. Neil leaned out of the window of his car to speak to the guard at the entrance gates. He showed his ID and asked Anna to show hers.

The guard checked a clipboard, then waved them through into the spacious courtyard in front of the magnificent building also known as the Eliza Wielopolska residence.

"I will park and wait for you," said Neil.

"Thank you so much, Neil," replied Anna. She got out of the car, climbed the steps to the ornate front door of the embassy, and crossed the marble entryway, to a reception desk. "Janet Clark to see the ambassador," she said to a young blonde.

"Of course," came the reply. "Please take a seat." The receptionist was pointing to a long low sofa and chairs against a highly decorated wall.

Within a minute or two, she was being escorted up the wide staircase to ornate double doors, which opened into the ambassador's large office, overlooking the magnificent gardens of the former palace.

"Ah, Miss Clark. Thank you for coming to see me so early in the morning," said the ambassador, a giant of a man, who stood up behind his desk with a welcoming smile. Sir Miles Sanford, was six foot four, with a ruddy complexion and thinning gray hair. He was dressed in a black pin-stripe suit, white shirt and what looked like a military tie.

"I'm pleased to meet you. Please take a seat," he continued, pointing to a large armchair in front of his desk.

"I'm pleased to meet you, Sir Miles," responded Anna.

"Well, you're going to be a pretty busy lady during your

assignment in Poland," Sir Miles continued. "The London Philharmonic visit is extremely important, and is the first cultural exchange between our countries for over forty years. I'm sure you are aware it is extremely important that we get it right. However, apart from helping to make this tour a success, I have been briefed on the even more important aspect of your visit to Warsaw. I wanted to agree a game plan for delivery of a package that we hope you will obtain over the next few days." The ambassador paused, looking closely at Anna for her reaction.

"I'm very much aware of my responsibilities during this visit," responded Anna. "I will do my utmost. If I succeed, what should I do with it?"

"Let me explain that in detail," responded the ambassador. "Immediately after you have the package in your possession, you should bring it to my residence, situated in Bagatela Street. Here are the directions and a map." He leaned over his desk and pushed a folder towards Anna. "You should do this any time, day or night," he continued. "There are permanent guards to my residence and when you present your ID, they will allow you to enter. They will then fetch my assistant who is on call twenty-four hours a day. You will accompany him to my office safe, and will witness the package being placed in the safe. Once this has been achieved you are free to leave, and you will have completed your mission." Sir Miles paused and waited for Anna's response.

"Will your assistant know who I am, Sir Miles?" asked Anna.

"Yes, and he has received full instructions. Incidentally, he's been with me for twenty-five years, and is totally trustworthy," responded the ambassador before continuing. "If circumstances permit, and that will be your judgment, Neil Jordan will be available to drive you to my residence or anywhere else you wish to go."

"Thank you," said Anna "Your instructions are clear. I hope everything will go smoothly."

"Well, Miss Clark, I hope we can get this wrapped up before

the orchestra's arrival."

"That is my intention, Sir Miles," said Anna.

With that, Sir Miles stood up from behind his desk and held out his giant hand, indicating that the meeting was adjourned.

"So good to meet you, Miss Clark. Good luck, and I hope to see you again shortly."

"Thank you," said Anna putting her hand into the ambassador's large paw.

After saying polite goodbyes, she descended the staircase, and exited into the courtyard, where Neil was waiting. She looked at her watch. It wasn't even 9:30 a.m., so she would have plenty of time to do some work, before heading for the university.

Within fifteen minutes, she was seated behind her desk at the British Council offices, and worked diligently until 11:45. She told Stefania that she had some errands to do and would be back after lunch, and made her way along Aleje Jerozolimskie to Nowy Swiat Street, looking carefully about her, to see whether anyone was following. Anna was not going to take any chances. She jumped on a tram going south, and after couple of blocks jumped off at a traffic light, ran across the street and onto a moving tram going north, working her way through a number of passengers standing in the aisle until she was able to slump onto a seat, pulling out her floppy hat. She took her APA instant guidebook from her bag, and got off the tram at Swietokrzyska Street, again carefully checking to see if she was being followed. Armed with her tourist book, she walked up the street to the twin-towered Baroque Church of the Holy Cross, quickly moving through the nave and out of a side door on to Traugutta Street, across from the main entrance of Warsaw University. It was nearly 12:10 p.m. She entered the large green, tree-studded quadrangle, intently studying her guidebook, and watching the lunchtime crowds of students, faculty, and the citizens of Warsaw as they crisscrossed the green lawns. She saw no signs of the police, or the "ferrets," but just after 12:15 she recognized

Professor Kopacz walking towards her, talking intently to a young man, presumably one of his students. Anna felt a knot in her stomach. She was all poised to follow the procedure to make contact with the professor, but she couldn't possibly do that if he continued to talk to the student as they got nearer. Suddenly, when they were thirty meters away they stopped. The student shook hands with the professor and walked off. Professor Kopacz continued to walk in her direction. When he got within a couple of yards, she stepped forward with guidebook opened and in hand.

"Excuse me," she said in Polish, but adding a slight twang. "Could you tell me the way to number 1 Karowa Street?"

The professor stopped in his tracks, and looked at her closely.

"Number 1 Karowa?" he repeated, just to make sure he had heard right.

"Yes, Professor Kopacz," Anna replied, clearly indicating that she knew him and the code.

He deliberately took hold of her guidebook, looked at it, and made a theatrical gesture with his right arm pointing across the plaza.

"Are you available to meet for lunch on Saturday?" he asked, all the while looking at the guidebook and chatting to her pleasantly with a smile.

"Yes, Professor, where and what time?"

"Could you meet me at the Blikle Café on Nowy Swiat at one?"

"Absolutely, I'll be there."

The professor smiled again, returned the guidebook, gave a slight wave and walked off briskly. Looking around again to make sure she was not being followed, Anna casually walked across the plaza in the direction that the professor had indicated. After five minutes or so she circled round back to Krakowskie Przedmieście Street, jumped on a tram, and was back in her office before one. She realized that her blouse was sticking to her back and she was trembling slightly. She had a quick sandwich and a coffee in the British Council cafeteria and returned to her desk, calm again and eager to get on with her work for the orchestra visit.

She had already arranged with Maggie and Stefania to go out for a Friday-evening date, and they had dinner at a café in old town. Although Anna thought the food and service was pretty awful, they had a fun evening, helped by some cheap Polish wine. She was happy to flop into her bed by eleven, and fell into a deep sleep.

She was awake very early in the morning, thinking about her forthcoming visit with the professor, and then, as she did most nights, she started thinking about her brother Jan in prison, only a couple of miles away. She had to find a way to get him out and to safety. She hoped everything would go smoothly with her mission and then she could concentrate on Jan.

All three women had breakfast together, with Stefania looking the worse for wear. She wasn't used to drinking wine, and had consumed a good amount. She clearly had a nasty hangover this beautiful Saturday morning.

"What are your plans today, Janet?" asked Maggie.

"I think I will take in a little sightseeing today."

"Sightseeing?" responded Maggie. "Better you than me. I've got a date with Johnny Cole from the embassy. We're going to Lazienski Park, and I intend to relax in the sun, perhaps have a swim, and if Johnny behaves himself, maybe have him for dinner." They all laughed.

"Well, you're all set then," said Anna lightly. "What are you doing, Stefania?"

"I'm going back to bed for a few hours. I feel awful. But if I can sleep it off, I will catch up with some friends later today."

Anna took her time getting dressed. She wore loose-fitting jeans, comfortable walking shoes, and a loose-fitting denim shirt. Sunglasses and her floppy hat completed her touristy outfit. She certainly did not look glamorous, and was confident that she would not attract attention.

Saying goodbye to the girls, she went out into the sunshine of a lovely July day. It was going to be a scorcher. She decided to walk to 35 Nowy Swiat and the Café Blikle, one of the oldest and most famous in Warsaw.

It was one of Anna's favorite cafés, oozing old-world charm and elegance with high ceilings and polished old wood tables, old prints and pictures on the walls. She hoped she would not be recognized. It would be crowded at lunchtime with locals and tourists and as such was a good location to meet Professor Kopacz. As she had been trained, she surveyed the street behind and in front of her, to see if she was being followed. To throw off any "ferrets" that might be in the area, she dodged into one of the faculty buildings in the university and out through a rear entrance, and then in and out of a couple of stores, finally spending ten minutes in the ladies' room at an art gallery a few doors from the café.

Eventually she arrived at the Blikle and saw Professor Kopacz at a small table just inside the doorway.

"Good morning, Professor. What a wonderful day."

"Good morning to you," responded the professor. "I really should know your name before we start talking."

"I'll give you some background, just in case we have to coordinate our stories. My name is Janet Clark. I was born and raised in Australia. My mother is Maria Kowalski, and our story will say that she is an old friend of yours from Poznan going back to when you were small children. She left Poland for Australia in the 1930s, and you haven't seen each other since. She knew, however, that you are a professor of physics at Warsaw University, and suggested I looked you up. To complete the picture, I should tell you that I am living in London, and have been sent to work with the British Council for the next three weeks as liaison director for the London Philharmonic Orchestra tour of Poland."

"Very good, Janet. Your Polish is excellent, hardly an accent at all. But, first, I must ask you, how are my friends Erik and Krystyna?"

"I'm afraid I have some sad news, Professor" said Anna somberly. "Krystyna died in an accident while leaving Poland. Professor Keller was shot, but fortunately, he has recovered. I've spent quite a lot of time with him recently. He has discovered a British branch of his family, who thought he had died in the Holocaust. So now, he has a new family to get to know, but of course he has been through an extremely traumatic time over the past few months. That is why he is determined that all his efforts not be wasted. It is my job to make sure this happens," Anna concluded with a firm voice.

"My God. How terrible. Krystyna dead. I can't believe it. Such a beautiful and cultured lady, I knew her from her early student days when Erik and I were new to the faculty here. Erik of course is uniquely brilliant. I have to tell you, Janet, that by asking me for directions to number 1 Karowa Street, I knew which package I was to give to you. Everything is in code, you know."

Anna nodded.

"There is also a number 2 Karowa Street package, which he meticulously copied from his number-1 package. It contains all of his notes, theories, charts, graphs and mathematical calculations, but unlike number-1 package, it does not include conclusions, solutions, and verification checks. Erik was always concerned that his work would fall into the wrong hands, and gradually, over the past decade, he decided that the Soviet bloc was the wrong hands. Both packages would take months to decipher. Of course, Erik working from his own notes, would speed up things dramatically. Any outsiders however trying to decipher the number-2 package would probably spend months, until coming to the conclusion that it is missing the vital solutions." He paused and gave a little smile.

"So brilliant, my friend Erik, but life has dealt him some deadly blows over the past few months, the loss of his sons and now the loss of his beautiful wife, and of course the loss of his homeland. I'm so relieved, Janet, that he has been discovered by members of his family." He paused, quietly thinking, with tears welling up in his eyes.

"You know Erik is world-famous," the professor continued, still eager to talk about his friend. "He was one of a group of research physicists who worked on nuclei and elementary particles, biophysics and hyperlinks in physics, with other famous Polish professors Marian Danysz, Jerzy Pniewski and Andrzej Solton. He was one of the originators of hyperlinks in physics, which was developed at this university with the discoveries of the first hyper nucleus and double hyper nucleus."

"I am sorry, Professor, but I don't have a clue what you are talking about, way over my head," said Anna with a laugh.

"Of course excuse me," replied the professor. "I understand, but Erik also worked with Leopold Infeld, famous for his papers co-authored with Albert Einstein, on the theory of atomic nuclei and of elementary particles, solid-state theory and statistical physics. Erik is a truly brilliant physicist, whose work will form the basis of many new discoveries in years to come. Unfortunately because of his brilliance he was plucked from Warsaw and sent to work in Moscow for many years, with the promise, which was not kept, that his research would be used for peaceful purposes. He gradually got more and more disillusioned and with the murder of his two sons – we all know it was murder – he finally made the decision to leave for good. I don't blame him. I was probably the only person in whom he confided about his plans, and when it came time to leave, he left his papers with me and I promised that I would get them to him when the time is right. And, Janet, it seems now the time is right."

The professor smiled quietly, and then leaned down next to his chair and moved a battered brown briefcase towards Anna.

She felt her heart pounding. "Is that for me?" she asked.

"Of course. If we need to meet again, however, I want you to know that I teach a class at the faculty of physics at 11:00 a.m. on Mondays, Wednesdays and Fridays. If you need to see me again for any reason, I would suggest you come to one of my classes, which are always held in Lecture Hall 3. I usually finish about twelve, so if you come a few minutes before the end and stand at the back, we will be able to talk immediately after my lecture. I think that would be better than trying to meet elsewhere."

"Okay, Professor, if we do need to meet again I will keep that in mind."

"Good," said the professor. "Now how about ordering something for lunch?"

They both studied the menu. Anna was feeling more relaxed now, was quite hungry. The restaurant was bustling and full. "What do you recommend, Professor?" asked Anna.

Suddenly from nowhere, they appeared. Four men, dressed in casual clothes, looking like any other customers. Two of them grabbed the professor and Anna on their shoulders, as they flashed their badges. Anna thought her heart would stop beating, as she saw that they were members of the SB Secret Police – the "ferrets." One of them said to the professor, "We would like both of you to come with us. Don't make a fuss in the restaurant and we won't use force."

Chapter 18

"What's this all about?" said Anna, feeling the panic rising in her chest. "I'm with the British Council. You can't arrest me."

"We are not arresting you, miss," said the leading "ferret," a large man with thick gray hair, pock-marked face and bad teeth. "We just are asking you to come down to our offices for some questions."

Professor Kopacz was trembling. All the color had drained from his face and he was speechless. One of the "ferrets" picked up the briefcase and Anna's handbag, as the others firmly gripped the professor and Anna and marched them out of the restaurant. The restaurant had gone deadly quiet. Nobody said a word; and, as had become the norm during General Jaruzelski's martial law, everyone had their eyes down avoiding contact with the "ferrets."

There were two black cars waiting at the curb. The professor and Anna were hustled to the separate cars, and pushed into the rear seats. Anna was protesting, but to no avail. They weren't interested that she was British, they weren't interested that she was at the British Council, and her comment about the London Philharmonic Orchestra tour fell on deaf ears. The cars moved off into the traffic. The two "ferrets" in her vehicle said nothing. Her inquiries were met with stony silence.

She sat back in her seat and realized that she had to think, and think quickly. She was shaking with fear. Did they know who she was? Were they arresting her for murder? Did they already know that she was Anna Kaluza and not Janet Clark? She would have to stick to her story about her mother and her childhood relationship with Professor Kopacz. But what about the papers in the briefcase? She would have to adamantly deny that she had any connection to the briefcase or its content. But would that leave the professor holding the baby? These thoughts were flashing through her mind as they sped through the streets. Sirens were blaring now to clear the traffic, making Anna even more nervous. The two cars drove into the courtyard behind the nondescript building on Stefana Batorego that was SB headquarters. Both Anna and the professor were hustled out of the cars and marched towards the rear entrance. The professor was stumbling. He was pale and shaking. Anna tried to comfort him with a slight smile. He noticed, but did not respond. Then they were separated, and pushed down some stone stairs through two heavy doors and into a large basement corridor with heavy metal doors on both sides.

Anna's captors opened one of the doors, making a large metallic echoing sound, and pushed her into a room. The room was small, windowless, whitewashed, with a large light hanging over a desk with two metal chairs facing each other. Anna noticed a small camera, high up in one of the corners of the room. There was no two-way mirror as far as she could see, and no other furnishings or lighting.

As her disastrous situation started to sink in, Anna started shaking with fear. She couldn't control herself but was conscious of the little camera in the ceiling staring down at her. She had to focus. "*Stick to the script,*" she said to herself. *That's what they said in London.* She forced herself to concentrate. "*Stick to the script. Use your Polish language to create doubt,*" *that's what they said.* "*Misuse words and use words out of context. Change your accent where possible.*" That's it, those were her instructions. "*Stick to the script, don't vary, create doubt.*" That's what she should do. *Focus focus focus.* Suddenly with another metallic clang the door was unlocked and two men entered, one of whom was carrying her handbag, and the briefcase. Anna stood up.

"Please take a seat, Miss Clark," said the older of the two men in Polish – a tall thin man with a sallow complexion, watery blue eyes, and wearing an ill-fitting suit. He sat down on the other side of the desk to Anna and pulled down the light, which was on a pulley and was now hanging directly over her head. The rest of the room was in deep shadow. The other man stood by the door nearly out of sight.

"My name is Jan Molinski," he said. "I am a major in the Sluzba Bezpieczenstwa, the Polish Secret Service, and I have a few questions for you. I strongly recommend that you cooperate completely."

"Of course," replied Anna as firmly she could. "But you do realize that I am in Poland working at the British Council as a member of the British Foreign Office, as the liaison director for the London Philharmonic Orchestra tour. I have to strongly lodge a complaint. It is completely against international protocol to arrest me in this fashion." She said this with as much strength as possible but her plea was falling on deaf ears.

"Please state your name, nationality, date and location of your birth," continued Molinski, ignoring Anna's protestations.

"My name is Janet Mary Clark. I am an Australian citizen, and I was born in Sydney Australia on 26th of June 1940."

"Have you been in Poland before?"

"No, this is my first visit."

"You speak nearly perfect Polish."

"My mother is Polish and came from Poznan. We spoke Polish at home. She only ever spoke to me in Polish and so I learned the language fluently at an early age."

"What is your mother's name and where did she come from in Poland?"

"Her name is Maria Kowalski. She was born and grew up in Poznan until she left for Australia in the 1930s."

"How do you know Professor Kopacz?"

"I don't. He was a childhood friend of my mother, when she was a little girl in Poznan," said Anna, keeping to her script. "My mother gave me his name and suggested I looked him up on my visit to Warsaw."

"And how did you look him up?"

"I just went to the university and by chance bumped into him."

"By chance!" said Molinski with sarcasm in his voice. "Just bumped into him, did you?"

"I did," said Anna. "And he suggested we meet for lunch, which is why I was at the Café Blikle."

"And why were you having lunch with him? What were you there to discuss?" said Molinski, now leaning in towards Anna.

"I don't know. We were just going to talk. He was keen to hear about my mother and catch up on old times, through me."

"And what were you talking about before we arrived?" asked Molinski.

"Nothing really," said Anna, beginning to feel the pressure. "I was just telling him about my mother, our lives in Australia, nothing much really," Anna continued rather lamely.

"Do you know Professor Keller?" shot back Molinski, surprising Anna.

"No. No. I've never heard of him," said Anna stammering a bit.

"I would like to see the contents of your handbag," said Molinski, changing the subject much to Anna's relief.

The other guard stepped forward with Anna's handbag and emptied the contents onto the desk. Molinski pushed the contents around in circles on the desk. He picked up her passport and looked through it carefully, without saying a word. He read the letter of introduction from the British Foreign Office that was folded inside the passport. He looked at the guidebook and shook out the pages to see if anything would come out. He opened her small purse shaking out loose coins, some zlotys, and two five-pound notes. He poked at a packet of polo mints, and looked carefully at the slim wallet containing her English credit cards – Diners Club and American Express. He picked up her camera. "Did you take any photographs?"

"Yes, I took a few sightseeing photographs, yesterday," said

Anna.

Molinski looked at the small pack of Kleenex, her lipstick and powder compact. He then handed her Kodak camera over to the other guard with a nod.

"All right, Miss Clark. Now tell me what was in the briefcase that Professor Kopacz was handing over to you?"

Anna felt herself trembling with fear, and her back was clammy. She tried to remain calm. "Professor Kopacz did not hand me any briefcase," she responded.

"We saw him push the briefcase toward you," said Molinski firmly. "What is in that briefcase, Miss Clark?"

"I don't know," replied Anna. "He didn't push the briefcase towards me or if he did, I didn't see him do it. The professor never mentioned his briefcase. I don't know what you're talking about," she said with a little panic in her voice.

"Were you taking delivery of something, maybe some papers, books, notes?" said Molinski, his voice rising.

At that moment, the door to the little room opened with a clang, and a shaft of light illuminated everything. A tall dark man in a blue suit came into the room and whispered something to the guard, and in that brief beam of light, Anna recognized the man as Roman Krinsky, the head of the SB, commonly known as the "King of the Ferrets." The dashing, handsome Krinsky was the son of a famous prewar Hungarian actress and a Polish count, a war hero. He was said to be the second most powerful man in Poland, and tipped as a successor to General Jaruzelski. The Polish public knew him for his ruthless reputation, and his womanizing exploits and scandals. He was married to a former Russian model who lived on his country estate near the Village of Lubice with his three sons. He had great charm and a flashing smile. Anna had never met him, but in her work as an ORBIS escort, she had often seen him at various government events when she was dropping off visiting dignitaries. His photo was also always in the papers, and he was often seen on television,

warning the public of subversive elements, and foreign inter-
ference in Poland's national affairs. He had played an important
role in helping General Jaruzelski impose martial law and clamp
down on the Solidarity movement. Like all Poles, Anna was very
afraid of him. Why was he coming into this interrogation?

"Well, Miss Clark," continued Molinksi, "if you're not going
to cooperate, we shall just have to see what's in the briefcase that
the professor gave to you."

"He wasn't giving it to me. I've told you, I've got no idea
what's in the briefcase. It belongs to the professor, and I assumed
it was just his work," said Anna pleadingly.

Molinski signaled for the briefcase to be brought to the desk.
"Well, we shall see," he said threateningly.

He released the clasp in the middle of the old battered
briefcase, opened it wide and turned it upside down so the
contents fell out onto the desk. Anna thought she was going to
pass out, she was so frightened. She felt beads of sweat running
down her back. There was no way out, she was caught and she
could very well end up in prison with Jan.

The contents spilled out on the desk. Anna nearly jumped for
joy. There were no papers, no notes, just two books on Poland's
churches, a couple of guidebooks in English, and maps of Poland,
Warsaw and Poznan. *Oh my God*, thought Anna. *The professor was
doing a dry run, just to make sure he was not being watched. How
clever.*

Molinski was talking. "Well, you see, Miss Clark, the professor
was giving you his briefcase after all, and apparently some guidebooks for your stay in Poland. How kind of him," he said
maliciously.

"I had no idea," said Anna truthfully. "How sweet of him."

She saw Krinsky moving in the shadows and whispering to
the guard again. He then knocked softly on the door. It swung
open, bringing in the shaft of light once again, as Krinsky left the
room. The guard came over and whispered something in

Molinski's ear.

"So, Miss Clark," said Molinski. "We appreciate your cooperation. I'm sure you understand, we are living in difficult times in Poland and we have to be very careful of subversive acts against the state." He then gave Anna a sickly smile. "You are, of course free to go now, but I am taking the film from your camera and will return the briefcase to Professor Kopacz." He stood up, pushing the light back up on its pulley towards the ceiling and widening the arc of light around the tiny room. Anna was so nervous and relieved she wasn't sure she could stand up steadily. She pulled herself together.

"Thank you," she said politely, but shaking with relief. The guard came to the desk and put all the guidebooks back into the briefcase and the contents of her handbag back together, which he then handed to Anna. "Please follow me, miss," he said, leading the way out of the room. Anna breathed a sigh of relief, as he led her up the steps into the courtyard.

"If you walk a couple of hundred meters to your left, you will come to Marszalkowska Street, which I think will take you wherever you want to go. Enjoy the rest of your day," he said as he quickly turned back into the building. Anna exited the courtyard and followed his instructions, wanting to put as much distance between herself and the deadly experience.

After jumping on a tram, Anna was at her apartment building within twenty minutes. She was still shaky and nervous, and was fumbling for the keys to the building, when Neil appeared at her side.

"Where the hell have you been?" he said testily. "I'm supposed to be looking after your security, and I lost you completely this morning."

"Oh, Neil," said Anna "I'm so pleased to see you. I was arrested by the 'ferrets.'"

"The who?" replied Neil, clearly confused.

"I'm sorry," said Anna. "The SB, secret police, the locals call them the 'ferrets,'" she continued with tears welling in her eyes.

Seeing her in distress, Neil calmed down. "You're trembling, Janet. What happened?"

"Let's go upstairs. I'll tell you the whole story."

They climbed the three floors and Anna shakily opened the door to the apartment. She called out Stefania's name, but received no response. Stefania must have felt better and had left the apartment. Anna motioned for Neil to sit down with her on the sofa. She was still feeling weak. She explained how she'd had a date with a professor at Warsaw University for lunch, a friend of her mother's, and out of nowhere the "ferrets" had arrived and arrested them both. They'd been taken to the SB headquarters, where she'd been interrogated. At the end of the interrogation, she was let go without explanation, other than thanks for her cooperation, "in these difficult times."

"That's outrageous," said Neil. "They can't just arrest an employee of the British Foreign Office. I think you'll have to tell BW on Monday, as I'm sure you want to lodge a formal complaint. I know the country is still under martial law, and the secret police have been particularly brutal, and paranoid, but they can't pounce on British nationals like this. It could be quite a scandal."

"I'd rather not make a big fuss now," said Anna, nervous that she would have to give a more detailed explanation to BW. "Please, Neil, don't tell anyone." Tears welled up in her eyes.

"Are you sure? You are still a little shaky. That's a terrible ordeal to go through," he said, reaching out for her hand to comfort her. Anna looked into his deep blue eyes, and saw his genuine concern. She noticed that he was dressed casually for the weekend. A white golf shirt, blue jeans and canvas boat shoes with no socks. Stefania was right, with his dark good looks and strong physique, Neil was a hunk.

"Do you mind if I go and have a shower," Anna said. "I feel grubby and sweaty after that ordeal."

"Of course not, you go ahead and I'll make you a nice cup of tea."

"Oh, that would be lovely. I won't be long,"

She climbed into the bath and turned on the shower. It didn't have much pressure, but the steady stream of hot water immediately started to relax her. She was washing herself with a flannel and soap, and suddenly felt totally fatigued, and leaned against the wall as she couldn't stop tears from gushing down her face. She stood there for quite a few minutes just sobbing, but gradually regained her composure. She climbed out of the bath, and put on her toweling robe. Tightening the belt, and drying her hair with a hand towel, she walked back into the living room. Neil had a pot of tea and a plate of biscuits on the coffee table in front of the sofa.

"Milk and sugar?" he asked.

"Mmm, thank you." Anna drank the hot tea thankfully, realizing how thirsty she was.

"Wow. It looks like you needed that. Have another cup," said Neil.

She gulped it down, and then leaned back into the sofa feeling the warmth of the liquid coursing through her stomach.

"Feeling better?" asked Neil.

"Yes. Much better." Her eyes were still puffy and red, but she was beginning to relax.

"You've had a really tough day. I might've helped, if you hadn't given me the slip this morning. I don't usually lose my charges, but I've got a feeling you've been well trained. I saw you dodging in and out of buildings on Nowy Street, but then I lost you. So I came back here and waited. I was pretty pissed, actually."

"I'm sorry, Neil" said Anna. She reached out and touched his hand in appreciation for his concern.

"Well, you can relax now, Janet," he said, gently pulling her towards him, and putting her head on his shoulders. She knew she was vulnerable, but she felt safe and warm in his arms. She closed her eyes. He stroked her hair and her cheek for a minute or two, and then leaned down, lifted her chin and kissed her softly on the mouth. She responded in kind, wanting more. He continued to kiss her on the mouth and then on her neck, and then her ear and her shoulder. He moved her body backwards onto the sofa, and knelt beside her, still kissing her, as he put his hand inside her robe and found her breasts. Her head was back, and her body arched toward him, as his mouth kissed her nipples and moved its way down her body opening her robe completely. He peeled off his golf shirt, undid his belt and dropped his jeans. Now he was kissing her firmly, as his tongue found hers and she hungrily responded. His hand was now moving down her body, caressing her tummy and then the inside of her legs. As his fingers started probing, she felt the wetness rising, and breathing heavily she pulled him on top of her, kissing him passionately, and letting out a whimper as he entered her. It had been a while, but Anna's animal sexual instincts were still there. Neil was strong, and Anna could feel his muscular arms around her and the strength in his body as she wrapped her legs around him. For the next two hours they made love, eventually landing up in a sweaty laughing embrace. And then dozing in each other's arms.

"My God, Janet. You are wonderful," he whispered in her ear. "You have an incredible body, but no one would know seeing you in those baggy clothes."

"It's better that way. I'm not here to be noticed, in fact exactly the opposite."

"I'll ask no questions then," said Neil with a somewhat knowing smile.

"I think we should both take a shower now," said Anna, changing the subject. "I'm starving as well. I had no lunch you know. How about taking me to dinner?"

"What a great idea."

They both got up from the sofa and headed to the bathroom

totally naked and admiring each other's bodies. Anna was nearly five foot ten, but Neil was probably six foot one, and she felt happy and comfortable looking up into his eyes. They showered together, soaping each other, and then dried off. Anna put on her bra and panties, picked up the rest of her clothes, and padded into her tiny bedroom, while Neil went back into the living room to get dressed. Leaving the M&S outfits in her closet, she put on a tight pair of jeans, and an apple green V-neck T-shirt which showed off her cleavage. She took a couple of minutes to add perfume and a little light makeup, and for the first time in days she felt feminine again.

"Wow," said Neil as she walked into the living room. "That's better. What a transformation."

Anna laughed.

"I'll take you to a little tavern in old town where they serve Polish food, but not that heavy stuff that they usually shovel down your throat. This is really good, you'll love it."

"Sounds fun. Especially with a man who knows his way around town." Anna threaded her arm into his as they closed the apartment door and headed down the stairs.

It was still hot but had cooled down a little from the brutal heat at midday, and a light breeze had come up. They took a slow walk up Senatorska Street into Old Town where they headed for Torbyd Tawerna, which Anna knew well.

It was early and the restaurant was not too full, so they were able to get a small table in the shaded garden overlooking the main Square Rynek Starego Miasta. They ordered a couple of Żywiec beers while they examined the menu. Anna took this opportunity to ask Neil about his background. He was two years younger than Anna, had joined the army at the age of eighteen and, after five years, transferred to OAS – Special Operations, eventually becoming an instructor on counterterrorism, security and VIP protection. He left the army after completing twenty years, but was soon recruited by the Foreign Office for special security assignments which included this mission to Warsaw, primarily to protect Anna.

"Part of my training, Janet," Neil said, "is not to ask questions but just to follow my mission instructions. But of course, I know you're not just here to facilitate the London Philharmonic tour. You seem to be well trained, because there are very few of my 'marks' that can give me the slip while under my surveillance. You are a pretty cool lady," he said with a grin.

"Well, thank you, kind sir," said Anna. "It's good to know that you are here to protect me."

The waiter came with their beers. "Do you know anything about Polish food?" asked Neil.

"A little," replied Anna. "My mother cooked her favorite Polish dishes for years when I was growing up. I never liked any of them."

"So, should I make some recommendations?"

"Oh, that would be great."

"Well, because it's so hot, I think we should keep it light, so I suggest, herring in cream, or oil and vinegar if you prefer, and then you might like to try the national dish, Bigos, which is sauerkraut with pieces of meat & sausage. They do that very well here, and it is not at all heavy."

"Sounds lovely, I will definitely take your advice," replied Anna, delighted that Neil had chosen some of her favorite Polish foods.

He ordered cold beet soup, followed by Golonka – pork knuckles cooked with vegetables. They had a very pleasant meal, chit chatting about their past, likes and dislikes, jokes about BW, but never getting too deep or too serious. A couple more beers and then coffee and schnapps finished off their meal.

The evening was warm and balmy as they walked back arm-in-arm to Anna's apartment building. On the entrance steps, Neil leaned in to kiss Anna. "I've had a wonderful time," he said, as he put his arms around her waist and pulled her towards him.

"So have I," replied Anna, as she put her fingers on his lips to stop him kissing her. "But I have got a hectic schedule over the next couple weeks, and I really don't want to complicate my life right now. It's been wonderful, Neil. You're a great guy and I hope you understand," she said with a warm smile.

"Yeah, I guess so," said Neil. "But I'll be around all day tomorrow watching you."

"Please, don't do that, Neil. Take the day off. I won't come to any harm and it is too hot for you to be chasing around Warsaw. However, I would really like to have you and your car available on Monday, if possible."

"Of course," said Neil. "Just tell me where and when."

"Could you meet me at 12:15 p.m. on Monday at the university? Please park on Obozne Street."

"Okay, I'll be there, and I will leave you alone tomorrow."

Anna leaned forward and gave him a soft kiss on his cheek. "Thank you. You are a darling. Goodnight."

She opened the door to the building, climbed the stairs and was relieved to find that neither Maggie nor Stefania had come home yet. It was still early but Anna was exhausted. As she was getting ready for bed, she thought about Professor Kopacz. She hoped he had been released. She felt sure he was giving her a message about meeting him after class. Anyway, she would find out on Monday.

Within twenty minutes she was in bed and fast asleep.

Chapter 19

Jan woke with a start. It was not yet light. He could hear the heavy boots marching down the concrete floor of the lower-level of block four at Mokotów prison. He shivered under his thin blanket, on the iron bedstead of his cell number 2840. An eight-by-twelve ice box, with a tiny basin, a wooden chair, small metal table and a hole in the floor to relieve himself. The only light came from a small barred window high up in the wall. He had been in this hellhole for nearly four months, after being released from the prison hospital in Kraków, and transferred to Warsaw. He had lost thirty pounds, and was becoming a mere skeleton of a man, with long matted hair, forcibly cut every six weeks, and unshaven for two weeks at a time. His emaciated body showed the signs of torture, bruising and red welts across his back, cigarette burns on the backs of his hands, and swelling around his half-closed eyes, as well as his feet and ankles. He prayed the boots would keep marching down the corridor. The thought of another interrogation nearly brought him to tears.

He didn't know how much longer he could take the abuse. Suddenly, his heart skipped a beat. The boots stopped outside his cell door. He shivered in fear, as the metal door clanked open and two guards came in. They wordlessly unlocked the shackle around his leg connected to a ring in the wall. "Stand up, Kaluza," said one of the guards, dragging him to his feet. "Quick, march," the guard continued, pushing Jan ahead of him and out into the corridor. As he half staggered past the other cell doors, he could hear prisoners moaning, whimpering and in some cases yelling in maniacal outbursts. At the end of the corridor two other guards unlocked an ironclad doorway, and he was pushed half stumbling up a staircase to the next floor, and then along another short corridor, to one of the interrogation rooms.

He stumbled along in fear, knowing what was coming. He was

pushed into Interrogation Room 3 where another guard grabbed him and shackled him to a large metal chair. A white spotlight was aimed at the chair. He was sitting there, blinking in the bright light. He could hardly see anything else in the room.

"Good morning," said the officer from the shadows. Jan recognized the voice of his tormentor, Major Larovski. He knew this was going to be another brutal session. "Prisoner 7747. This is your last chance to answer our questions. If you don't cooperate now, you will be subject to persuasive devices that will make our previous discussions seem like a tea party. It is up to you. Choose life or death."

Jan was shaking so hard, he didn't think he could speak. He'd been through quite a few of these sessions and genuinely couldn't answer the questions. They just didn't believe him.

"Do you know the whereabouts of your sister, Anna Kaluza?"

"No, I haven't seen her since before Kraków. I've told you this many times. I was in the prison hospital and then transferred to Warsaw. I don't know what happened to her and I don't know where she is."

"I shall ask you again, prisoner 7747. Do you know the where-abouts of your sister Anna?" With that, one of the guards cracked a short leather whip across Jan shoulders, drawing blood. Jan gasped in pain.

"No. I really don't know where she is," Jan managed to answer in a cracking, husky voice.

"Do you know Professor Erik Keller?"

"As I have already told you many times, I don't know Professor Keller, and I've never met him."

"I shall ask you again. Do you know Professor Erik Keller?" Before Jan could answer, a guard stepped forward and swung a withering heavy punch to his stomach. He gasped for air, and nearly threw up. Tears were running down his face. He couldn't breathe, and certainly couldn't talk.

"Answer me, you little prick," yelled Larovski.

"No. I don't know him," said Jan in a hardly audible whisper.

Major Larovski said something to two other guards in the room and they wheeled a metal table towards Jan; numerous electrical wires were hanging down from the table, with clips on the ends. They attached two of the cables to Jan's testicles, and two more to his nipples, and finally two more to his toes.

"This may be farewell, prisoner 7747. You've had your chance." He nodded to one of the guards, who switched on the electric current. As the power increased, Jan let out an agonizing scream...

Anna awoke, and shot up in bed. Her nightie was wet through, and sweat droplets were rolling down her face and neck. It was another nightmare, perhaps the worst that she had about Jan. She sank back on her pillow, terrified and yet relieved that none of it was real. But she wasn't sure. Maybe Jan was going through some sort of hell like this, less than two miles away from her comfortable bed. She lay quietly thinking as she recovered, and her breathing returned to normal. She had to get Jan out. But how? Who could she turn to? She racked her brains as the dawn light started to creep into her room. She got up and had a long hot shower, and by the time she got back to her bedroom she felt better.

After a leisurely breakfast with Maggie and Stefania, while they recounted their adventures of the night before, Anna got ready for her day out. She explained that she would continue her sightseeing, to incredulity and a low moan from the girls.

It was still hot but appeared to be cooler than the oppressive heat of the day before. Far less humid. Anna dressed in her usual disguise. She borrowed a baseball cap from Stefania and stuffed her floppy hat into her handbag. By 10:00 a.m. she was on her way.

As she left the apartment building she immediately saw the "ferrets." One opposite, leaning against a wall and smoking a cigarette, and another one just as obvious about a hundred meters to the right of the building. She ignored them and started walking quickly, this time through a couple of side streets to Elektoraina Street leading to Al. Jana Pawla. There she quickly engaged in her usual tactics, on and off trams in different directions. After about twenty minutes she was pretty confident that she had given the "ferrets" the slip. She took a tram south to the Warsaw Central Station on the corner of Al. Jerozolimskie and Jana Pawla, where she took off her sweater and stuffed it in her bag, and swapped Stefania's baseball hat for her floppy sun hat. She went to the ticket office and purchased a round-trip day ticket to Zyradow, which she had done countless times before. She had left herself slightly less than five minutes to get on the train and hurried down the platform, and making sure she was not being followed, jumped into a carriage. It being Sunday morning the train was not crowded. Once the train had left the station for the forty-five kilometer trip to Zyradow, Anna relaxed, looking out of the window as the train moved slowly out of Warsaw and into the sunlit countryside, taking in the colorful carpet of fields and meadows, the yellow rape crop, the ochre color of wheat and the dark green squares of growing vegetables. Avenues of beautiful trees and the endless greenery of forests and meadows reminded her of how beautiful Poland was in the summer. The train stopped a couple of times, but eventually arrived at Zyradow within an hour of leaving Warsaw. She descended from the train surveying the passengers to see whether she could see any "ferrets." There were none. She made her way through the station into Pilsudski Square. There, she found a rather battered taxi and instructed the driver to take her a few kilometers north to the village of Wiskikti. She wouldn't risk going all the way, so she paid off the cab in the central square and set off out of the village for the three kilometer walk to Kaskia Lodge, the former Kaluza-Zyradowski family estate. She passed little village houses and Skaksen buildings where thatchers were at work repairing a roof, and old men and women were sitting on chairs outside their houses, enjoying the sun and talking animatedly to each other. The last kilometer took her through the tree-lined drive up to the main house. When she arrived at the gravel-covered circular courtyard she turned left towards the gardener's cottage to find her mother. The lodge was looking a little decrepit and in need of repair, but still it still retained its air of majestic beauty. Not a soul in sight. Maybe the nuns and the orphans were at mass.

As she approached the gardener's cottage, she recognized the figure of her mother bent over her vegetable garden. Dressed in a long cotton skirt and matching top, with a traditional peasant scarf covered by a large floppy sun hat on her head, she was engrossed in her garden. Anna did not wish to surprise or shock her as she approached from behind so she called out softly, "Mother."

Maria turned, looked up and seeing Anna, a broad smile covered her tanned face. Still beautiful at seventy-three, but with her long blonde hair now turned white, and her body looking thin and fragile. Tears came to her eyes. She called out, "Anna! Thank God... You're safe. I've been so worried. I didn't know what had happened to you. Where have you been? What's been going on?" The words tumbled out as she took Anna into her arms and hugged her. The tears were running down her face, a sign of emotion that Anna had never seen before from her aristocratic Polish mother. Maria had always been proud, and strong, and had shown little emotion or affection for her children. Anna had always sought her approval and love, but she knew that it was only through Maria's extraordinary strength, that she and her brother Jan had survived the collective farm labor camp in Russia, the British Army camp in Uganda, and the first couple of tough years in Australia.

"I'm fine, Mother, there's nothing to worry about," said Anna encouragingly, feeling for the first time that she had to be the strong one. She had to learn to think differently about her frail, ageing mother.

"But we had the police here. And then those people from the SB," she said. "They said they were looking for you, and that they had arrested Jan. Something about smuggling..." She left the question hanging in the air.

"Come on, Mother, let's go inside and then we can talk," Anna responded, not really answering her mother's questions.

They went into the former gardener's cottage, and Anna saw the familiar furniture; many items taken from the Kaluza family home. Her mother, the former mistress of the seven-bedroom lodge and its eleven-hundred-acre estate, now lived in this modest home and felt very fortunate that she was able to do so. She was no longer the music teacher to the orphans and nuns who lived in Kaskia Lodge, although she helped out from time to time and organized and led the annual Christmas carol concert.

"Do you have any news of Jan, Mother?" asked Anna.

"I know he is in Mokotów prison," replied Maria. "The police were looking for you and said they had already arrested Jan. I can't believe that Jan would be involved in any smuggling ring. He would never do that. But they said that they had identified a group of employees at ORBIS, and they told me to inform them if you made any contact with me. Sister Agnes told me that there were a couple of SB people sitting in a car at the entrance to the driveway off and on for six weeks from the end of February when this whole mess began. Where have you been, Anna, and what have you done to your hair, and your eyes?" said Maria, apparently just registering the changes to her daughter's appearance.

"I've been moving around, Mother, and staying with friends. I changed the color of my hair and I'm wearing contact lenses to change the color of my eyes so that I'm not easily identified. Of course I had nothing to do with any smuggling ring, nor did Jan. But I'm avoiding the police and the SB until they can clear this thing up and realize that Jan and I are innocent," she said rather unconvincingly. "I'm reaching out to some of my contacts, in the hope that I can get Jan released," she continued in an optimistic tone. "Now, Mother, let's have some lunch together, and you can tell me all your news."

"Well, I've got some lovely salad here, and some ham. So maybe I'll make a little picnic, and we can eat it up on the hill."

"That's a wonderful idea; the weather is so beautiful, and it is not so hot today," said Anna eager to change the subject.

They busied themselves in the tiny kitchen, making a nice ham salad with some homemade dressing. Maria had the remains of a small chocolate cake which she said the nuns had given her on Friday, and she cut off two pieces to add to their picnic lunch. She had a bottle of mineral water in her tiny refrigerator and put everything into a small wicker picnic basket that Anna knew dated from the 1930s.

Anna grabbed the picnic basket as they made their way up the hill behind the lodge, where Maria laid out a blanket in the shade of the silver-birch trees on the edge of a densely wooded area. They sat down together and enjoyed their lunch, while Maria reminisced with her familiar story of how she and Anna's father and some friends had been having a picnic lunch a few days before Nazi Germany invaded Poland and started their bombing campaign of Warsaw. Anna's father, Marius, had left to join his regiment, and Maria, who at that time was pregnant with Anna, never saw him again. Anna also encouraged Maria to talk about Kaskia Lodge and the orphanage, the nuns, children, and the work they all did to maintain the large estate. Maria did not question Anna further on her problems with the SB, apparently satisfied with Anna's explanation. But, Anna realized that her mother was living in her own little world, ageing and apparently not in good health. She really struggled to walk up the hill, and was short of breath by the time they got to the top. She explained to Anna that she had suffered from a bout of bronchitis in March and was not really over it yet. They had a pleasant afternoon together talking and reminiscing. Anna found out that Jan's wife, Ava, had visited Maria and told her that she'd been allowed to visit Jan in prison, and that he was in good health although rather pale and thin. That was only four weeks ago, so Anna was relieved to hear that news. Jan had been suspended from his job at ORBIS, but Ava was receiving at least part of his salary, so she and the boys were surviving. She had also had numerous visits from the police, and the SB, all looking for Anna.

As the afternoon wore on, they wandered back down the hill, left the picnic things at the cottage and walked around the lodge and the grounds. Anna could see the fabric of the building needed considerable repair and the formal gardens had long since gone, but there was a large area of vegetable garden, which was well maintained. They saw a few of the orphans, walking on the grounds in the distance, but Anna was relieved they were not close enough to see her or greet Maria.

When it was time to go, Anna was again surprised at the warmth of her mother's hugs and kisses, and to see the tears welling up in her eyes. Anna promised Maria that she would keep in touch and would let her know if there was any further news on Jan.

The sun had disappeared behind some clouds, and the air had become heavy without the slightest breeze, as Anna made her way back to Wiskitki, where she caught a bus into Zyradow. She waited about thirty minutes for the next train to Warsaw, keeping a careful watch out for any "ferrets." However she was confident she was not being followed as she boarded the train. She passed the journey thinking about Jan in Mokotów, a terrible prison, known for its torture and severe conditions, whether in use by the Poles, the German Gestapo, or the Russians. The only encouraging news was from Ava. She would love to see her and the children. But she realized it was far too dangerous, since she was clearly at the top of the wanted list of the SB. She was also worried about her mother, living alone and in declining health.

So as she made her way back to the apartment, it was with a heavy heart, and she was overwhelmed by thoughts of what she could do to remedy the situation. She just got back before the sky opened up, and a violent thunderstorm drenched the city.

Chapter 20

Anna was up early on Monday morning, conscious that this could be a big day, make or break. Today she might succeed in her mission. The worst-case scenario could lead to her arrest, and she could maybe find herself in the Mokotów prison with Jan. That very thought made her head throb. She knew the "ferrets" would be outside watching for her, and so she suggested to Maggie and Stefania that they all go to work together. She borrowed a canvas holdall from Maggie, stuffed in her sneakers, socks, faithful M&S jeans, and a white blouse, and borrowed Stefania's baseball cap and backpack once again.

"What do you want that lot for?" asked the ever-inquisitive Stefania.

"I've got an errand to do at lunchtime, and I will need to change into some casual clothes," said Anna with a tone to discourage further questions. Maggie looked at her quizzically but said nothing.

It was just after 8:00 a.m. when they left their apartment. Anna immediately saw two "ferrets" about fifty yards from their apartment building, talking to each other, and further down the road, a black car with two men in it, certainly another "ferret" team. She felt confident having the two girls with her. They crossed through Ogród Saski Park to Marszalkowska Street where Maggie peeled off to go to the British Consulate offices, as Anna and Stefania walked on to Jerozolimskie Street and the British Council building. Stefania was chattering away, oblivious to Anna's thoughts and concerns. She felt certain that Professor Kopacz had been guiding her on how to meet up with him at the university, and she had taken in his instructions. But would he be there, lecturing as normal? Maybe he was in jail or being interrogated by the SB. Was it possible that they had let him go at the same time as Anna? If he was going to be giving his lecture as usual today, would he have the Keller papers with him? Wasn't it likely that he would be too nervous to do anything so soon after having been arrested? On the other hand, perhaps he would like to get rid of those papers as quickly as possible. All these thoughts were racing through Anna's mind. As they entered the courtyard of the British Council offices, Anna turned around and saw the two "ferrets" who had been following them since they left their apartment building. She knew that they would be there all day, waiting to see if she left the building. If she was going to get to the university she had to find a secure way to leave the British Council offices.

Anna spent the next few hours working diligently on the plans for the orchestra tour. She knew that Charlie Adams would be arriving tomorrow, followed a couple of days later by the full orchestra and entourage. As of tomorrow, Anna realized, she would be extremely busy, probably sixteen hours a day.

At 11:30, she left her office with the canvas holdall, and told Stefania she would be back in a couple of hours. She went to the ladies' room, and changed into her casual street clothes inside one of the stalls. Luckily, no one else was in the toilet area.

However, as she descended the stairs she walked right into Emily Paige- Madison. "We do have a dress code here you know, Janet," she said haughtily looking at Anna with disdain.

"I know, Miss Paige-Madison," responded Anna, "but I have to go out on a couple of errands for the London Philharmonic, and I didn't want to get my office clothes dirty," she continued without giving any real explanation.

Miss Paige-Madison let out a "humph" but didn't pursue Anna further. When she got to the ground floor, she asked the receptionist to send her holdall to her office, and then she went out the rear entrance into the courtyard, hopeful that there would be some vehicle from whom she could get a ride towards the university, without awakening the "ferrets'" interest. She was lucky. A gray van was making a stationery delivery, and Anna saw the driver coming out of the building and climbing into the driving seat. She quickly moved over to the van, gave him a big smile and asked whether he could give her lift into town. "Nowy Street will be fine for me," Anna said.

"All right, love, hop in," replied the jovial, red-faced driver. Anna climbed into the passenger seat and, as they left the building and entered Al. Jerozolimskie Street, she slid back into the seat and bent down as if to search for something in her bag. Five minutes later, the driver pulled up in the middle of Nowy Street and, thanking him with another big smile, Anna got out, and quickly jumped a tram going north.

She walked into the quadrangle of the university at noon and headed for the physics building. There was a lot of activity going on in the quadrangle, with large groups of students gathering in one corner. She was alarmed to see "Solidarity" banners being unfurled, and a significant police presence with a large number of SB plainclothes officers scattered around. *Oh God*, she thought, *This is the last thing I need today.* The demonstration, however, had not yet got underway, and she hoped she could get her mission completed before the demonstration escalated. As instructed by Professor Kopacz, she entered the physics building, easily identified Lecture Hall 3 and sneaked into the back just as the lecture was finishing and students were packing up their books and papers and filing out of the room. Three students had moved down to the front and were asking Kopacz questions. The rest of the lecture room emptied out, and Anna noticed the professor had seen her. As he disposed of the students' questions, one by one they gathered up their papers and left. At the same time Anna approached the professor.

"Janet," he said. "I see you understood my instructions."

"I was really worried, Professor."

"Me too. But I took comfort from the fact that I had only delivered some guidebooks to you, and even the SB could not find a reason to continue to detain me. They were suspicious, though. They'll be keeping an eye on me."

"There seems to be some sort of demonstration building up outside," said Anna anxiously.

"I heard something of the sort was going to happen today. You must be very careful; the SB is everywhere, so get away from the university as quickly as possible," said the professor. "I think this is what you're looking for," he said. Leaning down to his briefcase, he brought out a wad of papers, about five inches thick, wrapped up in twine. Anna opened her backpack, and the professor put the papers in.

"Thank you, Professor. If I need to contact you again, how can I get hold of you?"

"The safest way, would be to leave a telephone message with my close friend and colleague, Professor Galinsky. He'll pass on your message." The professor wrote down the telephone number on a piece of paper and handed it to Anna. "Please only contact me if it is extremely important or a dire emergency. I think you understand that I am being constantly watched, and I don't want to land up at SB headquarters again."

"Of course, Professor. I fully understand. I know that Professor Keller would be extremely grateful for the help that you have given me. Maybe we will meet again someday and we will be able to look back on this exchange with pride."

"I hope you're right, Janet," responded the professor with a smile. "Now get going. And good luck."

Anna hauled the backpack onto her shoulders and headed out of the lecture room at a fast pace. As she left the building and entered the quadrangle, she could see that the demonstration had started. A speaker was whipping up hundreds of students. They were chanting "Solidarity" and waving banners. The whole demonstration was now surrounded by a ring of police with riot shields, interspersed with easily identifiable "ferrets." There were students, onlookers, and possibly faculty, all mingling with the crowds. Anna needed to break through the ring and head for

Obozone Street, where she hoped Neil would be waiting with his car. The noise levels were rising and the shouting increasing. She knew it was only a matter of minutes before there would be a major confrontation. Some students were already trying to push through the police ring. Even though they didn't seem to be connected to the demonstration, they were being stopped. Anna's heart was pounding. How could she get out of this mess? At that moment, a group of about a hundred students broke through the police cordon, scattered and were being chased down by the police with flaying batons. As the demonstrators cheered them on, Anna ran as fast as she could, dodging students and demonstrators to join in the back of this group. In no time she was through the police cordon. She continued running towards the Obozone Street anxiously looking for Neil and his car. Where the hell was he? Suddenly she was facing a "ferret" right in her path. "Halt," he called out. She ignored him and continued running. "Halt," he said again, opening his arms to try and catch her. She ran around him, and continued heading to the street. He turned and chased her, just as she saw another "ferret" coming at her from her right. She tried to avoid him as well, and although her long legs were carrying her quickly towards the street, she felt him grab the back of her knapsack. She stumbled but didn't fall.

At that moment, she was aware of another body, flying fists, grunts and groans. She was vaguely aware of her assailant falling to the ground, and then Neil grabbing her hand and yelling at her, "Head for the rear seat." She saw the car with both the driver's door and the rear passenger door open. With Neil running at her side, she felt she was almost flying, he practically threw her into the rear seat of the car, slammed the door, ran around and jumped into the driver's seat. The engine was already running and within seconds he was roaring off down Obozone. "Keep your bloody head down," Neil yelled. "We've got company."

She could hear a police car siren, and felt Neil weaving in and out the traffic at great speed. Cars were honking at him, and she could even hear people shouting. Bagatala Street was only a few blocks north. With the police sirens wailing behind them, Neil executed a nearly suicidal turn into the street and the ambassador's residence. The car screeched to a halt at the barrier to the residence and the guard came to the driver's window.

"I'm delivering Miss Janet Clark in accordance with the ambassador's instructions," he said to the guard who nodded and immediately lifted up the wooden barrier. As Neil drove in, he yelled to the guard to close the iron gates. He drove round to the rear of the building and stopped. "You can come out now. We are on international territory." Anna climbed out of the rear passenger seat, shaking and almost unable to speak. "Thank you so much, Neil," she said in a husky voice.

"You look like shit," he responded with a laugh, "but you will be okay here."

Holding her arm in support, Neil escorted a still-shaking Anna and her backpack through a rear garden door into the ambassador's residence. They were greeted by a tall, thin, gray-haired man. "Delighted to meet you, Miss Clark. I am the ambassador's assistant, Alistair Cunningham. I would like you to follow me if you wouldn't mind."

Neil stood back as Anna shook hands with Mr. Cunningham.

She followed him through to the entrance hall of the beautiful 19th-century palace, and into a large comfortable library which also served as the ambassador's private office. Alistair Cunningham approached one of the bookcases, pressed a button on the wall and the bookcase swung open to reveal a large safe. He pressed a number of letters and numbers on the safe door, moved the heavy handle to the right and swung open the safe. Anna put her backpack on the floor and took out Professor Keller's papers – wrapped in twine, dog-eared, yellowed in places, and in small neat handwriting. She handed them to Cunningham. "The ambassador said I should watch you putting this into the safe," she said.

"Those were my instructions as well, miss." Cunningham took the papers and placed them in the safe, closing the door and moving the heavy handle to the left and pushing back the bookcase.

"Well, Miss Clark, I'm sure you'd like a nice cup of tea and perhaps a sandwich? The ambassador has been informed that you are here. He was at a reception with the Warsaw Chamber of Commerce, but should be back within half an hour or so. I have been instructed that he would like you to wait, if that's not too inconvenient."

"That would be very nice," Anna responded. "And I'm very happy to wait for the Ambassador's return."

"Make yourself comfortable, miss. Tea and sandwiches will be delivered shortly."

Anna sat back in a deep leather chair as the adrenalin rush subsided. But within a minute or two she felt elated. She had done it. She had completed the mission, and without too many complications. Even she felt surprised at the speed and ease at which she had managed to obtain Professor Keller's papers. Now she wasn't even sure why the SB was following her. Did they know of her mission? Unlikely. Otherwise she reasoned they would have held her at SB headquarters a lot longer. Well, she had done it, and she could concentrate on Jan. She had to get him out of that horrific prison, but at the moment she had no idea how to free her brother and get him out of the country. No easy task, but she had to find a way. She was deep in thought when she heard a soft knock on the door, and a maid entered with a silver tray containing small sandwiches cut into quarters – ham and cheese, cucumber, and egg, and a pot of tea. There were also a couple of slices of fruitcake and some chocolate biscuits, which she put down on the coffee table in front of Anna.

Anna poured herself a cup of tea with a splash of milk and two sugars, and sat back in the deep chair and contentedly munched on her sandwiches. Just as she finished eating her second slice of fruitcake, the door opened and Sir Miles strode in.

"Ah, Miss Clark, well done!" said the Ambassador with a broad grin on his face. "London will be delighted."

Anna stood up. "Thank you, Sir Miles. I must say it was easier than I thought, although I did have a couple of hairy experiences."

The Ambassador gestured to Anna to sit down, and lowered himself into the leather chair opposite.

"So I heard. The SB are not to be treated lightly. I think you were quite fortunate."

"Yes, I was lucky," said Anna. *Neil Jordan must have told him what had happened.* "Anyway, the job is done, and I am extremely relieved that it's over."

"Well, you can now concentrate on the London Philharmonic, and hopefully enjoy the music and the various events that will surround the tour prior to your return to London."

"I have got a lot of work to do, Sir Miles, starting with the arrival of the orchestra manager tomorrow," replied Anna. "But I hope everything goes smoothly."

"Then I'll have to get you back to your office as quickly as possible," said Sir Miles.

"Is it safe?" asked Anna. "I was hiding in the back of Neil's car, but I know we were being followed. Are the SB watching your residence?"

"No, I think we're all right," responded the Ambassador. "Jordan had removed the number plates from his car for your pickup. Although he was being followed by the police and maybe SB, he says he drove like a lunatic and was through the gates and in the back of our courtyard before any vehicles following him even entered the street. He is an expert at this sort of thing. We shall see, but we shall certainly continue to take protective measures. I have given Jordan the use of another embassy car and he has already left. My chauffeur will take you back to the British

Council offices, in my Jaguar. The rear of the vehicle has tinted windows, but I would like you to lay down as far as possible in the rear, just in case." He paused. "Have you finished your tea Miss Clark? Was everything satisfactory?"

"Yes, Sir Miles, it was delicious."

"So perhaps, you had better be getting back. We don't want to agitate Mr. Brookes-Walton, do we?" he said with a smile.

Within ten minutes she was at the British Council's offices, quickly exited the Jaguar and ran through the rear entrance, up the stairs to her office shouting, "I'm back," to Stefania as she ran by her cubicle. She grabbed the canvas holdall sitting by her desk and scurried off to the ladies' room. Two of the junior typists were chattering away as she locked herself in one of the stalls and quickly changed back into her work clothes. By the time she came out of the stall, the two young women had disappeared. She washed her hands and face quickly, puffed up her hair and with the holdall stuffed full of her M&S clothes, made her way back to her office.

Within a minute or so, Stefania came in to see her. "You may be in a bit of a pickle," said Stefania. "BW is looking for you, and Paige-Madison has been down here twice wanting to know where you were. I told her I didn't have a clue, and nobody else knew anything, other than you'd gone out on an errand. Anyway you'd better get up there and see what he wants. He's on the war path."

"I'm not surprised," said Anna. "Something about my dress code probably."

She was annoyed, but not really worried. She knew that she had the Ambassador behind her. She made her way upstairs and was given a rather cold welcome by Emily Paige-Madison.

"I'll see if Mr. Brookes-Walton is available, Miss Clark," she said as she disappeared into his office. She returned a couple of moments later. "Mr. Brookes-Walton will see you now," she said rather officiously.

"Ah, Miss Clark. Please take a seat," said Brookes-Walton. Anna noted that once again he was splendidly clothed and coiffed, in a blue suit, French blue shirt and a bright yellow tie. Anna sat down.

"Miss Clark, I don't know whether you fully understand the role of the British Council in Warsaw, and my role as the senior representative. For your information, I have diplomatic status and am on the Ambassador's list of staff as chief cultural attaché. While we have always been physically separate from the embassy, we work closely with our colleagues." He paused, looking at Anna pompously. "Now, you are here on a special short assignment, but as I explained when you arrived, an extremely important one. Not only is the London Philharmonic Orchestra tour an important milestone in the cultural relationship of our two countries, but also this tour has deeper implications for our diplomatic and trade relations. It is important, Miss Clark, that you adhere to the diplomatic protocol of the British Council of whom you are currently a member and representative. That means you cannot come and go as you please, without informing your assistant or our staff of your whereabouts, and you certainly cannot use the Council offices as changing rooms for you to put on weekend clothes, to go out on your personal errands. Do I make myself clear, Miss Clark?" he said sternly.

"I am sorry, sir," said Anna humbly. "I can assure you it won't happen again."

"I certainly hope not. You have an enormous amount of work to do in the next few days, and it will need all your personal concentration. I hope that is understood, Miss Clark?"

"Absolutely, sir," said Anna. "I will make sure everything runs smoothly from now on."

"Fine, Miss Clark, you can go now. But can you do something about your appearance? You will be the face of the British Council over the next couple of weeks. You are a pretty girl, but if you could just take a little more care in your... choice of clothes, er...colors and makeup..." BW trailed off, clearly embarrassed.

"I shall try, sir," responded Anna, smiling inwardly to herself.

Chapter 21

Tuesday. A cloudy day for a change. No sun streaming into her tiny bedroom, but Anna felt a sense of liberation, helped by the fact that she could now abandon her disguise, and dress to her normal taste. She stood naked in the bathroom after a shower, and admired her own athletic curvaceous figure. At forty-three, she felt blessed that there was very little change from a decade ago. Today she put on eye makeup, blush and lipstick, and let her dyed-auburn red hair down around her shoulders. She dressed in a figure-hugging gray skirt, orange silk top with a scooped-out neckline, wide leather belt, and high heels. It felt so much better, like she was coming out of hiding. She went into the kitchen to join Maggie and Stefania for breakfast.

"Cor blimey," said Stefania, in her usual exuberant way. "What have you done to yourself? You look incredible."

"Well, I've got Charlie Adams arriving today," said Anna, "and with the orchestra following on Thursday, I thought I better smarten myself up."

"You've done a great job, lass," said Maggie in her Yorkshire accent.

They were all laughing as the doorbell rang. Stefania went to open the door to find Neil standing there.

"I'm here to take you ladies to the office. I've also been instructed to escort you to the airport to pick up Mr. Adams later this morning, and will also be driving you around until you leave Warsaw, Janet."

"I love having you here, Janet," said Stefania. "We really get the royal treatment."

When they arrived at the Council offices, the receptionist took a double-take as Anna walked by.

"Wow! You look nice today Janet," she said.

"Thank you," Anna responded. "Big day today, the advance

guard of the orchestra is coming in," she continued, eager to give a reason for her appearance.

Almost immediately she bumped into Emily Paige-Madison.

"Good morning, Miss Clark," she said without any acknowledgement at seeing Anna following the dress code.

Anna decided to take Stefania with her to the airport, causing great excitement. It would be advantageous to introduce her as her assistant, and would limit conversation with Neil on the journey there and back.

At 10:00 a.m., Stefania was ready to go, armed for some reason with a clipboard and a pad. She also had her logistics information with her. "Just in case," she said dramatically. Neil was waiting in the courtyard with the gray Saab. Anna noted that he had not returned to the car that he had been driving yesterday when they made their dash to the Ambassador's residence.

The British Airways flight from London was on time and the three of them were standing in the roped-off Arrivals area, with Neil holding up a sign on which was written "Mr. Charles Adams." About thirty minutes after the flight had landed, a tall pleasant-looking, baldheaded man approached them.

"Good morning, I'm Charlie Adams," he said, looking directly at Anna.

"Welcome to Warsaw, Mr. Adams," Anna replied. "I hope you had a good flight."

"Yes, everything was on time. Very comfortable, thank you, and please call me Charlie," he said in an Essex accent.

"I'm Janet Clark, and this is my assistant, Stefania Piatkiewicz, and our driver for today, Neil Jordan," said Anna.

"Pleased to meet you all," said Adams, shaking hands with Anna.

They set off to central Warsaw, as Stefania handed Adams some tourist-guide information about the city, and also information about the Polish National Opera Theatre where the London Philharmonic Orchestra would be performing. Stefania was chattering away to Adams as they arrived at the Hotel Europejski on Krakowski Przedmieście, one of Warsaw's main streets. The hotel, the oldest in Warsaw, was a popular favorite of international diplomatic visitors, the media, and visiting artists. Adams deposited his luggage and returned to the lobby with only his briefcase. They were soon at the Council offices where Anna made all the necessary introductions. After Adams met Miss Paige-Madison, they were escorted into Brookes Walton's office.

After looking approvingly at Anna's appearance, BW indicated that she was no longer required. He clearly wanted a one-on-one with Charlie Adams. Full of his own importance, he wished to establish his credentials as the man in charge.

Anna waited outside his office until their meeting finished, and then took Adams and Stefania into a small conference room, where they got down to work. Starting with the arrival of the orchestra, Anna and Stefania laid out their proposed agenda, logistics, travel arrangements, hotel and eating arrangements, official events, details of their venues, and briefed him on the continuing government State of Emergency and clampdown on dissidents, demonstrations, and interaction with local residents. Adams had to be made aware of these constraints even if, as Anna hoped, they did not interfere with the orchestra tour.

Charlie Adams asked all the right questions. Anna took to him. He seemed a down-to-earth pragmatic, confident manager. He was clearly impressed with the details that had been assembled by Anna and Stefania, and made it clear that their planning would make his life a lot easier. Moving around eighty-five musicians, technical support, and even members of the Board of Directors who were on the tour, was not an easy task. It needed efficient management, people skills, and as he put it "a lot of good luck." And all that was before one note was played by the orchestra. A daunting task under any circumstances, but possibly more difficult inside a Communist country with limited infrastructure and understanding of Western expectations. They agreed they should meet the following morning to continue their review, after Adams had a chance to absorb all the arrangements, and request any changes he felt when necessary.

On Wednesday afternoon, Neil drove all three of them to the Teatr Wielki on Teatrainy Plaza Street, home of the Polish National Opera. The building was erected in 1825, but during the Battle of Warsaw in 1939 the theater was bombed. Only the classic façade survived. The building was restored, expanded and reopened in 1965, and had become one of the most inspiring and best-equipped theatres in Europe. Stefania had set up a meeting with the theatre manager, Emil Kaplinsky. Anna translated while Charlie Adams asked numerous questions relevant to the facilities for the orchestra who would be performing their last three performances in Warsaw on the 19th, 20th, and 21st of July. Kaplinsky had been well prepared and briefed, and appeared confident that the scheduled concerts would proceed smoothly. He gave them all a tour of the theatre, the front of the house, the technical support, dressing rooms and even the "green room." Anna thought the decor drab but not surprising for an Eastern European city.

When their meeting finished, Neil drove them back to the Hotel Europejski, and they had a drink in the bar followed by a light dinner. The following day was going to be hectic and challenging with the arrival of the orchestra, and getting everyone settled, briefed and comfortable.

Neil was at the apartment at 8:30 a.m. on Thursday morning to take Anna and Stefania to collect Charlie Adams and move on to the airport. For the first time in a week, the temperatures had cooled, and it was gray and overcast.

Anna asked Stefania if she was excited. "You know I am," she said. "I know you really don't have to include me in all of this, but it's really exciting for me, and a great experience. I just want to let you know how much I appreciate it," she continued as she gave Anna a hug.

They had a coffee in the lobby of the hotel, since they had plenty of time before the flight was due to arrive. Anna looked around, and was interested to see the variety of hotel guests mingling with some local residents. The place was buzzing, but Anna still picked out at least two "ferrets" sitting in lobby chairs behind newspapers, but watching the proceedings. She was a little apprehensive, because she knew there would be three ORBIS representatives at the airport, and she hoped to hell that she didn't recognize them and they didn't recognize her. Now that she was wearing more feminine outfits, she had some concern as to whether her red hair, green eyes and glasses were enough of a disguise.

After coffee, they piled into the Saab, and headed to the airport. They were to meet up with BW, who would be the official greeter on behalf of the British Embassy. Neil parked the car, and they walked into the Arrivals area, and made their way to a separate roped-off portion which had been allocated to the arriving orchestra. Anna immediately saw the three ORBIS reps, and breathed a sigh of relief. She didn't recognize any of them. She approached the most senior-looking of the three, a pretty petite young woman with black hair and clear gray eyes behind horn-rimmed glasses and introduced herself as Janet Clark, and also introduced Stefania and Charlie Adams. The ORBIS rep speaking English with a strong Polish accent, introduced herself as Marzema Nowak, and her two colleagues Adela and Nora who were from the Wroclaw and Poznan offices. Anna reverted to Polish, and found out that ORBIS had arranged for two passenger coaches, for the orchestra and entourage, a smaller passenger van for the visiting members of the Board of Trustees, and a large pantechnicon for the musical instruments, which would be parked overnight at the hotel, pending their departure to Wroclaw tomorrow. BW, standing with a prim-looking Paige-Madison at his side, ignored their conversation, but Anna still greeted him politely.

Anna looked up at the Arrivals board, and saw that special charter flights 1274 and 1275 had landed. About thirty minutes later, the orchestra, led by two airport VIP hostesses, started to enter the roped-off area from the Customs hall. Anna and Stefania stepped forward immediately and started to welcome the various members, asking them to stand aside to let the others come through. One of the hostesses brought over a small slim man with a shock of white hair and a big smile on his face. BW stepped forward.

"Good morning, good morning," he said with his eyes twinkling in great enthusiasm. "I'm Sir David Mandel."

"I'm very pleased to meet you, Sir David," responded BW to the great maestro. "It is my honor to welcome you and the London Philharmonic to Warsaw, on behalf of the British Council. I would like to introduce you to my assistant Emily Paige-Madison, and Janet Clark and Stefania Piatkiewicz, who are coordinating all of the tour arrangements, and also I believe you know the orchestra manager, Mr. Adams." Anna thought that BW was doing the introductions with considerable charm.

"Oh yes. Charlie, so good to see you. I'm sure you've got everything organized, and I know with you in charge we will have a very smooth tour," responded the maestro.

"Ah, there is our brilliant young soloist, Leonard Littowitz," said Mandel, seeing a thin pale, young man in his early twenties coming through. While the introductions were taking place, the roped-off area had been filling up. All the members of the orchestra and support team were through Customs, and then one of the airport hostesses led a small group out and brought them directly towards BW. A tall distinguished-looking gentleman led the group.

"Mr. Brookes-Walton, I believe? I am Sir Norman Farrow, the Chairman of the Board of Trustees, and I am here with seven other members of the Board. We are really looking forward to this incredible tour."

"Pleased to meet you, Sir Norman," responded BW. "We have arranged separate transportation for you and your group to take you directly to the Hotel Bristol, where I'm sure you will be very comfortable. You will be escorted by one of these delightful young ladies from ORBIS, the Polish National tourist office," continued BW pleasantly. Charlie Adams was starting to herd the orchestra out of the roped-off area and towards the front of the airport. As they came out of the area, Stefania was handing out yellow and blue tags, counting off the members of the orchestra, and allocating them to the "yellow" coach or the "blue" coach. The orchestra members were busily chatting away to each other laughing and joking in their excitement. Anna took in a variety of men and women of various ages and different ethnic backgrounds. There were a significant number of Asian women, two Asian men and one black face. Anna stayed back to make sure that Sir Norman and his group, together with Marzema from ORBIS, were escorted to the smaller black-windowed passenger van behind the two coaches. A tractor with six trolleys, loaded with luggage with blue and yellow tags, pulled up to the coaches. The orchestra filed onto the coaches according to whether they were "yellow" or "blue," and the Board of Trustees group climbed into the small van.

Anna went on the "yellow" coach, and Stefania on the "blue." BW and Paige-Madison were in the van headed to the Hotel Bristol. The whole process had taken nearly an hour but eventually they were on their way. On the drive into Warsaw, the ORBIS reps in their accented English, pointed out places of interest. Of course no comment was made about the paramilitary, armed and standing every half mile or so on the main road into the city. Probably neither the orchestra nor the Board of Trustees would have seen the paramilitary presence in the airport, or the watchful SB "ferrets" that Anna saw taking in the whole proceedings.

The two coaches arrived at the Hotel Europejski, and the orchestra disembarked while their luggage followed. They had already been pre-checked into the hotel, but all their passports were collected by the ORBIS reps and handed over to the reception. The rooms had been allocated, for the most part two to a room, and each member of the orchestra received a package of information, containing local sightseeing details, the rehearsal and performance agendas and the various events to which they had been invited on the tour, starting with a welcome dinner hosted by the Polish Ministry of Culture that evening at 6:00 p.m.

Anna and Stefania set up a table outside the ballroom, and worked up a table plan for the evening. By the time they had finished this plan, including the top table of dignitaries from the Ministry of Culture, and the members of the Board of Trustees, and not forgetting BW and the maestro, the event was ready to begin. Members of the orchestra filed in, choosing their names from the table plan, chattering and very relaxed. BW arrived early and after enquiring from Anna as to whether everything was organized and ready to go, stood by nervously, reading and rereading his notes for a speech, ready to greet the Minister of Culture, Lukas Kania.

Anna thought the ballroom itself was a rather shabby affair, with decor that needed a good lick of paint, and 1950s lighting and furnishings. Nevertheless, it would serve its purpose for the evening event, which Anna described to Stefania as "a rubber-chicken dinner."

Lukas Kania arrived with an entourage of five assistants. The minister himself was a small sallow-faced man with watery blue eyes and a drooping gray moustache. He was dressed in an ill-fitting gray suit, white shirt and red tie, and looked even more nervous than BW. The Polish government, and indeed the Ministry of Culture, did not host very many visiting foreign dignitaries, and a visit from the London Philharmonic Orchestra clearly intimidated them. Nevertheless, the evening began with a toast from BW in both Polish and then in English to his hosts. Kania responded in Polish, with a translator slowing up the proceedings as he gave an English version in accented English. The "rubber-chicken dinner" followed. The food was cold and generally unappetizing, but the members of the orchestra chatting away happily, didn't seem to notice. The dinner was followed by two long boring speeches, by BW and Kania. They both followed the same theme of honoring each other's country, declaring the long history of cooperation and understanding between the two countries, stressing the importance of the orchestra tour to the arts in Poland, and to strengthening ties between the two governments. This was followed by more toasts, and Anna was thankful when the evening finally came to a close about 9:00 p.m.

Anna was up early the next morning after a fitful night. She was thinking of Jan in Mokotów prison a couple of miles away. How was his health? Was he being tortured? And what could she do to get his release? Was it even possible? And over and over, she kept thinking about who would have the authority to grant his release. And how would Jan, Ava and the children get out of the country? She had to find an answer, but as she tossed and turned throughout the night, she had to admit she really didn't know where to start.

She had breakfast with the girls, and after issuing final instructions to Stefania for the preparation of the Warsaw events and concerts, she left the apartment with her suitcase packed for the trip to Wroclaw and Poznan. Neil was waiting for her downstairs, and drove her through the early-morning traffic to the Hotel Europejski. The ORBIS reps had done a good job, and had already organized the orchestra and the Board of Trustees to start boarding their coaches with all their luggage ticketed and identified. She joined the Board's coach, greeting each member pleasantly. It was a warm sunny day, and they had a clear drive out to the airport, where, after going through minimal formalities, they were taken out to their charter planes and within forty minutes were on their way to Wroclaw.

In Wroclaw the Board of Trustees and the orchestra had taken over the whole of the Hotel Monopol, one of the most prestigious hotels in Poland, built in 1892 in neo-baroque style. It was well located in the historical center of Wroclaw, a short walk from the opera house. Anna joined the orchestra for their afternoon rehearsal at the concert hall, and marveled at the way Sir David Mandel led the orchestra through Smetana's "Moldau." The two "ferrets" who had met them in Wroclaw said they were under instruction from the Ministry of Culture to assist the orchestra and the Board of Trustees with any questions that might arise during the tour. Anna could not imagine less likely proponents of the arts and culture. They were two large Polish thugs, and she knew their job was to keep an eye on everybody. However, they didn't seem to take a particular interest in her, which she found encouraging. One of the "assistants" stayed with the Board of Trustees while the other one joined the orchestra group. The ORBIS girls were the only people who looked nervous, but they catered to the orchestra and the Board of Trustees with confident broad smiles. The orchestra members and their support group seemed oblivious.

The Friday-evening concert was a sell-out, with thundering applause and a standing ovation. Everyone was delighted. The following morning, Sir David and Charlie Adams scheduled a further rehearsal, and Anna decided this would be her opportunity to see if she could find Wladyslaw Starzec.

When Anna had returned to Poland from Australia, after her divorce from Jack Gray, there was no shortage of suitors. An outstandingly beautiful woman of aristocratic bearing and background brought a cascade of men like bees to honey. However, for the most part, Anna had found the Polish men arrogant, chauvinistic, with bad teeth and terrible smoking and drinking habits. But one man had come into her life whom she

had found both physically attractive and intellectually interesting. An innocent friendship turned into a loving relationship
that lasted more than ten years. Wladyslaw Starzec was the
regional director of the Education Ministry in Wroclaw. He
worked at the Ministry in Warsaw four days a week for three
weeks out of four. Anna had first met him when she was driving
Ministry officials during an international education conference of
Eastern Bloc countries in the spring of 1971. He was a tall, good-
looking man with closely cropped gray hair, intense brown eyes,
and an athletic build from his many years as a university soccer
star. A former history and political science teacher, he'd been
seconded to the regional Ministry of Education, slowly moving
up the ranks until he became Regional Director. He was twenty-
five years older than Anna, with two grown-up children and an
ailing wife. Anna had always been attracted to older men as had
been evidenced by her past serious relationships and marriage to
Jack Gray. Wladyslaw's knowledge of Polish history and the
politics of the country intrigued Anna, and their love for each
other grew, but it was frustrating not being able to see him at
weekends. The relationship had ended the previous year when
he had taken retirement at the age of sixty-five and had returned
to Wroclaw permanently to look after his wife. Anna had always
known that their relationship would come to an end.
Nevertheless it was painful. But she accepted the situation in
good grace. She knew his home address, although she had never
visited him, met his wife or children, or even been in Wroclaw
with him. So just after 11 in the morning, having confirmed the
"ferrets" were with the orchestra and the Board of Trustees, she
found herself across the street from his apartment building at 12
Wierzbowa Street not far from Old Town. She hoped Wladyslaw
might have a contact in Warsaw who could help get Jan released
from jail. She hesitated however. She couldn't just knock on his
apartment door, meet his wife and come up with a story as to
why she was in Wroclaw and wanted to see Wladyslaw. But first

of all, she had to establish that he was still living at that address, so she crossed the street and entered the courtyard of the old seven-floor apartment building. There was a janitor's office on the right, and she knocked on the half-open door. A wizened old lady, holding a pail and mop, came to the door.

"Good morning," said Anna pleasantly. "Do you know if Mr. and Mrs. Starzec are in?"

"Mr. Starzec is out shopping," responded the old lady curtly, "and Mrs. Starzec is no longer with us, unfortunately," she continued, crossing herself quickly. "She died in January, you know."

Anna was genuinely shocked. "Oh, no, I didn't know," she responded. "I'm so sorry to hear that. Would you know how long Mr. Starzec is likely to be before he returns?" Anna continued.

"I saw him going out. I don't suppose he will be very long. After all, the poor man, he's only got himself to shop for these days."

"Yes. Of course. I'll return later," said Anna. She left the building and crossed the street, taking up a position which gave her an adequate view of both sides of the street and the entrance to the apartment building. After about twenty minutes she saw him, coming down the street carrying a Co-op shopping bag. He was wearing a faded check shirt with the sleeves rolled up and khaki trousers. He still looked big and strong, younger than his years but he was grayer, and now somewhat stooped. He was walking slowly and deliberately, like he had nothing really to hurry for, and was just going through the motions of life. Anna took in the scene, and felt sad for him. She had loved him for many years. About ten minutes after he had entered his apartment building, she crossed the street again, and asked the janitor whether Mr. Starzec had returned.

"Yes, he just came back," she responded. "Third floor, number ten."

"Thank you," said Anna, and she started trudging up the

circular stairway.

She stood outside apartment number ten and listened to her heart pounding. Was it the excitement of seeing Wladyslaw again? Or was it the possible opportunity of finding a way to free her brother Jan? She pushed the doorbell, which let out a dull buzz.

Wladyslaw opened the door. "Yes?" he said inquisitively, not recognizing Anna.

"Hello, Wladyslaw," Anna said.

"My God! Anna! I didn't recognize you. Your hair. You look different. Where have you been? I have been so worried about you." The words came tumbling out.

Anna laughed. "I know, I'm now a redhead instead of a blonde," she said. "I'm in Wroclaw for a few days, so I thought I would look you up," she continued easily.

"Well, that's wonderful, please come in," said Wladyslaw opening the door wide and ushering her in to his apartment.

Anna walked in. The apartment was dark, dreary and old-fashioned and it had a faint antiseptic smell. The furniture was worn, the wallpaper was faded, and heavy lace curtains kept out the light. They were in a living room, and she could see a kitchen off to the right. A partly opened door appeared to lead into a bedroom. The apartment was small, and the living room was cramped by bookcases, totally filled. There were piles of books and papers on the floor, particularly near an old-fashioned desk which stood by one of the windows.

"Anna, you look wonderful," said Wladyslaw with all his old charm and a happy smile on his face. "Please come and sit down," he said, indicating the sagging sofa on one side of the room. "Would you like a drink? A beer? Schnapps? Or tea or coffee?"

"Coffee would be fine. Let me come and help you," said Anna, following him into the kitchen, which was also dark and old-fashioned.

"I was just making myself some coffee. The water has boiled. I hope the instant will be okay," he rattled on.

"Of course, that would be fine."

He took out two cups and saucers and a coffee pot from a cabinet and put in some instant coffee, and poured in the boiling water. He had a small plate of cookies on the work surface, and put them all on a tray and carried them to the living room, putting the tray down on the table next to the sofa.

"Now, I want to hear all your news. It's been so long. But I have to tell you some sad news from my side. My wife died in January. You remember, she had been ill for a long time, but eventually she couldn't fight any longer," he said holding back the tears. "I tried to call you and tell you, but your office at first said you were out of town, and then that you had left ORBIS altogether. Then, a couple of weeks later, I got a visit from the SB. Scared the shit out of me. They told me that you and your brother were part of a smuggling ring: Your brother had been put in jail, and that they were looking for you. They wanted to know if you had been in touch with me and interrogated me about our relationship, which I assured them was strictly business. I told them I hadn't seen you for more than a year since I had retired, and that seemed to satisfy them and they went away. But, Anna, what is all this about?"

Anna laughed, confidently. "Oh, it's all a big mistake. They arrested a number of ORBIS employees for smuggling Western goods into the country. Jan had nothing to do with that. And of course, neither did I. In fact, neither of us knew anything about it. But he was arrested and has been in jail since the end of February. I left ORBIS and I'm now working for the Ministry of Culture. That's why I'm here in Wroclaw. I'm helping with the tour of Poland by the London Philharmonic Orchestra. A pretty big deal," Anna said, lying easily, as she sipped her tea.

"Wladyslaw, I'm so sorry that your wife passed away," continued Anna in a more serious vein.

"Yes, I think it was a blessing in the end. She really suffered the last few weeks," responded Wladyslaw solemnly.

"What are you doing these days?" said Anna, changing the subject.

"I'm keeping reasonably busy. I am an associate professor at the university, teaching one course of history and politics. It's not like the old days but it keeps me interested, and I have a good group of students. I also help with coaching the football team at a couple of junior high schools in the city, and serve on the Board of Biblioteka Ossolińskich. It has one of the most important collections of illuminated manuscripts in the world, dating back to the 14th century. Of course, I can now travel, because I have the time. I would love to come back to Warsaw, to see you, Anna," he said reaching out for her hand.

"That would be great," responded Anna warmly, but realizing life had moved on. She didn't want to hurt his feelings. "You must give me your phone number. I had your office number but have never had your home phone. I have just moved from my old address around the corner, but I don't have a phone yet. As soon as it is installed, I will let you have my new number." She paused, now thinking only about Jan.

"But, Wladyslaw, I could really use your help right now. I have got to get Jan out of prison, and I don't know whom to turn to, or who would have the authority to arrange his release. I'm not sure there's even going to be a trial. I made enquiries, but could get no help. Do you know any government people from your ministry days who could perhaps arrange his release? As I said, he is totally innocent of all these charges."

"Well, let me see. Getting someone released from prison is not easy, especially in Warsaw, and especially today. I'm still friendly with a couple of judges, one of whom is in Warsaw, but I really don't think either one would have the authority to arrange his release." Wladyslaw paused, his forehead creasing as he thought about the problem. "About the only person who could do that, just on his simple signature, would be the head of the SB, Roman Krinsky. If you could get to him you might have a chance, but he is considered cold and ruthless."

"I don't know Krinsky, but I know of his reputation. Ruthless, and quite a womanizer. But maybe you're right, he's probably the only person, who could release Jan without any questions being asked. The British Ambassador is hosting a cocktail reception at the embassy, for the London Philharmonic, some of their Board of Trustees, and no doubt many government officials. It's possible Krinsky would be there. I'll have to check, but thanks for the suggestion."

"I will make some discreet enquiries on your behalf, Anna, but you know one has to be very careful these day," said Wladyslaw. "You know I will do everything possible to help you. You can rely on me, especially now that I am a free man, a widower with no ties." He paused. "You know that I love you, Anna, and always will," he continued softly.

At that moment Anna believed him, but she had already come to the conclusion he would not be able to help her.

"Thank you, Wladyslaw," Anna said, as he squeezed her hand and moved closer to kiss her. She did not resist, as he pulled her closer to him, and she saw the softness in his deep brown eyes, and felt the familiar soft lips and probing tongue, as well as the smell of his skin, which set her heart pounding. But as his hands started caressing her breasts, and his breathing became heavier, she pushed him away. She was not going to encourage him. Not now. Not here, with the smell of his wife's sick room in the air. It had been over a year, since they had been together. Her life had changed. She had recovered from the pain of ending their relationship, and she knew that it was over. He was not the man she had loved either. He now seemed older and somewhat diminished and defeated. She had promised him that she would call, but she knew she wouldn't. Her focus was on Jan and nothing more.

"I've got to go, Wladyslaw," she said. "We have a sightseeing tour for the orchestra, and the Board of Trustees, and I have got to go with them," she continued as she got up from the sofa.

"Can I see you again while you're in Wroclaw?" asked Wladyslaw.

"I would love to, but I don't think so. We have a very busy schedule, and we leave on Monday morning for Poznan. But I'll call you when I get settled in my new apartment."

"Please do, Anna. I don't want to lose contact with you again. Let me know how you get on with Jan. I wish you luck."

He pulled her towards him and they kissed each other lightly on the lips as she made her way to the front door. They said their goodbyes, and Anna could see the disappointment in his face. He seemed to realize that their relationship would not be renewed.

Anna joined those members of the orchestra and Board, who were interested in the afternoon sightseeing tour. Wroclaw's location close to the borders of Germany and the Czech Republic was one reason why the city had frequently changed hands and nationalities during its long history. The city's architecture reflected its various rulers. Romanesque followed by gothic and the baroque from the Austrian Habsburg Dynasty when Silesia came under two-hundred years of Prussian rule. Seventy-five percent of the town, including many historic buildings and monuments, were destroyed during World War II, but a massive rebuilding program had restored many of the ancient parts of the city, including the main marketplace with its brightly painted gothic and baroque buildings. The tour eventually arrived at the Collegium Maximum, which forms the main building of the university, situated on the leafy banks of the River Oder. Anna was amazed at the beauty of these historic buildings and in awe of the magnificent Aula Leopoldina Assembly Hall, one of Poland's most beautiful baroque halls, where the flamboyant architectural details, trompe l'oeil paintings, frescoes and sculptures all harmonize perfectly. She really enjoyed the tour. She had never been to Wroclaw or Silesia, and this was her first exposure to its ancient history. However, as the tour progressed she couldn't help but notice the large police presence on the streets. Clusters of policemen in their pale blue uniforms at every one of their stops. She wondered whether extra police had been drafted in for the orchestra's visit. Wroclaw had been a center of Solidarity activity over the past couple of years, with many demonstrations, arrests and some bloody battles. Although the tour buses kept to the main streets, Anna was very much aware of the decrepit buildings that she could see down the side streets. There were grocery stores with long queues outside, and the people were poorly dressed. Old blue painted trams rattled through the main streets. Most of the automobile traffic consisted of tinny Fiat 125s and the East German Trabant. This was the real Poland, the real Eastern Bloc, looking significantly less prosperous than Warsaw.

The Saturday-night concert was another resounding success. Sir David was particularly pleased with the audience reception, as were the Board of Trustees.

The Sunday concerts were just as successful, and ended with a warm and genuine speech from the Mayor of Wroclaw, clearly delighted that such an important event in his city had gone so well.

On Monday morning, they headed for Poznan. Once again, the concerts were a resounding success, but Anna couldn't wait to get back to Warsaw, to check whether Roman Krinsky was on the invitation list for the Ambassador's reception on Friday night, and whether he had accepted. Her mind was preoccupied with how she was going to approach Krinsky and affect Jan's release from prison. Her fear of being identified as Anna Kaluza had diminished. She didn't want to be complacent, but the two "ferrets" who had accompanied the tour, took little interest in her, and she felt quite confident that she was accepted as Janet Clark from the British Council. It was therefore with some impatience that she assisted the ORBIS reps with herding the orchestra, entourage and the Board of Trustees onto their planes for the trip back to Warsaw. She was also looking forward to seeing Alex Campbell, who was arriving in Warsaw that day. Should she confide in him about her plans to use Roman Krinsky to release Jan? She knew this was contrary to her instructions from Tim Bevans, but she needed to talk things through with someone, and she had great faith and affection for Alex. Maybe he had a better idea.

By 2:00 p.m., the orchestra and the Board were back at their hotels. Anna was met by Neil who took her directly to her office. Her heart was pounding as she checked the invitation list and saw that Roman Krinsky had been invited to the Ambassador's reception and had accepted. She reviewed the plans with Stefania for the next four days in Warsaw. The orchestra would be rehearsing on Friday morning, would have a city tour in the afternoon and some members would be invited to the Ambassador's reception on Friday evening. On Saturday, they would be a further rehearsal and the first of four concerts at 8:00 p.m. that evening. This would be followed by two concerts on Sunday and a final farewell concert on Monday evening. All the plans and arrangements appeared to be in place, and Anna hoped that the few days in Warsaw would go as smoothly as the trip to Wroclaw and Poznan. As she was about to leave the office, she received a message to call Sir Alex Campbell at the Hotel Bristol. She got through directly to him, and was happy to hear his voice.

"Alex, welcome to Warsaw. Did you have a good flight?" asked Anna.

"Wonderful; no problems, no delays," he responded. "I hear you've been busy, and done a great job in every way," he continued, with a clear double meaning. "I'd love to get together, if you're free this evening."

"Absolutely, Alex. Just tell me where and when."

"Well, I thought you'd be the expert. Where would you

recommend?"

"I've heard the Bazyliszek Restaurant, which is on the Old Town Square, is supposed to be very good. Apparently there is a great view over the Market Square, and if you like duck, that is one of their specialties."

"Sounds great," said Alex. "I'll get the hotel to make a reservation for us at, say, 8:00 p.m., if that works you."

"Perfect, Alex. I'll see you there."

Chapter 22

Anna arrived at the restaurant right on time, having been back to the apartment to change. She was wearing a white skirt and pale blue silk blouse, high heels, and very little makeup. Large round sunglasses and her auburn hair down around her shoulders completed her attractive look. As usual, heads turned to follow her as she walked into the restaurant. She greeted Alex with a broad smile and a big hug.

Alex quickly got down to business, speaking softly in English, when they were seated at their table in a quiet spot on the terrace overlooking the ancient Market Square of the old town, which had been restored after the demolition of World War II.

"Anna, I must congratulate you. You're a real star in London. Tim Bevans was delighted to hear the news from the Ambassador that you completed your mission, much quicker than we thought. You seem very relaxed. Everything seems to have gone very smoothly."

"Not quite," responded Anna, speaking almost in a whisper. She then proceeded to brief Alex about her experiences with the SB, the continual surveillance by the "ferrets," and their wild dash through Warsaw's streets to the Ambassador's residence. She also told Alex about her arrest with Professor Kopacz, and her interrogation by the SB. She knew she had been lucky. But her recent tour with the London Philharmonic Orchestra to Wroclaw and Poznan had gone well and she was feeling much more comfortable.

"You were lucky the SB didn't realize who you were," said Alex, somewhat anxiously after listening to Anna. "Now you've completed your mission, I would hope there should be no more concerns prior to your departure next Tuesday."

"I hope so," said Anna. "How are you going to get Professor Keller's notes back to London?"

"I really don't know yet," replied Alex. "I met the Ambassador this afternoon, and he briefed me on a few possibilities suggested by London. He is sure that all our luggage will be thoroughly searched, and that includes all the orchestra's luggage, musical instruments and whatever, before we depart. He doesn't trust the diplomatic bags going to London, so my challenge is to come up with a solution between now and next Tuesday. I can assure you, I'm thinking about this very deeply, and assessing the risks of failure."

The waiter arrived with an enormous menu, and they both ordered drinks. At Anna's suggestion, Alex ordered the duck, while Anna chose the more traditional Polish pork. They agreed on a bottle of red wine from southern Poland and proceeded to enjoy a delightful meal in a beautiful setting. The evening was warm, and as the sun went down the reflections off the copper roofs of the buildings surrounding the Old Town Square were breathtaking. They chitchatted through the meal and then Alex asked how Anna was getting on at the British Council.

"I had a bit of a problem with dress code, and comments from Mr. Brookes-Walton and his assistant, while I was trying to look as understated as possible, until I got Professor Keller's papers. Brookes-Walton is rather pompous and over the top. By the way, I've been told that he has a boyfriend who works in the Russian Embassy," Anna said, with a smile and a raised eyebrow.

"I hear the Board of Trustees are delighted with the tour so far and are really looking forward to the next four days in Warsaw. I shall take note of Brookes-Walton's friendship with the Russian. Bearing in mind what happened in Vienna, that may or may not be relevant." Alex paused. "I have to ask, Anna, have you seen your mother and have you made any attempt to contact your brother?"

Anna smiled. "Yes, I went to see my mother, dodging the "ferrets" all the way. She was so relieved to see me, because she knew Jan had been arrested, and was told that there was a nationwide search going on for me. She didn't say too much but I know she has been frantic with worry. She's looking quite fragile these days, and has had some health issues, which worries me. I told her that Jan's arrest was a big mistake, and that I had changed jobs, but everything was fine." She paused, and let out a big sigh, before continuing in a serious tone. "I know Jan is in Mokotów Prison, just a couple of miles from here. It is so frustrating to be so near and yet so far. I've made no attempt to see him or his wife Ava or the children, but Alex, I do want to talk to you about Jan, and get your advice. I have been making some inquiries and it seems the one person who could obtain Jan's release immediately, is the head of the Secret Service, Colonel Roman Krinsky. He's going to be at the Ambassador's reception tomorrow night, and I'm thinking of trying to use my most charming approach to get him to release Jan. That is my only chance and I have to try, Alex," she said in a tight-lipped determined way, looking Alex in the eyes.

Alex was shocked. "Are you mad?! That's an enormous risk. You're walking right into the lion's den, and your chances of success must be slim. What do you think you would have to do to get him to sign a release form? You know what I mean, Anna. Are you prepared to go that far? And then, as soon as you mention the name Jan Kaluza, he will probably realize who you are and you could land up keeping Jan company in that prison. I think it's a terrible idea and, you will not only be risking your own life, but possibly this mission." Alex was irritated by what he thought was a hare-brained scheme. Still, he was amazed at how tough and focused Anna could be.

"But I've got to try something," said Anna with some desperation in her voice. "I can't let Jan rot in jail. Mokotów has a reputation for torture and death, and Jan has been there for four months already. God knows what he's been through. Ava was allowed to see him once, and my mother said that she said he was okay, but Ava probably wasn't going to tell my mother any bad news. I've only got four days and I can't think of a better scheme, can you?"

"You know, Tim has already told you that there will be an opportunity of swapping Jan for one of their people. You have just got to be patient."

"Alex, I am here now in Warsaw and probably not coming back," said Anna. "I've got to try to get Jan out. I can't wait for Tim Bevans. I don't know whether a prisoner exchange could take place in two months or two years or twenty years. I'm not sure how long Jan could survive. If I don't try, I will not be able to face myself if he rots in that prison for years or even dies."

"Let me speak to the Ambassador," said Alex, a little more sympathetically. "Maybe he's got some ideas that could work. I will do my best to help you, Anna, but I implore you not to put yourself and our mission in jeopardy."

After that, Anna really lost her appetite, even though their conversation moved on to discussions about the orchestra plans, sightseeing tours, and the Ambassador's reception. The evening drew to a close. Alex had a car from his hotel pick him up and he dropped off Anna near her apartment on the way. She gave him a big hug as they departed.

* * *

Anna and Stefania had an early Friday-morning meeting with Charlie Adams at the Council offices. There were some timetable changes to the sightseeing tours, and some adjustments to the orchestra's program on Saturday night. Anna had to get back to her apartment to get ready for the Ambassador's reception. BW had asked her to be there early, to make sure she could greet and meet the orchestra members, Sir David Mandel, and the Board of Trustees. Neil Jordan was still ferrying her around, and watching out for her. She was impressed by his dedication to the job, his composure and ability to choose the right time to speak or not.

Quite a significant achievement considering their intimate relationship. Anna found herself attracted to him in many ways. He was a real man. But, now was not the time.

It was 4:30 p.m. by the time she was "home." Maggie was out of the shower and half dressed as Anna arrived.

"I thought you'd be back earlier, Janet," said Maggie. "You're supposed to be there early aren't you?"

"I know I'm a bit late, but I'm a quick-change artist, so I'll be ready shortly."

Anna took a quick shower and had already laid out on her bed her outfit for the evening. A revealing turquoise chiffon dress, figure-hugging at the waist but floating down to her knees. The dress had a built-in bra, and it only took a minute for Anna to slip into it, and start working on her makeup. Her colored contact lenses had been irritating, not for the first time, but there was little she could do about it now. She had a pair of clip-on gold earrings and a matching necklace, which went well with her coloring and dress. With her hair swept up, she noticed that her natural blonde roots were beginning to come through her dyed auburn hair. *Only four more days,* she thought. She put on a pair of dull gold evening shoes that she had brought from London, which matched a small evening bag and she went into the living room.

"Janet, you look fantastic," said Maggie, greeting her with a big grin.

"Thank you, Maggie, so do you. I love that sparkling black shawl that you're wearing. I suppose I could really do with something to cover up my dress for the journey, but I don't have anything that will work."

"I have a black silk taffeta evening cloak; that might work. It will be a bit short on you, but at least it's something to take off when we arrive and put on when we leave the reception. Wait a sec, I'll go and get it."

She came back into the room with the cloak which had a hood

clasped at the neck and wide sleeves. Anna tried it on and although it was short on her and didn't cover her dress all the way to her knees, it did the job.

"Thank you so much, Maggie, you're really kind."

"Nonsense, this is a big night for you. The orchestra, and members of the Board. We've got to impress them all," she said.

They arrived at the embassy at 6:10, a little later than Anna had planned, but still in adequate time, to have a quick word with the Ambassador, check out the layout of the ballroom where the reception was going to be held, find out where the relevant toilets were located, and obtain a final list of attendees from Alistair Cunningham, the Ambassador's assistant. The beautiful embassy building was flooded in light, both inside and out. The 19th-century ballroom was a stunning sight. It had a decorated painted ceiling, multiple mirrors on the walls, and two large glass chandeliers hanging over the parquet wooden floor. It was another balmy warm evening, and two pairs of French doors opened out onto the terrace and its view of the spectacular garden. All in all, Anna thought, it was a fairytale location for what surely would be a glamorous evening. She was doing her best to stay calm and controlled. She knew Alex was right about Krinsky, but she had to take the risk. If all went according to plan, it was going to be a very long evening.

The Ambassador, Sir Miles Sanford, arrived with his wife. After greeting BW and a few other embassy and consulate officials, he saw Anna.

"Good evening, Miss Clark. You're looking very, ahem, elegant tonight," he said with his eyes focused on her cleavage. "May I introduce my wife Elizabeth."

Anna shook hands with Lady Elizabeth, a tall, horsey-looking lady, but with bright blue eyes and a pleasant smile. She was dressed in a long flower-printed dress that Anna thought looked more suitable for the opening of the village fete than an elegant Ambassador's reception. After a couple of "pleased to meet you's," the Ambassador and his wife moved to the entrance of the ballroom where Alistair Cunningham was standing with the task of introducing each arriving guest.

A steady stream of foreign Ambassadors, their spouses, consulates, Polish government officials, and members of the orchestra, together with Sir Norman Farrow and other members of the Board of Trustees, including Alex Campbell, arrived and were announced to the Ambassador by Alistair.

Anna circulated around the room, drawing plenty of admiring stares from the male guests as she spoke to members of the Board of Trustees, Sir Norman Farrow, and the Consulate General introduced by Maggie, all the while keeping an eye out for Colonel Roman Krinsky. Eventually, he arrived, without a lady on his arm. Anna's heart jumped; she was not sure whether it was from nerves at the thought of her task ahead... or Krinsky's outstanding good looks and sex appeal. Within a minute or so he was in conversation with some of the dignitaries. Anna made sure that she passed within his line of sight. She caught his eye and smiled, and he returned the acknowledgement with a smile of his own. As the evening progressed, and the canapés and the champagne flowed, she made sure that he saw her at least three more times, with an exchange of further smiles. However, he made no attempt to engage in conversation. The proceedings were interrupted by a couple of speeches from Sir Miles, and Sir David Mandel.

Alone for a couple of minutes, Anna walked through the French doors onto the terrace. She knew that Krinsky had seen her and she hoped he would follow. She was quietly sipping champagne with her heart pounding, when suddenly she realized that he was by her side.

"It's a beautiful evening in a beautiful setting," he said with only the slightest accented English.

She turned towards him as he gave her a big smile showing near-perfect white teeth, setting off his dark olive-skinned face with large brown eyes that she felt were looking right through her. His black hair was sleeked back, and flecked with gray. He was in the dress uniform of the SB; olive green with gold epaulets and a golden lanyard across one side of his chest to a button on his uniform. Anna thought he had enormous charisma and charm, even before he had said more than a few words to her.

"I was just thinking the same thing," Anna responded. "I don't think we could have chosen a more perfect evening. By the way, my name is Janet Clark. I'm with the British Council in Warsaw and I am responsible for organizing the London Philharmonic Orchestra tour of Poland."

"I am Colonel Roman Krinsky," he replied. "It appears your tour is going well. Everyone seems very happy, so I have to presume you're doing a good job," he said with a questioning smile. "Have you been to Poland before Miss Clark?"

"No. This is my first visit, but I'm enjoying it very much. We have visited Wroclaw and Poznan, both of which I found fascinating. Everyone has been very accommodating and helpful."

"Do you speak Polish, Miss Clark? I presume that would be helpful with your responsibilities?"

"I do. My mother was Polish, and although I grew up in Australia, she insisted that we spoke Polish at home, so I am pretty fluent, although my accent probably gives me away," Anna continued pleasantly.

Krinsky immediately switched to Polish and started rattling off a number of questions at her. She felt it was becoming a bit of an interrogation and so she decided to say so.

"I'm sorry, Miss Clark," said Krinsky. "It's probably because of my job. I am responsible for security, and we are living in difficult times, with some tough challenges."

"Of course, Colonel," said Anna with a smile. "I fully understand."

At that moment Emily Page-Madison appeared. "Ah, Janet! Mr. Brookes-Walton would like to see you, when you can spare a moment," she said looking directly at the colonel.

Dammit, thought Anna. *I need more time.* Page-Madison returned to the reception.

"I'm sure you are busy, Miss Clark," said Krinsky. "Maybe you'd care to join me for a light supper after the reception? We can talk more then."

"That sounds lovely, Colonel, and please call me Janet," responded Anna.

"Here's my card, Janet. I have an apartment on the third floor of a building just a few blocks from here. I'd appreciate it if you would enter through the rear entrance, as the front door to the building is closed at this time of day. The elevator will take you directly to the third floor. I need to reschedule some prior arrangements, but perhaps we could say 9:00 p.m.?"

"That would be wonderful. I look forward to continuing our conversation. But you must excuse me now," said Anna with a parting warm smile.

BW wanted to talk to Anna about tickets for the final performance. General Jaruzelski would be attending, and of course, he wanted to be amongst the dignitaries meeting the President, and his entourage. He asked Anna to secure six seats for his personal use.

Anna looked around the room and saw that Krinsky had followed her back in, but was now talking to some Polish government officials and other uniformed officers. He caught her eye and smiled, which she returned. She saw Alex Campbell across the room, and started to move towards him. She had not had time to say hello. But suddenly she froze as she heard the voice right behind her speaking in Russian. "Good evening, Anna Kaluza-Zyrardowski. I thought I might find you here." Anna's heart was pumping so fast that she thought she would pass out. She turned to face the big Russian.

"Sergei, what a surprise! I didn't expect to see you back in Warsaw," she said with a slight smile on her face, so as not to appear to have any connection to the Russian if any of the general guests were looking. Sergei looked older. His large, sallow, puffy face was the same, with his bushy eyebrows hooding his piercing gray eyes. But, his greasy gray hair was a lot whiter, or so it seemed to Anna, and his bulky body seemed somewhat stooped.

"Well, Anna, here I am. We need to set up a meeting."

"Why? We have nothing to talk about."

"I think we do. By the way, how is your mother these days? Enjoying her retirement at Kaskia Lodge?" he said in a clearly threatening manner.

"She's fine, thank you, but has some health issues, and is a little fragile."

"Health issues and a little fragile. Well, Anna, you see we have lots to talk about," he said emphatically. "We should meet tomorrow morning at our old rendezvous at 8:30. I am sure that will work for you, Anna."

Anna could hardly respond. She was totally terrified. So they knew she was here in Warsaw. At any moment he could inform the Poles and have her arrested and thrown in jail. He was also threatening her mother. He would know Jan was in jail as well. She knew that the Russians pulled the strings in Warsaw. He could blow her cover, but obviously he wanted something from her. He probably knew that Keller's papers were still in Warsaw. What else could it be? Anna's mind was racing frantically. She had no choice.

"I'll be there, Sergei." She smiled and turned away, and headed across the room to Alex.

"Good evening, Alex," she said. "I haven't had a chance to say hello."

"Good evening, Anna, you look beautiful, but have you seen a ghost?" he said with a look of concern on his face.

"I have," she responded, "but I'm fine. Don't worry, Alex. But it's good to know you are nearby. I think I am going to need your help over the next few days," she continued.

"That's why I'm here, Anna," said Alex, lowering his voice. "What happened?"

"Nothing to worry about. It is just comforting to know you are here," replied Anna with a smile for public consumption, now feeling a little more calm as she placed her hand on his arm. "I would like to keep in touch with you every day. Perhaps I could phone you at your hotel. I will be discreet, because your hotel room may be bugged, but we could meet somewhere public, if I need your help. Is that okay, Alex?"

"Of course. Feel free to call at any time. But, Anna, do not take any chances," he said emphatically.

Before Anna could respond, Maggie arrived. "Alex, I'd like to introduce you to my delightful new friend Maggie Mason. She is the assistant to the Consulate General in Warsaw, and has been really helpful to me during my brief stay here."

"Pleased to meet you," said Alex, with his charming smile on his face as he shook hands.

Their conversation was interrupted by an announcement from Charlie Adams of the times and the programs for the London Philharmonic Orchestra's performances for Saturday, Sunday, and the gala performance on Monday evening. He asked that any late special requests for tickets should be lodged at the British Council offices for the attention of Janet Clark.

Anna was unaware that this announcement was going to be made, but smiled sweetly to everyone who looked at her. Although the quartet started to play again after the announcement, this seemed to be the signal for the reception to break up. The Polish government ministers and dignitaries, and then, gradually, the Board of Trustees, the members of the orchestra, and foreign diplomats all expressed their thanks to Sir Miles as they left. Anna looked around and saw that Krinsky had already departed. It was not quite 8:30 p.m. Anna felt she should stay and be one of the last people to leave. She had plenty of time before her date with the colonel. She walked out on the terrace to get a final breath of fresh air. She didn't know if she was more fearful of the sudden appearance of Sergei, or the next few hours with Colonel Krinsky. Alex was right, she was going into the lion's den. She went back inside.

"Are you coming?" said Maggie. "We're going for a drink with a few friends from the consulate," she continued.

"Thanks, but no. I think I'll stay here with BW just to make sure he's happy with everything."

"Alright, luv. Have a nice evening, but if you want to catch up with us, we will be in the big bar at the Europejski."

BW was talking to the Ambassador as Anna approached. "Do you need anything else, Mr. Brookes-Walton?" Anna said politely.

"No, thank you, Janet. It seems everything is under control. The Ambassador put on a marvelous reception, and of course the British Council is most appreciative," BW responded for the Ambassador's benefit.

"Stefania and I will be in the office tomorrow morning. In case you need me for anything. We're meeting Mr. Adams to check that all the programs and plans for the next few days are in final order."

"Very good, very good," said Brookes-Walton pompously, more or less dismissing Anna.

It was time to leave. She picked up Maggie's black cloak, and left the embassy looking for Neil. She thought he could take her to Krinsky's building. She could rely on him to ask no questions. His Saab was one of the last few cars in the driveway and as he saw her he waved.

"Where are we going, Janet? Are you joining Maggie and the others?" Neil said.

"No, I have got a business appointment. She got out Krinsky's card. Can you take me to 84 Krakowskie Przedmieście? It's a government building, but the front door will be locked so we will have to enter through a small turning just off Królewska Street.

Do you know where that is?"

"Yes, I think so."

Within a few minutes, Neil was at the address; one of the government buildings which formed the row of important architectural buildings on Krakówskie Street. They had all been destroyed during the Second World War, but had been restored to their former glory, primarily occupied by government departments, but including the Hotel Bristol at numbers 42 to 44, and a magnificent palace in the middle of the block that was being restored to serve as the President's residence. The building Anna was visiting housed the SB Counterinsurgency Department, and apparently provided an apartment for Roman Krinsky.

"Would you like me to stay until your appointment is finished, Janet?" asked Neil, without a trace of innuendo.

"That won't be necessary, Neil. Thank you. I'm only a few minutes away from my apartment, and I don't know how long this meeting will last. This is very important to me, Neil. I know that I can rely on your total discretion."

He assured her that she could rely on him completely. "Please be careful, Janet," he continued. "This country is still under martial law, and I know from past experience that this can be very dangerous for foreign visitors."

"Thanks, Neil, I will be very careful, I promise." She opened the car door and as she got out pulled the hood of Maggie's cloak over her head as she made her way to the rear of the building, which was well lit and not at all menacing. There was a large glass ornate door, and a panel of numbers with buttons on the left hand wall. Only one button was lit up, and that was number 3. She pressed the button which created a buzz on the door which she pushed open. The entryway had a marble floor. She went up a couple of steps, to a steel-cased elevator. Again, only number 3 was lit up and she pressed the button. The elevator doors opened and she entered with her heart pounding. She was now in the lion's den.

The elevator slowly ascended. She had no idea what to expect, but despite her pounding heart and clamminess on her back, she was determined to stay calm and focus on her goal for the evening. Jan and only Jan.

The elevator reached the third floor and the doors opened. She was surprised to find herself right inside Colonel Krinsky's apartment. She stepped out onto a marble hallway.

"Good evening, Janet. I see you found your way. So nice of you to come," said Krinksy with a disarming smile.

"This is beautiful," responded Janet, with her own disarming smile. "I thought I would be visiting you in your office," she lied, all sweetness and naiveté. "This is magnificent," she continued, as the colonel led her from the hallway into a luxurious living room.

To Anna, it appeared to be like the presidential suite in a hotel. The living room was large, with a high ceiling and beautifully engraved moldings. A giant glass chandelier hung from the ceiling with modern flickering lights to give the impression of candles. A black polished Steinway was positioned on the left. There was a marble fireplace surrounded by two beige silk armchairs, and two large sofas with tasseled cushions and a large brown marble coffee table on which were books, papers and ornaments. At the end of the room was a bay window, covered by floor-to-ceiling silk drapes, a beautiful walnut desk in the bay on which was an ornate lamp and leather inbox, papers piled high and onyx boxes and letter opener. Two telephones, one of which was green, were also on the desk. A sideboard in the French Empire style was against the wall facing the fireplace, and a small round table had been set up in between, with a silver candelabra in the center, surrounded by little rosebuds. A bottle of Dom Pérignon and Walova Vodka were in ice buckets next to one of the chairs. Cut-glass champagne flutes, fine china, and a plate of dark Polish bread completed the place settings.

My God, thought Anna. *Is this how Communist officials look after themselves?*

There was only one door in the room, which Anna thought must lead to the bedroom and bathroom. She didn't want to think about that, not right now. The lights had been dimmed and the room resonated with low classical music on the stereo. The colonel was clearly going into full charm assault mode.

"Now, Janet, make yourself comfortable," said Krinsky as he helped to take off her black silk cloak. "I thought we could talk over a little light supper, without interruption," he said giving her another warm smile. "How about a glass of Dom Pérignon?"

"That would be lovely," said Anna. "Is this your permanent home?" she asked innocently.

"No, I live in the country, but I keep the city apartment above the shop so to speak, because I often have to stay in Warsaw for official reasons," he said as he poured her a glass of champagne. "I have got a little Polish fare for your enjoyment, Janet," he continued as he approached the sideboard, opened one of the cupboards, and took out two prepared plates of herring in cream sauce decorated with caviar. "I hope you'll find this to your taste," he continued.

"I'm sure I will, Colonel. It looks delightful."

"Let us sit down and enjoy," he said, as he politely pulled out one of the chairs.

Anna sat down demurely and sipped her champagne.

"Now, tell me all about yourself, Janet."

As they started eating, Anna launched into her script about her Australian upbringing, her Polish mother, learning to speak Polish at home, and the excitement of her first visit to Poland, conscious of course, all the time, that he had heard this story before, during her interrogation at SB headquarters. She also described the highlights of her sightseeing in Wroclaw and Poznan, as well as Warsaw.

He seemed confident that she had not recognized him from the interrogation.

"Well, now it's your turn, Colonel, you must tell me all about yourself," she said innocently. "You seem to have a very important job."

Much to Anna's amazement, he seemed quite willing to talk about himself and his background, stressing his aristocratic lineage, the death of his parents in the Second World War, his work for the Polish resistance against the Nazis, even though he wasn't yet into his teens, from which Anna surmised that Krinsky was a few years older than he looked. He described his military career leading to his current position as the head of the Polish National Security Service.

"We're living in difficult times in Poland, and we have a state of emergency because of certain elements that wish to bring down the government," he continued in a more serious vein. "It is my job to protect our citizens and the President, General Jaruzelski and our government. Many countries, particularly in the West do not appreciate how fragile our position is. We have to face facts, Janet. We have that big Russian bear sitting on our borders, watching our every move, and ready to pounce if they don't like the way things are going in our country. That is why we have to deal harshly with Solidarity, and any other movement that threatens our government and our way of life. If we look like we are failing, the Russians will move in," Krinsky said, with his face hardening and his voice rising with some agitation. Anna could see the power in his face and felt the deep penetration of his brown eyes. This was someone who could be ruthless and cruel. She shivered at the thought.

"I can see how important your job is, Colonel. I had no idea all these things were going on in Poland. You've certainly got your hands full."

They had finished their light meal, and he had poured out a couple more glasses of champagne. He had consumed four glasses of vodka as well as two glasses of champagne. Anna was determined to hold her drink, as he went over to the sideboard and removed from another cupboard a bottle of slivovitz and a plate of dark flat chocolates.

"Try some of these, Janet," he said pouring a small shot glass of the liqueur and pushing the chocolate towards her.

"Lovely," she said, helping herself to a chocolate and pretending to take a small sip. "Do you play the piano?" Anna asked, seeking to change the conversation and delay his inevitable advance at her.

"Yes. I have been playing since I was four years old. My parents were true music lovers, as well as accomplished musicians themselves, so they sat me on a piano stool at a very early age. Of course when the war started, I was unable to continue, and it was some fifteen years later that I found out that I could still play, albeit not as proficiently. But I like to play now. I find it relaxing although my time is limited. Do you play, Janet?"

"Very poorly, I am afraid. My mother was a piano teacher, so she tried hard to make a musician out of me, but I really didn't have the talent, and growing up in Australia I wanted to be outdoors all the time. I preferred sports in the open air to practicing indoors. She was very disappointed," Anna continued. Krinsky nodded as if understanding. It suddenly occurred to her that she should not have revealed information about her mother. She hoped that Krinsky had not taken note. "Would you play for me?" she asked, smiling demurely.

"It would be my pleasure," responded Krinsky with great gallantry and charm, getting up and moving over to the piano and turning off the stereo music. Anna followed him and leaned over the Steinway somewhat provocatively, as he sat down on the stool and started to play. She immediately recognized the piece. "Chopin Opus 28 Prelude #4."

A very sad piece, Anna thought. *An interesting choice.*

Krinsky was a talented pianist. He had a delicate touch and was totally absorbed in the piece he was playing. He was focused on the music, his eyes closing from time to time.

"Do you recognize this piece?" Krinsky asked, smiling at Anna.

"Of course! I love Chopin."

"There is an old Polish saying: 'A Pole listening to Chopin listens to the voice of his whole race.' I believe that's true. Frederic Chopin is a Polish hero and his music is certainly in all of our souls."

Anna found it hard to believe that this handsome and charming man, a talented pianist with obvious great feeling for the spirituality of music, was the ruthless enforcer of a military dictatorship.

"Well, that's enough of my showing off for one evening," said Krinsky with a laugh. "Let's makes ourselves more comfortable over there," he continued, picking up the slivovitz and the chocolates and moving over towards the sofa and the coffee table.

"Would you mind if I took off my uniform jacket? It's really quite heavy and warm."

"Of course not," Janet responded, making herself comfortable on the sofa. Krinsky sat down next to her, and she knew the evening performance was about to start.

"Tell me more about Australia, Janet," he said, leaning towards her with a soft smile and intense interest in what she was going to say. She rattled off a brief description of Australia, Sydney, the beaches, Alice Springs, the mountains, the Great Barrier Reef, a sort of tourist overview. He listened intently nodding from time to time, and reaching out to hold her hand.

"You seem to have one of the most powerful and important jobs in Poland," she continued, changing the subject and seeming oblivious to his holding her hand. "Can you decide who to put in jail or who to set free?" she asked as innocently as possible.

His face darkened, surprised at the question. "I can, of course. I just have to fill out one of those slips on my desk, but I don't. We keep strictly to the law and we follow due process in deciding who represents a threat to our society and who doesn't," he continued officiously. He clearly didn't like that question. She changed the subject.

"I've never met anyone so powerful, Colonel, it can certainly turn a girl's head," she said, clearly giving him a signal that she was in thrall to be in his company. He didn't miss it.

"I'm so pleased to have met you, Janet. You are so beautiful. I couldn't take my eyes off you at the reception. You outshone every woman in the ballroom," he said, turning on the charm.

"I'm so honored that you would even notice me, Colonel. Such an important man... and I'm just a junior employee at the British Council."

"Not true, Janet. I'm just an ordinary man at heart. And please call me Roman, none of this Colonel business tonight," he said moving in to kiss her.

Anna was surprised. His kiss was soft and tender. She leaned back. She didn't resist, but she also didn't respond. Despite the vodkas, champagne, and slivovitz, he didn't smell of drink. In fact she immediately noticed the smell of his skin, very manly and appealing.

"Let me show you the rest of my apartment," he said, gently pulling her up from the sofa. "By the way, these three pictures you see on the walls are by Polish artists from the late 19th century, who studied with the Impressionists in Paris. I was given them by one of my counterparts in Moscow. They were in the basement of the Hermitage in Leningrad, and had been languishing there for years. Unusual to get anything back from the Russians, you know," he said with a laugh. "They had probably been looted by the Russians at the end of the Second World War, so I feel quite happy that they're now back in their rightful place."

"They're lovely, Roman," said Anna. "I noticed them when I came into the room; very attractive, and you have lit them very well," she continued, keeping the conversation light.

Holding her hand, he led her out to the circular marble entryway which contained a door painted in the same decor as the walls, and thus not easily noticeable.

He opened the door and led Anna into a corridor, showing her a cloakroom, a beautifully decorated visitor's bathroom, a storage room and what appeared to be a staff bedroom. At the end of the corridor was a large stainless-steel and granite kitchen with a picture window overlooking Ogród Saski Park.

"My! Roman. This is all so beautiful. It's like living in a palace," said Anna, continuing the performance of the naive little girl.

"Yes. It's very comfortable, but I do have a lot of important meetings here, and I have to make sure that my visitors, especially those from foreign countries, are impressed and recognize that we Poles are sophisticated and modern."

"Of course. I'm sure that is very important to Poland's image," responded Anna helpfully.

Still holding her hand, Roman led Anna out of the kitchen and back into the corridor. There was a door that they had passed that they had not entered previously, which he now opened to reveal a large comfortably appointed bedroom. Anna immediately noticed that the drapes had been closed and the lights dimmed. The bedroom was dominated by a large bed, with an ornate carved headboard, side tables with cut-glass lamps, a thick carpet, and a couple of comfortable armchairs together with a chest of drawers again in the French Empire style.

"This is beautiful, Roman," said Anna enthusiastically. "Your whole apartment is exquisite."

"Thank you, Janet. You clearly have a good eye. Let me show you the bathroom." He led her into an en-suite dressing-room area and an enormous marble bathroom. She noticed that the dressing room was very masculine, with a row of suits and uniforms, neat shelves with shirts and sweaters and racks of shoes and some formal military boots. The bathroom had a large sunken bath, walk-in shower, a double basin and a vanity area. Mirrors covered the wall with the recess lighting reflecting the French gray marble.

"You're making me very jealous, Roman," said Anna. "Everything is so beautiful. I could live in the bathroom," she continued with a laugh.

"Well, you'll have to try it out," responded Roman with a suggestive smile, still holding Anna by the hand as he led her back into the bedroom. Anna knew that Krinsky was following a line of patter he had used many times before. Maybe not in English, but still... the well-thought-out seductive plans of a serial womanizer. But she had to admit, she found him very attractive. He exuded power and charisma, apart from his extraordinary good looks.

"You fit in here perfectly, Janet. Dressed up for the reception, and elegantly beautiful."

They were standing in the middle of the bedroom, and he gently pulled her towards him and kissed her. Again, soft and tender, but this time he started to kiss her neck and shoulders. She could feel the strength of his arms as he held her tightly, and this time she responded to his kisses, feeling her heart pounding. Now his tongue was probing, and his hands started to roam to her breasts. She felt aroused, and her breath was coming in shorter gasps. And then his hands were around her back, and she felt him unzip her dress which slipped down and pooled on the floor, leaving her naked, other than her panties. She stepped out of her shoes and put her arms around his neck as she started to kiss him passionately. She was nervous and excited at the same time; adrenaline was flowing. He started to take off his clothes, revealing a muscular torso, with black hair on his arms and chest. He gently led her to the bed, guiding her onto her back, all the time kissing her on the mouth, neck, and shoulders. Now his hands were roaming over her body, caressing her breasts and stomach while his lips found hers and his tongue probed. His fingers started to rub her through her panties, and she could feel her passion rising. Then she was helping him, as he removed her panties and took off the rest of his clothes. Now she eagerly wanted him. His hands roamed and caressed her whole body and his fingers probed, as she arched back towards him. Then he was inside her, and their bodies were writhing and rhythmically moving together. Anna was now responding with full passion, sighing and groaning as he eventually brought her to a climax. He continued to kiss her as he rolled her on top of him. She twisted from side to side, feeling him deep inside her, and, then bathed in sweat, they moved in unison as they climaxed together. Anna laid in his arms, completely spent, listening to his racing heart beat and looking into his handsome face with those deep, brown penetrating eyes.

"My God, Janet. You're really something. What a tiger! The little innocent lady is quite a lover," he said with a laugh. "That was wonderful."

"You are, what we call in Australia, a real hunk," responded Anna. "I get the feeling you may have done this before, Roman. You seem to be a real expert, but how could a girl resist?" she continued cheekily.

He lifted her head off his chest and kissed her again. This time soft and tender.

"I would like to see a lot more of you, Janet," he said, apparently genuinely. "How much longer will you be in Warsaw?"

"Just a few more days. But maybe I could get a posting at the British Council," she said, clearly eager to accommodate his wishes.

He held her and kissed her again, and started to caress and arouse her. They made love again, this time more slowly. Afterwards they dozed for a bit in each other's arms.

"You are incredible, Janet," he said. "If there is anything I can ever do for you in Warsaw, at any time, just let me know."

Anna saw her opening.

"Well, Roman," she said with her heart pounding. "Perhaps you could help a friend of mine. He was arrested some months ago, for smuggling. I know that he didn't do it, but his case is not coming to trial. He was a school friend of mine in Australia, and I had hoped to see him when I got to Warsaw, but I found out that he is in Mokotów prison. Perhaps you could get him released?" she said smiling, as innocent as possible.

"If he is not involved in some big crime or mafia-style gang, perhaps I can help," responded Roman. "What's his name?"

"Jan Kaluza."

Anna could feel him immediately stiffen as he raised himself up on one elbow.

"Jan Kaluza," he repeated. "You know Jan Kaluza?"

"Yes," Anna said. "We went to school together."

She saw his face harden and his eyes narrow and she could feel her stomach tighten with nervousness.

"I was right," he said with his voice rising. "You and Kopacz. He has something of Professor Keller's that you want, doesn't he? I knew there was some connection." A look of realization came over his face. "You're Anna Kaluza! You're not Janet Clark," he shouted, his face now red with anger, and veins pulsating on his forehead. "You're wanted for murder. You want to see your brother Jan? I can arrange that. In fact you can keep each other company in Mokotów prison. You thought you could fuck me, and get me to sign a release? You stupid little bitch. You're crazy!"

He grabbed Anna in a vicelike grip on her wrist and started to drag her off the bed.

"I don't know what you're talking about, Roman," Anna cried, panic stricken, desperately trying to free herself. "I'm Janet Clark. You've made a mistake!"

"No I haven't. But I can assure you, we will find out everything. You'll have plenty of time to think about things in prison. I'm going to make a call now, and in twenty minutes, you will be on your way to keep your brother company," he responded, screaming at her with a vicious look on his face.

Anna was trying to twist away from him, but to no avail. Even though she was resisting with all her strength, he pulled her off the bed and slowly dragged her half stumbling out of the bedroom and into the living room towards his desk. They were both naked and Anna had no answer to his considerable strength. Her panic was rising. She knew that once the "ferrets" arrived, she was doomed. They would torture and maybe kill her, but if not, she would be tried for murder and sentenced to death. She realized that her effort to get Jan released was foolhardy. Krinsky was too clever, too ruthless and too worldly to fall for her attempts at seduction. He seemed to guess what she was thinking and continued to yell at her. "You thought you could fuck me, to get your brother out of prison. Who do you think I am, some schoolboy, who you could wave your tits at and seduce?"

He had dragged her across the room, and now slammed her into his desk. She was now pinned, with her back across the desk, as he leaned over her to the green phone. Her free hand desperately roamed the back of the desk, looking for some object she could hit him with. As he picked up the phone, her hand found the onyx letter opener on his blotter. She had one chance. She could not waste a second and as he was distracted by her writhing under him, and picked the phone off its hook, she plunged the letter opener in his left eye, and deeply into his brain. A look of horror appeared on his face. He immediately released the vicelike grip on her wrist, and started to slide down her body to the floor. He let out a death rattle from his throat, and then was still.

Anna looked down, and knew he was dead. She started to shake uncontrollably as she leaned against the desk. Tears were running down her face and she was moaning quietly to herself. She was aware her wrist was throbbing, and her naked body was blotched red and hurting from Krinsky's rough treatment. She didn't know how long she stood gently rocking herself, but after a while she started to recover her composure somewhat, looking around the room as her surroundings came into focus again.

Now her thoughts turned to escape and survival. She bent down, and trying not to look at Krinsky's face, she withdrew the letter opener from his eye. A trickle of blood and fluid ran down his face onto the carpet. She went over to the table where they had been dining, and picked up a napkin, using it to wipe the blood and fluid and her fingerprints from the letter opener. She proceeded to use the napkin to wipe clean her champagne glass, water glass, knife, fork and spoon, the arms of her dining chair, the plate of chocolates, the shot glass for the slivovitz, and other objects that may have had her fingerprints on them. When this was completed, she went back into the bedroom. Krinsky's clothes were in a pile on the floor, as was her dress and shoes. Grabbing her panties from the bed, she quickly put them on, and went into the bathroom and looked at herself in the mirror. Her tearstained face was red and puffy, her mascara had run, and her hair was a mess. Using a small hand towel she ran cold water in a basin and washed her face. She was still shaking. Unpinning her hair, she let it fall to her shoulders. Her wrist was red and bruised and some of the blotches on her skin looked angry. Drying herself quickly, and wiping her fingerprints off the faucets and basin, she returned to the bedroom, put her dress and shoes back on, then walked back into the living room to collect her black cloak and handbag. She hoped she had thought of everything and had left no trace of her visit. There was nothing more she could do. Exhausted and still trembling, she had to get back to her apartment. She gave one last look round the living room and then left, careful to wipe her fingerprints off the door handles and the elevator button as she left the building.

It was not yet midnight, but there seemed to be very little traffic as she walked quickly up the side turning until she got to Wrzosowa Street, a mere ten minutes from her apartment.

Keeping the hood of her cloak well over her eyes she hurriedly made her way home. A late-night bus and some cars passed but there was nobody on the streets. As she approached the apartment building, she crossed the street because the two "ferrets" were in their car as usual. But she saw they were both asleep. A lucky break, and so she was relieved to let herself back into her apartment. Maggie and Steffi had not yet returned. *They must be having a good night out,* she thought.

Undressing and painfully climbing into the shower, she cleansed herself from her lovemaking with Roman. Hot water soothed her bruises. She knew that Krinsky's murder would create a national manhunt for the perpetrator. Could they connect her to the murder? Jan was still in prison, and she was no nearer getting him released. What would tomorrow bring? She was too exhausted to think about it and flopped into her bed knowing she faced another problem; her meeting with Sergei tomorrow morning in the park.

Chapter 23

She awoke with a start. Her mind was racing. In her subconscious state she had devised a plan. A last chance for Jan. Could the Russian do it? Would he do it? Could this be a way out for her? A new life at last?

She looked at her watch. It was just past seven and the apartment was dead quiet. Her window was wide open, but the curtain didn't move. There was hardly a breath of air. It was going to be another scorcher. She turned over in her bed and felt a stab of pain in her ribs. Her left wrist was red and swollen and her hip and thigh were also aching. Last night's horror entered her thoughts, and she started shaking with fear and felt a knot in her stomach tightening. She couldn't help herself as she relived the sight of the letter opener pushing through Krinsky's eye and into his brain. Her breathing was coming in short bursts and she thought she was about to have a panic attack. She turned against the wall, forced her eyes shut, and willed herself to clear her mind of these terrible thoughts. She must concentrate on Jan now, and somehow push the previous night's events and the possible consequences from her mind.

Slowly, she sat up on the edge of the bed, wincing in pain from her bruises. But she pushed herself to her feet, and padded out of her bedroom to the bathroom. She closed the door quietly, took off her nightie and looked at her naked body in the mirror. She saw a large red weal across her left ribs, and a big purple bruise on her right hip. There were some other red blotches on her torso and hips, and her wrist was a mess. Luckily there were no marks on her face, neck, shoulders, or legs. She washed her face with cold water and used a cold flannel to dab the puffiness around her eyes, and her bruised ribs and hips and felt some relief. She cleaned her teeth, and vigorously brushed her hair, which was a matted mess from the night before. After adding a light touch of makeup and a spritz of perfume she felt better. She quietly padded back to her bedroom, and put on her bra, panties, shorts, a baggy T-shirt, and socks and sneakers. She had a man's handkerchief, which Neil had given her and she had yet to return, and she wrapped it round her swollen wrist tucking it in carefully, completely covering the red swelling. Moving around had helped her aches and pains, and she felt revitalized as she quietly exited the bedroom for the kitchen area, where she made herself a cup of black coffee with a liberal amount of sugar. It was just after eight but the apartment was still quiet. She guessed that Maggie and Steffi were probably still in a deep sleep after last night. When she finished her coffee, she left the apartment, closing the door as quietly as possible behind her.

As she reached the street, she was immediately hit by a blanket of humidity. Nevertheless, she started jogging up and down in place, warming up, knowing that the "ferrets" in the car across the street were watching her. As she started jogging down Bielanska Street towards Ogrod Krasinskich Park, she saw one of the "ferrets" get out of the vehicle. However, he decided not to follow her, perhaps not relishing the thought of running in this heat. He got back into the car.

The "ferrets" had become bored, and lazy. They were fed up watching Janet Clark and seeing nothing untoward. She headed across Swierczewskiego Street and into the park. Passing the Museum of Archaeology, she jogged along and passed the Narodowa Library, to the tree-shaded picnic area in the extremities of the park. She was more than five minutes early, so she jogged around in a circle, eventually coming back to one of the picnic tables at the back of the wood where she sat and waited. There were very few people in the park at this hour. Within a few minutes she saw Sergei coming towards her from Swietojerska Street. He was wearing brown linen trousers, sandals and a cream shirt, already drenched in sweat. His normal pale puffy face was red as a beetroot and he was wiping his forehead with a large handkerchief as he approached.

"My God, Anna, what a day. A heat wave in Warsaw is like a hot wet blanket. So uncomfortable," he said with a friendly smile, panting from the minor excursion of walking across the park.

"I don't like it either, Sergei," she said pleasantly. "So I have taken it easy this morning. I have been jogging really slowly."

Sergei took out a plastic bottle of water from his hip pocket. He took a large gulp, and passed it to Anna.

"Here, have a taste of this. It helps," he said.

"Thank you," responded Anna, helping herself to a slow drink.

"We don't want to stay around here too long. So I will get straight to the point. I think you are in Warsaw to collect something that belonged to Professor Keller. Am I right?"

"Yes."

"And that is…?"

"More than thirty years of Professor Keller's notes, formulas, calculations, quantum mathematics, and solutions relative to nuclear-fusion theories."

Sergei's eyes widened and his mouth opened. Anna could see the excitement moving up his flabby body.

"What!" he said incredulously. "That's a goldmine of information. Why didn't you tell us?" he continued with his eyes narrowing.

"I didn't know what I was supposed to collect, and I didn't know if I would be able to get hold of the papers."

"Have you got the papers now?"

"No."

Sergei's face dropped and his eyes hardened. "Well, are they available or not?"

"I know they are available, and I will be able to get them on Tuesday morning, just before I leave the country," she said coolly and confidently.

"Have you told MI6?"

"Yes. They are hoping I can deliver them on Tuesday."

"This could be the most important delivery we have ever made," he continued, hardly able to conceal his excitement.

"I know," responded Anna. "I've been told that all the papers are in Professor Keller's code. Whoever gets them will have the job of cracking the code, which may take weeks or even months. He did that, apparently, as a form of security for himself and his family, designed to work whether he landed back in Moscow or in London."

"We have the best code breakers in the world. I know that will not be a problem," said Sergei arrogantly. "Your job, Anna, is to deliver them to me, and then you will be providing lifetime security for your mother in the idyllic setting of Kaskia Lodge," he continued with a menacing leer. Anna ignored the veiled threats.

"I'll deliver the papers to you, Sergei, but I expect something from you in return."

"Really. And what might that be?"

"My brother Jan is in Mokotów Prison. He was arrested in February as part of a raid on a ring of smugglers working for ORBIS. He is totally innocent, but he's unlikely to get a trial. I want to know whether you can get him out of jail."

"That may be possible," said Sergei warily. "You should have asked your friend Roman Krinsky, last night at the reception. He is head of the SB and could have him released within an hour."

"I don't know Roman Krinsky," Anna responded, trying to keep her voice from trembling.

"I saw you speaking to him a couple of times," said Sergei.

"I spoke to many Polish dignitaries and officers and I can't remember who was who," continued Anna, trying to sound casual.

"He was the tall handsome colonel in the olive-green uniform."

"Sergei, I spoke to officers in pale blue uniforms, gray

uniforms, and olive-green uniforms. I don't think I remember him."

"Well, anyway, I will speak to him on Monday morning. I don't think it should be too much of a problem to get your brother out of prison," he said with a slight smile on his face.

"But he is under Polish jurisdiction. Could that make it difficult?" she asked anxiously.

Sergei let out a belly laugh, revealing his yellow teeth and mopping his brow as the sweat continued to drip down his face. "Of course he is under Polish jurisdiction. But let us say we have an arrangement. If Mother Russia wants something or someone from the Poles, they are always most accommodating. So, as I say, I don't think it will be a problem."

"There is another part of this request," said Anna. "Jan's wife, Ava, and their two children will need to leave Poland safely on Tuesday morning. I'm going to give you their address. I'm sure they don't have passports, but I hope you could get them out of the country. Is that possible?" she asked, trying to conceal her fear and concern.

Sergei paused, looking into space as he was thinking.

"I suppose I could have a couple of my people put them on the ferry to Stockholm. But without papers and passports they would not be let into Sweden, unless you can arrange for them to disembark in Stockholm, perhaps into the hands of the British," he said.

Anna could now see how important this transaction was to Sergei. This might be the highlight of his career. He would be a hero in Moscow and could retire in comfort to his dacha, at least until the code breakers found out that vital links, solutions and analysis in Keller's papers were missing.

"If you bring Jan to the Victoria Hotel lobby at eleven on Tuesday morning, and confirm to me that Ava and the children are on their way to Sweden, I will hand over Keller's papers."

"What will you tell MI6?"

"I will tell them that my source was unable to deliver as I had been promised. They believe that it is a long shot in any event, so I don't think they will be too surprised."

"Okay, Anna, we have a deal. You know you can trust me. I've always delivered in the past. You just make sure that you get those papers, and your brother and his family will be safe," he said, clearly excited.

"Right, Sergei. I will see you at eleven on Tuesday morning at the Victoria Hotel. If there is any reason to believe you cannot deliver, please get a message to me. I shall be at the London Philharmonic Orchestra concerts tonight, tomorrow evening, and for the gala event on Monday evening."

Anna took out a little purse from her pocket, from which she retrieved some zlotys, pencil and a small notepad. She wrote down the Hotel Victoria address on Krolweska Street, as well as Ava's address. She gave the note to Sergei. He looked at the note quickly, and nodded.

"We have spent too long talking in this park, Anna. You leave first, and I'll follow in a few minutes. I will see you on Tuesday unless you hear otherwise."

Anna said goodbye and started jogging back across the park; checking to see that Sergei was not following her, she jumped into a public phone box outside the Museum of Archaeology. She took out a piece of paper with a phone number on it, put zlotys in the phone and dialed. The phone started ringing. "Please pick up, please," she said to herself, her heart pounding. After what seemed like an eternal delay, she heard a voice say.

"Yes?"

"Professor Galinski?"

"Yes."

"I am Anna, a friend of Professor Kopacz; he gave me your number."

"I see."

"Will you tell him that Anna would urgently like to see

number 2 Karowa Street, and I hope he can join me tomorrow at the 11:00 a.m. Mass at Kosciol Sw. Krzyzy. Can you get this message to him?" Anna asked anxiously.

"Yes. I think so. He lives in the apartment below me," Galinski replied, in an amused voice.

"Oh, that would be wonderful. Thank you so much," Anna responded, breathing a sigh of relief. "I appreciate your assistance, Professor. Goodbye," she said politely, as she hung up the phone.

Anna was back in the apartment within fifteen minutes. Steffi and Maggie were up and about, padding around in their nighties in the kitchen.

"Good morning. You were up early," said Maggie quizzically.

"Yes. I couldn't sleep. It was too hot, so I thought I'd get out for an early jog, but, boy, is it humid out there," replied Anna.

Stefania looked a little pale and worse for wear, obviously hungover.

"You girls got in late. Did you have a good time?" said Anna.

"Yeah, we had a great time. Didn't get back till after two. Those musicians really know how to party. It was amazing. Flute players, violinists, percussionist, they were all the same. They can party like mad," said Maggie, laughing. "We had a really good time, didn't we, Stef?"

Stefania nodded, still half asleep, and not in a chatty mood.

"What happened to your wrist?" asked Maggie, looking at Anna's makeshift bandage.

"I slipped on the embassy steps. I'm not used to those high heels. I fell on my hand, and I think I sprained my wrist. But it's okay, I wrapped it up for the day. It's a bit swollen. I could really do with a cup of coffee," Anna continued, changing the subject.

"Okay," said Maggie. "I will make you some toast and coffee. I know Neil is picking you and Steffi up at 10:30 so you better get a move on."

"I'll just pop into the shower and get dressed. I won't be long," said Anna.

Fifteen minutes later she was dressed, made up, with her hair on her shoulders, and ready for what the day might bring. Her elation at making progress on her plan to release Jan was tempered by her fear of what the day's news might bring. Would Krinsky's body have been found yet? Would the police or the SB be able to connect her to the murder? She shuddered at the thought as she put the final touches to her makeup, and went back into the kitchen.

Anna had just finished breakfast and a second cup of coffee when the doorbell rang. Neil announced that he was downstairs in the car.

"We'll be back this afternoon to change for this evening's concert," said Anna to Maggie. "Are you coming?"

"No thanks. I don't want to spend my weekend sweltering in a concert hall with no air conditioning," responded Maggie with a laugh.

Neil deposited Anna and Stefania at the British Council's offices. There was a skeleton staff on duty, but Anna immediately went to the reception desk to check the Warsaw newspapers for any news on Krinsky. There was nothing. Too early, she decided.

They worked hard on ticket requirements, logistics and timetables for the transfer of the Board of Trustees and the orchestra to the concert hall. Charlie Adams came in later, and confirmed everything was set up from his end. All they could do was hope that it went smoothly.

Anna and Stefania went back to the apartment to change later in the afternoon. The humidity was nearly unbearable and they both wore the lightest clothes possible, although Anna chose a long-sleeve blouse to cover her wrist. They arrived at the Teatr Wielki early to greet all the dignitaries, consular general officers, and the press. The concert, a Beethoven evening, including the "Eroica," was well-received. Everyone was pleased. As in Wroclaw and Poznan, the orchestra got a standing ovation.

Alex had joined other members of the Board of Trustees, and Anna made sure she could spend a few minutes with him.

"I think I'm going to need your help, Alex. Are you up for lunch tomorrow?" said Anna.

"Yes," replied Alex. "What do you need, Anna?"

"I'll fill you in tomorrow. Say lunch at your hotel at one?"

"Of course. That'll be fine. I'll see you then," responded Alex, as he joined the rest of the trustees leaving the concert hall.

Stefania had looked pale all day and was eager to get home to bed. Anna was also exhausted after a traumatic twenty-four hours. She knew that the news of Krinsky's death would come out shortly, and that all hell would break loose. The thought that she might be arrested or even interrogated caused her to shake uncontrollably. But she tried to think positively. Only two more days and then she hoped Jan would be leaving Warsaw. Nevertheless, she did not have a good night, tossing and turning, and waking in fear when she heard the wail of a police car siren. Her hip and other bruises were still painful as was her wrist. She was awake well before six, but couldn't go back to sleep. She lay in her bed, thinking through her plan to collect Keller's papers and get them to Sergei. She would have to hide them in the apartment for a day or two. She also knew she would have to tell Alex about Krinsky and her plan for Jan and the family. Would he help? Some things she couldn't reveal. It was going to be difficult.

Anna got up, had a shower, and was dressed by nine. Stefania and Maggie were still in their nightclothes when they came into the kitchen area to see Anna making a large breakfast for them.

"It is Sunday. So I thought I'd make you some eggs and bacon. We can have a leisurely breakfast today. It's too hot to rush about, so we can take it easy. What have you girls got planned for the day?" asked Anna.

"I have been invited to have lunch, by one of the violinists from the orchestra," said Steffi rather sheepishly.

"You never said anything," said Maggie laughing. "What a sly one you are," she continued, with a dig.

"What are you doing, Maggie?" asked Anna innocently. "Are you out all day?"

"Yes, I am heading to the Lazienki Park again, with some friends from the consulate. We hope to have a swim and picnic. It should be fun. What about you, Janet?"

"I have arranged to have lunch with Sir Alex today. I'm going to take him on a little sightseeing tour this afternoon. And then another concert this evening. Steffi is helping me for this afternoon's matinee, aren't you?" Anna said.

"Of course. I'll be there and take care of everything," said Stefania.

"I will see you girls later then," said Anna, getting ready to leave.

She went through her usual evasion tactics just in case the "ferrets" were in the mood to follow her, and was at the Kosciol Sw Krzyza Church ten minutes before eleven. She looked around anxiously for Professor Kopacz, as she settled into a pew three rows from the front of the ornate alter where the priests and the choir were gathering. A couple of minutes later she saw him enter from Krakowski Street. He was carrying a co-op shopping bag, and came and sat next to her.

"Good morning, Anna. I got your message, and everything you require is in this bag." He spoke in a whisper.

"Thank you, Professor. I'm really most appreciative. I hope you weren't followed here," Anna responded, also in a whisper.

"I don't think so. The SB has got other things on its mind today. Roman Krinsky has been murdered. Haven't you seen the papers?"

"No," said Anna. She purposely had put off buying a newspaper until after the mass and her meeting with the Professor.

The mass started, and Anna gradually calmed down. In fact she enjoyed the service. It brought back her childhood memories in Australia. It had been so long since she'd been to mass, but she felt a certain tranquility which gave her strength to face her fears and the horrors of Krinsky's death.

Her daydreaming was interrupted when Professor Kopacz whispered to her. "I'm going to slip out as soon as the mass finishes. I want to be lost in the crowd as much as possible. I suggest you wait until the very end and leave through the rear door over there. It will take you into a courtyard, which will lead you to Traugutta Street. If you need me again, remember you can contact me through Professor Galinsky. Otherwise, Anna, I wish you luck and when you next see Professor Keller, please give my best wishes to my dear old friend."

"I will. Thank you once again for all your help. I hope we meet again in better circumstances, when Poland frees itself from the current regime." She leaned over and gave the professor a peck on the cheek.

After leaving the church she bought a newspaper from a cafe bar down the street. The headline screamed of Krinsky's death:

Krinsky Dead.
Head of SB Murdered.

Colonel Roman Krinsky, 55, the Chief Executive and Commander of the SB, was found stabbed to death in the small apartment that he maintained above the offices of the SB counterintelligence department on Krakowski Street. It appears he was killed by either an intruder or someone with whom he had an appointment.

The article went on to describe Krinsky's background and career, including the fact that he was the son of Count Alexander Krinsky and the well-known 1930s Hungarian actress Ilona Dioniski, both of whom had been killed in the Second World War. The article also described Krinsky's important role in controlling the recent Solidarity uprisings, and maintaining public order. It intimated that Krinsky was General Jaruzelski's right-hand man, in line to succeed him. The article also included a statement from his wife, the beautiful Moscow model, Tanya Sakharov:

"My husband told me he was attending a reception at the British Embassy last night, and then had a late meeting at his offices. He said he would stay overnight in the apartment above his office and would return home on Saturday morning. He has been working very hard recently, and with all the responsibilities of maintaining public order, he often has to stay overnight at the Department. When I hadn't heard from him by lunchtime, I got worried and decided to call Police Commissioner Stepinska. My family and I are in a state of shock over our loss and this gruesome act of violence. We are confident that the police will do everything possible to apprehend the responsible parties."

There was a small picture of the beautiful Tanya Sakharov with two young boys of about ten and twelve years old. The article concluded with a quote from Commissioner Stepinska:

"We are following a number of leads, and are using all our resources, to apprehend the killer. I shall be making a further public statement within the next forty-eight hours."

Anna read the article over and over again, her hands trembling as she held the *Trybuna Ludu* newspaper. She bought a copy of the *Zycie Warszanwy* paper as well, and compared the two articles. They were more or less the same, not giving much away but indicating a quiet confidence from the commissioner. As she finished reading, she heard the wail of police sirens. Maybe it was her imagination, but it seemed police cars were everywhere, sirens screaming. There was nothing she could do but wait, and pray that she had not left any clues that would lead the police directly to her, and that she would be out of the country before they even thought of her. Was this wishful thinking?

She clutched her Co-op shopping bag tightly and hurried back to the apartment. She knew the apartment would be empty, and went straight into her bedroom and pushed the bag under her bed.

It was nearly 1:00 p.m. as she entered the lobby of the Hotel Bristol for her lunch with Alex. She took a moment or two to pull herself together before walking into the bar. Alex was waiting.

"Good morning, Anna. How do you manage to look cool and composed in this boiling-hot weather?" asked Alex with smile.

"I don't feel at all cool," replied Anna. "In fact, I feel all my clothes are sticking to me, and I'd like a nice long cold cocktail."

"Well, I think that can be arranged," said Alex cheerfully. "Would you like a drink here or shall we order one at our table? I made a reservation for a quiet table in the corner over there."

"I'm happy to have my drink at the table. That quiet spot is a good idea."

Alex introduced himself to the maitre d' in Polish, and they were seated at a pretty pink-clothed table in the corner of the dining room, which was nearly empty this hot Sunday.

They sat down and the waiter presented them both with the menus, and took their drink orders, a vodka and tonic for Anna, and of course a scotch whisky and water for Alex.

"Okay, Anna," said Alex, lowering his voice and looking very serious. "I have to ask you. I hope you have nothing to do with Krinsky's murder, which is splashed all over the newspapers. I warned you to keep away from him and I trust you listened to me."

Anna started shaking, and tears welled up in her eyes, as she looked down to the table.

"Christ, Anna, what have you done?" asked Alex, with a look of horror on his face.

"I should have listened to you, Alex, but I had to try and get Jan released, so I went to his apartment..." Anna stopped, her voice shaking and unable to continue for a moment, as she relived the horror of Friday night. "He realized who I was," she stammered, "and was calling the SB to come and get me. He said I was wanted for murder, and he would put me in Mokotów Prison with Jan, and he would make sure that we told him everything." She paused, trying to hold herself together. "He made it clear that we would both suffer the most painful torture. He had me in a vice grip on my wrist. It's still swollen. I wrapped it up," she said, showing him the handkerchief around her wrist. "I didn't have a choice. It was either him... or death for myself and Jan. I stabbed him with a letter opener through his eye..." She stopped again as her voice cracked and tears started running down her cheeks. Alex immediately handed her a handkerchief.

"My God, Anna. This is a disaster. The city is now swarming with police, all looking for Krinsky's killer. Did anybody see you? Do you think you left fingerprints all over the place? Who do you think knew you had a date with Krinsky?" Alex rattled off these questions, his mind running ahead to damage control. Without waiting for an answer he continued, "If they haul you in, Anna, they could arrest half the British Council, or people from the Consulate General's offices..." He trailed off, but then continued still keeping his voice low but now really angry. "This could turn out to be a major diplomatic disaster. I told you not to get involved with Krinsky."

"I don't think anyone knew of my date with Krinsky. In fact he told me he would cancel some prior engagement in order for us to meet at his apartment. We had drinks and a light supper, which was already set up, probably for someone else. I did everything I could to wipe off any fingerprints. I hope I succeeded. I know it's only a few hours, but I haven't heard from anyone in the police, SB, nor the 'ferrets.' So I'm praying that Krinsky's murder will not be connected to me."

"This is your second killing in Poland in four months. How did you become so proficient?" asked Alex, somewhat sarcastically, but showing genuine concern.

"I'm not proficient. I had some training from the MI6, but I just had to respond to life-and-death situations. I'm now a trembling, nervous wreck, Alex," responded Anna with tears still in her eyes and her voice shaking.

Alex was thinking rapidly. "If you are arrested, I will try the diplomatic route to get you out. But it would be really difficult if that happens. I promise you, however, I won't speak to the Ambassador or anyone else unless the police come after you."

"Thank you, Alex. I know I can always rely on you," Anna said, reaching out across the table for Alex's hand. "I do need your help, however, with Jan and his family."

"Did you manage to do something for Jan?" asked Alex incredulously.

"Yes. I believe he is going to be released from prison on Tuesday morning, and will be able to travel with us to London. But, he doesn't have a passport, so I wondered if the Ambassador could help somehow."

"My God, Anna. How did you manage that? Do you think this will still happen now that Krinsky is dead? Security will be a nightmare. They are going to be watching and checking everybody leaving the country, unless they make a quick arrest. And that might be you," Alex continued emphatically, his mind racing.

"I can't be a hundred percent certain, but I think Jan will be released. But I will need some other help as well, Alex," said Anna, pleading now.

"More help? You're kidding. I don't know how we're going to get a passport, let alone additional help. What else do you need?"

"I need to get Ava and the children out of Poland on Tuesday morning as well. I believe I can get them on the ferry to Stockholm, but I know they have no passports or papers, so they won't be allowed to enter Sweden. Would it be possible for the British Embassy people to meet them off the ferry and take responsibility for them, putting them on a plane to London?"

"Anna, these are enormous tasks. I've got no idea whether this can be arranged or not, but I certainly can't help you unless I talk to the Ambassador directly about this. Tim Bevans and the people in London are delighted that you have successfully completed the mission in Warsaw, so there should be some goodwill towards you... and perhaps an effort to help you with Jan and his family. But I can't guarantee it. I'm sure it will raise hackles at the Foreign Office, but I will do my best."

"Thank you so much, Alex. I don't know what I would do without you. You've been my rock and support since Kraków. Without you I would be in a Polish prison or dead. I just hope that I can keep ahead of the police for the next forty-eight hours."

At that, the waiter came and took their order. Alex ordered a bottle of cold Chablis, and they both had cold salmon and salad. Neither of them was feeling particularly hungry.

Chapter 24

The Sunday-evening concert, Haydn's "Symphony No. 94," and Liszt's "Années de Pèlerinage," with soloist Leonard Littowitz, was another resounding success. Standing ovations for the orchestra and conductor. However it was a sweltering-hot evening, and Anna was delighted to get back to the apartment and take a cool shower before flopping into bed.

She had another disturbed night, partly because of a massive thunderstorm that shook the whole building around 2:00 a.m., after which she found it very difficult to sleep, reliving yet again the horrors of Friday night, her mind racing with fear about the possibility of her being arrested and interrogated. She was up early, even though this Monday was going to be a quiet day. She had planned to only spend a few hours in the office, partly at the request of BW who wanted to say goodbye before she departed to London. She was unable to shake the feeling of acute fear. There could be a knock on the door at any minute with a visit from the Warsaw police.

She tried to think positively. Only twenty-four hours to go, and she would be packing for a return journey to London. Would Alex be able to help? Having gotten this far, and if Sergei delivered Jan tomorrow, she had to find a way of getting him out of the country. She decided that if Alex couldn't help, she would stay in Warsaw, and go into hiding with Jan, and try to escape to Finland or Sweden. It would not be easy. She was praying that Alex would come through. Meanwhile she had to prepare for the gala this evening.

Another black-tie and uniform event, and evening dress for the ladies. She would wear the same outfit as for the British Embassy reception the other night. Was that the best thing to do? Would somebody recognize her and put her together with Roman Krinsky? Only Neil Jordan knew of her date with Krinsky.

Could she trust him, given the massive headlines and coverage of his murder? It was no use worrying, she decided. There was nothing she could do but wait.

The storm had finally broken the oppressive heat wave, dumping inches of rain on the city, and cooling everything down. It was a cloudy but pleasant day and a great relief from the excessive heat of the past few days. Anna got dressed for her last day at the British Council and made breakfast for the girls who came sleepily into the kitchen at around eight.

"Last day at the office for me," Anna said jauntily to Maggie and Steffi.

"We're going to miss you," responded Maggie. "Aren't we, Steffi?"

"I'm feeling really sad this morning," said Steffi. "You have taught me so much, and have been wonderful to work with. The least snooty person in the British Council," she continued.

"Well, you've done a great job, Steffi. I think you are much more appreciated now, and I know that BW has asked you to stay on for a new twelve-month contract. Have you decided yet?"

"Yes, I decided to stay. I think it will be a great experience, and I'm enjoying Warsaw and my Polish is improving every day. Maggie has been a wonderful house mum to me, so I'm really happy here at the moment."

"I think that's a good decision," said Anna. "Meanwhile we have got the gala to worry about tonight. The President, General Jaruzelski, and a whole lot of dignitaries and military people."

"Did you see all the stuff in the papers, about the murder, Janet?" asked Maggie. "I think he was one of the officers you were talking to at the British Embassy reception. Really good-looking."

"Yes, I saw the headlines. I guess he was one of the big cheeses in Poland. I may have spoken to him at the embassy reception, but quite frankly, Maggie, I spoke to so many people in uniform, I can't remember one from the other."

"Well, by all accounts, he was one for the ladies. Had a girl in every port so to speak. So maybe this was a crime of passion," said Maggie with a big laugh. "Anyway, hope it doesn't put a damper on your gala concert tonight. Police and security will be everywhere."

"Gosh, I hope not," responded Anna, nervous and wanting to change the subject. "The government must be quite embarrassed just as our countries are making an effort to melt the ice. I don-t expect anyone will be eager to talk about the murder. In fact, just the opposite."

Anna, couldn't help herself, her hand was shaking and she dropped her teacup, which shattered on the floor.

"Hey, don't worry, Anna, I am sure the gala will go off just fine," replied Maggie, helping Anna pick up the broken pieces of china.

"Mind if I use the bathroom now?" asked Steffi, changing the subject to Anna's relief.

"You go ahead. I'm all finished and ready to leave when you are," responded Anna.

Anna went into her room, sat on the bed and tried to calm down. She got out her suitcase. She was debating whether she could pack Professor Keller's papers, but decided they wouldn't fit, so she would have to continue to carry them in the Co-op shopping bag. In the meantime, she made sure they remained hidden under her bed. About fifteen minutes later, Steffi yelled out that she was ready to leave. It was just after nine. They left the apartment, to find Neil Jordan waiting for them outside. Anna immediately noticed that the "ferrets" were no longer there. Their car was gone for the first time in nearly a month, and there was nobody in sight that could even be a "ferret." *That's interesting,* she thought. *Probably they've been called off to help in the hunt for Krinsky's murderer. How ironic,* she told herself. *They have been sitting there, looking at me all the time.* She quietly smiled to herself as she got into Neil's car.

Anna and Steffi worked diligently, making sure that the gala program was in place and that they had covered every possible issue. They then discussed the logistics of moving the orchestra, the Board of Trustees and Anna to the airport for their departure tomorrow. They knew there would be a lot of security and probably delays. Their charter flights were scheduled to depart at 3:00 p.m., and they thought they should allow two and a half hours for Customs and Passport Control, and getting the orchestra's instruments and other luggage on board. They agreed that departure from the Hotels Europejski and Bristol should be at noon. If all went according to plan, she should have no difficulty in being at the Hotel Bristol in time. Steffi agreed to make sure everyone was given the departure time and details for checking out of the hotel and delivering their luggage.

At 11:00 a.m. she presented herself in Emily Paige-Madison's office, for her meeting with BW.

"Good morning, Janet. I shall just see if Mr. Brookes-Walton is free to see you now. Please take a seat for a minute or two," said Paige-Madison gushingly friendly and polite, now that Anna was leaving.

Within a minute or so, she was ushered into BW's office.

"Ah. Janet, thank you for sparing some of your valuable time on what I know is going to be a very busy day for you. I wanted to tell you personally, how delighted I am with the way that the orchestra tour has progressed. It has, of course, been an outstanding success, and has done much to cement the UK's political outreach to Poland. I think it may well serve as an example of creating warming relations with other countries behind the Iron Curtain," he said in his usual pompous manner. "You will be leaving us tomorrow, returning with the orchestra and the Board of Trustees to London, but I wanted to thank you for the excellent job that you have done over the past few weeks. I can assure you it is much appreciated, and I have told London how happy I am with your performance."

"Thank you very much, Mr. Brookes-Walton. That's very nice of you," Anna responded politely, hoping her fear and stress wasn't obvious. "Of course, whatever I've achieved has been done as part of a team effort. Stefania has been particularly helpful, and working with Charlie Adams has been an absolute pleasure."

"That's very generous of you, Janet. I hope that everything goes smoothly tonight and for your departure tomorrow, and that we have the opportunity of meeting again." With that, he stood up, immaculately dressed as usual. He extended his hand which Anna shook firmly.

"Thank you very much, sir. I appreciate your support." Anna left his office, and stopped to say goodbye to Emily Paige-Madison, and returned to her office, checked the agenda one last time, and then went to lunch. Forty-five minutes later she went back to her office and cleared everything out, leaving Steffi with all the necessary files and other information covering the tour. She put her own personal things into a small shopping bag.

"I'm going back to the apartment now, Steffi. I think I will have a rest to be fresh for this evening's proceedings. You come back early as well, so as we have plenty of time to meet and greet at the Teatr Wielki. You can dress up tonight in your most glamorous outfit," she said with a laugh.

She went down to the reception and checked out the daily newspapers. The Krinsky murder was still front-page news. There was a long article about the funeral arrangements to take place on Wednesday, which would be with full military honors at the Koscial Karola Boromeusza church and the special military cemetery in Powazowski. There was not much additional news other than to say that the police were exploring various leads, and that Tanya Sakharov was secluded at their country estate and had requested privacy and respect from the media. Although Anna's heart was pounding as she avidly read and reread the article, there really was no more detailed information than yesterday's news.

Neil was waiting in the courtyard. Anna got into the car, and felt a sigh of relief, like the last day of term, breaking up from school. She had completed the MI6 mission, and she hoped to be reunited with Jan soon and to have him and his family safely transported to England.

"The Ambassador called me into his office today," said Neil, as he drove slowly out into the street. "I've had some pretty tough assignments, Janet, so I know to a certain extent what you're going through. It's never easy, but particularly when other people's lives are involved. As part of my training, I never ask questions, so you don't have to respond. However, tomorrow morning, I shall give you my passport and a suitcase full of my clothes. I understand you will need them, for someone else to take my spot on the return flight to London."

Anna looked at Neil, opened-mouthed. She couldn't speak for a moment. She never thought Neil would become part of her plans for Jan's escape. She looked at him with tears in her eyes. "My God, Neil, that's amazing. I've been praying that the Ambassador would come through. What you're doing is saving the lives of a whole Polish family. I can never thank you enough."

"All part of the job, Janet, you know that. When we get the call, we follow orders without question."

"Neil, you've been wonderful throughout my visit to Warsaw," she said genuinely as she thought about what a great friend and protector he had been to her over the past few weeks. She would really miss him.

"It's Mark."

"Mark?"

"Yes, my real name is Mark Evans," he said with a smile on his face. "Maybe we'll have a chance to get together in London. I really enjoyed our time together. You are an incredible woman, Janet, and I would love to get to know you better. I don't want to lose contact," he continued purposefully.

"Thank you, Mark. That would be great," responded Anna. "But how can you get out of Poland without a passport?"

Neil laughed. "Don't worry. I've got five more. The embassy will get me out of the country, maybe to Sweden, Finland, or south through Hungary or Czechoslovakia. It will probably take a week or two, but I'm confident I will show up in London." He paused. "Would you give me your phone number?"

"I'm not sure where I'm going to be located. But don't worry, Neil or Mark," she laughed. "You can find me through the FO, or 'the firm.'"

"I will. You can bank on it," he responded.

They were now back at the apartment, and Anna suddenly felt very tired.

"What time do you need me in the morning?" Neil said.

"Ten-thirty will be fine."

"I will come at the normal time, around eight-thirty and take the girls to their offices one last time. Forecasting some rain for tomorrow as well, so I think they'll appreciate the ride."

"That would be very nice. You really are a sweet man," said Anna leaning in and kissing Neil fully on the lips. "I'll see you later," she added, trying to keep her response upbeat as she dealt with so many conflicting emotions.

Anna went up to the empty apartment, and immediately started her packing. All her clothes, except for what she needed for the gala concert, and to travel back to London tomorrow. She left the shopping bag, with the Keller Krakova two papers, under her bed. She would not bring those out until she was ready to leave in the morning. *God,* she thought, *is this going to work? Will Sergei bring Jan? How near are the police to making an arrest?* She shuddered as she tried to put all these thoughts from her mind. She was able to rest for an hour, and was just finishing getting dressed in her "embassy dress," as Steffi arrived back.

"Wow. You're dressed already, and you look smashing," said a gushing Stefania. "Can you help me, Janet, I haven't got a clue how to dress for a posh evening like this. I got my one navy blue silk dress, which I hope works, but I don't know what to do with my makeup or hair."

"Don't worry, Steffi, you're going to look sensational. I'll help you if you need me," said Anna, noting how excited Steffi was about the event. "Get going. We've got to be there early, as you know."

Steffi ran off to her bedroom. Twenty minutes later, she was dressed, and Anna decided she really did need some help. Her dress was a bit too big, and her flat chest did not help.

"Okay, Steffi," said Anna with a laugh. "Let's turn on the glamour." She started by handing Steffi fistfuls of Kleenex. "Right, stuff those in your bra and we shall see what that looks like." Steffi obliged, and it did help.

Anna got a wide black leather belt, from her suitcase, and put it around Steffi. It tightened the dress on her body, and gave her figure some shape. Next she started on her hair. Her straw-colored mane hung limply on her shoulders. Anna swept it up and pinned it. That made a big difference, as Steffi had a nice face and small flat ears. Then she turned to makeup. She gave her a good foundation, and some pale rouge to brighten up her complexion. Finally, she put on lashings of blue eye shadow and mascara, to accentuate Steffi's blue eyes. She admired her handiwork, and pushed Steffi into Maggie's bedroom where there was a full-length mirror.

"Well, madam," said Anna, "what do you think?"

"Crikey." Steffi exclaimed with her eyes wide. "That's fantastic. I feel wonderful, just like a film star."

"And that's exactly how you look. Going to turn a lot of heads this evening."

Within fifteen minutes they were at the Teatr Wielki. They busied themselves with their tasks for the next half an hour or so, checking with the caterers, making sure the champagne, wines and spirits had all been delivered, and arranging for sunshades to be pulled down over the large windows so the guests could appreciate the beautiful chandeliers hanging over the "long bar" where the reception was to be held. Charlie Adams found Anna in the bar area.

"Good evening, Janet. Is everything set?"

"Yes. No problem, as far as I can see."

"The Ambassador and the Board are going to come backstage at the end of the concert to meet with Sir David Mandel, and Leonard Littowitz. It would be helpful if you could escort them to the backstage area. You know the exit door, it's the one hidden under the box over the right stage. It's got 'no admittance,' in Polish of course."

"We will be standing there at the end of the concert," said Anna. "I assume one of the Ambassador's aides will be leading the group to that door."

"Yes, that's all arranged. Okay, got to rush off now. See you after the concert."

Within five minutes, the Ambassador, Sir Miles, the Consulate General, BW, and their aides and assistants all arrived, looking somewhat nervous, Anna thought. She knew there was a lot riding on this evening, and a lot was expected from the British group.

Soon, the Board of Trustees arrived, including Sir Alex Campbell. Anna was excited to see him, and tell him of her conversation with Neil and the arrangements tomorrow.

Alex came straight towards her with a serious look on his face. "Have you seen the TV news?" he asked.

"No," replied Anna. "We don't have a TV in our apartment."

"The Krinsky murder is still front and center. They announced that the police were going to make an imminent arrest."

"An imminent arrest?" Anna felt fear grabbing the pit of her stomach.

"It looks like they are about to pounce. Have you seen any sign of the police?"

"No. I don't even have the "ferrets" watching me anymore," responded Anna. She was beginning to tremble. "What should I do?"

"There's nothing you can do, Anna. Stay close to me this evening, and pray that whoever the police have got in their sights isn't you."

"You know about Neil Jordan and the passport?"

"Yes, I was able to get help from London and Sir Miles. You have a lot of friends and supporters in high places, for what you have achieved here. But I also have to say, London wants to avoid a major diplomatic incident, and so they agreed to see it through, and hope that your plan works. Of course, I haven't told anyone about Krinsky. That's another issue which will have to be discussed when you return to London. If you ever get to London." Alex wasn't pulling any punches. It was clear that he, the FO, and MI6 were unhappy with Anna's extracurricular activities, but they probably thought it would be worse if they didn't try and help Anna.

"Oh, Alex, I can't tell you how grateful I am." She was shaken by his news and his clear disapproval. Tears welled up in her eyes, although she was doing her best to avoid having her mascara run.

Alex ignored her emotional response. "It is very important that the evening goes smoothly. I shall be joining the Board of Trustees when they go backstage after the concert. Please stay close to me. I shall need your help."

For the first time, Anna noticed that Alex was holding a black canvas tote bag. She had a good idea what was inside. She also realized that Alex must have come up with a plan to get the Keller papers out of the country.

"I will be at the exit door to the backstage, at the end of the concert, and will keep as close as possible to you the whole time," said Anna.

The long bar was now filling up with diplomats, Polish

government officials, and other dignitaries. Canapés and drinks were being passed around, and Anna politely spoke to as many people as possible. Stefania was glued to the Ambassador's group and the Consulate General and his aides. Every now and then, she took off at a great pace on an errand with a determined look on her face. Anna found it very difficult to keep her composure, but forced herself to smile and put on the charm as necessary. She was relieved when there was an announcement accompanying a large gong that the concert would commence in ten minutes. Government officials, guests and dignitaries moved to their seats. Anna hung back to make sure that everything was in order and to answer any questions.

With the audience seated, and within a few minutes of the beginning of the concert, there was a ripple of excitement and chatter as the President and his entourage arrived outside the concert hall. They were met by Emil Kaplinsky, the manager of the Teatr Wielki, Sir Miles Sanford, BW, Sir Norman Fowler and some Polish government officials who had come earlier to the reception. General Jaruzelski, in white tie and tails and with a wide sash in the Polish colors across his chest, his wife, Foreign Minister Stephan Olszowski, and the Minister of Culture Lukas Kasia were escorted up the steps to the theatre and beyond to the large presidential box. Waiting to greet the President, was Sir David Mandel, Leonard Littowitz, the UK Consulate General, a couple of aides, and Anna standing unobtrusively in the corner in case she was needed. BW acted as translator as he introduced the President to the waiting line. The President, in his usual dark glasses, and with what Anna thought was a Cheshire Cat grin, spoke politely to each individual as he walked down the line. He and his entourage then entered the seating area of the presidential box as Sir David Mandel and Leonard Littowitz were ushered down a rear staircase to prepare for their entrance on stage.

A spontaneous ripple of applause greeted the President as he took his seat. He applauded back, smiled, nodded and waved.

Anna had been standing in the corner watching the proceedings, and thinking that Roman Krinsky would probably have been invited to this important event. Her heart was pounding and she was trembling at this thought. Sir Alex's news about an imminent arrest had shaken her confidence. She wasn't sure she could continue to function. Would the police come and arrest her now, or after the concert? Was she being watched or closely tailed throughout the evening? "An imminent arrest." Who else could it be but her? Her daydreaming was interrupted.

"Are you all right, Janet?" asked BW. "You're looking rather pale."

"No, sir. I'm fine, just a bit tired. A little stressed you know."

"You can relax now, Janet. The show is about to begin. I'm just going down to make my speech," he said, clearly reveling in the importance of the occasion.

The orchestra was warming up, and the entrance of Sir David Mandel and Leonard Littowitz brought on enthusiastic applause. They were followed by BW, elegant as always if not a little over the top with his bright purple bow tie and silk handkerchief. A polite applause followed him.

"Your Excellency, government ministers, Ambassadors and honored guests, it is my privilege to welcome you on behalf of the London Philharmonic Orchestra to this gala evening, celebrating the completion of a highly successful tour of Poland and the first of what we hope will be many cultural exchanges between our two great countries. As the Director General of the British Council for Cultural Affairs in Poland I extend, on behalf of Her Majesty's government, our sincere thanks for the welcome and support given to the London Philharmonic Orchestra on this historic tour. We sincerely hope you will all enjoy this outstanding evening of music. Thank you very much." BW received an enthusiastic response from the audience. He then exited the stage, and Sir David Mandel tapped his baton on his music stand and the program erupted in a burst of glorious music.

The atmosphere was electric, and the orchestra seemed to bond with the audience. The program of Mozart and Strauss in the first half received a standing ovation. The second half of the concert was devoted to Leonard Littowitz and a brilliant performance of Rachmaninov's "Concerto No. 2," and finishing with Frederic Chopin's "Étude in E major Opus 10." This brought the audience to its feet in a roar of appreciation, and bravos. Sir David Mandel and Leonard Littowitz left the stage three times only to return for further bows, as the audience continued its standing ovation. Sir David acknowledged the orchestra and got them to rise to receive the applause. It was a full five minutes before the cheering died down. Anna, watching from a standing position near the "no admittance" door, noticed that the President and his entourage left the box immediately after the concert finished. At last the audience started to file out, in a high level of excitement, laughter and talking. Eventually there were just a few stragglers and the Board of Trustees remaining in their seats. Anna signaled to Sir Norman Fowler, to follow her through the "no admission" door to visit backstage. She gathered the group and souvenir programs and gift bags from the Polish Ministry of Culture, and led them through the door, then immediately attached herself to Alex, who was carrying his black canvas tote bag. Charlie Adams met the group and asked them to follow him to the "green room" where Sir David and Littowitz were waiting. There was an enormous hustle and bustle going on stage. The large Steinway piano was being lowered through an enormous trapdoor to below stage, music stands were being cleared away and Charlie Adams' team were collecting musical instruments and music, chatting to each other in loud Cockney voices. Most of the musical instruments were being loaded into large container storage units with open fronts and shelves on which various sizes of instrument were being placed and tied down. There were two large trunks marked "music one" and "music two" gradually being filled with each batch of music inside sturdy canvas folders tied together with a ribbon and identified on the front. This feverish activity was going on as the Board of Trustees made their way across the stage to the waiting maestro.

Anna stuck to Alex like glue. As they passed the music trunks, Alex whispered to Anna, "Create a diversion for me. Turn on the charm and get their attention." Anna nodded in response.

"How do you manage to keep track of all those instruments?" she asked one of the burly assistants to Charlie Adams. She stopped and provocatively leaned against one of the instrument containers looking inside.

"We know them all pretty well, miss. But we do tag each one, just to make sure that the right instrument gets to the right musician," he responded with a laugh. Two other of Charlie Adams' "boys" came over to have a good look at Anna.

"He doesn't have a clue really. Just guesses and hopes for the best," said one in a loud Cockney voice.

"It's true, miss," said the other one. "It's a flaming miracle that the musicians get to play the right instruments. I'm sure it's all going to go wrong one day," he said with a loud belly laugh.

Anna laughed with them, as she saw Alex putting two additional canvas music folders into the "Music Two" trunk. She said a few words of thanks and with a broad smile walked off towards the green room.

The Board of Trustees were already there, congratulating Sir David Mandel and Leonard Littowitz. The room was full of flowers, and champagne was being poured, accompanied by lots of laughter and English chatter.

Alex sidled up to Anna. "Thank you. That was very helpful." Anna noticed that Alex was still carrying the black tote bag, but it was now empty and folded up in his hand.

The green-room party went on for another twenty minutes.

BW was buzzing from trustee to trustee, chatting to everyone and making sure the Ambassador spent time with every member of the board as well as the maestro himself. Anna stood unobtrusively as possible in the corner of the room, now eager for the event to end so she could escape back to the apartment. Stefania had already departed with a group from the Consulate General's office including Maggie.

Finally the party wound down and Anna handed out the souvenir programs and gift bags to each trustee. Charlie Adams appeared, and escorted the Board of Trustees through the theatre to the waiting bus that would return them to the Bristol Hotel. BW followed the Ambassador and his wife out of the theatre, leaving Anna and Charlie Adams to confirm that everything was under control. "Thank you, Janet. We seem to have a resounding success on our hands, and tonight's gala concert was really amazing. I don't think I have ever heard the orchestra so sharp and enthused. Are you able to get back to your apartment okay?"

"Yes, thank you, Charlie, and congratulations on an incredible evening. You and your team were wonderful."

Charlie escorted Anna out through the theatre to a side entrance where the ever-reliable Neil was waiting in his car. He drove her back quickly to the apartment building, through the dark wet streets, with hardly another vehicle in sight. She half expected to see a line of police cars outside her apartment and breathed a sigh of relief when she saw nothing, not even the "ferrets." She thanked Neil again, with another sincere kiss.

"See you in the morning, Neil. Thanks again for everything."

She made her way upstairs and was relieved to find that the girls had not yet returned. More celebrations with the orchestra perhaps! She felt like a nervous wreck and was happy to flop into bed hoping for sleep that would not come.

Chapter 25

The midsummer dawn came early. The gray light turned to pink, and gradually the sun came up, flooding her bedroom with golden light. Anna had been tossing and turning all night, jumping at every sound. Police sirens in the distance sent a shudder through her body. She expected a loud knock on the door, following a screech of tires, from a number of police cars sent to arrest her. However, the knock on the door did not come. At six-thirty, she could stay in bed no longer. She was feeling exhausted, heavy-eyed, and dry-mouthed. She quietly padded into the bathroom, took off her nightie, noting that her bruises had now turned yellow, and the swelling on her wrist had subsided. She got into the shower, and turned it on full force, reveling in the sharp hot spray, which slowly revived her as she relaxed under the warm water and steam. She tried to clear her head. No arrest as yet. She should just keep to her plan, and pray that all the pieces fell into place. Would Sergei show up with Jan? Could she trust him? Had he arranged for Ava and the children to take the train to Gdansk, and board the ferry to Stockholm? She must be positive. She had got to make this work. Sergei would come through for the Keller papers. She knew this would be the crowning glory of his career, and he would move heaven and earth to have Anna deliver those papers into his chubby hands.

She got out of the shower, feeling revived, and went back into her room, and got dressed for the trip home to London. She dressed modestly, beige slacks, white blouse and a brown cotton sweater, as the last thing she wanted to do was attract attention to herself at the airport. She finished her packing, pulled out the Co-op shopping bag from under her bed, stacked the bag and her suitcase near the door, and carefully checked the room, to make sure she had left nothing behind. She then went into the kitchen and started making breakfast for herself and the girls. Just before 8:00, Maggie appeared, looking hungover and squinting in the bright light of the sun-filled living room.

"God, you're up early and all bushy-tailed," she said to Anna. "Didn't you party last night?"

"No. By the time I left the theatre, I was exhausted. Neil brought me straight home."

"Well, we had one hell of a time. Singing and dancing at the Europejski bar. One of the pianists from the orchestra played for over an hour, and we had a real old-fashioned singsong. Vodka, whisky and beer by the bucket load. I can't imagine what the final bill is going be, but it was great fun. I'm sorry you missed it, Janet."

"No problem, Maggie. We will meet up again soon." Anna was getting quite tearful as she went over to Maggie and gave her a big hug.

Stefania came shuffling into the kitchen, her eyes half closed. Her makeup from last night was not totally removed and smeared over her face. She looked awful and clearly felt so.

"Have you heard about the party last night, Janet?" she said, croakily. "I'm really feeling awful. Do you think you could give me a cup of black coffee?" Anna poured some coffee into a large mug and pushed it towards Stefania, who picked it up with shaking hands. "I'm not used to these wild parties, you know," she said to Maggie and Anna. "I don't think I can handle all this drink and lack of sleep. Maybe I am just not strong enough." Maggie and Anna were roaring with laughter. "You may think it's funny, but I feel really ill, and I've got to be at work within an hour."

"Okay, Steffi," said Anna taking control. "Go and have a really hot shower to revive yourself. We've got to get you up and out within the next half an hour, so go to it."

Steffi staggered off to the bathroom.

Anna finished her tea and toast, and looked around the sunny living room. Her eyes stopped at the sofa, remembering the afternoon fling with Neil. This apartment held fond memories for her. It had been a rewarding but frightening time for her in Warsaw, but her Polish roots had kicked in, and somehow she had felt comfortable and at home here.

She was snapped out of her reverie and jumped at the buzz of the doorbell and a knock on the door. Too soft for the police she thought immediately. As she approached the door, there was another slight knock and Neil's voice. "It's just me." Anna opened the door.

"I thought you would want to see these," said Neil handing over the morning newspapers to Anna. "I'll be waiting for the girls downstairs."

She quickly opened the state-controlled *Trybuna Ludu*. The front-page headline, covered the whole masthead of the newspaper:

Krinsky Murder. Arrest Made.

The Police Commissioner Jan Stepinska, announced early this morning that Lena Podolski, 31, had been taken into custody and was helping the police in their enquiries into the brutal murder of Roman Krinsky, the late head of the SB.

Lena Podolski is the arts critic of TV P1. It has been established that Ms. Podolski had known Colonel Krinsky for about six months. They met on a regular basis, including meetings at Colonel Krinsky's apartment above the SB counterintelligence unit on Krakowski Street. Ms Podolski is married to Captain Pyotr Podolski, an officer in the SB, who was arrested at the beginning of March on the orders of Colonel Krinsky in connection with a widespread corruption investigation involving the Warsaw police and members of the SB. Captain Podolski is being held in Mokotów Prison, but no charges have been brought against him as yet. It is believed that the investigation is continuing.

It is alleged that Ms. Podolski had a nine o'clock appointment on Friday night at Colonel Krinsky's apartment. Earlier in the evening he was at a reception given by the British Ambassador, Sir Norman Fowler, at the British Embassy for the London Philharmonic Orchestra which has just completed a very successful tour of Poland.

Police Commissioner Stepinska said that Ms. Podolski claimed that Colonel Krinsky had cancelled their appointment due to some security issues, believed to be related to members of the Solidarity movement. No charges have been brought as yet, and Commissioner Stepinska has said the investigation continues.

In the middle of the article was a photograph from some publicity head shot, of the very attractive Lena Podolski. Anna could see that she had long dark black hair hanging to her shoulders, a pretty smile showing even white teeth, and pale clear eyes.

Anna was shaking as she finished reading the article. She turned to the other newspaper, *Zycie Warszawy*, which contained the same photograph, and more or less the same report, but the story shared another big headline about the imminent announcement of the lifting of martial law. After years of protest, strikes, battles with the police and army, death and prison, it appeared Lech Walesa and the Solidarity movement had won. Government reforms were now inevitable.

Anna looked closely at the photograph. Lena was young, too young for Roman Krinsky. She was playing with fire. Was she having an affair with him? Or was she just trying to get her husband released from prison, for a crime that probably he had not committed. Possibly it was both. Anna hoped that she had an alibi. But "the investigation continues." Would Lena's arrest give a breathing space for Anna to get out of the country before the police connected her to the murder? It was only a matter of hours now, and she would be on her way. And now she felt tremendous guilt. This innocent woman had been arrested for a crime she did not commit. Would she be able to prove her innocence, or would the police commissioner not care as long as he could announce an arrest.

The girls came out of their respective bedrooms, dressed for work, and ready to go.

"My God, Janet, you look like you've seen a ghost. What's the matter?" said Maggie.

"I'm fine," responded Anna, recovering quickly. "Just a little overcome at leaving you girls, and I think I'm a bit stressed out now we are at the end of the tour. But I'll be okay," she continued in a more jovial manner.

There were further hugs and kisses and goodbyes. Just as Steffi was about to leave, Anna asked, "Hey, Steff, could I have your baseball cap as a souvenir?"

Steffi looked a bit surprised. "Of course, Janet. You can have anything of mine if you want."

Steffi rushed back into her room, and came out with the slightly grubby off-white baseball cap which she pushed into Anna's hands.

"Thanks so much," said Anna. "I'll see you at the Europejski before 12:00. I'll be with the group from the Hotel Bristol. I hope you and Charlie will be able to get the orchestra and equipment loaded up by the time I get there."

"I'll do my very best," said Stefania earnestly, as she gave Anna a peck on the cheek.

Maggie came over and gave Anna one last hug. "Do be careful, luv," she said, "and please keep in touch."

With that the girls, a little late now, swished out of the apartment door. Anna was alone. She was packed, and had nothing to do until Neil returned for her at ten-thirty. She went over to the window and discreetly looked down on the street. No sign of police or "ferrets." Nothing. She sat down on the sofa and re-read the articles about the arrest of Lena Podolski. She could understand Lena being the initial suspect, but surely she had an alibi, and surely the police would have found something to indicate she was not the murderer. She started pacing up and down, thinking of Lena, Jan, Sergei and Ava. Every few minutes she looked at the clock; time was passing excruciatingly slowly. She had to calm down. She sat down on the sofa and picked up the newspaper again.

She read a long article in the *Trybuna Ludu*, which she knew was the mouthpiece of the government, about the lifting of martial law. No firm date was given, but the article made clear that the official announcement would be within the next week or so. Anna realized this was a momentous time for Poland, reform, and even future freedom. How would the Russians react? Would the Jaruzelski government really release a number of Solidarity prisoners from prison? Would, as the article said, the government sit down with Lech Walesa and negotiate the Solidarity reform demands? Would the streets remain peaceful? What a fascinating time. Was the Russian grip on Eastern Europe starting to crack? Could Poland engineer reforms without the big Russian bear taking control politically and militarily? She read the rest of the newspaper from cover to cover. For the most part, the content was biased reports about economic successes in Poland and Eastern Europe, and critical articles of the United States and Western Europe. Anna smiled to herself. She been reading this sort of nonsense for the whole of the fifteen years she had been in Poland. A few short months in London had opened her eyes to the events in the real world. She jumped again at the sound of police sirens. She stopped reading. Two or more getting nearer and nearer. She held her breath. The noise slowly receded.

Neil, as usual, was early. It was not yet ten-thirty when he knocked on the door softly to announce his arrival. She was happy to see him, and had an urge to kiss and hug him for what he had done for her over the past few weeks.

"Come in, Neil. I am still going to call you Neil. Mark will have to wait," Anna said. "You are early, but I don't want to get to the Hotel Victoria much before my appointment at eleven.

Would you like a cup of coffee, we have plenty of time?"

"Okay, Janet. That would be nice."

"Are you sorry to be leaving Warsaw?" asked Neil.

"Well, in some ways I am," replied Anna. "But I'm also eager to get back to London."

"I know, it must be a big day for you. Here's my passport. Keep it in a safe place until you need it. I have got my suitcase in the car downstairs with a bunch of clothing, and I thought I should throw in a shaving kit and some other normal stuff."

"Oh, Neil, I can't tell you how much I appreciate everything you're doing for me," Anna said, getting very emotional.

"I'm pleased to be of help, because I really do think of you as someone special."

That did it. With tears in her eyes, Anna leaned into Neil, put her arms around his neck and kissed him fully on the lips. He quickly responded and pulled her towards him.

He was kissing her on the lips, her neck and shoulders, and as she became aroused she responded in kind. His hands started to roam over her body.

But the next few hours could be the most crucial in her life, so she gently pushed him away.

"We'll have to take a raincheck," she said with a smile. "To be continued. Maybe in London; soon, I hope." She got up from the sofa and smoothed her clothing.

"Let's finish our coffee and get out of here," she said.

"I'm going to take you up on that London date. As soon as possible."

They both downed their coffee. Neil finished off a biscuit, and they were ready to go.

Anna went into her tiny bedroom and retrieved the suitcase and Co-op bag.

"Here, give me that," said Neil, grabbing the suitcase. "Been doing some food shopping?" he asked cheekily, looking at the Co-op shopping bag.

"You could say that," said Anna, laughing. Anna grabbed Steffi's baseball cap which she stuffed into the Co-op bag along with her floppy sun hat.

She closed the apartment door behind her and they descended to the street, loaded up Neil's Saab, and were soon outside the austere Soviet exterior of the Hotel Victoria, opposite the Saxon Gardens and Pilsudski Square twelve minutes before eleven.

"Neil, I hope I won't be more than about half an hour. I will take your suitcase and the Co-op bag into the hotel. I shall leave my case in the boot of your car. When I come out, I will have someone with me, wearing your clothes. We would then like to head over to the Hotel Bristol as quickly as possible."

"No problem, Janet. I'll be waiting here. There is plenty of parking." With that, he got out of the car and retrieved his suitcase, a small battered brown leather one, and the Co-op shopping bag and handed them to Anna. "Good luck."

"Thanks," said Anna, now feeling very tense and shaky. She went into the lobby of the old hotel, a little dowdy and rundown, and looked around. No sign of Sergei and Jan at the moment. There were two clusters of deep leather chairs in the lobby, and a number of people coming and going. She confidently walked past the lobby reception, and headed to the restaurant, where the glass doors were closed and the sign said, "Open for lunch at twelve noon." A member of the staff in a black jacket walked by and Anna asked where the ladies' room was located.

"Down this corridor and turn right," he said, pointing. "It's just past the gents, madam. You can't miss it."

"Thank you," said Anna. Jan would need to change clothes somewhere without being interrupted. If the restaurant didn't open until twelve, it was highly unlikely that there would be any ladies using the restroom.

She returned to the lobby and sat down in one of the leather chairs, and waited, the leather suitcase at her side and the Co-op bag on her lap. She looked at her watch, ten-fifty-eight. No sign of Sergei or Jan. Her stomach was knotted as each agonizing minute passed. It was now past eleven, still no sign. Another five minutes went by. "Oh my God," she said to herself. "He is not going to come. What am I going to do?" She started to tremble again. She didn't have a plan B. If Sergei could not deliver Jan, should she stay in Warsaw or should she go? It was now eleven-ten. Still no sign. She realized Neil would be starting to worry if she didn't appear. Should she go and tell him? No, she couldn't move. She had to stay longer and pray.

People were coming in and out of the hotel lobby, and now a group of Russian tourists were blocking her view. Another few minutes passed. Suddenly she saw them, the large, flabby Sergei, wiping his sweaty brow, with a handkerchief and holding onto the arm of an elderly, scraggy man, in ill-fitting clothes. At first Anna couldn't believe what she was seeing. Sergei wasn't with Jan? At least it did not look like Jan. She got up as they both approached.

"It wasn't easy, Anna," said Sergei, stressed and serious. "There were some delays this morning. Since our friend Krinsky is no longer with us, nobody wanted to take responsibility and sign the release papers. But I got it done and I'm delivering your brother, just as you requested."

"My God, Anna, it's really you," said Jan falling into Anna's arms with tears running down his face.

She couldn't believe it. Jan had lost at least twenty pounds since she had last seen him in February. His hair, cropped very short, was nearly white. His eyes were sunken into his head with dark black circles underneath. He had a few days' stubble on his gray white beard, and as she hugged him, she could feel his ribs through his thin clothes.

Tears were running down Anna's face as well. "Oh, Jan, what have they done to you?"

"I'll be fine. Don't worry. I just had no idea I would be released. I saw Ava and she said the police and the "ferrets" were looking for you. And now you're here. Beautiful as ever, but now a redhead?"

"None of that matters now, Jan. We're going to have a long day and I have to get you into better shape."

"Thank you so much, Sergei. How about Ava and the children?"

"They are on their way to Gdynia. They will be taking the ferry in about an hour to Karlskrona. This ferry service runs twice a week and takes ten hours. The Gdansk—Stockholm service takes nineteen hours. I thought it better to get them to Sweden as quickly as possible."

"Thank you, Sergei. That is wonderful. I really appreciate it. Now, here is your bag of goodies." She handed over the Co-op shopping bag. She took out the baseball hat and her floppy sun hat. Sergei had a brown briefcase with him and he took out the thick wad of Keller's papers and put them into the case, handing back the empty Co-op bag to Anna.

"I hope this is the complete package, Anna," said Sergei suspiciously.

"Of course it is," replied Anna confidently. "It's exactly as I received it."

"I know you understand how important it is that your friends in Moscow are happy with this delivery. Especially because of the extra favors I have done for you." Sergei couldn't avoid the standard threatening language.

"I'm sure everyone is going to be very happy, Sergei," said Anna, eager to terminate the conversation and focus on Jan.

"You have one more task to complete this saga," said Sergei, taking out a folded piece of paper from his pocket and handing it to Anna. She opened it and paled as she read the content.

"I can't do that, Sergei," she said earnestly with her stomach starting to knot again. "It would be impossible."

"I'm sure you will find a way, Anna. You will have plenty of time. Until the end of next month. Opportunities will arise, and you have been well trained to take advantage of opportunities. You didn't really think that handing over these papers would be the end. We don't like loose ends, Anna, as you know. If you don't get this job done by the end of August, your mother's privileges at Kaskia Lodge will be ended, and she will join your friend the former Assistant Defense Minister, in a comfortable Gulag in Siberia," Sergei continued, with a cold leering look on his flabby face.

"What's this all about, Anna?" asked Jan. "Why are you talking about mother, and Kaskia Lodge. Who is this man anyway?" Jan continued anxiously.

"It's nothing, Jan. No problems. We've got to get moving."

Turning to Sergei, Anna said, "I'll get it done."

"I'm sure you will, Anna," responded Sergei, cold as ice.

"We have to go now," said Anna. "I have a very tight timetable, but I want to thank you for your help," she said, eager to be appreciative and leave him on a positive note.

Sergei couldn't resist one last dig. "I have held up my end of our bargain, Anna, now you must get the job finished. We shall be watching you."

Anna picked up the suitcase, and the empty Co-op bag. "Come on, Jan, follow me... Goodbye, Sergei, and good luck."

Jan looked bewildered and confused, but after months in prison, he was used to taking orders and responded without question. Sergei marched off quickly, clutching his briefcase tightly. Anna and Jan headed for the ladies' restroom. Anna cautiously looked in. It was empty. She beckoned Jan into the old-fashioned tiled bathroom.

"Now, Jan, here's the score. Sergei had Ava and the children picked up this morning. They should be in Gdynia now. He has arranged for them to board the ferry to Karlskrona in Sweden. I am arranging for someone at the British Embassy, in Stockholm, to meet the ferry and take responsibility for Ava and the kids. The British Embassy will arrange for their flight to London, which is where we're going now."

"London," repeated Jan, clearly confused.

"Yes, but we need to get you cleaned up, and looking at least somewhat like the British passport I am going to give you, which is in the name of Neil Jordan. I have been in Warsaw, working with the British Council in connection with the first Polish tour of the London Philharmonic Orchestra. We have two charter planes to take us and the orchestra back to London this afternoon. But, we expect that we will all be questioned and searched at Warsaw airport before being allowed to board our aircraft. You have got to stick close to me, Jan. Follow my instructions, and only speak English. You have to pretend you do not understand Polish, and also that you're suffering from stomach flu, which we hope will explain your current appearance. Think you can handle that, Jan?"

"You arranged for Ava and the children to leave Warsaw," responded Jan, focused on his family. "That's incredible, Anna. We are all going to leave this damn country. Anna, you are amazing. What you've done today, is nothing less than a miracle." Tears were pouring down Jan's cheeks as he hugged Anna.

"Yes, well, we will have plenty of time to talk about that, but I need to know that you can handle the next few hours and have the strength to see this through. We have to make this plan work, otherwise both of us will be in Mokotów Prison. I hope you understand that."

"Yes, Anna, I get it. Don't worry. I'll do my part, but do you think you could get me something to eat? I'm really feeling weak through lack of food."

"Okay. I'll do my best, but in the meantime, get out of those awful clothes."

Jan stripped down to his worn underpants. Anna could see the remains of bruises on his back and shoulders, and now saw how thin and ill he looked. His muscular athletic body had shriveled.

"Here, Jan, I think these will work." She retrieved a black cotton roll-neck sweater, gray jeans, white socks and worn sneakers. She also took out a small travel bag, containing a can of shaving cream, razor, and a small tub of Brylcreem. "Why don't you shave first, Jan, and then I shall apply some makeup, to take away that prison pallor, and then we'll see if these clothes fit."

Anna filled one of the basins with hot water, and Jan proceeded to wash his face and neck and arms, before lathering up his face and completing his shave. Anna took out a small makeup bag from her purse. She also retrieved Neil's passport, and compared his photo and physical information with Jan. They were about the same height and if Jan hadn't shrunk away to nothing, their physique would have been not dissimilar. Facially, however, there was no resemblance. Neil's face and skin looked darker even on the black-and-white photo, and he was clearly dark-haired. But Anna had no choice, she had to make this work somehow.

She took out a compact of light foundation from her makeup bag and as discreetly as possible dabbed it onto Jan's face, ears, and neck. She stepped back to admire her handiwork. She wasn't convinced, but it did help, at least taking away Jan's prison pallor. All she could do for his hair was to carefully use her mascara and eyelash brush to darken his short cropped hair as much as possible. The gray jeans were the right length but far too baggy. Luckily, she found a belt in Neil's suitcase, and tightening it to the last hole, pulled the waist band in about three inches. The socks and sneakers did not present any problems, and the black cotton sweater covered the pulled-in waist of his jeans. To finish off the disguise, she firmly put Steffi's baseball cap on Jan's head. She stepped back and gave him a good look, in comparison with the passport photo. At best, she thought Jan looked like a sick thin version of Neil, but there was no more she could do.

"Right, Jan, you look like a new man," said Anna encouragingly.

"I may look like a new man, but I don't look or feel like Jan," he responded, looking at himself in the bathroom mirror.

"Don't worry, we'll get you back to your old self in no time. Now, we're going over to the Hotel Bristol to pick up the Board of Trustees of the London Philharmonic and then we will cross the street to the Europejski Hotel where we will join the full orchestra and their entourage, and head to the airport. If anyone asks who you are, which they probably will, tell them you're a member of the orchestra, and you're suffering from stomach flu, and Janet is looking after you. Have you got that?"

"Yes, sure. But who is Janet?"

"I am Janet Clark, from Sydney Australia. MI6 gave me a new persona in London."

"Are you still working for them? You will have to tell me what happened in Kraków, and how you got to London." Jan was coming out of the fog of prison, and one-million questions were now filling his head.

"I promise you, when we get to London, I will explain everything. But let's just focus on getting out of Warsaw." Anna closed Neil's suitcase, and shoved Jan's awful clothes into the Co-op bag. "Okay. Let's go. We're running late." Anna looked at her watch. It was eleven-forty. She still had to pick up the Board at the Bristol and get over to the Europejski for the twelve noon departure. They marched back through the hotel lobby and out into the street. She immediately saw Neil, parked about thirty meters from the hotel entrance. He came towards her, and grabbed his suitcase and the Co-op bag, and opened the boot of the car and the rear doors.

"Get in quickly," he said. "The police are looking into every vehicle outside of the hotel and taking down license numbers. Get your heads down and let's get out of here."

Anna and Jan did as they were told, and jumped into the rear seats of the car. Neil started the engine and drove the one block down Krolenska Street to Krakowski Przedmieście. Within a couple of minutes they were at the Hotel Bristol. The small van was outside the main entrance, already loaded and the Board were milling around on the sidewalk. Neil came to a halt behind the van and Anna got out of the car.

She quickly approached Sir Norman Fowler. "I'm sorry, Sir Norman, but one of the orchestra members has the stomach flu and I have been helping him get ready for the journey."

She nodded towards Jan. "We were getting a little anxious," said Sir Norman. "But we only have to cross the street to the Europejski and then head off to the airport." He turned to the group on the sidewalk, including Alex, who was looking at Anna intently. "Alright, we can board the bus now. Make sure you have all your personal possessions. Janet will come with us and we will meet up with full orchestra across the street."

The driver started the van and they edged out into the traffic doing a U-turn to bring the van in front of the Europejski. The final bags were being loaded on to the two coaches, and Steffi and Charlie Adams were running up and down the sidewalk, issuing instructions. Neil had followed the van and was parked right behind it, awaiting instructions.

Janet approached Charlie and Steffi. "Are you all ready to go?"

"Well, nearly," replied Steffi. "We're just waiting for Sir David Mandel and Leonard Littowitz. They have been doing a radio interview at the hotel, and they are late. But I just got a message that they will be with us in five minutes. We're just loading the final orchestra members onto the buses now. I've checked every name. Everything is in order."

"Well done. That's a relief." Anna went over to Neil and leaned in through the car window. "We have got about five minutes. Do you think you could somehow get a sandwich and some fruit or cake or something for our passenger?"

"Sure. Just keep an eye on the car will you?" responded Neil as he got out of the driver's seat. He quickly disappeared into the hotel.

"Jan, stay in the car. Neil will be driving us separately to the airport. We'll be following the van and coaches."

Amazingly, within a couple of minutes Neil returned, with a wrapped ham sandwich, an apple, and a bottle of water. He handed it to Jan who eagerly opened the packaging and started munching.

"Thank you, Neil," said Anna. "I need another favor from you. Would you please get a message to Sir Miles at the Embassy? The message is, 'The package will be arriving at Karlskrona on the Ferry from Gdynia at 9:00 this evening, and not in Stockholm.' This is really very important, Neil, a matter of life and death," continued Anna, with desperation in her voice.

"Don't worry. No problem," responded Neil.

Sir David Mandel and Leonard Littowitz arrived on the sidewalk, apologizing and flustered. They were the last two on the coach. Everything and everyone was now loaded, and Anna joined Neil and Jan in the car. They eased out into the traffic and headed for the airport.

The convoy picked up speed. Anna immediately became aware of the number of police, paramilitary, and "ferrets" on the streets. Cars, vans and even bicycles were being waved down and searched. There was clearly a major security effort underway. *The investigation continues*, Anna thought, repeating the press comment. The weather had clouded over, and it looked like rain.

Jan dropped off to sleep, the stress and traumas of the day taking their toll. Anna was lost in thought, thinking ahead to the airport and the passport and Customs ordeals still to come. The traffic was light however, and soon the lead coach pulled up to the airport departures building, moving right to the end in the same spot where the orchestra had arrived some two weeks earlier. There were the same three ORBIS representatives on the sidewalk.

Anna and Jan got out of the car, as Neil retrieved both Anna's suitcase and his own from the trunk. Steffi was leading the orchestra members into the terminal, and Anna hurried forward to herd the trustees group to follow. Porters arrived with large articulated luggage containers into which they were loading the baggage. The musical instruments would have come directly last night or very early this morning.

When everyone was assembled in the large drab and poorly lit passport and Customs area, the senior ORBIS rep, Marzema Nowak made a brief statement, in English.

"We would ask you to be patient, ladies and gentlemen. Passport Control will review everyone's passport in groups of ten. Please stay behind the red lines until there is space at one of the booths. When you pass through Passport Control, you will hand over your visa document and then enter the Customs area. Your luggage will be lined up against the walls. Please select your luggage and carry it to one of the eight metal tables. You will be required to show your passport again, and your luggage will be searched. Once this is completed, you will be able to pass through to the Departure Lounge for boarding of your charter flight. Are there any questions?"

Everybody seemed to understand. Steffi and Neil found Anna.

"Well, I don't think there is much more we can do here," said Steffi with tears welling up. "Have a good flight, and please keep in touch, Janet."

"Thank you, Steffi. Of course I will," said Anna giving Steffi another hug.

"Same for me," said Neil. Anna gave Neil a real tight hug and kissed him on the cheek.

"I hope to see both of you again soon," said Anna. "Thanks for everything."

With Jan closely at her side, Anna joined the group slowly being filtered through Passport Control. She noted that Alex was keeping very close and signaled her thanks with a smile. Eventually it was their turn, but Anna held back to make sure that Jan got through safely. He went up to booth number 8.

The passport official looked at Jan, and then at the photo.

Jan said in English, "Stomach flu. I feel very sick," rubbing his stomach and making a face. The official nodded, removed the exit visa document, and stamped the passport. He was now through into the Customs area, where he joined Alex. Anna followed within a minute or two. Jan and Alex had already introduced themselves.

There were armed paramilitary officers standing around the walls of the building, together with police in their blue uniforms, some SB officers and plain-clothed "ferrets." Every now and then one or more of the orchestra members was asked to follow an officer to an office in the corner of the building. There they were being questioned, but most were released after a few minutes. She noticed a female ginger-haired violinist from the orchestra being escorted to the bureau, and shortly thereafter, another female orchestra member with deeper red hair. Anna's heart jumped. *Oh God. They are looking for a redhead. Of course. They must have found traces of my hair on the bed, on the sofa, or on the carpet.* She had piled her hair up under her floppy sun hat, so there was no red showing at the moment, but if she was asked to remove her hat they would surely want to interrogate her.

"Okay," said Anna to Jan. "Let's find our luggage and keep close together." They retrieved their bags, and when a couple of officials were free, moved forward. Anna was holding Jan's arm, as they dragged their bags to two adjacent metal tables. She made a big show of helping Jan place his suitcase on the table. "He has bad stomach flu," she said in Polish. "He's really ill." She returned to her own table and put her suitcase in front of the official.

"Stomach flu. Many people have problem. The hot weather," said the Customs official to Jan in broken English. "Passport, please." Jan handed over the passport. The official looked at Jan, and then at the photo. Anna could see he was not happy. "Wait here, please," he said as he took the passport over to one of the SB officials watching the proceedings. Anna could see that this officer was clearly very senior. He looked at Jan's passport, handed it back to the Customs official and started walking over to Jan. Anna's heart was pounding. When he was within a few feet of Jan, there was suddenly a commotion two tables down.

Alex was yelling at a Customs official. "Keep your grubby hands off my personal effects. You can search my bag without making such a mess can't you? It's disgusting, and you don't even have gloves on. We're just tourists. We should not be treated like this." The official protested, and then Alex pushed him. That did it, the SB official changed direction and went over to the table where Alex was, still protesting loudly in Polish. Both the SB and the Customs officials were angry. "Come with me now, sir," the SB official said forcefully, leaving no room for argument. Alex was escorted over to the office and the Customs official carried his bag behind him.

The official in front of Jan had now been abandoned. Anna moved over to Jan, offering him a drink of water, and appearing to hold him up. The official looked at Jan then said again, "Stomach flu," nodding to himself. "Okay." he signaled for Jan to close his case and pass through. Anna nearly cried out in joy.

Now it was her turn. "What you do in orchestra?" the official said to her in broken English. She replied in Polish, "I have been organizing the tour for the British Council."

She handed over her letter of introduction from the Foreign Office. He read the document and nodded. After a brief look in her case, he handed her back her passport, and said, "You can go through now."

She sighed with relief. Thank God her passport photo was black and white, and that he did not ask her to remove her hat. She went over to Jan. "You did well, Jan. Let's mingle with the crowd now."

They joined the orchestra members and some of the trustees

who had already cleared Customs. No sign of Alex though, or the redheaded ladies.

Anna was still anxious, and keeping an eye out for all contingencies. Twenty minutes later all the orchestra members, trustees and others had cleared the Customs desks. Two airport officials arrived and manned the desks at the exit door to the tarmac. One of them made an announcement over the PA in English. "We shall shortly be boarding the aircraft. There is no assigned seating, and you will be given your seat number as you pass through the desks. Please keep your luggage with you and leave it on the sidewalk as you exit. It will be loaded onto the aircraft. Thank you." A few minutes later, the exit door was opened. It had started to rain. *Neil's forecast had been right after all*, thought Anna. The group marched across the tarmac to their waiting plane. Still no sign of Alex. Anna helped Jan up the steps to the aircraft, and they found their seats in Row 12.

The luggage was being loaded. It was a slow process. The pretty English stewardesses were helping everyone get seated. Then Anna saw a vehicle coming out from the terminal towards the plane. Her stomach knotted again, as she saw the SB senior official sitting in the passenger seat. Then another vehicle followed, pulling up at the steps to the aircraft. Alex and the two redheaded orchestra members got out. The SB official got out of his car, and came over to Alex and the ladies. Anna could see them speaking and nodding to each other. Eventually the SB official shook hands with Alex and the orchestra members and gave a slight wave and smile to them as they ascended the steps to the aircraft. The door was closed, the engine started, the pilot made the usual announcements, but Anna was too tense and excited to listen. The plane rattled down the runway and took off. They were on their way to London.

She gripped Jan's hand, and they looked into each other's eyes. Tears were running down their faces. They didn't speak. They didn't have to. They had always had a complete understanding of each other, and mutual love and devotion. They had survived a Russian labor camp, a five-day rail journey to Baghdad in cattle trucks with no food or water, a British Army camp in Uganda, a new life in Australia, marriage, divorce and an ill-fated decision to move back to Poland. And now, another chance. Free at last, and hopefully their past lives would no longer haunt their future. For the first time in weeks, Anna relaxed with a sigh of contentment and gratitude.

Chapter 26

The flight started the descent into London Heathrow, through a cloudless blue sky. The change in the sound of the engines woke Jan, who had slept for most of the flight.

"There's London. It's vast, isn't it?" said Anna.

"Is that the River Thames?" asked Jan.

Anna leaned over towards the window. "Yes, and we are passing over the Tower of London, and you can see the Houses of Parliament just ahead. Wow! It really looks beautiful in the sunshine."

The pilot announced the imminent arrival of the flight, as the noise of the wheels coming down caused a slight shudder in the plane. Within a couple of minutes the pilot executed a perfect landing and a few minutes later they were at their gate at Terminal 2. An airport official was there to guide them to a separate Baggage Claim and Customs area. Alex was with other members of the Board as they awaited their luggage.

"Alex, you were there for me again," said Anna. "We can't thank you enough for creating that shindig in the Customs area in Warsaw. I think one of the "ferrets" was unhappy with Jan's passport photo, and if you hadn't started the fracas with that Customs official, we could have had a major problem."

"I saw what was happening, so I started shouting and gave him a shove. Luckily that seemed to divert attention from the officer that was heading your way," responded Alex.

"They marched you off. What happened?"

"They took me to that office in the corner of the Customs hall where there were some police officers and your friend the "ferret." The Customs official followed us in. I apologized profusely. I told them I had a hangover from the festivities of the night before, and I assured them I loved them both and I loved Warsaw, and it would never happen again," Alex continued, with a chuckle. "Eventually, after your "ferret" friend asked me a long list of irrelevant questions, I think he realized that I was not a real threat. He calmed down and offered to take me directly out to the plane. Two young musicians were also being released. I realized that their interrogation was probably to do with Krinsky's death, but they quickly satisfied their interrogators. I started chatting with them amicably and kept it going until we got to the plane," said Alex.

"I think you may have saved Jan's life, and maybe even mine. Not for the first time, Alex," Anna said, emotionally.

Two men approached them.

"Good afternoon, Sir Alex. We've met before. I'm Lewis from the Ministry of Defence. This is Detective Sgt. Fuller, from Special Branch. I've been told that you may have some papers for me. Bob Fuller is here to escort Miss Anna Kaluza and her brother to the Middlesex Hospital."

"Good to see you again, Lewis," said Alex. "Follow me and we'll see what we can do. In the meantime, Anna, I'll say goodbye. I think Jan probably needs a good rest after his ordeal, but I'll be in touch within the next few days. Good luck, Jan."

The luggage was arriving on the carousel, as two large container trolleys were wheeled into the baggage-claim area. Alex, with Lewis in tow approached Charlie Adams.

"Charlie, I'd like to introduce Mr. Lewis. We would like access to your music trunk number two. Could you open it for me?"

"Music trunk number two? Yes, of course, Sir Alex," said Charlie with a puzzled look on his face. He walked over to the second trolley, peeled back the tarpaulin cover, and opened the two padlocks on the large trunk.

"These two trunks just contain the orchestra's music. There's nothing else in there. The Polish Customs officials went through them before we left," continued Charlie as he lifted the lid.

Alex looked inside at the neatly stacked folders of music. He dug down maybe a foot or so on the right-hand side of the trunk and came out with two canvas-covered music folders tied with red ribbon. Professor Keller's papers had finally left Poland and were on their way to their originator. Alex handed the papers over to Lewis.

"I believe this is what you are looking for. Everyone is going to be very pleased," he said with a smile. "Thank you, Charlie," he continued, to a bemused Charlie Adams.

"Thank you, Sir Alex!" said Lewis empathetically. "If you would like to find your luggage, we can escort you through Customs and Passport Control. You will save yourself some time," he continued.

"I think I'll follow the normal procedure. I have a few thank-yous and goodbyes, and I don't want to create any speculation as to why I am able to walk out directly. I am sure you understand." "Of course, Sir Alex. I will make sure that these papers get delivered immediately."

Alex returned to the luggage carousel and quickly found his suitcase.

Meanwhile Anna and Jan had retrieved their bags and were escorted out by Fuller. There was an ambulance waiting in a side road, around the corner.

"I don't understand why I am being taken to hospital," said Jan. "I just need to know that Ava and the children are safe."

"I know, Jan. We should hear something in about three or four hours. But in the meantime, I think they just want to check you out and make sure you are healthy enough to be out in the wide world," responded Anna cheerfully. "I'm coming with you. I shall stay with you as long as necessary, Jan."

"Thanks, Anna. I better start speaking in English again and see if the locals can understand my Australian accent," said Jan with a smile.

Even with the ambulance bell ringing, they still had to fight the evening traffic, and it took over an hour to get to the Middlesex Hospital in central London. When they arrived,

Detective Sgt. Fuller told them to stay in the ambulance while he went for assistance. He returned within a minute or two with a couple of white-coated hospital officials, followed by two large men in dark gray suits. Clearly police bodyguards. They helped Jan out of the ambulance, and within a few minutes he was lying in bed in a private room in new blue pajamas provided by the hospital. Shortly after, a doctor and nurse entered the room.

"Good evening, Mr. Kaluza. I am Dr. Rylands, and this is Nurse Cox," he said, introducing himself and a smiling blonde nurse. "We are not going to prod you around very much this evening. We will just give you something to eat, take your vital signs, and give you a light sedative so as you can have a good night's sleep. Tomorrow we will do some blood tests, and give you a general physical. If all is well, we'll be able to discharge you very quickly," he continued with a reassuring smile.

"And you must be Anna Kaluza," the doctor said, oozing charm, while he gave an admiring look at Anna. "You're welcome to stay for the next couple of hours or so, until Mr. Kaluza can get some well-earned sleep."

"I would like to stay, until about nine-thirty if possible, because we are expecting an important message. I know Jan will sleep soundly once we hear positive news. I hope that will be okay, Doctor," Anna continued, returning the doctor's smile.

"It's nearly seven-thirty now. So we can hold off on the sedative until later," he said turning to his nurse as a silent instruction.

"I'm feeling fine, Doctor," said Jan, speaking in English for the first time. "A good sleep would be great, but otherwise I'm sure I'll be fighting fit within a day or two."

"We certainly hope so. But I would ask you to be patient," responded the doctor with a little more authority.

Despite Jan's protestations, he dropped off to sleep within five minutes of the doctor and nurse leaving the room. He was awakened when the nurse returned and took his blood pressure and other vitals.

The hospital dinner came, but Jan had very little appetite. Anna was sitting in the room but declined the offer of hospital food. Jan fell off to sleep again.

At about nine-ten, there was a soft knock on the door. Anna opened it to find Fuller with a folded piece of paper. "This was just delivered, miss," he said. Her heart was pounding as she opened the message:

Ava and children safe in Sweden. Will arrive in London tomorrow afternoon.

Anna nearly jumped for joy. "My God, I did it. Keller's papers, Jan and the family are all out of Warsaw," she said to herself.

She gently woke Jan. "Ava and the children are safe in Sweden. They will be in London tomorrow afternoon. We can have a family reunion tomorrow evening, Jan," Anna said, trying hard to contain her emotions.

Her pale thin brother pushed himself up in the bed, and threw his arms around her as tears ran down his face. "Anna, you've done it. You saved us all. I can't tell you how proud I am of you and how grateful."

Anna was crying as well. "We will be a family again. I have just got to get Mother out of there. It will be my final challenge," she continued with a laugh, through her tears.

"I know you will sleep now, Jan, so I'm going to leave you for the night, but I'll be back about nine-thirty in the morning." She leant over the bed and gave her brother a kiss on the cheek. She left the room, noting the two bodyguards were positioned outside. Detective Sgt. Fuller was sitting in a chair a little way down the corridor. "If you are ready, miss, I have got instructions to take you to your flat."

"That would be wonderful," replied Anna, suddenly feeling totally exhausted. She couldn't wait to get back to her little pad and crash out.

* * *

Frank did his best to avoid the evening traffic jams, and eventually delivered Alex to his St John's Wood apartment.

Julia was waiting. "Ah! Alex, thank God you're home safe and sound. No blood or traumas this time, I hope," she continued with a little sarcasm in her voice.

"No. No problems this time. In fact a very pleasant visit. The orchestra outdid themselves. They were spectacular, and the last couple of nights in Warsaw were amazing. The audience really loves classical music. Standing ovations, apparently throughout the tour. As to the other matters, all went smoothly. I'm sure Tim will be delighted." Alex was saying all of this as he took Julia in his arms and gave her a warm kiss and embrace.

"I hope the SIS is satisfied, and they won't be calling on you again."

Alex laughed and changed the subject, asking about Julia's day and enquiring about the children. He unpacked and was relaxing with a scotch and water when the phone rang.

"Alex. Welcome home. I just received a delivery from our friend Lewis. I just wanted to call you immediately, to tell you how grateful I am, and how delighted everyone is that the mission has been completed. Well done. I would love to have lunch with you and hear how you so cleverly got the papers out of Poland. How about Friday at one at the Savoy Grill?" said Tim in one long sentence.

"It's great to be home, Tim," said Alex. "Lunch on Friday sounds good. Of course it was Anna that bore the brunt of the load, and successfully retrieved Keller's papers." He paused. "I look forward to seeing you."

* * *

Anna was back at the Middlesex Hospital just before nine-thirty on Wednesday morning. However, she couldn't get into Jan's room because he was undergoing various tests.

Nurse Cox asked her to wait in the corridor. "We won't be long. Just doing a few straightforward tests."

Despite the smiling assurance, Anna was nervous. She knew that Jan had been through hell, and she could see the physical impact just by looking at him. She hoped that he had been strong enough to withstand the abuses of the past few months.

After about ten minutes, Dr. Rylands appeared. "Ah! Miss Kaluza. We were just doing a few tests on Jan. We will have the results later today. I would also like to send him down for some x-rays later this morning. He is suffering from malnutrition, and may have a couple of cracked ribs, although I believe they are healing. We will be checking all his vital functions, and looking at his kidneys and liver. Although he is now painfully thin and weak, I can see that basically he has a strong physique. I hope that all he will need is rest and some good, nutritious food. You can go in now, but he is still very tired, and I think you should let him rest as much as possible."

"Thank you, Doctor. I won't spend long this morning. I hope to return later this afternoon with his family."

Dr. Rylands nodded and hurried down the corridor.

Jan was looking a little stronger. He admitted to being exhausted still, but said that he had slept well for the first time in months. He was ecstatic about seeing his family. Anna told him that "The Firm" had given her a generous allowance to go shopping with them tomorrow for clothes, shoes and everything else that they would need, and she would return to the hospital later with the family.

She had also received a call that morning from MI6 asking her to come to a debriefing session at 3:00 p.m. the next day. She was not looking forward to that. She knew that she would have to tell them about Krinsky.

She returned to her flat and waited for Detective Sgt. Fuller to phone her as arranged. It was just before two-thirty when the phone rang.

"Good afternoon, miss. Your guests are now in London. We should be at your flat within an hour or so," said Fuller in his gruff Cockney voice.

"Wonderful. I hope they have enough English to understand that you are bringing them to see me, and that Jan is in London, safe and healthy."

"It's alright, miss. I speak Polish. That is why they put me on this gig," said Fuller, clearly amused.

"Of course. I should have thought of that. Are they excited?"

"Excited, miss? They're over the moon. You will see for yourself."

"Wonderful, Detective. See you soon."

There were many tears, hugs, kisses and laughter, when Ava and the children arrived. This was repeated, but even more so, when Anna escorted them into the hospital room. Jan was sitting up in bed, looking a little more rested but still pale and wan. Everyone was talking at once as Jan and Ava shared their experiences. When dinner came, not only did Jan eat every morsel, but so did Ava and the children, obviously finding hospital food extremely tasty. At eight o'clock, Nurse Cox came in and requested the guests leave Jan to rest and sleep.

Fuller was waiting to take Ava and the children to temporary accommodation in Clapham. The apartment was in a low rise 1930s block of flats, with a small balcony that looked over a grass-covered front yard. The kids thought the flat was the height of luxury, turning the hot and cold taps on and off, and opening and closing the refrigerator. Anna knew that they had endured a long day. She handed over her recent purchases and left them to their own devices. Detective Sgt. Fuller had assured her they would be safe, and that the apartment was being watched by Special Branch.

The next morning, Anna escorted the family to the hospital

and after more tears, hugs and kisses left them chatting merrily. Dr. Rylands had confirmed that while Jan was suffering from malnutrition and might have some kidney damage as well as cracked ribs, nothing was life-threatening and with a little rest and good nutrition, should be able to rebuild his strength very quickly.

Anna was delighted to hear this news, said her goodbyes, and quickly got a cab outside of the hospital and headed towards the MI6 headquarters.

She arrived with plenty of time before her debriefing session. She was escorted to the familiar basement interview room.

Almost immediately, Bob Stewart entered. "Good afternoon, Anna. Welcome back. I hear you did an outstanding job. Congratulations, everyone seems very happy here."

"Thank you," said Anna. "I'm pleased to be back in London," she continued modestly.

"Well, Anna, I think you know the format, so I would like you to give me a full account of your stay in Warsaw, your acquisition of Keller's papers, the release of your brother from jail, and your return to London," said Stewart, turning on the tape recorder.

Anna proceeded to give a full description from start to finish. She commented on the orchestra tour, working at the British Council, the various personalities with whom she interacted, her meetings with Professor Kopacz, her acquisition of Keller's papers, the help provided by Neil Jordan, and how with the aid of Colonel Roman Krinsky, she had been able to engineer the release of her brother Jan from Mokotów Prison. Bob Stewart listened intently without interruption. Then Anna dropped the bombshell.

"I spent the latter part of last Friday evening at Colonel Krinsky's apartment. I know that Mr. Bevans had told me not to attempt to get my brother Jan released from prison, and Sir Alex Campbell warned me in Warsaw to keep away from Colonel Krinsky." She paused, gathering her thoughts, as she started to relive her nightmare. "However, I know, as does much of the Polish population, being arrested and interned by the SB is no picnic. I was worried sick about my brother, and felt that I could not leave Warsaw without making an attempt to get him released. The one man who could do that with a quick signature on a piece of paper, was Colonel Krinsky. That evening, he signed a green release form for Jan. I think he was showing off, making sure I would understand how powerful he was in Polish politics. However, after I had secured this release form, Krinsky asked me a number of questions. Perhaps I appeared to be a little too eager, or naive. In any event, it suddenly dawned on him that I was Anna Kaluza, Jan's sister. He grabbed me by the wrist, tighter than a vice. You can still see the yellowing bruises around my wrist now." She stopped to show Stewart, who nodded. "He started to drag me across the room to his desk, and telephone. I didn't have the strength to fight him as he pulled me half stumbling across the carpet, until he positioned me against the desk and was leaning over me to get to the phone." She stopped, unable to continue for a few moments. When she continued it was in almost a hoarse whisper. "He screamed at me, that I would be imprisoned with my brother within twenty minutes. I was sure this was a death sentence. I had to get free from him and stop him making that call. I was pinned back on his desk. He had his arm across my throat as he picked up the phone." She stopped again, as tears fell from her red swollen eyes. She slowly pulled herself together and continued in a whisper. "My hand felt around the desk, looking to grab something to hit him with. I felt a letter opener, and as he was distracted dialing, I plunged it into his eye." She paused again. "The knife must have penetrated his brain, because he slid to the floor. I had killed him." She stopped and was shaking and crying, unable to continue.

"What? Killed him?" said Stewart, clearly shocked to hear this news.

Anna continued slowly. "As you can imagine, I was in a

complete state of shock." She stopped again, reliving the nightmare before continuing in a hoarse voice. "I gradually recovered, cleaned up as best I could to avoid leaving finger-prints or clues, left his apartment, and made it back to mine." Anna now continued in a stronger voice. "Of course, Krinsky's death was front-page news. Police cars and sirens were all over the city for the next few days. I was counting the hours until I could leave Warsaw, and was praying that Krinsky's signed release for Jan would still be valid, and that I could arrange through some friends in Warsaw for Jan's wife Ava and his two children to leave Poland." She paused, thinking carefully as she weaved her lies around the facts. "It wasn't until Tuesday morning that I was able to have Jan released and start Ava and the children on the journey to London. I was relieved and terrified at the same time. We still had to get through Warsaw airport, which turned out to be a harrowing experience. On Tuesday I read in the papers that the police had arrested someone in connection with Krinsky's murder. No charges have been made at the present time. Of course the person arrested is totally innocent." She paused again. "I feel very bad about that. I hope she will be released soon."

"Is that all, Anna?" asked Stewart.

"I know that Mr. Bevans and the SIS will be disappointed in my taking matters into my own hands, against advice and instructions. I'm sorry that I had to kill Colonel Krinsky, and that my actions could prove to be an embarrassment to Her Majesty's government. I can only say that blood is thicker than water and I believe that if I had not been able to obtain Jan's release he might well have died in prison. I hope there will be some understanding of my feelings and consequent action in Warsaw."

Bob Stewart was stunned. All he could say was, "You murdered the head of the Polish SB, on your own, in his private apartment?

Before Anna could answer, Tim Bevans marched into the

interrogation room, red-faced and livid.

"What the hell have you done?" he said, his voice rising. "I had no idea that getting your brother out of jail involved murder. What were you thinking? You could have jeopardized this whole mission, and caused a major diplomatic incident. That might still be the case. You are extremely lucky that you haven't been arrested and charged with murder!" he continued, glaring at Anna. "If that had been the case, your brother would have probably stayed in jail and had the key thrown away and you might have joined him." He paused, looking like he was ready to explode. "Your training, Anna, as a part of the MI6 team, is always to act in the best interests of Her Majesty's government. In this business, your personal or family interests come second. You know that." Bevans was furious, pacing up and down in front of her.

"You did well retrieving Professor Keller's papers. But... but..." Bevans stammered uncharacteristically. "...murdering the head of a foreign service in cold blood because of your family problems cancels all of your achievements." Bevans cut through the air as he waved his right arm, gathering his thoughts for the next onslaught.

"We shall have to consider how we deal with your breach of trust and orders," he continued, now in his cold diplomatic voice. "In the meantime, until I get the broader picture, you will be suspended. Your suspension can run concurrently with some vacation time that you have due. I don't want your actions or your suspension to be known by your colleagues at this time. You will call Mr. Stewart every morning to report on your daily plans. You will be under surveillance 24/7. You will hand over your passport to him. Within four weeks you will be informed of our decision on your future in the service. Do you understand?" Tim continued glaring at Anna.

As an afterthought, Bevans added in a cold hard voice, "That is two murders you have committed in Poland over the past few months. You better pray that this Krinsky murder does not lead to a major diplomatic row. If it does, we might send you and your family back to Poland."

Tim Bevans did not wait for a response and marched out of the room.

Anna looked at the exit door, in shock with her mouth open. *Oh, no,* she thought, *back to Poland to the death penalty after all of this.* Her stomach tightened into a knot of fear.

"You've been given your orders, Anna," said Stewart with a frosty expression. "You should comply to the letter. Tell your superiors, for the time being, that you have got two weeks' vacation. This will give you a chance to settle your brother's family. I understand that within a few days they will be moved to a safe house in Ealing. I'm sure you will have more than enough to do over the next week or so getting them settled." He continued in a somewhat softer tone. "But, frankly, Anna, you are in deep shit. Your position in MI6 does not include a license to kill, and you may well face prison in this country."

"I'm so sorry about all of this. I know I took an enormous risk. It was certainly against advice, but I just had to try to help Jan," said Anna, trying to make her case.

"Anna, I have just got one more question," said Stewart, getting back into interrogation mode. "With Krinsky murdered, and the police rushing around Warsaw looking for his killer, how did you manage in that chaos, to get Jan released, and have his family put on a boat for Sweden?"

"Sheer luck, I suppose," said Anna. "Perhaps nobody wanted to question a release authorization signed by Colonel Krinsky just before he died. Anyway, it all worked out," Anna said, eager to end the conversation.

"Yes. I would say extreme luck," continued Stewart, with a troubled expression his face. "Okay, Anna. You can go as soon as I arrange for your 'protection' escorts. They will be with you day and night, until further notice."

"I understand. Thank you," said Anna.

Chapter 27

Alex arrived at the Savoy, a few minutes before one o'clock, and after a quick wash and brush up in the cloakroom, made his way to the grill where Tim was waiting.

"Good to see you, Alex," said Tim. Alex thought his friend looked really drawn and tired. "Mario has a nice quiet corner table for us," continued Tim as the maître d' ushered them both towards the back of the restaurant. Tim and Alex recognized many of the diners and waved to them as they passed their tables.

They ordered pre-lunch drinks and chose the menu items. Tim was eager to get straight to the point. He leaned in towards Alex, and spoke softly but quickly. "Alex, did you know that Anna killed this Colonel Krinsky?"

"Yes, Tim," replied Alex, also speaking quietly. "She told me and I was absolutely flabbergasted. I had warned her to stay away from Krinsky. I told her she was playing with fire and could jeopardize our mission, but unfortunately, she didn't listen to me."

Tim nodded and continued. "This could blow up into a major diplomatic row if the Polish police or Secret Service are able to link Anna to Krinsky's murder. She was very foolish to even attempt to get Krinsky's help. It should have been obvious that Krinsky would put two and two together. The amazing part of the story is that she actually pulled it off. I'm still not sure how she achieved this. Did she give you any details?"

"No. But, I did find out about her Krinsky meeting and I read the Warsaw papers. She told me that she went to Krinsky's apartment with a view to turning on the charm and convincing him to sign some sort of release for her brother. Colonel Krinsky was a well-known womanizer, apparently not above disposing of the competition for the women of his choice, by putting their boyfriends, lovers or husbands in jail. Not a very savory character, even though he was thought to be General Jaruzelski's closest aide. He was also a very tough but capable front man, dealing with the Solidarity movement street protests. He was married to a Russian former model. He had two young children and lived in a country estate south of Warsaw. The police have arrested someone who is 'helping their enquiries.' The lady in question is supposed to be Krinsky's current girlfriend, whose husband he put in jail a few months ago."

Tim nodded as he took in all this information. "Clearly not an officer and a gentleman. But nevertheless, his high profile could prove to be extremely embarrassing should Anna come under suspicion," said Tim.

"I know," responded Alex seriously. "By the time I found out what had happened, it was too late to do anything other than try and help Anna succeed in her quest. I asked the Ambassador for his help and I know he contacted the FO in London, and I presume you and your team for approval. He offered up Neil Jordan's passport. I think you know who he is. In addition he contacted the embassy in Stockholm and arranged for some of their people to meet Ava and her family when the ferry arrived and take them under their wing, even though they had no passports or formal papers."

"Yes, I was in the loop on all those plans, Alex," replied Tim, "but by God, we certainly had no idea that she had murdered the head of the Polish Secret Service. If we had known that, we might have taken a different decision. If we had been given the opportunity to weigh the diplomatic impact of helping or not helping her, I think quite frankly, she would have lost out. Nevertheless, the deed is done; I have suspended her while we decide her fate. This is a major breach of protocol and our operating mission. She is in deep trouble." Tim paused. "I don't want anyone in the department to know what transpired in Warsaw at the present time. Meanwhile, we will keep our ears close to the ground in Poland, and piece together some of the missing elements of the story. I know I can count on you, Alex, to keep all of this under your hat,"

"Of course," said Alex earnestly.

"Now, you must tell me your part in this whole operation and how you got the papers out of Warsaw," Tim continued.

As they were eating lunch and enjoying a couple of glasses of Chablis, Alex told him the whole saga.

The rest of the lunch and the conversation was amicable enough. As they were completing their coffee, Tim asked, "What are you going to be doing for the next few weeks, Alex?"

"I shall be in Scotland for a week or so. I have some business in Edinburgh, and Julia is going to join me. Laura is going to spend a few days with us, and Mark is coming home from Kentucky for a couple of weeks. So it is going to be business and pleasure. I hope to get in some golf and maybe a little fishing."

"Sounds great, Alex. I'm afraid I won't have any leave until the end of August. Things have been so hectic recently, I'm not even sure I'll be able to get away then. Gail is not very happy with me at the moment. However, I would appreciate it if you could keep contact with Anna just to see what she is up to. Let me know if there's anything you think would be of interest to us."

"Of course. I was planning to meet with Anna, and her family and also to see Keller again shortly. Do you have some concerns about Anna?" said Alex.

"Not really. Nothing at the moment, but we need to do a little homework while she is suspended," said Tim amicably. But Alex knew there was something nagging at Tim's conscience.

"We're planning to move Jan and his family into a safe house in Ealing next week, after we've had a chance to debrief him. When he's had a couple of weeks to rebuild his strength and settle his family, we shall reallocate some responsibilities for him, probably at Lambeth. He's been a loyal operative for many years and I think he will be useful to us," said Tim.

"That's good to hear," responded Alex. "The poor guy has

been through hell and high water, and deserves a break."

* * *

It had been a tough couple of weeks for Anna. She had to contact Bob Stewart every morning and tell him of her plans for the day, and if she wished to leave her apartment she knew she had two escorts as company, a man and woman from Special Branch. One of them was always seated in the corridor outside the entrance to her apartment, and the other one in a car across the street. She was having many sleepless nights as she worried about the outcome of the review on her future with MI6. So far as she knew, there had been no diplomatic explosions connecting her to the murder of Roman Krinsky. But it was early days yet and anything could happen. The thought of being sent back to Poland or tried and jailed in the UK was terrifying.

She was miserable and depressed. She really had no friends in London. She had not been in the city long enough to make friends. Even though she had worked for a few weeks at MI6 headquarters, she had been sent on a survival course and then back to Warsaw. She had lunch with Alex, but it was a strained meeting, not relaxed and enjoyable; the Krinsky murder hanging over them. Her only salvation was Jan. At the weekends she had gone to Ealing, to help him and Ava settle into their new home, and joined in the excitement. She had not told Jan of her current predicament, in accordance with instructions she had received from Bob Stewart. But in any event she didn't want to add to his pressures as he settled into a new job, in a new city, in a new country with a new identity, for himself and his family. Other than those outings, she spent a lot of time reading and went to the cinema a couple of times, but generally felt lonely and depressed.

It was late afternoon on a stormy August Thursday, when the doorbell rang. She opened the door to find Neil Jordan standing there with a big grin on his face, and a bottle of champagne in his arms. Anna was overwhelmed at the sight of a friendly face and couldn't stop the tears. As soon as he came into the apartment she threw her arms around his neck and hugged him tightly. "Oh, Neil," she said. "I can't tell you how happy I am to see you."

"It wasn't easy," said Neil. "Nobody in 'the firm,' knew Janet Clark, and to find out where Anna Kaluza had gone, took nearly a week. But I'm good at that sort of thing," he continued. "And so I tracked you down at last. You're supposed to be on vacation, or so they told me, but I see you've got company in the corridor outside and across the street. So I gather you may not be having a great vacation."

"You're right, Neil. This is no vacation. I have some problems with 'the firm.' I am confined to barracks, so to speak, until they decide my fate. So seeing you has made my day. Tell me, what are you doing in London?" she said as she motioned Neil to sit with her on the sofa.

"I got back from Warsaw, at the beginning of last week, via Helsinki. I hung around really to see how the Krinsky investigation was progressing. As you know I don't ask questions, but I thought you might be interested."

"Absolutely, of course," responded Anna eagerly. "What is happening?"

"The country is consumed with politics and the future of the Solidarity movement. Apparently there are negotiations going on between Solidarity, Lech Walesa, and General Jaruzelski's government. In addition, there is a new acting head of the SB, who released Capt. Podolski a couple of weeks ago from prison, the same day as the police commissioner announced all charges against Lena Podolski were being dropped and that she was to be released immediately. The commissioner said that the Krinsky murder investigation is continuing and they are pursuing other leads. However, since that announcement there has been complete silence, so I don't know whether they have other leads or not." Neil looked at Anna, waiting to see if she would add to his comments. But Anna said nothing, even though she nearly jumped for joy on hearing that Lena had been released.

"So, Neil," she said, changing the subject, "as I said... what are you doing in London?"

"I think I have to call you Anna, and I think you will have to call me Mark. We are no longer on a working assignment. I like the name Anna, so let us deal with our real identities," he continued with a laugh. "I really came to London to see you but also to pick up a new assignment."

"I'm flattered, Mark. You couldn't have come at a better time." "Unfortunately, it's taken so long to find you, and now I'm off tomorrow on my new assignment."

"Oh no," Anna responded with genuine concern. "Not now, just when we found each other again. Where are you going and for how long?"

"I can't really be specific, but I signed a two-year contract for work in the Gulf States."

"Two years! That's a lifetime," Anna said, with tears welling up in her eyes again. She didn't want to lose him. She had developed some deep feelings, and he was the only contact with the outside world she had at the moment. Separating for two years would be very painful.

"Let's not dwell on that at the moment, Anna," said Mark. "Let's enjoy the champagne and celebrate the fact that we finally found each other, and we are safe in London. Do you have any plans for this evening?"

"Plans! You must be kidding," responded Anna, laughing.

"Okay. It's bucketing rain out there, so how about a quiet meal here together."

"That would be lovely," said Anna. "I've got eggs, cheese, and some salad. I should be able to whip something up for us."

"That won't be necessary. I'll pop out and get some scrumptious food from Harrods. I can be back within an hour and then we'll put it all together. Do you have any wine in the house?"

"No," said Anna. "I finished the last bottle of Chardonnay yesterday."

"No problem, I'll get a couple of bottles at Harrods."

"It's pouring out there, Mark; are you sure you really want to do this?"

"Sure. But I'll try and persuade your friend downstairs to do a little chauffeuring for me!" Mark said. "But just in case, lend me an umbrella." Anna went to get the large golf umbrella she had found in a closet in the apartment.

"I'll be back within an hour; maybe earlier if I can get a lift." He leaned in and gave Anna a warm kiss on the lips as he left.

Anna decided that this would be a special evening after all, so she laid up the small dining table in the living-room area, found a couple of glass candlesticks and some candles and lit them, and dimmed the lights, giving a warm glow to the room, fighting back the gloom of London in the rain. She then changed into a slim-fitting white skirt and blue T-shirt, put on a silver necklace and earrings, freshened her makeup and teased her hair. She had just finished when Mark returned, amazingly in less than an hour.

"I flashed my ID card to Jimmy, your pal downstairs, assured him that you weren't going anywhere, and he took pity on me because of the rain and we nipped over to Harrods. He waited while I rushed around the food hall and then drove me back. So here I am as dry as a bone, and here is your umbrella unused!" he said with a look of achievement on his face. "Boy have I got some goodies for us tonight." He carried two heavy Harrods bags into the kitchen area and started unpacking. Two bottles of Chablis, smoked salmon, two lobsters, a cucumber salad, white asparagus, half a dozen mini patisseries, and a tub of coconut vanilla ice cream. "This should keep us going, I think," he said in triumph.

"My God, Mark! This is incredible. It must have cost a fortune," said Anna, wide-eyed.

"Well, we're worth it," he responded, laughing.

The food was delicious and as they enjoyed every morsel, they talked about their childhoods and life experiences. But Anna couldn't bring herself to tell Mark the whole story. She kept partly to her script, describing herself as Australian and filling in all the details of her childhood, education, teenage years, and her first marriage to Jack Gray. After they had finished dinner, cleared the plates and tidied the kitchen, they took the remains of the champagne and sat down on the sofa. It was the first time Anna had relaxed for weeks, and she felt warm and protected as she snuggled into Mark's shoulder. They said nothing as he held her closely and gently kissed her forehead, lips and then her shoulders and neck. She turned her face to him and responded, and soon the passion was rising. She took him by the hand, rose from the sofa and led him into her bedroom. He slowly undressed her, kissing her gently, until she was standing only in her panties. She did the same for him and when he was down to his shorts, they climbed into bed. His hands started to roam over her body and soon their kissing became more passionate, and they made love holding each other as if there were no tomorrow. They slept and made love into the night and early morning. She was still in a drowsy sleep when she awoke and saw him getting dressed.

"What time is it?" she said huskily.

"Just after seven," he replied. "I'm afraid I've got to go."

She watched him silently as he got dressed and said nothing, although she felt her emotions rising and tears welling up. She realized that they had something special together and believed their feelings for each other were genuine. Not only because of their circumstances, or the fact that they had been through some hair-raising ordeals. This was deeper than that, but once again Anna was losing the love of her life.

"I don't like long goodbyes," he said as he bent down over the bed to kiss her. "I love you, Anna, and whatever happens I will return. I promise it will be as soon as possible. I shall keep in touch – somehow."

Tears were running down her face now. There was nothing more to say. She kissed him back. "Be careful out there, Mark. I need you back in one piece."

Mark grabbed his things, and took one last look at Anna as he left.

* * *

When Alex got home that evening, Julia told him that Erik Keller had been on the phone and wished to speak to him. Alex returned his call. Erik asked whether it would be possible to spend a few days in the Scottish countryside after the week in Edinburgh, and could Alex recommend a hotel. Alex thought for a moment. "Of course, Erik. I think you would enjoy Ardbeg House. It is a country-house hotel on the way to Perth, about an hour or so north of Edinburgh. Lovely countryside, and great hiking and fishing."

"That sounds lovely, Alex. Thank you. I shall arrange for a reservation." Then came a request that took Alex by surprise. "Do you think it would be possible for Anna to join me?" Alex couldn't help himself. He felt a pang of jealously. A few days with Anna at the beautiful Ardbeg House. Perhaps Julia was right – was there a romance developing between Erik and Anna?

"Anna? Er… Erik, I will have to get permission from Tim Bevans, but I will get back to you as soon as I've spoken to him. If he gives the okay, I could have Anna picked up on Monday week at Edinburgh Airport and brought into town where we can all have lunch. I will have Frank take you both up to Ardbeg House. I know you will have your bodyguards watching over you, and they can make their own arrangements at the hotel. I'm sure you and Anna will have a wonderful time."

"Well, we are good friends and kindred spirits."

When he got off the phone, Julia was eager to hear about the arrangements. She had considered Anna and Erik "an item" for some time now, and thought they were very well suited. As she said to Alex, she felt they both deserved some peace and happiness after their respective ordeals. Alex didn't agree. He thought that Keller represented another father figure for Anna, or maybe he was just jealous. He phoned Tim to get approval for Anna's trip. Tim responded that approval would be granted, but she would need to be "escorted" to Edinburgh, and then be under the protection of Keller's bodyguards.

* * *

Anna was in a deep depression all day, not helped by dreary gray damp London weather, until the phone rang at about seven. It was Alex. After some chitchat he told her that he was off to Scotland for a couple of weeks. Then came the good news.

"Erik Keller would like you to join him for a few days at a lovely country-house hotel, Ardbeg House. It is near Perth and a great place for hiking, fishing and is in spectacular countryside. What do you think?"

"Oh my God, that would be wonderful, Alex," said Anna, her heart leaping for joy at the thought of getting out of her 'house arrest' for a few days. "But will Mr. Bevans let me go?" Anna continued anxiously.

"Yes, I got his approval. You will be accompanied to Edinburgh by one of your protectors, and then handed over to Erik Keller's bodyguards. I will have Frank, my chauffeur, collect you at Turnhouse Airport on Monday week. I'm arranging a family luncheon in Edinburgh, and you will be able to join us before going off to Ardbeg House."

"That's fantastic," responded an excited Anna. "Thank you so much, Alex. You've cheered me up no end." She paused before asking tentatively, "Do you have any news from Mr. Bevans about my MI6 review?"

"No, I'm afraid not, Anna, but obviously nothing is going to happen in the next couple of weeks or Tim would not have given his approval."

"Alex, I know I will enjoy every minute of my first visit to Bonny Scotland," she said with a laugh. She couldn't believe her good luck. A trip to Scotland and a few days with Erik Keller.

* * *

The week in Edinburgh went well. Erik found the city fascinating and was eager to explore its history, palaces and ancient buildings, despite being followed continuously by the two bodyguards, and wearing a bulletproof vest, which he strongly objected to. He continuously thanked Alex and Julia for their kindness and hospitality and expressed his appreciation for being welcomed into the family.

The following Monday, Frank was at Turnhouse, Edinburgh Airport to pick up Anna. Unfortunately it was a dark and dreary day, with no sign of sun. Alex had booked a private room for lunch at the new La Petite Maison restaurant just off Princes Street. He had invited a few cousins, and with Laura and Mark the total group was sixteen. Anna had bleached out her red hair and her natural blonde was growing in. She looked happy and relaxed. Erik was all smiles and was beginning to look very English, wearing a tweed jacket, gray trousers, green shirt and a woven wool tie. Lunch was a great success and didn't break up until after 3:00. After many thank-yous and hugs, Anna and Erik departed, followed at a distance by the two bodyguards in their own vehicle. Throughout lunch, the family had been unaware of the bodyguards. They had checked out the restaurant before the lunch had started, and had positioned themselves at a table with a clear view of the private room.

The weather cleared up and was warm and pleasant for the

rest of the week. Alex had a couple of meetings at the Edinburgh offices, but also had a day's golf at Muirfield with Mark, and had gone fishing with three of his executives. Julia had enjoyed catching up with some of her old Edinburgh friends and visiting her charitable Boards. Friday was the last day before their departure back to London. Laura had already left to catch up with friends in Italy and Mark had flown back to the US the day before. Alex was chairing a meeting on new product development when his assistant came into the boardroom and whispered in his ear. He excused himself to answer the phone in his office, and picked up the phone. It was Tim.

"Alex, how quickly can you get to Ardbeg House?"

"About an hour or so, depending on the traffic. What's up?"

"I need you to leave immediately, Alex. It's very urgent. I'm at Northholt at the moment on my way to Edinburgh. I shall be met by a police helicopter which will get me up to Ardbeg House. But probably it will take at least an hour and a half or so. I don't know, but maybe every minute will count," Tim continued in a very anxious voice.

"Okay" said Alex. "I'll drop everything and leave immediately. But what is this all about?"

"We think Anna is a double. Possibly KGB. If so, I'm concerned that she may kill Keller."

"What!!" responded Alex, in shock. "Anna. Are you sure?"

"I can't talk now, Alex. However, I'm pretty sure. Do me a favor and please call Erik Keller now, tell him to wait for you in the hotel lobby. We are trying to reach his bodyguards. I hope you can drop everything and get moving."

"I'm on my way, Tim. I'll see you later." Alex immediately phoned Ardbeg House and asked for Erik Keller or Anna Kaluza. After an excruciating minute or two he was told they were not in their rooms, and were not in the hotel. He asked if the reception knew where they had gone. Some inquiries were made and the doorman said that they were dressed for hiking and were aiming to climb to the Polmont waterfall about four miles from the hotel. Alex returned to the boardroom and excused himself, explaining that something extremely urgent had arisen. He called for Frank to bring the car around to the front door, and within a few minutes they were driving through the Friday traffic, and heading for the road to Perth.

Frank sped up the motorway, and they arrived at the hotel in about seventy-five minutes. The local Perth police were already there. Alex introduced himself to the senior officer. He said he had just received a message that Tim Bevans would be arriving in the grounds of the hotel within five minutes or so. Alex went to talk to the doorman and established that the bodyguards had followed Erik and Anna when they left for the hike. At least Erik had some protection.

Alex heard the sound of the helicopter before he saw it. The clackity clack of the rotor blades got louder and then the black police Sikorsky came over the hill, and hovered over the large rear manicured lawn of Ardbeg House. The copter slowly descended as the wind from the blades bent the rose bushes around the edge of the lawn. Alex turned his head against the wind and the dust. The blades were turning slowly when the door opened and Tim jumped out. He approached Alex and the Special Branch inspector.

"Good morning, Inspector. Stevens isn't it?"

"Yes, sir, good morning to you."

"Do you know Polmont Falls? How far are we?" Tim continued, not wasting a minute.

"Yes, sir. Just over those hills. Maybe four or five miles. You can see the track heading from the paddock over there. That goes through the woods and beyond you come to the rocky trail up to Polmont."

"Okay," responded Tim. "Alex, I would like you and Inspector Stevens to join us on the helicopter. I may need you to intercede with Anna and the professor. Let's get going; we can't waste a second."

He turned on his heel, and with Alex and the inspector following, made his way back to the copter. Alex and Stevens followed Tim into the bird, and were handed headphones. Apart from the pilot, there was a police officer from the SWAT team, dressed in black fatigues, and holding a rifle with a telescopic lens. The other passenger was Bob Stewart, who Alex recognized from Lambeth. As they boarded, another officer, whom Alex presumed was from MI6, disembarked. Tim had a last few words with him.

"Okay, Stevens," said Tim. "Show us the way, please." The pilot opened the throttle and the helicopter ascended slowly and then wheeled over towards the woods, following instructions over the intercom from Stevens.

Alex looked down. They were only a couple of hundred feet above ground and they quickly covered the distance across the paddock to the woods where the footpath disappeared. Within a couple of minutes, they were over the woods and Alex could see the footpath starting to wind its way up the increasingly rocky ground towards Polmont Falls, a couple of thin streams of water cascading off the top of the escarpment and down the rocky banks to a fast-flowing stream of whitewater. They were quickly approaching, and Alex could see Anna and the professor standing next to each other on a rocky ledge overlooking the falls. About thirty yards further down the hill were the two bodyguards. As the helicopter approached, all their heads turned, and Alex saw the bodyguards withdraw their handguns from their clothing.

"Can you circle around and land above them?" said Alex to the pilot.

"No problem, sir."

"I'd like you to hover about twenty feet above ground, until I tell you to land," continued Tim. The pilot wheeled above and around the little plateau from which the falls were gushing.

Tim switched on a mike connected to a megaphone outside of the helicopter.

"This is Tim Bevans. Please move away from that ledge, Professor, immediately! Anna, move away from the professor and raise your hands where we can see them," he continued.

The professor looked confused and appeared to say something to Anna. She nodded and motioned him to move away as instructed. She also put her hands in the air, as if surrendering.

"Mullen and McNicol, please move towards the professor and Anna Kaluza. Keep Anna covered at all times. We shall join you in one minute," said Tim, addressing the bodyguards.

The two bodyguards, with guns drawn, approached Anna and the professor, who had now moved fifteen yards away from the waterfall and was standing still with fear on his face. Anna didn't move.

Tim told the pilot to land the helicopter and cut the engine. Within a few seconds the door was opened.

"Anna," said Tim, holding the megaphone, and now approaching them on the ground, followed by the sharpshooter, rifle at the ready, Alex and Stewart. "Keep your hands in the air, but I want you to kneel on the ground." Anna nodded and did as she was told.

As soon as the professor saw Alex, he looked relieved and marched towards him.

"What is going on, Alex. Why the helicopter, why the police, is there some trouble?"

"Nothing for you to worry about, Erik. Just stay close to me."

Anna was now surrounded. Tears were running down her face, as Tim and Alex approached.

"You needn't have worried. I could never harm the professor, whatever the consequences," she said through her sobs to Tim. Then looking at Alex.

"I'm so sorry, Alex," she said. "Somehow, I'm glad it's over," she continued, now almost unable to speak, and shaking uncontrollably.

Tim and Stewart approached Anna who was still kneeling on the ground, and helped her to her feet.

"Right, Anna," said Tim. "I think we have a lot to talk about."

Stewart then clamped nylon handcuffs on her wrists as he pulled her arms behind her.

"I don't understand, Alex," said the professor. "Why is Anna being arrested?"

"I'll explain later, Erik, when we head back to Edinburgh."

Tim went over to the two bodyguards, and told them to make their own way back to Ardbeg House. He informed them he would be going straight on to Edinburgh airport and then back to London, with Anna.

Anna and the professor squeezed into the helicopter and within a few minutes they were back on the hotel grounds. Tim, Alex, Stevens and the professor disembarked. Tim issued further instructions to Stevens and the Special Branch team. He then took Alex aside. "I know this is all very distressing for you, and for the professor. However, we believe Anna is a double agent working for the KGB, and she may have received instructions to kill Keller. We're going to take her back to London, and hopefully get the whole story. I know you're going back to London tomorrow, Alex, but I'll be in touch with you later in the week. Among other things, we've now got to check whether the professor's papers are genuine, or whether she was helping the KGB and has delivered fakes. The professor hasn't had a chance to start sorting the papers out. That could occupy him for months, apparently, so it may take a considerable time to get to the bottom of this whole nasty mess." He put his hand on Alex's shoulder.

"I'm just dumbfounded," responded Alex. "After all Anna has been through, it seems incomprehensible that she was risking life and limb for the KGB."

"More or less as an afterthought, we decided to interview Ava," said Tim. "She was absolutely terrified when we brought her in, thinking that she might be arrested or deported and separated again from her husband. Anyway, she described how she was able to leave Warsaw with her children and make it to Sweden. She said three Russians came to their apartment and her description of the leader fitted an old-time KGB agent. We showed her some photos and she picked out the suspect. When she said that two of them had used their authority to help them board the ferry, even though they had no papers or passports, it was clear that the Russians were behind this. Putting two and two together, it appears that these arrangements were instigated by Anna, who clearly was going to deliver something valuable in exchange. We came to the conclusion that it could be the Keller papers and the professor's death."

"Oh my god, Tim," responded Alex. "I'm going to have to tell Keller, and when I do, I am sure he will be as shattered as I am. I will also have to tell Julia. Will that be alright?"

"Yes, of course," said Tim. "But please tell them both to say nothing for the time being, and I would ask you not to spread this news to anyone else."

"Absolutely. But please let me know how things progress. I would hate to believe that all our efforts in Poland have been for nothing."

"I have got to get moving. I want to get Anna back to London as quickly as possible. Have a good trip home, Alex. I promise we'll speak soon."

Tim turned and headed for the helicopter, and as he climbed in, Alex could see Anna looking at him through red-rimmed eyes with a forlorn expression on her face. The rotors started up, and within a few moments the helicopter wheeled away towards Edinburgh.

Chapter 28

Alex, Erik Keller, and the family returned to London, which, over the next week, suffered through a heat wave. A thick brown cloud of pollution hung over the city for days. There was no word from Tim Bevans, and Alex found himself anxious and agitated. How were MI6 handling Anna's interrogation? He hated to think about it, but what sort of pressure were they putting on her? He didn't even know if MI6 employed torture, but even the thought made him very worried. He was shocked and angry at Anna, but he still couldn't believe that there wasn't some reasonable explanation. She had put her life at risk twice, helping Keller to defect from Poland, and then retrieving his all-important papers. How could she be working for the KGB, and risk her life for the MI6? It just didn't add up.

But then, in the back of his mind was the thought that maybe she had taken him for a ride as well. The tearful damsel in distress at the door of his hotel bedroom. The silhouette of her incredible body in the light of the bathroom. The plea for help in Warsaw. The hugs, the smiles, her hand reaching out to his, was it all part of the KGB training? The well-known Russian "honey trap." Alex Campbell had built a career on his judgment of people, his executives, workers, customers and suppliers. He was always confident of his judgment, but now he wasn't sure. Anna had lied to him, and so had broken his trust. Were there other lies? Could he believe anything she told him? He felt a protective closeness to Anna, maybe more than he should have, but had he been tricked by her charms, or was there some unknown explanation for her double-agent life? He was hurt and uncomfortable about the future.

* * *

It was the following Monday morning, after a much cooler and wet weekend. He had just got to his offices in Sackville Street, when Heather came in to tell him that Tim was on the telephone.

"Good morning, Alex," said Tim. "I hope you had a good weekend, despite the weather. I know you're anxious to hear where we stand with Anna."

"Yes," responded Alex, a little testily. "I've been waiting to hear from you."

"Well, we've spent the last week doing a number of interviews, and checking and crosschecking her responses."

"And—?" interjected Alex.

"I think we should meet so I can bring you up to date. Are you free tomorrow afternoon, say at three, at my Northumberland Avenue office?"

"I have an appointment tomorrow afternoon, but I will cancel it," replied Alex. "I'm very keen to see you as quickly as possible. Are you sure that Anna is a "double?" I can't believe she has been working for the KGB."

"Yes, Alex. She has definitely been a "double," working for the KGB. However, that is not the full story, and it is not quite as dark as it seems. I will give you the full picture tomorrow."

"Okay. Fine. I look forward to seeing you then, Tim."

Alex had spoken to Erik Keller a couple of times during the past week. Keller was as anxious as Alex to hear news of Anna. He told Alex that he had begun the preliminary work of sorting and decoding his papers, with the intention of initially rewriting all his notes in Polish and then having them translated into English. When Alex asked whether Keller was confident that these papers were his, and were real and not fakes, the professor laughed. He assured Alex that these were the original notes that he had coded over a period of thirty years, and that they were certainly not fakes. That response gave a little relief to Alex. Anna had therefore retrieved the papers from Warsaw in accordance with the MI6 plan. He didn't know where the KGB came into this, but if they had helped Jan's wife and family to escape to Sweden, she must have given something in return.

The cooler temperatures and the rain had cleared out the humidity, and the sun had returned as Alex arrived at Northumberland Avenue at two-fifty. After signing in, he was escorted up to Tim's office. Tim's large window overlooked the sun-splashed Houses of Parliament, Westminster Bridge, and a sparkling River Thames – an incredible sight on a beautiful day.

"Make yourself comfortable," said Tim, motioning Alex to one of the sofas near the naked fireplace. "I've ordered some tea."

"Thank you. That's very nice," said Alex settling into the sofa and eager to hear Tim's report.

"Alex. Let me get straight to the point. We have spent five days interviewing Anna. We have made her tell her story three times and have given her polygraph tests on two separate occasions. So, we have established that she has been telling us the truth. We have also established that her brother, Jan had no idea of her connection to the KGB. Having said that, she has confessed to being a double agent throughout the past fifteen years. What we had to establish was what damage she has done to MI6 and the UK during this period, how active an agent she had been for the KGB, and what she provided to them in exchange for spiriting Jan's family out of Warsaw, and on the ferry to Sweden." He paused, gathering his thoughts, as Alex interjected.

"Fifteen years!! Unbelievable." He still couldn't believe this was happening.

"Over the last five days, we have, by necessity, interrogated Anna for up to five hours at a time. We pushed her to repeat her story over and over again, so we could check for changes, untruths, and also ascertain whether her responses were part of her training by the KGB. It has been traumatic and wearing for all concerned." Alex nodded, but didn't interrupt, as Tim continued. "She has been apologetic, tearful, pleading, and sometimes angry at our continued persistence. Her focus has been to get us to understand her predicament." Tim paused, as the tea arrived and then continued.

"Anna was recruited in Sydney, just after we had persuaded her to join MI6 and work with us and her brother Jan. The KGB, of course, used other tactics. According to Anna, and I want to stress, Alex, that we do believe all of her explanations, the KGB pointed out that she was a Russian citizen, having been born in a labor camp south of Stalingrad, and that if she wanted her mother, Maria, to enjoy a quiet life in Warsaw, she should enthusiastically accept their offer. If she accepted, the KGB would arrange for her mother to return to the family estate Kaskia Lodge, and live on the property. If Anna didn't agree, the KGB implied that the Polish authorities might believe that Maria had returned to Poland to spy for the West. This could lead to prosecution and maybe jail."

"Nice people," interjected Alex sarcastically. Tim nodded in agreement.

"So as they say, Alex, Anna was between a rock and a hard place. She certainly had no desire to get involved with the KGB, but she felt she had no other alternative. She was desperately frightened that the KGB threat against her mother was real and could easily be initiated. So she felt she had to agree."

Alex nodded.

"She was given an intense training course; much more physical, and detailed than our own training. Of course, we didn't see Anna as a major agent." Tim paused, taking a sip of tea, and gathering his thoughts. "As you know, after Burgess and Maclean, our Eastern European network had been decimated; we were eager to rebuild, but we had to start from the bottom with young and inexperienced personnel, who would initially carry out minor duties. Anna and Jan filled that bill. The KGB had other ideas. They saw Anna as a very attractive, sexy young woman, who they could use in their many "honey trap" missions, which, for the most part, were aimed at Eastern European politicians and military personnel. The Russians don't trust their allies too much and like to keep a watchful eye on their friends, sometimes entrapping them. Anna knew she already had a job lined up in Warsaw through us, which would involve driving visiting dignitaries. She told the KGB that her brother Jan worked for ORBIS, the Polish tourist agency, and that he had arranged for her to get a similar job as a driver. That was perfect, from the KGB's point of view."

"Yes, I can see that," interjected Alex.

"However, it should be said that the KGB probably also regarded Anna as a very junior player, who they would use from time to time when a suitable occasion arose. Unlike us, the KGB made no payments for her work, but apparently they did follow through and arrange for Maria to move back to the family estate. When Anna got to Warsaw, she was introduced to her handler, an old-time KGB agent, Sergei Malenkov," Tim continued. "He has been her handler throughout the past fifteen years. He's been in the KGB for over forty years, and survived the Stalin purges, the Second World War, and even the siege of Stalingrad. He is a major in the KGB, and should have been retired by now."

"Malenkov, Malenkov, I know that name from somewhere," said Alex, with a puzzled look on his face. "But I have to ask you, Tim, when you said the KGB saw Anna as a prospective "honey trap" agent, was she supposed to sleep with her victims? Was Anna one of these Russian "sex sparrows," who were trained for that purpose?"

"No, Alex, Anna was never a Russian "sex sparrow." They would never use someone like her, despite her physical attractions. Although she'd been born in Russia, she grew up in Australia and is and was Western in all her attitudes. I'm sure they realized that even if they had wanted her for that role, she would never have agreed under any circumstances. No, it appears that her "honey trap" days were all talk and little action. Undoubtedly, she gave her victims the come on from time to time, plying them with drink, and encouraging them to hope that they would land up in bed with her. She says that never happened. We believe her."

"So, do you know what she did for the KGB?" asked Alex.

Tim nodded before continuing, "Anna had a number of minor missions over the years, for the KGB, and she really didn't have a very important role in Warsaw. Occasionally, bad behavior by some Russian official or military man, engineered by Anna, would lead to a dismissal or transport to the Gulag. This was the sort of mission that she was given. We also didn't use her very much. However, Malenkov did have regular meetings with Anna, and she was supposed to inform him of all her driving jobs as they related to any Eastern European or foreign dignitaries. She said that she studiously avoided giving him information that she was passing on to us, such as it was. According to Anna, Malenkov never questioned her reports. However, and here's the big issue, Alex." Tim paused again, letting out a big sigh. "She was the source of the leak about Keller."

"What!" said Alex. "Oh no! Anna was the leak?

"She says that passing the information on was done innocently, and we believe her," continued Tim. "She says that she had no idea who Professor Keller was, and when she was given the mission to join the group in Kraków, she thought there was no harm in telling Malenkov. Keller, after all, was Polish and he had never been interested in the movement of Polish officials. At that time, she had no idea Keller was going to defect. When Jan was shot, she thought it was the KGB. She was then determined to carry out his part of the job, which was to get Keller across the border. Jan knew that Keller was to be picked up in Czechoslovakia and taken to Vienna. Of course, Alex, she was only able to succeed with your help." Tim paused and took a big gulp of tea.

"Oh God! What a mess," said Alex.

"Yup! We believe that Malenkov and the KGB put two and

two together. They certainly didn't want him to defect to the West, with all his incredible knowledge. They wanted him out of the picture, and they saw this as a golden opportunity. He was well known and respected in Poland, and so I believe that they didn't want to kill him on his home turf, with the public outcry that it might bring at a time of the burgeoning growth of the Solidarity movement and so soon after the death of his two boys. Incidentally, Alex, there has been no public information about the death of Krystina Keller and the two soldiers."

"Really? They kept it under wraps. Maybe they didn't want to expose the Keller name."

"Could be," said Tim. "However, disposing of Keller outside of Poland was an attractive alternative. And it was an immense stroke of luck that he somehow survived the assassination attempt. I now believe that the KGB was behind this, but we don't understand at the moment who the assassins were, and more importantly who they work for. That is a mystery still to be solved."

Tim paused again. "Would you like some more tea?" he said to Alex.

"No, thanks, I'm fine. I'm just trying to absorb all of this."

Tim poured himself another cup, leaned back into the sofa, and continued. "Well, we are not finished yet. Now, we turn to Anna's Warsaw mission," said Tim. "She did an incredible job of retrieving Professor Keller's papers. He is now working on sorting out those papers. In fact, he has asked for Anna's assistance specifically to complete this task, which is a bit ironic considering she was the one who passed on the information that nearly led to his death." Tim gave a grim smile before continuing. "Nevertheless, what I believe she didn't tell you, was what really happened in Warsaw that enabled her to get Jan and his family out of the country. You know that she foolishly engineered an invitation from Roman Krinsky to visit him in his apartment. She naïvely believed that she could seduce Krinsky and get some sort of release documents from him. She was of course, foolhardy and stupid, and her actions nearly jeopardized her whole mission to Poland." Tim paused and gave a big sigh, before continuing. "We were not amused. Of course, this became a much more explosive issue when we found out that she had actually murdered Krinsky in his apartment. The fallout from that action might still cause a major diplomatic incident." Alex could see Tim's cheeks reddening as he continued this part of the story. "She behaved like a reckless idiot," he said, almost to himself.

Tim paused again. "Apparently, at the Ambassador's reception, she was cornered by Malenkov, who she hadn't seen for some months. He, of course, knew that Keller had survived, and that Anna had been successful in helping him defect to the West. He had also guessed correctly, that the only reason that Anna had returned to Warsaw, was to collect some important information that Keller had probably left behind. He is a smart old fox, that Malenkov," said Tim with a slight chuckle. "He demanded to meet Anna the next day. He probably wanted to establish whether his theory was true and if so, whether he could use the leverage of Maria again, to carry out his orders. She saw a meeting with Malenkov as the last opportunity she had of helping her immediate family. She had killed Krinsky, but was no nearer helping Jan get out of jail. She had one last card to play." Alex leaned forward totally amazed at this part of the story, but also silently seething that Anna had lied to him. Tim continued. "She had discovered that the amazing Professor Keller had created not one, but two apparently identical coded packages of papers. The only difference between package one and package two, was that package two did not have the vital information of the solutions to the various nuclear-fusion theories, experiments and trials that was the crux of the whole of Keller's research. Because it was in code, and the notes were so extensive, it would take very qualified code breakers and physicists, many months, if not years, to realize that the package was worthless. Anna says that when she met Malenkov, she offered him a deal. Get Jan released from jail, and put Jan's family on a ferry to Sweden, in exchange for Keller's papers. Malenkov apparently eagerly accepted. He knew that the KGB would have no difficulty in getting the Poles to cooperate." Tim paused.

"Well, you have to admit, Tim, that Anna is one hell of an operator. Playing, with fire, but quick and nimble," said Alex.

"That's true. That was the deal. On the morning you left Warsaw, Malenkov delivered Jan directly from prison to the Hotel Victoria, having already arranged for Ava and the children to start their journey to Sweden.

"Of course," continued Tim, "Malenkov had to extract his final pound of flesh. He told Anna that she would have to finish off the KGB mission, namely killing Keller. He gave her until the end of August. If the mission was not completed, her mother Maria would be arrested, put in jail, and probably prosecuted. Might even end up in the Gulag. Anna apparently agreed, but now tells us that she had no intention of following those instructions. She realized that she was putting her mother's life at risk, and that may well be the case right now. However, she said that she couldn't even contemplate killing Keller."

"Is there any possible way you could help Anna's mother?" asked Alex, relieved to find out that Anna was genuine, despite her lying to him.

"I have been thinking about this. Anna is suspended from 'the firm.' But, possibly, in a couple of weeks or so, we may be able to put the word out to a known KGB source, that she has been arrested and suspended by MI6. From that leak, perhaps the KGB will recognize that she cannot carry out the final Keller mission. It is then possible that they won't bother with Maria. It is also possible that whatever Malenkov said to Anna, they really did not intend to arrest and prosecute Maria. After all, what do they gain by that? But of course, these are all unknowns at the moment. I have to complete a full report and pass it up to my minister, the FO and the PM's office. We shall have to see how things progress. But her actions are a major breach, Alex, which if pursued could lead to jail time."

"I understand" said Alex, trying to digest this part of Anna's story.

Tim continued. "Anna gave Malenkov the number two version of the Keller papers, and then joined your group at the Hotel Europejski for the journey to the airport and subsequently to London. I gather that you were not aware of these arrangements and that Anna told you a different story." Tim paused, with a questioning look on his face.

"My God, Tim, that's amazing. No of course I had no idea of that part of the story. In fact, Anna told me that she had Roman Krinsky sign a release paper for Jan, before she killed him. She told me that she was able to get Jan out of prison with the signed release, and that some of Jan's friends had arranged for the family to leave Warsaw, and get the ferry to Sweden. I believed her. Of course, Anna never spoke of Malenkov or about two sets of Keller papers. I checked with the professor, to see whether the papers that he has in his possession were not fakes. I phoned him last week, actually, and he laughed when I questioned him. He assured me that they were real." He paused. "What happens now, Tim, with Anna?"

"Well, we shall be keeping her for a few more days at least. We need her to list and remember every single mission she carried out for the KGB. This is going to take a lot of work and in the end we may not get the full list. However, this will allow us to assess the impact of her working for both MI6 and the KGB. As to legal action, criminal action, or whatever, that won't be up to me. It will be the minister and his team who will decide. Of course, everyone is very concerned, but at the same time, we have to admit we are delighted to have both Professor Keller and the Keller papers under our protection in the UK. Personally if I am asked, I will seek lenient treatment for Anna. She will definitely have to leave 'the firm.' We couldn't possibly use her again, even though she clearly has considerable talent. However, we must recognize that it's possible she will be prosecuted for spying for the KGB."

"That would be a pretty grim outcome," said Alex, now eager to help Anna, yet again, "given the fact that she risked her life twice. If required, I would be available as a witness to her dedication and bravery. I do, however, recognize that she took an enormous risk in Warsaw. That was extremely stupid and foolhardy. On the other hand, I think she was correct in recognizing that once she left Warsaw, the chances of Jan being released from jail, in a reasonable state of health, were much diminished. A pretty noble effort I must say."

"You're right," responded Tim. "Who knows what one would do under similar circumstances? However, working for the KGB for fifteen years cannot be taken lightly."

"When do you think you will know the outcome?" asked Alex.

"I really don't know, Alex. It could take weeks or even months. However, you can rest assured we are not going to keep Anna cooped up here during this period. I shall try and work something out over the next week or so."

"Thank you, Tim," said Alex warmly, as he rose from the sofa realizing their meeting had come to an end.

They shook hands, said a few pleasantries, and Alex left, still feeling anxious and concerned.

Alex was deep in thought as he descended in the elevator to the ground floor and an awaiting Frank. As he was driven back to his St John's Wood apartment, he tried to rationalize the thinking of the minister and his advisers who would be reviewing Anna's case. He wondered whether he should make a personal call to Maggie, the PM, but decided going around and above the minister was probably not a good idea. However, he determined that if the worst case scenario arose, he would definitely make a personal appeal to 10 Downing Street.

When he got home, he told Julia what had transpired. She kept asking him what outcome he expected, and he had to tell her in truth he had no idea. He also phoned Keller who sounded very concerned. "If the government treats Anna badly, like they could do in Poland, I may not cooperate. Perhaps they will wait years, to find out what is in the Keller papers," Keller said, his voice rising and agitated.

"Now, Erik, let's just wait and see," said Alex in a calm voice. "This is not Poland; she will be treated respectfully and will receive the full benefits of the law. Of that I am certain. I promise you, Erik, I shall call you as soon as I have some news."

Alex was pleased that he had a full calendar over the next two weeks with lots of meetings and the announcement of the Campbell Group's half yearly results, with the usual round of press and analysts.

It was the beginning of the third week in August when Alex got a call from Tim. "Good morning, Alex. I have some good news for you about Anna. If you're free, why don't you come over to my office at Northumberland Avenue this afternoon?"

"Of course, Tim, I can be there at four-thirty. Would that work?"

"Absolutely. See you then."

Alex put down the phone, with his heart pounding and a sense of excitement mounting. Tim had sounded quite buoyant, so Alex felt he could assume that there would be no worst-case scenarios for Anna.

At four-thirty on the dot he was once again in Tim's office.

"I was called to the minister's office this morning to hear the result of the preliminary enquiry into Anna's case. The minister said that he and his panel had considered all the written reports on Keller's defection, and the successful operation in retrieving Keller's papers. They also reviewed the transcripts of the pre-Warsaw interviews, of Anna and yourself, and the recent interrogations of Anna following the revelations about the KGB connection. They have come to the following conclusions. One, that Anna, aided by yourself, had done an outstanding job in helping Keller defect, particularly after the shooting and arrest of her brother Jan. They considered her determination and bravery beyond the call for a junior agent. Two, Anna had completed her mission to retrieve the Keller papers, with professionalism and persistence, following instructions to the letter. Three, the decision to engage with Roman Krinsky, against your advice, had shown a lack of discipline and disregard for the basic tenets of MI6 protocol. Her actions could have jeopardized the mission, and the safety of her colleagues. It could have and may still result in a major diplomatic embarrassment for the UK government. They believe that this warrants disciplinary action against Anna. Four, her relationship, and support of Professor Keller is considered extremely important for his cooperation with the UK government, the decoding and translation of his papers and the development of a working relationship with his peers in the UK and possibly our allies." Tim paused, as Alex waited for the other shoe to drop.

"The net result of these deliberations, Alex, is that Anna is to be dismissed from her responsibilities at MI6 without current or future financial benefits, but she will be reassigned to assist Professor Keller in the translation of his papers, and we hope, become a long-term assistant to the professor as he establishes himself in the UK and works with our nuclear establishment. The minister and the panel recognized that there were mitigating circumstances which they considered to be understandable in her enlistment by the KGB in Australia in 1967, and her subsequent work for them as an agent in Warsaw. We believe there was minimal damage to the UK, and little if any impact on her relationship with MI6. They have therefore concluded that there will be no further legal action or prosecution of Anna," Tim concluded with a broad smile on his face. "I think, Alex, we can all be pleased with this result."

"That's wonderful news, Tim," said Alex with a similar smile, and a sense of relief. "I have to let the professor know as quickly as possible. I'm sure he will be delighted, particularly if Anna is going to be his assistant. Has she been told?"

"Yes, Alex. She was told about half an hour ago, and is in fact on her way here. She should be with us any minute. She has been under house arrest in her apartment since this whole business began. I know it will be a great relief to her, and her brother, of course," said Tim with a grin. "I think we should have a drink to celebrate, don't you. I have some Campbell's Scotch in my cabinet."

"Absolutely, Tim, this definitely calls for a 'wee dram.'"

Tim poured out a couple of glasses of Campbell's Scotch, just as there was a knock on his office door and his secretary entered, followed by a casually dressed, but beautiful Anna, her blue eyes sparkling, and her blonde hair cascading over her shoulders.

As she saw Alex with Tim, the tears started rolling down her face. "Oh, Mr. Bevans, I can't thank you enough. What a relief," said Anna with a broad smile, even as the tears kept rolling. "And, Alex, I feel your support, even when we are not together. It has been a great comfort to me. I phoned my brother Jan at Lambeth, and of course he was overjoyed to hear the news. I don't know how to thank you both," she concluded with a tremble in her voice and her lips quivering.

Unable to speak, Anna threw her arms around Alex, mumbling her thanks over and over again.

Alex stood there rather stiffly and embarrassed, holding Anna close to him, while Tim looked on with a mild smile on his face.

"Well, Anna," Tim said. "You are going to be escorted back to your apartment now. I would like you to pack all your possessions tomorrow morning, and be ready to be transferred to a new location near Reading. We're moving Professor Keller into a new safe house in Amersham. I understand it's a beautiful 1920s country house in two acres of secluded gardens. Its location at the end of a lane will allow us to provide excellent ongoing security. I'm afraid you will have to get used to watchtowers, electrified fences, and barriers to and from the property. But, I think you will see it is worth it. Our people will be as nonintrusive as possible, but one thing is certain, you can feel perfectly safe from any prying eyes, or foreign threats. Initially we intend to meet with you once per month, to follow up on the KGB information you provided to us, as we complete our own investigations, and then just to report on progress with the professor's efforts on decoding and translation. I am sure, Anna, that you will do an excellent job as his new assistant. We know that we can rely on you for executing instructions to the letter, when appropriate," Tim concluded with a wry smile.

"I can assure you, Mr. Bevans, that I will give my new assignment my total commitment," Anna responded, now less tearful, and full of enthusiasm.

Tim buzzed his intercom, and his secretary escorted Anna from his office. "Good luck, Anna. We shall see you soon."

Tim then turned to Alex.

"The Keller mission continues. It could go on for years you know. But as far as the 'little job' that I asked you to do in February, that has come to an end, Alex. It was a job very well done."

"Thank you, Tim, and thanks again for all your efforts for Anna. I think she deserves it. However, Tim, I think I'm finished with your 'little jobs!'"

It was time to go, and Alex shook hands with Tim as he left his office. "Please keep in touch. Perhaps we can get together for dinner soon."

Chapter 29

Sergei Malenkov! Wiesenthal, Vienna. Alex shot up in bed, baked in a cold sweat. Not the usual panic he felt when he revisited the liberation of Bergen-Belsen, and the SS major who had lunged at him with a knife. His shoulder still throbbed occasionally, forty years later. No, this was a sudden realization that he had seen Sergei Malenkov's name in the Wiesenthal papers on Franz Steuben. The pieces of the jigsaw were beginning to fall into place. He looked at his bedside clock. It was three-fifty a.m. Julia was snoozing quietly. But Alex had to get up now. He put on a robe as he could feel the autumn chill in the apartment.

He went into the living room and looked down on a wet and windy Prince Albert Road. Hardly any traffic, but a police siren in the distance. He sat down to try and think how the pieces fitted together. Sergei Malenkov was one of the officers interviewed by Steuben after the battle of Kiev. They subsequently escaped, and Steuben had two of the guards shot, and was nearly court-martialed himself. Alex knew that Steuben spoke fluent Russian. His mother had been connected to the royal Romanov family. Could the connection in Kiev over forty years ago have led to the attempted assassination of Erik Keller in Vienna? Was Steuben a Russian spy? A major in the SS. A hero of Stalingrad. It seemed unlikely, but possibly Steuben was hedging his bets. Have a connection with the NKVD, just in case the Führer's Third Reich did not last a thousand years. Was it possible that Malenkov had been in Stalingrad, and had arranged for Steuben to make his miraculous escape? Was he returning the Kiev favor? The rest of his group had been killed. No witnesses. Had they maintained a relationship right up to the present day, and had Malenkov used Steuben, now known as Karl von Schuyler, to dispose of Keller? A third-party killing, outside of the KGB. No leaks, no finger-pointing. Very clean, very tidy. But a bit of a stretch.

Alex's mind was racing as he thought through each event and possible linkage. He would have to phone Tim Bevans. Perhaps he could dig into Malenkov's background.

He said nothing to Julia, but after breakfast, phoned Tim directly on his private secure line. It had been four weeks since they had last met. He told Tim of his revelation about Malenkov.

"Tim, I am now convinced that Wiesenthal was right about Steuben. Von Schuyler is such a powerful man in Austria, it is highly unlikely that anything is going to happen that could lead to him getting indicted, but it would be interesting to see how far these inquiries go. Do you think you could find out more about Sergei Malenkov and particularly if he was in Stalingrad at the same time that Steuben was captured, interrogated and made his miraculous escape?"

"That's very interesting, Alex," responded Tim. "Sounds like you had a busy night," he continued. "We probably have a file as thick as your arm on Malenkov. I shall have our people look into it, and see if we can piece together any connection to the attempted murder of Erik Keller. Incidentally, he is making good progress in sorting out his notes and apparently Anna is proving to be an excellent assistant. Our 'boffins' are pleased with the progress."

Ten days later, Tim phoned back. "We have some interesting information on your friend, Alex. I can't say that we have the full answer to the puzzle, but there certainly seems to be a connection. Why don't you come over on Thursday and I'll fill you in."

The weather was awful on Thursday. Rain was teeming down, knocking the leaves off the trees. London traffic was snarled and Alex arrived late at the Lambeth headquarters. Alex was ushered into a small conference room next to Tim's office. While he waited, he stood at the window, looking at the gray and angry Thames, and the Houses of Parliament nearly obscured by sheets of rain.

The door opened and Tim entered, accompanied by a dark haired fresh-faced young woman.

"Good afternoon, Alex, may I introduce Melanie Coleson from our Russian Research desk. She has been looking into Sergei Malenkov. Please take a seat. Melanie, over to you."

"I'm pleased to meet you, Sir Alex," said Melanie. "I have done a lot of research into the background of Major Malenkov of the KGB. He has had a long and fairly distinguished career. One of his claims to fame appears to be that he has survived the numerous purges, arrests and investigations that wracked the KGB and their predecessors, the NKVD, since the Stalin era. He should be coming up to retirement very soon. Perhaps the Keller affair will prove to be his last assignment."

Melanie opened a thick file which she had taken out of a ribbon-enclosed folder. She extracted a few pages stapled and stamped in red, "Top-Secret."

Melanie started reading. "Sergei Malenkov was born in 1918 in a small town outside of Moscow. His father served in the military, and survived the First World War. Sergei joined the NKVD in 1938, after completing a short, specialist training course, linked to Moscow University. At the beginning of the Second World War, he was assigned to the Soviet 40th Army, which was part of the invading force that marched into eastern Poland. He was then assigned to the regional headquarters of the NKVD in Kiev and remained there during the German onslaught and encirclement of the city in August/September 1941."

"Ah, Kiev," interjected Alex. "Our first possible connection."

"Maybe," said Melanie. "There is reference to his capture and escape with four other officers after interrogation by the SS. He stayed with the retreating 40th Army, and I can confirm that he eventually was posted to Stalingrad and survived the German attacks and siege throughout the winter of 1942/43."

"Connection number two," interjected Alex again.

Melanie continued. "There are references to his responsibilities as part of a group of interrogating officers, but nothing that would link him to Franz Steuben."

"That's a pity," said Alex. "Is there any reference to his working with SS officers or out-of-the-ordinary results of interrogations?"

"I'm afraid not," replied Melanie, pausing before continuing her narrative. "After Stalingrad, he followed the Red Army again, as they advanced through Poland and into Germany, and his group were involved in prisoner interrogations, the capture and separation of SS officers and, towards the end of the war, concentration-camp commandments."

"Nothing there" said Alex.

"No," said Melanie. "After the war, he married Lyudmila Mikelova in 1947, who worked for the Ministry of Culture, assigned to the Bolshoi Ballet, and subsequently the Kirov Ballet. During this period, Malenkov had an office job in Moscow, but in 1949, he and his wife started a series of overseas missions, where they were invariably attached to the Cultural Department of the respective Russian Embassy, which is the normal location for their KGB agents. He and Lyudmila had a little girl Tanya, in 1951. Unfortunately, Tanya died of leukemia in 1960. Sergei and Lyudmila divorced in 1963 and he has never remarried. He returned to Moscow in 1967 and was posted to Warsaw, as Assistant Secretary of Culture at the Russian Embassy. It was at this time that he was responsible for Anna Kaluza, as her handler, as well as four other KGB agents."

"Were there any special references about Anna?" asked Alex.

"No," responded Melanie. "Pretty mundane stuff. None of his assignments, postings or KGB work has been of much interest to MI6. Really, our paths didn't cross throughout his career, until we recently found out about his connection to Anna. He was sent to Vienna in the middle of February 1983 and could possibly have a connection to the attempted murder of Professor Erik Keller."

"Looks like it to me," said Alex, as Melanie continued.

"However, we have no evidence of that at the present time. We do know that the KGB will use outside agents for kidnappings, murder and assassinations from time to time, where the target could cause embarrassment to the Russian government or lead to suspicion of Russian KGB involvement. Use of third parties in these circumstances has proved to be quite successful." Melanie paused. "We are continuing our research into Malenkov and we are also working with the Wiesenthal Center on the Steuben background."

"Thank you," said Alex. "I think there are a number of connections."

"Melanie," said Tim. "That was very interesting. There appear to be a number of questionable coincidences and possibilities that might ultimately be tied together."

"I agree," said Alex.

Tim nodded and continued. "We're going to forward Melanie's summary to our people in Vienna and also through them to the Vienna police. They say that they are still investigating the 'murder' of Gustav Bauer. We don't know how hard they're trying, but this information might prompt them to follow-up on the investigation. We will have to see Alex, but we should certainly keep prodding for answers," said Tim, rising to his feet.

"And thank you again, Melanie," said Alex graciously. "I hope your work will lead to the completion of the jigsaw."

* * *

Anna heard from Mark on a regular basis, albeit not directly. She received postcards from various locations: Abu Dhabi, Kuwait, Jeddah, Sana, and even Jerusalem and Beirut. The postcards came in brown envelopes, addressed to people around the UK she didn't know but forwarded on to her. They contained cryptic messages which she realized were in code. Tiny little indentations under various words translated into messages such as "I love you," "You are so beautiful" and "Thinking of you."

However in the spring of 1984, a large postcard arrived, with a picture of the Baha'i Temple in Haifa. The code was much too complicated for her, so she asked help from Erik Keller, and for the first time explained her relationship with Mark. Keller was delighted that Anna had a love in her life. He translated the cryptic message in the postcard. "Please meet me at Antibes station, at noon on September 7th. All arrangements made for one week fantastic vacation. Can't wait to see you. If you can't make it, please reply to sender."

Anna looked at the large brown envelope and on the back found a name and address in Barnsley, Yorkshire. Mark's postcards had been addressed to various people scattered around the country and started with "Dear Mother" or "Dear Brian" and other names. She realized that whatever Mark's mission, his location and identity was highly sensitive. She was over the moon. She would move heaven and earth to make sure she made it to Antibes for the rendezvous. She sought advice from Alex and then appealed to Tim Bevans. Amazingly quickly she got clearance and a new passport in the name of Emily Paxton, just in case. But no escorts or bodyguards.

She counted off the days during the summer, and took the first flight out of Heathrow to Nice on September the 7th. She was in a taxi and on her way to Antibes station by eleven and arrived with ten minutes to spare. She stood in the entrance, not sure where Mark would come from but within a couple of minutes he arrived in a drophead Renault sports car, looking fit and tanned, and with an enormous grin on his face. He jumped out and Anna ran into his arms laughing and kissing him at the same time. He threw her case in the trunk and they drove off with a roar. He had reservations at the Voile D'Or hotel on Cap Ferrat. They had a fantastic week together, visiting Nice, Cannes, Monte Carlo, and driving into San Remo in Italy for shopping and the Saturday open market. Anna had never been to France or any other country in Europe other than Poland. The French Riviera was like a fairytale to her, and she couldn't stop gushing about the beauty and ambiance of every place they visited. She loved every minute of it, and was amazed at his lavish generosity. He bought her clothes, jewelry, bags and shoes. He also bought himself some fancy Italian shirts and shoes. When she questioned him about all the spending, not to mention the expensive hotel they were staying at, he laughed and told her she was worth it.

Of course, he wouldn't discuss his work, but he did tell her he was being employed as a construction engineer. This was said with an impish grin on his face. They ate, drank, and made love throughout a week of beautiful balmy days and warm evenings. Anna was in paradise with a man who had become the love of her life. When the time came to part, he assured her he would continue to keep in touch with his "postcards" and hoped that they would be able to meet up again somewhere in Europe again soon. He dropped her off at Nice airport, as she tearfully told him to take care.

* * *

There were a number of developments throughout 1984. Keller completed the decoding of his notes and Anna helped him translate them from Polish into English and recorded the complete package on tape. Keller continued his research, working closely with the UK nuclear establishment. Although he wanted to focus on nuclear energy for peaceful purposes, he devoted some of his time and gave a number of lectures and seminars on his nuclear-fusion theories in relation to the UK nuclear-defense strategy. Anna blossomed, in a new life without stress and trauma. Her brother Jan proved to be an able and valuable resource for MI6, and was promoted a couple of times. He seemed to relish his new life in London and his family was very happy. At the end of 1984, MI6 heard that Sergei Malenkov had retired, and had moved to a dacha in the country. Tim Bevans surmised that the KGB had finally decoded and translated all of Erik Keller's notes only to realize that they were worthless without the practical solutions to his theories. The murder investigation of Roman Krinsky continued to grab the headlines in Warsaw for a few weeks in the summer of 1983, but with the lifting of martial law, release of political prisoners, and Solidarity negotiations with the government, there was less interest in Krinsky's murder, as he was very much a figure of the brutal immediate past. Early in 1985, his beautiful widow remarried, to a leading Polish film producer.

The saddest news of the period came from Kaskia Lodge. Maria developed pneumonia in the winter of 1984 and shortly after, passed away from congestive heart failure. Anna and Jan were devastated, particularly because neither of them could return home for the funeral. They had to rely on Maria's sister's family to take responsibility for all the arrangements. In one respect, however, Anna could breathe a sigh of relief. Malenkov, in the end, had taken no action against Maria, and now that he was retired and she had passed away, that chapter could be closed.

In December 1984, Professor Keller was invited to the United States. The visit was to be a six-month sabbatical, hosted by the University of Chicago, where Professor Keller would give a series of lectures on his nuclear-fusion theories, and as a guest of the US government meet with the Pentagon and the US nuclear establishment. He was also scheduled to give some additional lectures across the country. He and Anna flew into a freezing Chicago on 21st January. The sun was blazing, and steam was rising from Lake Michigan. They were given a royal welcome and transferred to the Ritz-Carlton hotel on Michigan Avenue, where they would stay for a week as guests of the University of Chicago, doing some sightseeing, but also attending some meetings and private functions. The professor and Anna were overwhelmed by the beauty of the city, with its outstanding architecture, as well as the warmth and generosity of their hosts. The University of Chicago had been at the very foundation of nuclear science and quantum mechanics since the early 1940s. At the end of the Second World War, Enrico Fermi and his scientific team conducted the first self-sustaining nuclear chain reaction. Over the following decades, a large number of discoveries and scientific breakthroughs made Chicago one of the world centers of molecular and atomic theory, garnering a number of Nobel Prizes. Now, Professor Keller had the opportunity of meeting these distinguished scientists. He gave some outstanding lectures, despite his somewhat heavily accented English, and almost immediately was embraced by the faculty and students alike. He and Anna were given a comfortable apartment at the university and that became their base, as they travelled to Washington for high-level meetings with the Pentagon and the nuclear establishment and then to San Francisco, where he gave a series of lectures at Berkeley, followed by a visit to Los Alamos in New Mexico. The weeks flew by, and the schedule was extensive. Both the professor and Anna were overawed by the beauty, size, prosperity and modernity of the United States. To go from the fear, drabness, and confinement of the Communist system in Poland to the freedom, opportunities, and excitement of the USA was like going from one planet to another. They loved every minute of it, and were a little sad when they had to return to England.

But a few weeks later, Anna was off to Rome to meet up with Mark for another wonderful vacation. She felt that if they were able to spend more time together, they would know if their love for each other was deep enough to face the test of time. So, she was extremely upset when Mark informed her that he had agreed to extend his contract for another year. "This is an offer I can't refuse," he said. "I'm making so much money that I will be able to come home with enough funds to set up my own security

company. Then, I promise, Anna, I shall never leave you again."
What could she say?

At the beginning of August 1985, Tim called Alex.

"Good morning, Alex. Have you read about the wine scandal in Austria?"

"Yes. I read something about it last week in one of the trade papers. Somebody has been adding chemicals to their white wines. Not really my field, Tim."

"I know," replied Tim. "But we have just been informed that the scandal is enormous, and will certainly have political implications. Furthermore, our friend Karl von Schuyler may be involved in a big way. I thought I'd let you know that we have asked for a full report from our friends in Vienna. When I have a more detailed picture of what's going on, I will give you a call and we can get together."

"Whew! That's very interesting, Tim."

Over the next couple of weeks, Alex read a number of reports in the English newspapers about the expanding wine scandal. It appeared a number of Austrian wineries had illegally adulterated their wines using the toxic substance diethylene glycol, a primary ingredient in some brands of antifreeze, to make the wines appear sweeter and more full-bodied. Many of these wines had been exported to Germany, some of them in bulk which were then illegally blended into German wines.

The toxic compound was found in a significant number of different bottlings, and the DEG findings immediately became a full-scale scandal requiring action by federal authorities in both Germany and Austria. On July 9th, the Federal Ministry of Health in Bonn had issued an official health warning against the consumption of Austrian wines. It became impossible to sell Austrian wine on any export market.

As the weeks went by, the press coverage in the UK continued. In September, an in-depth article appeared in London's *Financial*

Times, describing how some Austrian exporters had entered into long-term contracts with supermarket chains in Germany to supply large quantities of wine at a specified quality level. The producers ran into problems as a result of some weak vintages. The 1982 vintage in Austria was plagued by these problems. When this led to insufficient quantities of wine being available to fulfil the contract, some producers started to search for methods, including illegal ones to correct the wines. By using diethylene glycol, it was possible to effect both the impression of sweetness and the body of the wine. The *FT* went on, that the recipe must have been drawn up by a knowledgeable wine chemist working for a large-scale producer. The article also confirmed that the Vienna Police Serious Fraud Squad had been investigating possible illegal adulteration of wines since learning of some minor infractions in 1983. Chief Detective Investigator Fritz Muller confirmed that investigations were continuing and that he confidently expected arrests and prosecutions would follow shortly.

At the beginning of September, Alex read Vienna's *Kronen Zeitung* and *Ö* newspaper:

> *Chief Investigator Muller of the Vienna Serious Fraud Squad investigating the wine scandal, confirmed that the police had detained 20 people for questioning over the past week, including Otto Nadrasky, a 58-year-old chemist from Grafenworth in lower Austria, who acted as a consultant to some major wine producers. Chief Investigator Muller confirmed that he expected further arrests at a high level in the industry, followed by multi-prosecutions.*

Another article reported:

> *The sea of poison wine has spilled into Austrian national politics, shaking the foundations of the government of Chancellor Fred*

*Sinowatz, as Conservative opposition leaders called for Agriculture
Minister Gunter Haiden to step down, for failing to report the
scandal until months after it was first known. Mr. Sinowatz
emerged from a "wine summit" of senior ministers and aides to
announce that Austria would rush through new wine control legis-
lation before the autumn harvest. The FPÖ, members of the current
government coalition, have been keeping a low profile, possibly
because Karl von Schuyler, who controls approximately half of
Austrian wine production and exports, is known to be a major
funder and active political adviser to the FPÖ. Herr von Schuyler
has not been available for comment.*

Alex, of course, was fascinated by these articles. He phoned Tim,
who confirmed that the press reports were in line with information he was receiving. However, at this stage there had been
no arrests directly connected to von Schuyler, although Tim felt
the noose was tightening. It would now seem highly unlikely that
von Schuyler or his companies were not involved somewhere in
the scandal.

A couple of weeks later, Alex was in Vienna himself. The trade
magazine *Spirits* hosted an annual meeting for spirits-industry
executives and major distributors. The annual meetings were
held alternatively in major American cities and major European
cities. In 1985 the location happened to be Vienna. The program
consisted of a welcoming cocktail party, usually hosted by a
major national or international drinks company, and then a full
day meeting, including panel discussions on industry issues
broken up by a lunch addressed by an internationally recognized, active or recently retired, political figure. The evening
event was a formal dinner, which invariably included senior
political figures from the host country and as would be expected,
the finest wines and spirits that were on offer. The meeting termi-
nated after breakfast the next morning when the executives
would leave for their home countries.

Alex found himself back at the Palais Schwarzenberg where the meeting, lunch and dinner were to be held. However, his main interest was the opening cocktail reception to be hosted by none other than Karl von Schuyler in the courtyard of his 18th-century office building. This arrangement of course, had been made months before the breaking wine scandal. As of mid-September, no charges had been brought against von Schuyler even though the rumors were flying. An embarrassment for the organizers, but there was nothing to be done other than proceeding as planned.

The reception started at six, and Alex arrived promptly. The cobblestone courtyard had been covered with a large wooden floor carpeted in green matting, under an enormous tent with chandeliers hanging from the fabric covered ceilings, and wood-paneled sides with large candelabra sconces on the walls. There were of course a number of drinks stations, and on both sides of the tent a large display of VS Imperial brandies and VS Group schnapps. White lilies and mimosa covered every corner and the beauty and fragrance was nearly overwhelming. The hosts Karl von Schuyler and Katarina were greeting guests at the entrance. Von Schuyler looked tanned and healthy, immaculately dressed in a pinstriped navy blue suit, white shirt and orange and blue tie. Katarina was wearing a pale gray cocktail dress, her blonde hair swept up in a bun, and her ample cleavage covered with a magnificent diamond and emerald necklace with matching earrings.

"Sir Alex," said von Schuyler, greeting Alex with a warm smile. "So nice to see you again. I'm pleased you were able to come."

"Wouldn't have missed it for the world. An opportunity to visit Vienna again," responded Alex, oozing charm.

"May I introduce you to my wife Katarina," continued von Schuyler.

"Pleased to meet you. I've heard so much about you,"

responded Alex continuing the charm offensive.

Taking advantage of the few seconds that he had with von Schuyler, Alex said, "I am so sorry we were unable to do anything with your schnapps range. But our research showed that the market was too small in the US, for both of us."

"Yes, that was disappointing," replied von Schuyler.

Alex jumped in, "With this terrible wine scandal going on, I expect you have got plenty on your plate at the moment."

Von Schuyler's face hardened immediately. His cold gray eyes seemed to stare right through Alex. "Very time-consuming, unfortunately. Of course I am not personally involved in this regrettable situation for our industry. But obviously the culprits must be brought to justice," he continued but, Alex thought, not convincingly.

"I have no doubt that all the participants, big or small, will be flushed out by this major investigation," Alex replied, staring back directly into von Schuyler's eyes. "The truth will come out, as they say, even if sometimes it takes months, years or even decades," said Alex with a slight smile. He could see von Schuyler's confidence and arrogance starting to wilt.

"You'll have to excuse me, Sir Alex. Perhaps we can catch up later."

Alex nodded as Karl and Katarina turned towards other arriving guests.

Even though Austria's wine scandal was the top-of-mind issue of the meeting, the organizers kept to their program and the focus on worldwide spirit sales and distribution, tariffs, taxes, marketing and advertising. While the meeting and the various speakers were interesting, Alex found the true benefit was the opportunity to meet with his peers from around the world and sharpen his considerable skills at networking for the benefit of the Campbell Group. From his personal point of view however, the most intriguing and perhaps enjoyable part of the whole trip was seeing von Schuyler as his empire began to crumble.

On October 8th, the dam finally broke. A dawn police raid, led to the arrest of Karl von Schuyler, and his chief winemaker Jean-Robert Du Sable. Tim was on the phone to Alex early in the morning.

"I've just heard the police have arrested von Schuyler and his chief winemaker. They have been charged with masterminding the whole scheme. He has issued a statement through his lawyer, denying all the charges, and has been released on bail. There is a hearing scheduled in three weeks. His winemaker, Jean-Robert Du Sable, has also denied all charges. I'm expecting a full report from Vienna in the next couple of days, but I understand that the police and the prosecution believe they have a watertight case. I'm sure there will be some fireworks in the next week or so. It will be interesting to see whether the government will let von Schuyler swing, or find a way to rescue him. I'll keep you posted, Alex."

Over the next week the "fireworks" happened as expected. The Austrian Wine Institute announced that they had accepted the resignation of Karl von Schuyler, a former president, from the board. A similar announcement was made by the women's board of the Vienna Opera accepting the resignation of Katarina von Schuyler. Twelve winemakers, from various wineries owned by von Schuyler, were arrested and charged with adulterating various wines for export. The next day the *Österreich* newspaper had a lead story about Otto Nadrasky, the wine chemist who had signed a written statement, saying he had been hired by the Von Schuyler Wine Group. With his help they had incorporated the diethylene glycol into their bottling lines. He went on to say that he had submitted his invoice for consulting services to Jean-Robert Du Sable and had received payment and a signed acknowledgement.

Tim phoned again a few days later. "Not too much to report yet, Alex, but I just heard from our people that the Viennese police have asked the court for a search warrant for all von

Schuyler's wineries and residences. This has not been announced, of course, but apparently they're marshalling a major force to carry out the search in the next few days. Von Schuyler is in big trouble and I have a feeling we've only seen the tip of the iceberg. So far, no government minister or official has come to his rescue. In fact from what we've seen it appears that the government is distancing themselves from him and behaving as if he was a stranger with no political connections whatsoever. As they say, 'this gets more interesting by the day.'"

When von Schuyler and Du Sable were arraigned in the middle of November, the prosecution laid out a long list of charges. These included willful adulteration of Austrian wines for the domestic and export markets using the toxic chemical diethylene glycol. The levels of diethylene glycol in some of the tested wine products could have potentially health-damaging properties including brain and kidney damage. As a result of these illegal actions, a total of 270,000 hectoliters of wine, equivalent to more than seven months of Austria's total wine exports, had been destroyed. The cost of doing this in an environmentally acceptable way in Germany alone exceeded six million marks. There were a number of other charges listed, including mislabeling, falsification of quality certificates, and obstruction of justice. The cost to the economy of the collapse of Austrian wine exports was very significant. A number of health claims against von Schuyler and his companies by residents of Germany, Austria, France, Italy and the US, were already being filed.

The lawyers for the von Schulyer group, and Karl von Schuyler and Jean-Robert Du Sable pleaded not guilty to all charges and asked the court for six months in which to prepare their defense, due to the complications and extent of the case being brought against them. The court granted them four months, and the hearing was to resume in mid-March 1986.

The week after the hearing, it was announced in the Austrian newspapers that the Viennese police had raided all the wineries owned by the von Schuyler group, their offices in Vienna, and his residence in Carinthia, Schloss Lendorf near Klagenfurt and his elegant apartment over the company's headquarters in Vienna. Chief Investigator Fritz Muller of the Vienna Serious Fraud Squad, who had been leading the investigation, stated that they had removed boxes of files, computers and computer tapes. Three weeks later, the police announced that the search of von Schuyler's home in Carinthia had revealed a secret room, in which there were AK-47s, Uzi automatic pistols, Glock and Mauser pistols, hand grenades, stun guns, teargas, rubber truncheons and knuckledusters. They also discovered a 1979 BMW motorcycle. Inspector Otto Langer, the Chief Inspector of Homicide of the BK, was now investigating a possible connection to the murder of Dr. Gustav Bauer at the Allgemeines Krankenhaus hospital in Vienna in February 1983. The police also announced that Katarina von Schulyer was helping them with their enquiries.

Alex had become an avid reader of the Austrian and German newspapers and magazines. Between the extensive coverage of the scandal in both countries, and reports from time to time in the British press, together with regular calls to and from Tim, he developed a comprehensive understanding of the wine scandal and the various legal cases that were unfolding. In December, *BILD Zeitung* from Germany published a photo spread under the title, Who is behind the Austrian wine scandal? The four-page spread gave a reasonably accurate history of Karl von Schuyler and the development of his business and political success over the past twenty-five years. There were numerous photographs of von Schuyler at various ages, on horseback, at a black-tie event with Katarina at the Austrian Wine Institute, when he was chairman; pictures of the happy couple on the Riviera just after their marriage, and of course the inevitable pinup photographs of Katarina as Miss Austria. The article implied that given von Schuyler's position in the wine industry, he was the obvious suspect to be the mastermind behind the use of diethylene glycol. The German public appeared to love the specter of the Austrian multimillionaire winery owner and developer, now apparently under indictment and facing criminal charges in the Austrian courts.

In January 1986, just after the New Year, the Viennese newspapers had a new banner headline, "Katarina File for Divorce". The unfolding story was that Katarina had filed for divorce, citing physical and mental abuse. The articles were careful to point out that Katarina had absolutely no knowledge of her husband's possible involvement in the diethylene glycol scandal, or possible criminal charges arising from the murder of Dr. Gustav Bauer in 1983. The article also stated that Katarina was continuing to cooperate with the Viennese police, both the fraud department and homicide.

Alex and Julia invited Professor Keller and Anna to dinner in late February. Alex took the opportunity of telling them both about the unfolding developments in Austria. Although Keller had seen some mention in the British press, he did not realize that there could be a connection to his attempted assassination. Both he and Anna were wide-eyed as Alex explained, for the first time, the possible connection of Karl von Schulyer not only to the assassination attempt, but also to Franz Steuben, the SS major who was responsible for liaison with the Siemens company and other suppliers of equipment and chemicals to the concentration camps, including Auschwitz and Plaszow, where Erik Keller's parents had perished. This information had a dramatic effect on both Keller and Anna. The color drained from Keller's face, and Alex felt that maybe he should have kept that information to himself. But if Karl von Schuyler was charged with the murder of Gustav Bauer and it was proved that he was really Franz Steuben, then the connection to the Keller family, and indeed the Kornmehl family, was very relevant.

Tim had offered Alex the opportunity to view all the information coming from Vienna, most of which was top secret. As the month progressed, Alex dropped by the Lambeth headquarters a couple of times a week. Usually, he spent a half an hour or so in a small private office next to Melanie's department. The case against Karl von Schulyer and Jean-Robert Du Sable started in mid-March. The rats were clearly leaving the ship. The prosecution produced a number of witnesses, including ten winemakers, who all confirmed that they were instructed by Du Sable to work with the chemist Otto Nadrasky, on incorporating the diethylene glycol into the wine-production bottling. Two of von Schuyler's winemakers had resigned in protest, but the others, under threat, had complied. They all said that they had been threatened physically if they didn't fall into line. When Du Sable took the witness stand, he claimed that von Schuyler had devised the scheme to meet the commitments of the large export contracts they had with Germany and other markets. He said that von Schuyler was a chemical engineer by training and was quite knowledgeable about DEG. Another witness was Adolph Schatner, who had formerly owned a family winery in Bagram. He filed a statement accusing von Schuyler and his black-suited security personnel of violent threats, which forced him into selling his winery. He also stated that he believed von Schuyler and his security team were behind a major fire in Burgenland, after which von Schuyler made a number of winery purchases at knockdown prices.

The trial went on for three weeks. Von Schuyler declined to go into the witness box. His main defense was that he knew nothing about the diethylene glycol scheme, and that his chief winemaker Du Sable was the mastermind. His lawyers tried to make the case that von Schuyler was far too powerful and rich to be involved in such an illegal operation. Why would he risk his reputation and fortune on such a scheme? If he had been unable to supply the wines as per his contract with his German importers and others around the world, he could have easily paid compensation and not risk everything. The jury was not convinced, and unanimously found him guilty. The judge stated that he would pass sentence in late June.

In the meantime, Otto Langer, was building a murder case against von Schuyler, and Alex was able to read the buildup of evidence. By the early summer of 1986, the coalition between the FPÖ and the socialist SPÖ government was fractured. It was open warfare within the FPÖ itself. Georg Haider, the charismatic young leader, was challenging Norbert Steiger, the more moderate leader of the party since 1980, and the man who had the full support, both financial and political, of von Schuyler. It was now clear that the government was not going to help von Schuyler in any way. In fact, they were now eager to see his downfall and elimination from the political establishment. Among the evidence that Otto Langer put together was a statement from 88-year-old Dr. Sigmund Papen, stating that he believed Frau Astrid von Schuyler, Karl's aunt, had been asphyxiated. At the time of her death, she was suffering from dementia and congestive heart disease. Von Schuyler had been adamant and, according to Dr. Papen, threatening in his demands for a death certificate from natural causes. The doctor confirmed that he had complied, but it had worried him for these past thirty years. At the time of Astrid's death, Karl had only been in Austria for a few weeks, and so Langer decided he would look into von Schuyler's background in Argentina. Working with the homicide police in Buenos Aires, he obtained a number of photographs of von Schuyler in the 1950s. A young man playing polo, driving drophead sports cars, and with both male and female friends at restaurants, bars and black-tie galas. This didn't look like the lifestyle of von Schuyler, and although there was a physical resemblance, Langer was not convinced. He therefore sent photographs of Karl in the 50s, horseback riding on the Riviera, and at similar public events. The impish grin and smile was always present. After a few weeks, he heard from the Buenos

Aires police. They had traced three former friends of Karl von Schuyler. Each one stated that the photographs were not of their friend and even though there was a physical resemblance, they were adamant that this was not the same man. The Buenos Aires police then sent a dossier to Otto Langer based upon the disappearance of Karl von Schuyler in rather unusual circumstances in 1956, after the sale of the family winery in Mendoza. Included in the dossier were photographs of Karl, his father and the general manager of the winery, Wilhelm Schmidt. Studying the photograph of Wilhelm Schmidt through a powerful magnifying glass, Langer believed he could detect a permanent grin. Was Karl von Schuyler really Wilhelm Schmidt?

When Alex read this, he called Tim, suggesting that Inspector Langer pay a visit to Simon Wiesenthal.

"The Wiesenthal files were passed to the police a couple of weeks ago," responded Tim.

"I understand this Inspector Langer and his people have been going through the files since then. Apparently, the police now have enough evidence to charge von Schuyler with murder. Of course, we know that Gustav Bauer not only didn't exist, but was really Professor Keller, who he tried to kill. It is becoming clear that von Schuyler was Franz Steuben and was more than likely a multiple murderer, so I am disinclined to inform anyone about the Bauer incident."

"I agree with you, Tim," said Alex. "I've read enough about SS Major Franz Steuben to realize that he was a dyed-in-the-wool Nazi. Although, as Simon Wiesenthal said, it's not been possible to prove that he actually pulled the trigger during his multiple interrogations or his work at the concentration camps, but he was a willing instructor and a willing supporter. It's about time he was brought to justice."

The next two weeks brought a further flurry of activity, which Alex followed closely in the Austrian newspapers. First it was announced that Viktor Eigner had been arrested and was helping the police with their inquiries. Within a few days, five other members of von Schuyler's security team were arrested. The judge in the wine scandal announced a delay in the sentencing of von Schuyler, and the newspapers surmised this was because of the possible murder charges to come. However, the five members of the security team were released after a couple of days and no charges were brought against them. Alex then read in the reports from Vienna to MI6 that the police were interviewing von Schuyler's butler, Ernst Wenger. This was followed by a long article in the *Österreich* newspaper about Katarina, and her role as they described, the "trophy wife" of Karl von Schuyler. Mainly it was a piece about their lavish lifestyle, the Lendorf Estate, and their integration and acceptance into Austrian politics and high society. The public always like a story about how the mighty have fallen, but the piece also referred to Katarina's cooperation with the police, and her almost eager desire to provide damning evidence against her estranged husband. "Anonymous sources" also commented on her divorce proceedings, and the fact that she had suffered much physical and mental abuse over the years by von Schuyler.

A few weeks later, the FPÖ formally withdrew from the coalition with the SPÖ. Georg Haider took control of the party and moved it immediately to the right, with inflammatory speeches about immigration and Austrian nationalism. This was open warfare within the FPÖ, but Norbert Steiger, the leader of the party, lost out. The moderate wing was disintegrating. It was clear that Karl von Schuyler was no longer the power behind the throne of the FPÖ, and the government no longer needed his services.

At the end of June, the German *BILD Zeitung* published another photo spread under the title, Who is the real Karl von Schuyler? The first page was dominated by two photographs next to each other of SS Major Franz Steuben, and a youthful Karl von Schuyler. Both photos had very similar poses with the almost identical grin on both faces.

The description of the photos was of Steuben, at Plaszow concentration camp in Poland in 1943, and von Schuyler at a Wine Institute event in 1964. The facial expressions were uncannily alike. The article went on to describe the disappearance of Franz Steuben at the end of the war, and the appearance of Karl von Schuyler in Klagenfurt, Austria in 1956, just after Austrian independence. In between there were photographs of the von Schuyler family wineries in Mendoza, Argentina and a highlighted photograph of Wilhelm Schmidt the general manager of the Mendoza winery sitting next to Gerhard von Schuyler and his son Karl.

A week later, the Vienna newspaper had an op-ed piece about Karl von Schuyler and the wine scandal, and the possible criminal charges being pursued by Otto Langer and the homicide department of the BK. The gist of the article, however, was that Karl von Schuyler was likely a former German Nazi. No relation to the distinguished von Schulyer family of Klagenfurt in Carinthia, and not a true Austrian. A convenient explanation which passed off this bad behavior to a "foreigner." On the same date, the newspaper also carried a cartoon showing two vultures chained to a perch and each other, with the faces of Karl von Schuyler and Du Sable looking very miserable. They faced an open gilded birdcage, with a canary sitting on the roof with the happy face of Katrina. The title of the cartoon was "The Canary Sings." Apparently, the canary was singing very loudly. From the reports from Vienna, Alex read that both Ernst, the butler, and Katarina had informed the police about a few phone calls with a Russian – Sergei. The Austrians thought Sergei might be Sergei Malenkov, a known KGB agent who had served as Cultural Secretary at the Russian Embassy at the beginning of 1983.

A few days later, Otto Langer and a police squad carried out a dawn raid on the Lendorf Estate, and arrested von Schuyler again. He was charged with murder. He had been living in seclusion, awaiting his sentencing for the wine scandal, but now he was in even deeper trouble. At his arraignment, he was charged with the attempted murder of Dr. Gustav Bauer outside the Imperial Hotel, in Vienna in February1983, masterminding the subsequent murder of Dr. Bauer at the Krankenhaus a few days later, the murder by asphyxiation of his aunt Astrid von Schuyler in 1956, arson and intimidation in connection with his acquisitions of numerous wineries in the 50s 60s and 70s, income-tax evasion, falsification of accounts, falsification of visas and passports for his security employees, the maintenance of an arsenal of weapons without permits and licenses, and a slew of lesser charges. Although his lawyer pleaded not guilty on his behalf, to all charges, he was remanded in custody without bail. The judge said that he considered von Schuyler a flight risk who could attempt to leave the country. Tim phoned Alex to tell him of the charges.

Ten days later, Tim was again on the phone to Alex. "I have some news from Vienna, Alex," he said gravely. "Von Schuyler has been found dead in his cell. My sources tell me that he committed suicide by swallowing a cyanide pill. That was the old way the Nazis often chose to leave this earth. So it appears we will never hear a guilty verdict in connection with von Schuyler's actual and attempted murders, and we will never know how many deaths he was responsible for during his interrogations and in the camps. But I guess he won't be missed."

Alex was shocked to hear this unexpected news. It took him a minute or two to collect his thoughts.

"So the Franz Steuben/von Schuyler mystery comes to an end," responded Alex. "I'm glad the world finally caught up with him. For Professor Keller and to a lesser extent myself, it provides closure for our family of Holocaust victims. Thanks for letting me know, Tim. I shall pass on the information to Erik Keller"

A couple of weeks later, Alex hosted a small family dinner which included Keller and Anna, in the private dining room at the L'Ecu De France restaurant on Jermyn Street. Anna, had asked Alex if she could bring her friend Mark Evans. Alex of course agreed, and immediately recognized Neil Jordan, but said nothing. He could see that this was a romantic relationship, so Julia was wrong about Anna and Erik Keller being "an item." Laura happened to be in London for a visit, and Alex added Jan and Ava to the small dinner party. Julia played the gracious hostess. After an enjoyable meal and some excellent wines, Alex related the Franz Steuben, Karl von Schuyler story. He finished by saying, "SS Major Franz Steuben had a role in the establishment of the gas chambers in Auschwitz, Plaszow and probably other camps. Erik Keller's parents died at Plaszow, as did many of our Kornmehl family. Steuben has taken his own life, the Nazi coward's way out, but although it took forty years, justice I believe has now been done." He then slowly raised his wine glass looking around the table. *"L'chaim.* To life."

Roundfire

FICTION

Put simply, we publish great stories. Whether it's literary or popular, a gentle tale or a pulsating thriller, the connecting theme in all Roundfire fiction titles is that once you pick them up you won't want to put them down.

If you have enjoyed this book, why not tell other readers by posting a review on your preferred book site. Recent bestsellers from Roundfire are:

The Bookseller's Sonnets
Andi Rosenthal

The Bookseller's Sonnets intertwines three love stories with a tale of religious identity and mystery spanning five hundred years and three countries.
Paperback: 978-1-84694-342-3 ebook: 978-184694-626-4

Birds of the Nile
An Egyptian Adventure
N.E. David

Ex-diplomat Michael Blake wanted a quiet birding trip up the Nile – he wasn't expecting a revolution.
Paperback: 978-1-78279-158-4 ebook: 978-1-78279-157-7

Blood Profit$
The Lithium Conspiracy
J. Victor Tomaszek, James N. Patrick, Sr

The blood of the many for the profits of the few... *Blood Profit$*
will take you into the cigar-smoke-filled room where American
policy and laws are really made.
Paperback: 978-1-78279-483-7 ebook: 978-1-78279-277-2

The Burden
A Family Saga
N.E. David

Frank will do anything to keep his mother and father apart. But
he's carrying baggage – and it might just weigh him down...
Paperback: 978-1-78279-936-8 ebook: 978-1-78279-937-5

The Cause
Roderick Vincent

The second American Revolution will be a fire lit from an
internal spark.
Paperback: 978-1-78279-763-0 ebook: 978-1-78279-762-3

Don't Drink and Fly
The Story of Bernice O'Hanlon Part One
Cathie Devitt

Bernice is a witch living in Glasgow. She loses her way in her
life and wanders off the beaten track looking for the garden of
enlightenment.
Paperback: 978-1-78279-016-7 ebook: 978-1-78279-015-0

Gag
Melissa Unger

One rainy afternoon in a Brooklyn diner, Peter Howland
punctures an egg with his fork. Repulsed, Peter pushes the plate
away and never eats again.
Paperback: 978-1-78279-564-3 ebook: 978-1-78279-563-6

The Master Yeshua
The Undiscovered Gospel of Joseph
Joyce Luck

Jesus is not who you think he is. The year is 75 CE. Joseph ben
Jude is frail and ailing, but he has a prophecy to fulfil...
Paperback: 978-1-78279-974-0 ebook: 978-1-78279-975-7

On the Far Side, There's a Boy
Paula Coston

Martine Haslett, a thirty-something 1980s woman, plays hard on
the fringes of the London drag club scene until one night which
prompts her to sign up to a charity. She writes to a young Sri
Lankan boy, with consequences far and long.
Paperback: 978-1-78279-574-2 ebook: 978-1-78279-573-5

Tuareg
Alberto Vazquez-Figueroa

With over 5 million copies sold worldwide, *Tuareg* is a
classic adventure story from best-selling author
Alberto Vazquez-Figueroa, about honour, revenge and a
clash of cultures.
Paperback: 978-1-84694-192-4

Readers of ebooks can buy or view any of these bestsellers by clicking on the live link in the title. Most titles are published in paperback and as an ebook. Paperbacks are available in traditional bookshops. Both print and ebook formats are available online.

Find more titles and sign up to our readers' newsletter at
http://www.johnhuntpublishing.com/fiction

Follow us on Facebook at
https://www.facebook.com/JHPfiction
and Twitter at https://twitter.com/JHPFiction